and

MEMORY OF FIRE

Book One of The World Gates

"What a fun book! *Memory of Fire* grips from the opening
paragraph, snagging the reader on a fast and furious tale
that is at times heroic, at times poignant,
and at all times entertaining."
Elizabeth Haydon

"Lisle's richly realized characters defy easy classification and are
the complex products of their convoluted environments."
Robin Hobb

"A literal walk through the looking glass into worlds of
adventure and romance."
Susan Sizemore

"Lisle seems to be an author unlikely to write
a sloppy or stupid book."
Chicago Sun-Times

"It's always a delight to read Holly Lisle's books . . . And
Memory of Fire is Holly Lisle at her best."
S.L. Viehl

Also by Holly Lisle

MEMORY OF FIRE
Book One of The World Gates

HOLLY LISLE

BOOK TWO OF THE WORLD GATES

The Wreck of Heaven

An Imprint of HarperCollinsPublishers

EOS
An Imprint of HarperCollins*Publishers*
10 East 53rd Street
New York, New York 10022-5299

Copyright © 2003 by Holly Lisle
ISBN: 0-380-81838-8
www.eosbooks.com

First Eos paperback printing: April 2003

Eos Trademark Reg. U.S. Pat. Off. and in Other Countries, Marca Registrada, Hecho en U.S.A.
HarperCollins® is a trademark of HarperCollins Publishers Inc.

Printed in the U.S.A.

10 9 8 7 6 5 4 3 2 1

Matthew, with all my love

Acknowledgments

My deepest gratitude to:

Sheila Viehl and Robert A. Sloan—for first-draft read-through and critique. Your comments helped immensely.

Diana Gill, whose edits challenged me to find the story's deeper layers. Thank you.

Matthew, who managed to see in three seconds what I'd missed for a whole year, and whose brilliant suggestion gave the story new heart. You're wonderful.

All the writers and readers in the Forward Motion Community (*http://hollylisle.com*), who have been endlessly supportive through this grueling process. Onward!

My kids, who are fun and funny and encouraging, and who talk about writing intelligently, and offer good suggestions, and bring me stuff when I'm on deadline. I love you.

The Wreck of
Heaven

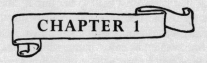

CHAPTER 1

Copper House, Ballahara, Nuue, Oria

MOLLY McCOLL tightened the laces on the heavy silk bodice and shrugged into the brocade overgown. Alive, she thought. I'm alive. *I'm alive!* I was dead, and now I'm alive, and I'm back in Copper House. She tried on a smile, but it didn't seem to fit.

She remembered dying all too clearly—remembered taking her sister's kid through the gate between the worlds, only too slowly, because she'd been unwilling to do what she had to do. And her hesitation had almost cost three-year-old Jake his life.

Saving him *had* cost her hers. The healing that would have been so effortless on Oria had, on Earth, required her to take every bit of Jake's pain and all of his injuries into her own body. To absorb them. On Earth, she'd been only human, stripped of downworld magic and Vodi power. And on Earth she had died.

But now she was alive again, brought back by the Vodi magic. Brought back to Oria—and in her head, the voices of long-dead Vodian whispered remembrance of their own deaths and rebirths and deaths again.

Molly had only been alive again for a few hours—at least she could only remember the last few hours. She felt out of place in her own skin; she could not remember how she had arrived at Copper House. Her first memory was of stumbling naked through the forest. Her only clues about her return were the leaves in her hair and the dirt under her fingernails.

The sleek, heavy gold necklace purred around her neck almost as if it were a cat held to her throat. She didn't want to think about the necklace, or about being the Vodi; she didn't really want to think about being alive, or why that was wrong. She wanted to enjoy being with Seolar. She wanted to be in love, and happy, and carefree in a world as far from the trailer park in Cat Creek as any human being could conceivably get.

"You weren't born to be carefree," she muttered at her reflection in the mirror. The mirror only emphasized that truth. On Earth she'd been of average height, moderately attractive, and clearly human. Oria had changed that, and her unexpected return from death had changed it even more. Her hair now fell to her waist, its color a copper so glossy it looked metallic. She'd grown both taller and thinner—she guessed she stood around six feet now, but couldn't be certain since she lacked any mechanism to convert local measurements to those familiar to her; she was still short by veyâr standards. The bone structure of her face had new angles, high cheekbones, and a sharp little chin. Her eyes stared back from the mirror, impossible emerald green, deeply slanted, and enormous. She still, thankfully, had the right number of fingers and toes. She glanced at the twelve-string guitar leaning in the corner of the room and tried to imagine learning to play all over again with the surfeit of digits on a pair of veyâr hands.

"You look breathtaking," Seolar, who was her beloved and the Imallin of Copper House, said softly. She could have said the same of him. His gold skin, darker gold hair, and jet-black eyes, his height and his grace gave him the air of some otherworld angel. Even the golden brown tattoos that curled and spiraled across his cheeks only added to his beauty.

She turned to him and smiled uncertainly. "Do I?"

"I swear it." The smile he gave her in return trembled at the corners, and she saw brightness in his eyes. He closed the distance between them with three steps, and pulled her into his arms. "Never leave me like that again. I was lost without you. I died inside, and only when you appeared on the balcony tonight did I start to breathe again."

Inside of Molly, the darkness descended. "I'm the Vodi," she whispered.

"I know. But I love you."

She nodded. "But I'm the Vodi." She pulled back so that she could look into his eyes. "Do you know what sort of lives my predecessors lived?"

"I read the old records. After you . . . after you died . . ." Seolar turned away from her and looked out the window at the last vestiges of twilight, at pale wisps of gold and pink streaked across the indigo sky. "I did little else but read, trying to understand."

"Then you know what happened to the Vodi."

"They were hunted. Mercilessly, by terrible enemies." He turned back to her. In a hoarse voice, he continued. "They died again and again. But that will not be your fate. I won't let it."

Molly said, "I hope you can stop it, Seo. You can't see the pictures I see, or hear the voices of the others. The necklace holds them close to me, and when I close my eyes and let them show me, I can see where the other Vodian went before me. They still have their horror. They're hollow—they're ancient shells, and all that's left of them is the death and the pain and the fear. I close them out as much as I can. I don't want to go where they have been." As he turned to face her again, she added, "Not again, anyway."

"No. You are my love. You are my heart and s—" His voice broke off, and an expression flashed across his face that worried Molly. "You are my heart and soul. I'll keep you safe." He put an arm around her and led her out of their suite. "While you dressed, I told Birra to have a meal brought to the solar. I know it's your favorite room, and I thought your first night back, it would be pleasant to have a private dinner among the flowers and beside the little waterfall. It should be ready now."

Molly smiled up at him. "That sounds wonderful." The pressure of his hand on the small of her back and his wondrous warmth and presence steadied her. She needed steadying; glad as she was to find herself alive, overjoyed as she was to be in Oria, in Copper House, in Seolar's embrace, she could not shake either the darkness inside her nor an ugly hollowness that seemed to echo in even the smallest moment of silence. Death had changed her, and not in good ways. "That sounds wonderful," she repeated. And she wished it did. But far back in her mind, darkness moved and shifted and whispered. Far back in her mind, the enemies of her dead predecessors had opened their eyes and were yawning and stretching and sniffing the air, sensing fresh meat, and while Molly hungered for the ordinariness of dinner and the charm of an indoor waterfall and the sweet scents of out-of-season flowers in a room where she could look out at the moonlight on snow, she could not hide herself from the hunters that stalked the periphery of her mind.

She could not hide herself from the life she'd been born to live, from the duty that only she could fulfill, from the hand of Fate that held her in its harsh grip.

She wondered how she would manage to eat and converse with that ball of dread knotting her belly.

Seolar guided her through the private passageways that kept them out of sight of guests and servants alike; they slipped through the secret panel in the solar into a fairy realm, with thousands of slender tapers lining the walls and stuck in candelabras worked in between the flowers and the plants—in the still fish pond opposite the little stone bridge that spanned the stream, floating candles by the hundreds, flickering and golden.

On the patio where the two of them had shared their first meal together, a little table, empty plates, and empty glasses already waited. "The food will be along as soon as we call," Seolar said. "I didn't want it to chill."

"This is so beautiful," Molly said. "How did you manage it so quickly?"

Seolar laughed. "I put a hundred servants and soldiers to the task. Had they not been able to do the job, I would have commanded two hundred."

Molly found a genuine laugh inside herself. "It's good to be the king," she muttered.

Seolar raised an eyebrow.

Molly shrugged. "A line from a . . . from an entertainment back home."

"I like hearing you laugh."

Molly grinned at him as he held her seat. "It felt good. I'm so glad to be here."

Seolar rang a bell, then took his seat across from her. "I dread asking for fear of bringing to mind great pain, or great sorrow, but . . . did you suffer?"

Molly shook her head. "No. Not once it was over, anyway."

"What happened?"

"I was stupid. I hesitated leaving the scene of the battle—you know of the battle?"

"Yaner was most thorough in telling us what happened."

Molly said, "He would be. My sister told me to flee the scene of the battle and take her son, Jake, to safety in the other world. She had the gate already in place; I could have gone easily. But I waited because I was afraid that I might not be able to get back here. I hesitated, and a blast hit us. It hit her son—tore him almost in two—just as I finally stepped into the gate. We went through to Earth, but while we were between the worlds, I felt a force keeping Jake alive. Once we reached the other side, though, I knew he would die. I could feel it, and the closer I came to Earth, the more horrible it became. And if he died, it would be my fault." She closed her eyes and took a deep breath, and felt tears start down her cheeks.

"You don't need to tell me," Seolar said.

"But I do. You have to know, because I almost cost us . . . us." Molly got hold of herself and continued. "I didn't save another little boy once, and I knew that if I let Jake die when, had I done what Lauren told me to do, we would have both been safe, I could never have lived with myself. So when we crossed over, I took his injuries into myself. They weren't survivable. He lived; I died."

"I'm sorry," Seolar said, and put his hand over hers.

"Me too. It didn't have to be that way."

"I'm sorry for every terrible thing that ever happened to you." He leaned forward and kissed her. "Never again, my love. Never again."

Molly heard footsteps, and a cleared throat. She opened her eyes and Seolar moved back. Birra—dear Birra—stood before her with a covered silver tray. "Imallin," he said, and bowed. He turned to Molly, his expression carefully polite. "And . . ." His voice faltered, his body went rigid, and the tray dropped to the tabletop with a horrific crash. His hands flew to his face, he dropped to one knee, and from his mouth erupted a keening that on Earth would have had every dog in a one-mile radius howling in sympathy.

Seolar put a hand on Birra's shoulder, and said, "Enough, man! Catch yourself in hand."

Birra put his forehead to the floor, and said, "Relieve me, my Imallin. I dare not confess what my eyes tell me they see. Relieve me of my post—I have gone mad."

"She's real," Seolar said. "That's why I did all this. She's real, she's back with us, and this time we'll keep her safe."

Birra lifted his head just high enough that he could peer over the table. "Vodi?" he croaked. "Is it really you?"

Molly smiled. "Birra, it is. I had a long way to come to get home, but I'm here now."

Birra looked from Molly to Seolar and back to Molly. Tears slid down his tattooed cheeks, and he mopped them with his braids. "How?" he asked, and immediately retracted the question with a vehement shake of his head. "No, I step above my place to ask such a thing. Oh, Vodi," he said, "I would have sold the sun itself to bring you back to us, had it been mine. Anything you would have of me, you have only to ask. Thank all the little gods you have found your way back." He rose, took a deep breath, and seemingly more composed, looked at the mess on the table. "The kitchen has more of everything," he told her. "I will bring you food undisturbed by my . . ." He gave Seolar a doubtful look. ". . . foolishness."

"I'm sorry, Birra," Seolar said, picking up on the cue. "I should have told you. But I thought you would think me mad unless you saw her yourself—and she was dressing. And then I was so excited about my idea I forgot what a shock her presence would be to you."

"Lucky it did not slay me, truth be told."

"Indeed." Seolar had the grace to look chagrined. "Perhaps you had best warn the rest of the staff before we send for anything else—I'd hate to spend the rest of the night picking up dropped food and shattered plates."

Birra gathered up the mess and vanished down the path, and Seolar said, "By tomorrow the House and the village will be decked in ribbons, and by the next day, all of the land, I think."

Molly said, "It makes for quite a homecoming." She sighed. "Lauren doesn't know."

"Your sister? You haven't told her?"

"I woke up in the forest not far from here. I had no way to reach her or tell her. But if we're going to do what our parents planned for us, I'm going to have to find a way."

"I'll take care of it," Seolar said. "I don't want to take the chance of you going on your own."

Molly would have argued, but in truth she didn't want to take that chance either. "Send someone reliable to her," she said. "Perhaps Yaner—Lauren knows Yaner."

"Of course."

Molly heard a scuffling down the path, and turned to find a handful of servants peering at her through the arching branches of the trees and the lace of the ferns. She smiled at them and they prostrated themselves, then turned and fled.

"The word is out," Seolar said. "I could punish them for

such impertinence . . . but I won't. We thought the veyâr were doomed; that they want to see for themselves that we once again have hope, well . . . I won't blame them for that."

Molly smiled. "No. I'm sorry I so stupidly took hope away from them, even for a little while."

Seolar kissed her again.

When the food came back, it tasted wonderful, and Molly discovered that she was ravenous. She ate seconds of everything and thirds of the delicious fruit dessert.

Seolar watched her eating long after he'd finished with an expression of bemusement. "I don't know why I'm so hungry," she said. "Maybe coming back took a lot out of me." She frowned. "Well, no—there was nothing in me . . ." She shrugged. "I feel like I haven't seen food in a year, though, and this is so wonderful. And I'm so grateful the kitchen made extra."

Seolar leaned his chin on one cupped hand and said, "Do you think you'll be this hungry at every meal now? I may have to find more cooks." He grinned at her and Molly laughed.

"I don't know. I don't think so. It's just that this is the first thing I've eaten. And I didn't even know I was so hungry."

"There's more if you want it," Seolar said.

Molly leaned back in her chair and sighed. "You know, I don't think I do. Finally."

Seolar's smile broadened. "Good. Because I don't think there was that much more."

Molly laughed, then leaned forward. "In the next few days, we'll have so much to do. But tonight—tonight we don't have to do anything in particular, do we?"

"Certainly not. Why?"

"Because I would love so much to listen to some beautiful music and dance with you. Could we do that?"

"You had only to ask, my love." Seolar looked toward the main door to the solar, and started to say something. Birra's voice floated back to them before he could utter a sound. "I am on my way to get the musicians, Imallin. They shall be only an instant."

Molly sighed and smiled into the silence, truly content.

In that silence, in the stillness of her mind, she heard the heavy, slow flap of a leathery wing, and her happiness melted away like snow on hot pavement. She froze, concentrating. Had she heard something, or had she only imagined it?

She closed her eyes and concentrated. And there it was again. Flap. A pause. Flap. It came from a distance, and she knew she did not yet hear it with her ears, but she could not doubt that it was real. She opened her eyes and looked at Seolar and said, "Something coming."

"Something?"

"Hunters," she said. "they're coming. They know I'm here, and they're looking for me."

"What kind of hunters?"

Molly dreaded even saying the word. "The rrôn," she whispered.

Cat Creek, North Carolina

Crocuses on the lawn, the first hints of daffodils pushing heads above the dirt, and a splash of insanely yellow forsythia running along the side of the house next to the driveway. It looked so cheerful, and so ordinary, Lauren Dane thought as she pulled into the drive.

"Okay, puppy boy," she told Jake. "You're going to help me carry groceries into the house this time, right?"

Jake gave her a little smile. "I help," he said. "I'm a big boy."

He sat quietly in the car seat while she unfastened him, then stood still while she put the plastic bag that held the bread over his arm. She loaded up with most of the rest of the bags, clamped her keys between her teeth, and said, "C'on, Jake. Ess go."

He followed close behind her, like an obedient little lamb. Lauren wanted to scream. She wanted to cry. Jake had never been an obedient little lamb. Never. In fact, he'd always seemed to her to be a cross between a caffeine-hyped kitten and the cartoon Tasmanian devil. She hadn't seen any part of the little boy she recognized for the last two weeks—not since something awful had happened to him going through the world gates and Molly had died in the process of fixing it.

Lauren wanted her busy, stubborn, fun little guy back. She wondered if he'd ever make it back—he'd finally started talking again, but he didn't chatter. He didn't get into things. He didn't run around. He stayed where she put him, did what she told him, and nothing more.

Lauren shifted bags to one hand, unlocked the front door, shoved it open with a hip, and swung the groceries down to the foyer floor.

She turned to find Jake plodding up the front steps to the porch, the arm with the bread on it carefully lifted to keep it from dragging on the ground.

"You doing all right?" she asked him.

"Yes." He held the rail with the opposite hand and was doing what Lauren thought of as the Modified Wedding Walk going up the stairs—left foot, step together; left foot, step together. Cautious.

"I'll be right back, then," she told him as she ran down the stairs. "I have to get the rest of the groceries." Lauren hurried—loaded the rest of the bags on one arm, praying that the flimsy plastic handles wouldn't break, slamming the trunk, and hurrying back to the house at as close to a run as she could manage.

She needn't have worried. Jake, once inside the door, went to the foot of the stairs leading up to the second floor and sat on the first step.

"All right," Lauren said. "Let's get all this stuff into the kitchen. Come on."

He shook his head and sat watching her.

Lauren sighed. "Jake, I have to put the food away. The ice

cream will melt, and a lot of this needs to go in the refrigerator. Can you carry the bread to the kitchen for me?"

He still sat where he was, shaking his head.

Well, okay. He was obedient except for that. He wouldn't go down the hall—not for love, not even for ice cream.

She leaned down, kissed him, and took the bag of bread. "Okay. I'll put things away and then be right back. Stay there."

"Nooooo!" he wailed as he saw her start to leave.

"I'm just going down the hall. Everything is okay, monkey-boy. Really."

"Nooooo," he said. The back of the foyer terrified him. The giant mirror that hung on the wall there terrified him. She could get him into the kitchen if she picked him up and carried him, and the only time she got a show of spirit from him anymore was when she tried to carry him down the hall. Then he turned into a hellcat, if only briefly, and she felt like she had her little boy back.

She had too many groceries to put away to voluntarily engage in a fight, though. "I have to, kiddo. I'll be fine. And so will you."

"NOOOOO!"

Lauren took a deep breath, preparatory to just picking up the bags and heading down the hall and letting him scream. Behind her, someone knocked on the front door. She turned. Pete Stark stood there, still in his deputy's uniform.

Pete was second-in-command of the two-man Cat Creek Sheriff's Department. He was, as well, a newcomer to the Sentinels, which had been—until Lauren returned to Cat Creek—a closed and secretive cell of a hereditary group of guardians, whose family associations had reached back for generations. Lauren's own family had been Sentinels longer than they'd been Americans—and they'd been Americans well over a hundred years.

The Sentinels stood at the world gates and fought to prevent—and if necessary, repair—damage from magic that rebounded from other worlds in the worldchain back to

Earth. They lived dangerous lives, and frequently died young. Hidden away in small towns, spending their days as florists and insurance salesmen and bank clerks and housewives, they kept the ancient secrets of the world gates and the magic that lay on the other side of them—because anyone could be taught to use the gates, and those who traveled down the worldchain gained the power of gods, if not the wisdom.

And magic used downworld rebounded upworld, often with horrific results.

The Cat Creek Sentinels had suffered major losses recently. Nine of fourteen Sentinels—including the traitors who caused a magic-borne plague that had killed over three hundred people in Cat Creek alone, and millions worldwide—had died in the past month. The survivors had sworn Lauren in as their replacement gateweaver, and had taken Pete mostly because he was a friend of Eric MacAvery—Cat Creek's sheriff and the head of the Cat Creek Sentinels—but partly because he knew too much about the Sentinels and world gates to be permitted to walk away.

In spite of the somewhat shotgun-marriage manner in which he'd joined, Pete had taken to the duties and responsibilities of a Sentinel with an enthusiasm and a dedication that surprised everybody.

Only Lauren seemed to wonder at his competence in tight spots. Only she seemed to notice layers to him that lay below the surface, or to suspect that he was more than he seemed. She thought he was trustworthy, for what it was worth. Actions spoke truth where words lied—and he'd saved Eric's life, and had risked his own many times in many ways.

She liked the look in his eyes. Her gut said, *He's okay. He's one of the good guys.*

But which good guys?

"Hey," she said, opening the door. "Are you where you could take a minute or two and sit in the hall with Jake so that I could put groceries away?"

He looked startled. "Well . . . I suppose. I came by to talk to you, but . . ." He shrugged at her, smiled at Jake, and sat down on the stairs beside him. "You want to play? Cars? Or horsey? Or something?"

Jake sat there staring at Pete like Pete had two heads.

"Right back," Lauren said, and hauled her groceries down the hall before Pete had second thoughts.

He'd been by almost every day since the funeral. She saw him when she answered calls to check on the Sentinel gates around the town, too, and when they bumped into each other on the street. In a town that—since the influenza epidemic— housed only a few more than seven hundred people, not running into someone became difficult.

He wanted to be with her, to spend time getting to know her; he wanted to help her get past all the awfulness of the past couple of months—and maybe the year before that, too. He liked her. For that matter, she liked him.

But he wasn't Brian, and could never be Brian. And Brian had reached back from death to save Jake's life, and had told Lauren that he would always love her, and that he would be waiting for her. That didn't leave Lauren with a lot of room to move on with her life.

She was at such loose ends. She owned the house outright, and with government money that came in monthly, she and Jake could afford to live without her working, even though to do so they had to live very small lives. It wasn't such a hard thing to live a small life in a place like Cat Creek.

But her life had been planned to be so much more. Until Molly's death, she had been one-half of a partnership born to save Earth from self-immolation and prevent the escalating collapse of the worldchain of which Earth was just a single bead. She'd spent thirty-five years of her life heading toward a destiny of unimaginable wonder, had in a single day at the end of that thirty-five-year trek discovered not only who she was and who Molly was, but what their parents had planned for the two of them, and that her life mattered in huge ways she couldn't even fully conceive . . . and in the same day, Molly had died and she'd lost the sister she'd only just found and the future she'd spent her entire life hungering for. And that same bitter death had rendered her parents' sacrifice of their lives years before futile—for if Lauren and Molly couldn't carry out their parents' plans, Lauren's mom and dad had died for nothing.

Lauren jammed cans onto the shelves of the pantry and the fruit into big wooden bowls lined along the counter and refused to let the tears come. Shit happened. It happened to everyone, and if it didn't seem fair that so very much of it had happened to her, well, no one with any sense had ever tried to claim that life was fair, had they? Or even that anyone ought to try to make it fair. She still had Jake. She had a place to live, a little bit of money, the time to give her little boy what so many young mothers didn't have. She had a lot, and she would not succumb to the temptations of self-pity. She would not. She loathed whiners.

She could hear Pete out in the foyer talking to Jake. Reading him a story, she realized. "The Little Old Lady Who Was Not Afraid of Anything"? She winced. That had been one of Jake's favorite books prior to . . . well, everything. But he couldn't seem to stand the suspense anymore, and when the pumpkin said, "Boo, boo!" he always burst into tears, even if the pumpkin said, "Boo, boo!" very quietly.

"He hasn't been doing too well with that one lately," she yelled.

"He's hanging in with it right now," Pete called back. "Has his hands over his eyes, but I'm going light on the dramatic presentation."

"He cries at the pumpkin."

"I'll take it easy."

Suit yourself, Lauren thought, annoyed. If he has a fit, though, you're going to deal with both of us.

Bread in the freezer, muffin mix on the shelves, flour and Toll House morsels and brown sugar on the baked goods shelf at the top.

"He DOES NOT!" Lauren heard Jake shout suddenly.

"The very scary pumpkin say, 'BOO! BOO!,' not 'I gots a cookie!' "

Lauren stopped putting things onto shelves and listened.

"Right here," Pete was saying. "See—it says, 'The very big, very orange, very scary pumpkin says, "I have a cookie in my tummy." ' "

"You a dumbass," Jake said. One of Brian's words. Usually Lauren found a little bit of comfort in hearing Jake using Brian's words, in the same way that she found comfort in knowing that he now remembered his father—but she wasn't sure how Pete would take being called a dumbass by a three-year-old.

Pete was laughing. And an instant later, so was Jake. She leaned against the counter and put her head down on it and cried. It was the first time Jake had laughed since the accident, since the awfulness—and by all rights she or Jake's father should have been the ones to make him laugh, and instead, he was laughing at the man who seemed to want to take his father's place.

Lauren wanted to be happy with that breakthrough. A part of her was—hearing Jake laugh again was like music from heaven. But a big part of her was hurt and jealous and—yes, she admitted—bathing in self-pity.

Dammit.

She straightened up, wiped her eyes on the sleeve of her sweatshirt, and took slow, deep breaths until she got over it. Brian was dead, and he couldn't be there for his son anymore, though he sure as hell had been there when it counted. Molly was dead, and she couldn't be there for Lauren, or the plan. Mom and Dad were dead, and shitty as that was, they'd been dead for a long time.

And if Lauren didn't get her ass in gear, the ice cream was going to melt all over the floor.

She heard footsteps in the hall and turned to see Jake riding on Pete's shoulders—and Pete had gotten him through the back end of the foyer and past the dreaded mirror without so much as a whimper.

"Mama, Pete did the story wrong," Jake said, and he had a real smile on his face. "He said . . . he said . . ." Jake started to giggle, "that the very big, very scary, very orange pumpkin said he gotted a cookie in his tummy." He wrapped his arms around Pete's eyes and leaned over his head, laughing again, laughing so hard his head bobbed up and down and his belly shook. "But the pumpkin 'spose to say, 'BOO! BOO!' " Jake did those 'boos' with the tremendous vigor Lauren always used to give them when she read the book. "An' I say Pete is a dumbass."

Lauren winced and said, "I heard."

Pete grinned at her. "He has his opinions, doesn't he?"

"He does." She smiled at his son. "This is the happiest I've seen him. Since . . ." She shrugged.

"He's a tough little guy," Pete said. He swung Jake down to the floor, and Jake ran to her and hugged her around the thighs.

"Can I help?"

Lauren handed him a soup can and pointed him toward the floor of the pantry. "Right there," she said. "Put it away, and come back for the next one."

Pete said, "I wanted to let you know that a new Sentinel came in today. Girl named Darlene Fullbright. Eric asked me to stop by and let you know, maybe run you by so you can set up her gate. She was going to be staying with June Bug, but apparently Darlene is allergic to smoke, and June Bug said that at her age she's not going to be told to go outside her own doors to smoke—the two of them did not get off on the right foot at all."

Lauren smiled a little. "I don't see June Bug being any too happy about someone suggesting that she make any changes, frankly. And anything involving those damned cigars of hers . . ."

"She's a character," Pete agreed. "Want me to run you by? Soon as you put up the rest of your groceries, of course."

Lauren shrugged. "I might as well. I have to give Jake

a bath this evening, but that's the biggest event I have going."

"We could do something together. Go get something to eat—over in Rockingham or Laurinburg or down in Bennettsville. You don't need to be spending every evening alone. You've been through a lot—and I have the feeling that, like ol' Jake there, you could stand to laugh a bit."

Lauren thought wistfully of the evenings that she and Brian had gotten dressed up—Lauren in a pretty dress, Brian in his blues with his service ribbons proudly displayed—for special events on base at Pope. She could close her eyes and see him standing in the living room of their little base housing duplex, flight cap in hand, smile on his face. She hadn't worn a pair of hose or a dress for anything other than funerals since Brian's death.

Maybe it wouldn't hurt to take Pete up on his offer—maybe it was time that she thought of high heels as something other than shoes to wear when people died.

But would that be leading Pete on? She wasn't a free woman. She was a widow, but a widow under special circumstances—she would never be a free woman.

Yes, she decided. Knowing that Pete liked her, and would like to date her, she couldn't accept something that he would look at as a date with a clear conscience. "That's sweet of you," she said.

"But . . . you're going to turn me down." Pete smiled sadly. "I swear, Lauren, I could see the whole thing running across your face while I was standing here looking at you. You wanted to go, you considered going, and then something changed your mind. What?"

"Brian."

Pete closed his eyes, took a slow breath, and blew it out with the air of a man trying to find patience he didn't have. Lauren expected him to tell her that Brian was dead, that wedding vows were only until death—and instead he just nodded. "All right, then," he said.

Lauren discovered that she'd wanted him to try to argue her out of it. What the hell did that mean?

She turned away, put the last of the groceries in their places, balled up the plastic bags, dumped them into the trash, and wished that she could understand herself.

At her feet, Jake said, "Oh, no. Mama. No."

Lauren turned to see what was bothering him. She couldn't see anything. She took a step forward and moved into a spot of air so icy, so terrifying, that she almost shrieked. But in her mind something whispered, *Get the man to leave. I have news for you.*

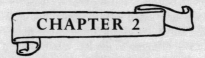

CHAPTER 2

Cat Creek

L AUREN FROZE in place, trying desperately to think. She picked up Jake and held him close, and whispered in his ear, "Hush, puppy, everything is going to be all right." She stroked his hair and moved out of the ice blast that almost had to be one of the Orians.

"Mama, the guy wants to talk to you," Jake said, and started sobbing loudly. "Let's go. Come on, Mama. Let's go."

Lauren headed out of the kitchen toward the front of the house, bypassing Pete, who turned with a bewildered expression on his face and came after her.

"What's wrong?"

Lauren said, "I don't know. Jake's been having—if he were older I'd say he had panic attacks every time we came to the back of the house. He has a bad reaction in the foyer by the mirror, of course, but he also gets panicked in the kitchen. He won't go in there on his own, and he tries to talk me out of going back there."

Pete looked chagrined. "I'm sorry. I didn't know. I thought bringing him back would help him get past being afraid of the mirror . . ." He patted Jake on the shoulder, and Jake turned his head away and buried his face in Lauren's hair.

"Go 'way."

Pete looked at Lauren. "He's mad at me?"

Lauren, showing Pete to the front door, gave him an

apologetic smile. "He's gotten very good at laying blame recently. The person who gets him into a situation he doesn't want to be in becomes the enemy—at least for a little while. Usually it's me, since I'm the only one he's with all the time." She shrugged as she opened the door for Pete, and with Jake still clinging to her like a barnacle on a boat, said, "He doesn't hold grudges, though. He's a pretty cool little guy that way. Next time he sees you, he'll be fine."

"But we were having such fun," Pete said, stepping out onto the porch.

"Yep. And then he realized that you got him to go into the kitchen, where he knew he didn't want to go—so in his eyes, you became just another sneaky adult." Lauren stepped far enough out onto the porch that Pete had to clear the doorway completely. When she was sure he'd committed, she took a half step back in and said, "I'll have to get the gate for the new girl later. It isn't like she has to have it right this minute, anyway. She can just be off duty when she's home until I have a chance to get over there. I think I need to make sure Jake is calmed down and okay right now."

Pete, who clearly couldn't figure out how he'd been steamrolled onto the porch, started to protest. Then he nodded. "Yeah—go ahead and get him feeling better. I'm sorry, little guy. I didn't want you to be scared."

Jake yanked his head around so he was facing away from Pete.

"He'll get over it," Lauren said, stepping into the foyer and closing the door.

Pete stood on the porch for a moment, the flummoxed expression not leaving his face. Then he turned and walked down the steps. Lauren locked the front door—her fellow Sentinels had an unnerving habit of knocking to announce their presence, then coming on in if the door wasn't locked. Those small-town habits didn't bother Lauren most of the time.

Now, however, an uninvited guest—rather, a second uninvited guest—could be a problem.

"I'm not coming back to the kitchen," she said when she saw Pete pull the black-and-white out of the drive. "If you want to talk to me, you're going to have to come up here. My kid is afraid of the kitchen."

She saw a shimmer at the back of the hall—something transparent moving toward her. She waited, and the thing took shape. It was one of the veyâr. Because it remained translucent and kept itself toward the back of the foyer away from the bright outside light, she had to guess at color, but she thought it was one of the blue-green ones.

"I have news," the veyâr said. Lauren could now hear its voice, but it sounded to her like it was calling to her from the end of a very long, echoey tunnel.

"So you said." Lauren held Jake tight against her chest. His little body had gone rigid, and she could feel him shaking with fear. "Make it quick. You're scaring my little boy."

Veyâr faces were hard to read—Lauren could only guess at the emotions that flashed across this one's tattooed visage. He looked nervous, timid, and at the same time almost excited.

"Brief. Yes. I will be brief. The Imallin sent me—you must come to Oria to carry out your destiny."

"My destiny died with my sister," Lauren said quietly. "I don't have a destiny anymore."

The veyâr snapped his wrists emphatically by shaking them up and down; Lauren had no idea what that gesture meant until he said, "No, no, no. Your destiny is reborn. The Vodi has returned to us."

"You found a new Vodi?" Lauren asked, trying to make sense of what he was saying.

"No. Your sister. The Vodi. She is alive."

Lauren felt something twist in her gut. Anger. Fear. Something dark and ugly. "I buried Molly," she said, her voice dropping and getting softer as the anger grew. "She's dead. I can take you to the grave if you'd like. But I'm not going to be dragged into Oria with my little boy for some farce you people thought up. Without Molly, I can't do anything that matters."

"And without you, neither can she," the veyâr said. "She gave me a message for you. She said you would know that it was from her, that this was something that only the two of you would be able to make sense of. She told me that your parents planned for her to be the warp, and you to be the weft."

Lauren stared at the veyâr, disbelieving. "Explain yourself."

"I cannot. I can only relay what she told me to tell you. She said your parents planned the two of you to weave our worldchain back together, and she was to be the warp, and you the weft." He shrugged—that gesture, at least, Lauren could make some sense of.

Your parents planned for her to be the warp, and you to be the weft.

Yes. That was it precisely—the analogy that they had implanted through magic in Lauren's and Molly's minds. That image had exploded to life, along with a thousand other connections, when Lauren and Molly finally met and touched. In the same day that it came to life, though, Molly died, without having an opportunity or a reason to share that information with anyone else. Lauren had never told anyone— had never said a single word about what had passed between the two of them. Perhaps the veyâr had ways of reading her mind—she wouldn't put that past them. But somehow . . . somehow this felt real to Lauren.

Could Molly be alive?

No. Of course not. Lauren had been to the funeral, seen her sister lying in the coffin, watched June Bug Tate quietly fall apart standing there staring at Molly's body. Jake was alive because Molly had given her life to save him.

Warp and weft.

She took a deep breath and asked the veyâr, "How? How is she alive?"

The veyâr said, "She is the Vodi. She wears the necklace of all the Vodian who lived before her, and it protects her the way it protected them. She is alive, and she and the Imallin beg you to come to Oria."

"He's bad, Mama," Jake said, his face pressed into her neck. "Make that bad guy go away."

Lauren leaned against the wall and stared at the veyâr, rocking her son against her body and patting him on the back as if he were still a baby. Warp and weft—the threads that would weave the dying worldchain back together. Her parents had left that message with Molly, they'd left it with Lauren—and here it was, come back to haunt her.

And if Molly truly still lived, then the plan lived, too. Lauren's parents hadn't died for nothing. Lauren still had a destiny. The world she loved and wanted to leave for Jake and Jake's eventual children still had a chance.

And if the plan still lived, then the Sentinels might be a problem, and other things might be a problem, and Lauren and Jake, unprotected in the old family house, were sitting ducks for anything that came looking for them with an eye toward rectifying a situation that Molly's funeral hadn't quite handled. Shit.

Copper House would be a safe place for her and Jake—at least for the length of time it would take for her to determine whether Molly was alive and whether any real danger threatened them. Copper House lay through the gates, downworld in Oria, and it had been built to ward off the magics of the oldest and most deadly of the dark gods. The veyâr might be edging close to extinction, but it wasn't because they'd failed to take adequate precautions in covering their asses.

If Molly lived, Lauren had an obligation to go to Oria. She had a duty. She had work to do—and she couldn't turn her back on it, because she of all the people in the world had been born to do the things she had to do. Molly—half-human, half-veyâr—had been conceived and born at enormous personal cost to Lauren's mother. Lauren wasn't sure if her parents had actually figured out their plan before or after they discovered that Lauren could weave gates, and that she had a real knack for weaving them to places she'd never been. She knew, though, that even among gateweavers she was a rarity.

Lauren looked around the house that had belonged to her parents—that now belonged to her—and realized that if the veyâr told the truth, she was going to have to leave it behind, maybe forever. She didn't want to do that. Her mother had planted the daffodils and the crocuses, the phlox and the forsythia, the dogwoods and the azaleas. Her father had built the bookshelves and the window seats, fixed the front porch and made the porch swing, and done things up in the attic that Lauren still hadn't completely figured out. This was the only place in the world that she could truly claim as home. She didn't belong anywhere else.

"I'm going to have to bring Jake with me," she told the shadowy veyâr.

"Bring him."

"You don't understand. I can't get him anywhere near a gate without him going completely to pieces. Something awful happened to him related to Molly and gates, and I don't want to cause him any more pain."

The veyâr looked sympathetic—at least Lauren interpreted his expression and body movements as sympathy. He said, "The little boy will be safer in Copper House than here. The Imallin told me to be sure you knew that forces aware of the return of the Vodi—and of the import of that—have already begun to gather. They will know your relation to her. They will understand your importance. And if they cannot get to her—and they cannot, because she is safe in Copper House—they will come after you."

"No," Lauren said, but she already knew the truth in his words.

"Please. For your safety, for our worlds—for our people. Please come. She needs you. *We* need you."

Lauren tightened her grip on Jake, and stroked his hair.

"Go back. Tell her that I'll be there as quickly as I can. I need to take care of a few things before I leave here—I can't know how long I'll be gone, and I'll need to make arrangements."

She couldn't tell any of the Sentinels she was leaving, though. She couldn't trust them to be on her side if they knew Molly was alive. Except for Pete, maybe. She thought she could trust Pete. She needed to make sure he had her keys, that he could get into her house, pay her bills if she couldn't get back quickly enough . . . and she needed to be sure that he could keep the rest of the Sentinels from coming after her if she couldn't return to Earth promptly.

Lauren wouldn't have to worry too much about packing for a journey; the veyâr would take care of everything she needed while she stayed in Copper House. Once she left the veyâr stronghold and began to carry out her duties, she would have magic to provide for most of her needs. She'd have to have a couple of Jake's favorite toys. She'd need her picture of Brian. Beyond that . . .

She'd been staring at the floor, and she looked up to tell the veyâr that she would be along in a day or so—and he was already gone.

Lauren took a deep breath. Molly alive. Maybe . . . and if she was alive, how? And how did her being alive relate to the Sentinels' flat prohibition against bringing anyone back from death—or against the sick twist Lauren got in her gut when she even thought about using magic to resurrect the dead?

But those were details she could only know when she got to Oria. First she had to get there.

Lauren listed the things she needed to accomplish. A note and a key to the house shoved through a little gate into Pete's apartment, left on the table where he'd find both when he got home—and some sort of plausible lie to put in the note; put the house services on hold; get someone trustworthy to keep an eye on the house; put Bearish and Mr. Puddleduck and the Crashable Cars in a backpack with Jake's flannel jammies and Brian's photo.

And the letters. She wasn't leaving home without the letters she and Brian wrote to each other when he was stationed overseas.

She could do all of that in an afternoon. Rocking Jake in her arms, she realized that she could very possibly be out of the house before it started to get dark.

She didn't want to be. But the faster she got to Oria, the faster she would know the truth. And then maybe she would find that it was all a lie, and she could come back home.

But inside, she knew the veyâr had been telling her the truth. She could feel it, like the coming of a storm. Molly was alive again, and the two of them had work to do.

Cat Creek to Copper House

Lauren got the gate for the new girl out of the way simply because she didn't want to leave things undone. She had her paper stopped, left a note in the mailbox for the postman, turned the thermostat in the house down so that it would kick on and keep the pipes from freezing if Cat Creek had a late frost. She checked to make sure all the doors and windows were locked, that her car was locked away in the storage building to the back, that her private gates in the storage building were all shut down and blocked with her personal key.

All that, and twilight was just settling around the town. She wasn't ready to go.

"But I don't know that I'll ever be ready to go," she told Jake. "The big question is, do we ever get to come back . . . and I can't answer that one for us."

Jake, used to being the listening part of conversations that made no sense to him, gave her a tentative smile and focused on the words he recognized. "Go?" he asked. "Go to Hardee's, get biscuits?"

Lauren said, "Not today, Jake-o. Today we have other things to do. Time to go visit your aunt Molly."

That meant nothing to him. Well, he'd only met her once, under the worst possible circumstances; no reason to think her name would stick. Going through a gate would ring a few of Jake's bells, though. Lauren got her little overnight bag, slung it on her shoulder, and went to the hall mirror. She had Pete's note all ready. She read it again, looking for flaws.

Pete,

Sorry to beg a favor from you without warning, but Jake and I have to go to Charlotte. Brian's parents are going to be in town for the next few days, and have called from out of the blue and asked that he go visit them. Since there is no way in hell he's going to see those people without me around, I'm going to be out of town for the next few days. The Sentinels can get coverage from the gateweaver in Vass if you have an emergency before I get back. I'm not going to leave a phone number—this is something I have to do, and it isn't open for negotiation or time limits.

Please pass on my apologies to everyone. I would have done a more graceful job of this with more warning. I'll be back as soon as I can. Meantime, please keep an eye on the house for me, and eat anything perishable that you want from the fridge.

Thanks,
Lauren

It looked okay to her.

Lauren let Jake sit on the bottom step at the front of the foyer to wait for her. She went to the huge mirror at the back, took a deep breath, and rested one hand against the glass. She stared into her reflected eyes and concentrated on Pete's kitchen table, and after a moment she could see a tiny flash of green shimmer in the eyes of her reflected self. She called that fire to her, and beneath her splayed fingertips felt the mirror begin to purr like a happy cat. She unfocused her eyes just a bit, and the picture she saw changed—no longer a dark-haired woman standing with her hand on a full-length mirror in the hallway of an old house. Now she saw a neat, almost bare kitchen, the card table in the corner wiped clean and with a tiny handful of unopened bills placed at an exact ninety-degree angle in Pete's little apartment across town. She looked at this kitchen through a green glow—a haze of pale, cold fire. She didn't want to just shove the letter through, in case he was around, so she concentrated on pivoting her view to take in the rest of the kitchen.

His pantry, doorless and with neat wire shelves that she knew he'd installed himself, was terrifying. Lauren had lived within the military system, and she'd still never seen anything quite so compulsively neat. He'd alphabetized the cans, and cans occupied a different set of shelves than cereals and baking goods—which he actually had. Go figure. Not the typical bachelor.

She got a full-circle look at the area, and if he was around, he occupied some corner where he could see her. So she shoved the letter through the surface of the mirror, feeling the sensual pull of the paths spun between the worlds. Then, because she wanted him to see the letter, she made sure that it didn't line up at a right angle, but instead looked like she'd tossed it from the other side of the room and only barely hit her target. She dropped her key ring on the table beside the letter.

She pulled her arm back, and the fire she'd summoned died away. She turned to find Jake curled up on the bottom stair, his arms wrapped around his face. He was whispering "No, no, no . . ."

"Oh, Christ," Lauren whispered. She hurried to his side, crouched beside him, and pulled him into her arms. "Hey. Monkey-boy. Jake-puppy. It's okay. It's all right. Nothing's going to hurt you. I have you." She kissed him, and rocked him, and waited.

After a long, long time, she felt him relax.

Lauren wanted to throw up. This was the kid she was going to drag through a gate; this was the kid she was going to put face-to-face with the woman who'd almost gotten him killed, in the world that had almost killed him. She closed her eyes and tried to think of anyone, anywhere, that she would trust with the life of her child. And there was no one. Not one single person. Pete came closer than anyone else— but Lauren suspected Pete of harboring a secret, and until she knew what it was, she wouldn't take any chances with him, either.

We have to go, she thought. I have to do this, because if Molly and I succeed, we will save this world for all the generations that follow—and revive the worlds above it, and protect the ones below it. If I don't go, the next screwup, the next disaster, the next slip, could be the last, and everyone on the planet but the few who can find or create gates will die.

I have to go.

I cannot leave Jake behind.

I cannot wait until he's ready, because he might never be ready, and Molly and I don't have forever to do what we have to do.

She held her son, and rocked him in her arms, and silent tears ran down her cheeks. She hated what she had to do, and what it would do to Jake, and she hated feeling like a bad mother, and she hated her lack of options. For a moment she hated her parents for giving her such a burden to bear.

Then, because she knew the weight she carried, and because she would not shirk her responsibilities, she carried Jake back to the mirror and rested her free hand on the glass and summoned the fire that would carry her through realities. She summoned the world of Oria with its vast, ancient forests, and closed in on the walled village built around the magnificent Copper House, and drew herself a circle of fire in the center of the cobblestone street in front of the palace, between the two tall, blue-skinned veyâr guards who stood at either side of the door.

Then, her little bag of personal items on her shoulder and Jake clinging to her hip, frozen rigid with panic, she pushed gently against the mirror glass, and felt it give, and the universe beyond welcomed her into its embrace.

For a time that was no time and an eternity, while the music of the universe vibrated and strummed every cell of her body, she fell and floated and soared and the universe streamed by her, and she touched her own immortality and her soul commingled with Jake's. It's okay, she told the universe and Jake, all in a breath and a thought, and somehow she made it okay. She moved within the pain and the terror he held in his tiny body, and smoothed off the edges so that it was still his pain, which he had earned, and which was his by rights—but now he could face the pain.

Magic. Through the gates lay magic; the building blocks of the universe and the birthplace of godhood. For that time outside of time, she was pure spirit, the weight of her body fallen away to nothing, and she and Jake flew like eagles and angels.

Then the universe pushed them out the other side, and she and Jake were standing in front of the two veyâr guards, who, unprepared for their eruption from nothingness, howled and lowered weapons into attack positions.

"I'm the Vodi's sister," Lauren screamed, and clutched Jake tight. Should have thought of something besides her own convenience in making the gate, she realized. Those spears had hellish sharp points, and they were too close. She could summon a spell and blast both of the guards to oblivion—but they were supposed to be on her side. She willed them to move their spears to an upright position, and when they did, though she could see their muscles bulging as they fought to keep her at spearpoint, she said again, "I'm the Vodi's sister. I'm here because she sent for me."

They stared at her, and one of them turned his head fractionally, while still staring at her, and shouted, "Guest for the Vodi; claiming to be her sister."

She didn't push past them. She could have, but she didn't choose to make enemies. Something had them frightened and on edge—she should have recognized the signs as she watched them through the mirror. Guards walked the parapets of Copper House and squatted atop the towers along the wall that ringed the city. Soldiers, armed and watching the skies, and now some of them watching her.

Lauren looked up.

Dark shapes soared high overhead. She would have thought them vultures, or maybe ravens, but the scalloped trailing edges of their wings and the whiplike length of their tails made her realize how very high above they soared. She counted a dozen before she turned to the guards who watched her. "Rrôn," she said, and shivered.

They nodded. "Gathering since the Vodi returned. They want nothing good."

"No," Lauren agreed.

Humans called them dragons, and had known them as dragons when they lived on Earth, and had feared or worshiped them. With reason. They were creatures out of nightmare. She'd seen three one terrible day, and had killed one. She was tempted to use the magic she controlled in Oria to create some weapon to shoot them out of the sky. Except magic that dealt death had echoes that flowed upworld; if she killed one of the rrôn here, something terrible would happen to a dozen innocents back on Earth—or perhaps to a hundred or a thousand who were less innocent. No one understood how magic moved between the worlds well enough to predict the echoes that any action could cause.

But everyone could point to correlations—a healing spell that spawned remissions, a murder that spawned a killing spree.

She would kill nothing using magic unless she had no other choice. She left the rrôn to their circling and turned her attention to the front gate, where an amber-skinned, golden-haired veyâr stepped through the front arch of Copper House and walked toward her.

King of the castle, she thought. Master of an empire. He wore a simple tunic of deep red velvet, black breeches and soft, low black boots, and he had neither crown nor scepter. But he wore power, and that gave lie to the simple clothes, the unadorned braid hanging down his back, the fact that he carried about him no symbols of power.

His men turned to him and offered deep bows; he responded with a nod.

This, then, would be Seolar, Molly's love.

Lauren waited, not bowing. Seolar, when he reached a spot between the two guards she still held at bay, stopped and studied her for a long, still moment. Eyes of jet black, enormous, without scleras, looked into hers and she felt as if her life had been laid bare for everyone to see. She was, to the veyâr, one of the old gods. But, dammit, the veyâr had presence. She could roast this fellow with a word and a wave of her hand, but he outclassed her on a scale that defied measurement.

"You favor her in a hundred ways I cannot even define," he said after a moment. Then he bowed to her, gracefully and deeply, and said, "Quickly, please. Inside—the rrôn arrived a while ago, and the Vodi has not been herself since their coming. They watch all we do, and I fear they may know the Vodi's Hunter has arrived."

Lauren spared another glance at the sky and saw that the rrôn now circled closer. She held Jake tighter, clutched her shabby little carry-on bag, and hurried after the master of the castle, feeling small and insignificant and nervous.

Through doors of solid copper, beneath arches bound in

copper, over floors banded in copper, past copper spun into lamps and fountains and banisters and balustrades, she followed the veyâr, who set a fast pace.

She stepped at last into a generous library, with books that lined the walls to a height of three stories, with walkways all around and spiraling staircases up and down, and in the corner one fine, grand fireplace. And in front of the fireplace, taller than she had any business being, and with the delicate bones and impossibly green eyes that marked her as having veyâr blood, stood Molly.

Lauren saw her sister, and tears filled her eyes. Molly hurried across the room and hugged her and Jake.

They stood that way for a while, rocking back and forth, and finally Molly pulled away a little. Lauren swung her bag to the ground and shifted Jake over to her other hip. She shook her head and smiled, lost for words.

"Kind of hard to figure out what to say, isn't it?" Molly offered at last.

"Aside from 'Jesus, it's good to see you,' yeah. Kind of hard." Lauren shook her head. "But . . . Jesus, it's good to see you."

Cat Creek

Pete got home late. He hadn't intended to stop by work, but after Lauren turned him down again—and then shooed him out of the house in such an abrupt fashion—he didn't feel like going home and brooding about it. And Eric had needed help with one thing and then another, and they'd gotten to talking and had a few laughs, and then had taken off for Bennettsville for a couple of drinks and a couple of steaks.

He thought he'd go straight to bed. But on his way past the kitchen, he caught a glimpse of something out of place from the corner of his eye. He stopped, internal alarms going off. Put his hand on the butt of his Browning, held his breath, and listened. He could hear nothing. He tried to figure out what about the dark kitchen had set him off, and narrowed it down to a splotch of white on the kitchen table.

He hadn't left anything on the kitchen table. More than once, knowing exactly how he'd left a place and being able to spot changes had saved his life. And he hadn't started getting sloppy.

He edged back around the corner into the kitchen. It was empty, but someone had been there. He saw a piece of paper and a key ring.

Check for bombs first? Dare a light switch?

He decided to read the note. Put on gloves and a filter mask, because stuff that just showed up where it had no business being could turn out to be lethal.

Preparations taken, he read the note. He felt better—after all, at least Lauren had liked him enough to trust him with her stuff for a few days. But just when he'd decided to feel flattered, he looked at her keys and his stomach knotted and the hair on the back of his neck stood up.

She hadn't just left her house key. Or even the house key and a key to the mailbox. She'd left her full key ring—including her car key. And this wasn't a spare key ring. This was *her* key ring, the one with the picture of the Sainted Dead Husband in one side of a Lucite frame and Jake as a baby in the other.

Pete started running scenarios in his head—no one had come through the door, disturbing the little telltale he always left. The only way in through the windows was to break one, and after a quick inventory of the rest of the apartment, he cleared windows as a possible point of entry. So Lauren had used her little mirror trick to deliver the note. That wasn't the problem. The problem was, had she done it of her own free will, or under duress? And if under duress, then from whom? Another rogue Sentinel? One of the enemies Lauren had no doubt left in Oria? Or one of *his* problems, who'd seen him with her and decided she and Jake would make nice leverage?

Or . . . had she just made a dumb mistake? Left him her

ring and taken her spare? He wasn't immune to tendencies to assume the worst, to seeing disaster where none existed, or even to going off half-cocked—though he'd gotten better about that over the years.

So what should he do?

First, he decided, he'd check her place. Look for signs of forcible entry to the house, her car, out back in the storage shed; check for evidence of a struggle inside.

Next, check out the in-laws. Where were they, what was their story?

Then . . . well, depending on what he found, maybe a visit to a few old friends. Carefully, of course. But for certain sorts of problems, especially people going missing for nasty reasons, he had just the right sort of friends.

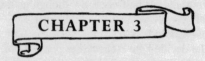

CHAPTER 3

Above Copper House, Ballahara, Oria

THE RRÔN SPUN and spiraled in the sky above the hunkered-down copper-clad dwelling, with Rr'garn over all of them. Master of the dark rrôn—the hunters, the destroyers—Rr'garn wore the scars of a hundred deaths between his wings; each had burned him and hardened him until he was cold as death itself, free from the burdens and the hungers and the dreams of life. He breathed power, sang power, flew power; he no longer even slept, and so had shed the last frailty of dreams.

He arched his neck and set his wings to best advantage, knowing the spectacle he made as he soared and enjoying the awe he inspired.

He would ascend to Master of the Night Watch. He had decreed it, and his rrôn would fight to put him in the seat of power. He drank the deaths of worlds, and already his belly cried out for the next great meal. Never had a rrôn been as magnificent as Rr'garn, nor would another ever equal him. Even his allies trembled in fear at his passing.

Cowering inside the copper barriers, the first real threat to the aims of the Night Watch in more than a hundred years shook off the lingering pains of her first death. He yearned to feel her heart beating, to feel the air moving through her lungs, to hear the mouse-quick dance of her thoughts. But she and her thoughts eluded him. He knew she waited inside the barriers of Copper House; his spies swore to that. He heard she had an ally—a sister with terrifying powers of her own. His spies swore to that as well. What he did not know was what this new Vodi and her sister would do. He felt trouble coming; he sensed that this Vodi was not the timid, shy little creature the previous Vodian had all been. Everything about these two new players reeked of uncertainty.

In that uncertainty lay the potential for disaster.

If the problem stood to be disastrous, the cure was simple enough. Destroy the Vodi, slaughter her sister. And promptly, before they started to work against the Night Watch.

Rr'garn held in his mind a memory of the Vodi's thoughts, that he had caught before she found a way to shut the dark gods out of her mind. The one his spies called the Hunter was another matter. Neither he nor any of his could mark the Hunter at all; she still resided among the truly living.

But subtlety would be best if his warriors could manage it. Treaties with the other dark gods hung in the balance; and if he were too zealous, Rr'garn could give away his hunt for the head seat on the Night Watch before he was ready for the war that would ensue when he decided the time was right to claim it. So—no armies of rrôn sweeping down and leveling Copper House. Instead, one special soldier, sent alone into the halls of Copper House, who could neatly destroy the Hunter and bring out the Vodi, whose death would take a great deal more effort.

Rr'garn liked that plan. And he knew which soldier would be able to accomplish the task.

"Watch the place," he told his wing-second, Trrtrag. "If anything changes, shout me. I'm after Baanraak."

Trrtrag eyed him as if Rr'garn had lost his mind. "Baanraak? He stepped away an eon ago. He'll devour you before he returns to the Night Watch."

"Devour Rr'garn?" Rr'garn said. "Baanraak has grown large in your mind after all these years. And he is clever, or I would not spend the necessary time to seek him out. But . . . fearsome? I think not. I hear he suns himself like an old lizard, and has reduced himself in his old age to eating voles and insects." Rr'garn added, "I don't want him to return to

the Night Watch. I just want to hire his . . . talents. He stands
to lose even more than we do if these blisters undo our work
or re-life Kerras."

"Luck, then, that you find him," Trrtrag said, "and that
you make him see reason before he rips out your throat and
melts down your gold."

Rr'garn thought Trrtrag lacking in reverence toward him.
He had heard one among his number might be disloyal,
harboring plans for his own advancement. "I'll take your
luck," he said, thinking he would deal with Trrtrag upon his
return. He set his wings into the last of the day's thermals
and spiraled upward, nostrils flared wide, mind and body
stretched tight as bowstrings, searching for the oldest of the
dark rrôn, the deadest of the dead.

Copper House

Molly sat in her suite across from Lauren, resting in a broad,
soft chair, but she held her body rigid with tension. She
stared out the window closest to her, looking up, and said
nothing.

"What are they doing out there?" Lauren asked.

Seolar, standing at the window, shrugged. "They're flying. Circling. There are neither more nor less of them than
there were an hour ago."

"There's one less," Molly said, and both Seolar and Lauren jumped. She'd said almost nothing since they entered
the suite—and Lauren guessed that had been half an hour
earlier.

Seolar turned away from the window. "I have good eyes,
and I didn't see one leave. My vantage point is better than
yours. How can you be sure?"

Molly's face held no expression. She turned away from
the window and closed her eyes, but her body didn't relax in
the slightest. "My love, you truly do not want to know."

Seolar said, "My love, truly I do."

Lauren sat in the middle of a conversation that felt like it was about to become a lovers' quarrel. She squirmed and looked at Jake, asleep on the couch—no reprieve there. She couldn't leave without him, and she couldn't very well use him as an excuse. So she sat, cringing inwardly. Molly· didn't want to talk, and had grown quieter and more withdrawn the longer the rrôn circled Copper House, and as Lauren watched her sister watching them, she started to get the feeling that Molly knew something of what was going on.

Now Molly stood and removed all doubt. "The one who left," she said, an edge on her voice and anger in every line of her body, "is named Rr'garn. His mind is cold and harsh, ugly and crowded with plans worse than the worst thing I've ever thought." She turned to Lauren and said, "He thinks he and his monsters up there need to kill both you and me as quickly as possible, because we're going to be a problem."

Seolar stood with his mouth hanging open—no more attractive an expression on the face of a veyâr than on a human, Lauren noticed. "How do you know that?" he asked Molly after a moment.

The anger seemed to drain from Molly's body, almost as if someone had pulled a plug and let it spill out. "I can hear him," she said. "I don't know how. I can hear bits and pieces of what all of them are thinking . . . or maybe feeling. I don't know which. But their minds echo in mine even now. It's almost as if they and I are strings tuned to the same note, and the finger that plucks them vibrates me."

Lauren studied her sister. Molly looked sick, as if just admitting this was more than she could bear.

"Molly?" Lauren stood and went to her sister's side. "Hey, it's okay. You tell us what they're thinking, we'll use that against them."

Molly looked down into Lauren's eyes, and for a fleeting instant an expression of pure grief flashed across her face. Then it was gone, and Molly managed a smile. "But you see," she said, "they can hear me as clearly as I hear him. Or they could. I think I've managed to close them out now, but not before they found out more about me than I wanted them to know." Her voice dropped to a whisper. "And having seen inside me, they still think that I'm like them. Or that I will be, given enough time and enough deaths." Molly shuddered and wrapped her thin arms tightly around herself.

Lauren hugged her. "You aren't evil, Molly. You aren't like those things. It's some weird trick that you can hear their thoughts."

Molly took a deep breath, smiled at Lauren, and nodded. "You're probably right. I'm still kind of . . . shaken up after what happened. I'm feeling lost. And that monster knew it—knew that I was just back, that I was still under the effects of everything that happened to me. I hadn't even considered the possibility, but this probably will go away. In the meantime"—she turned to Seolar— "you need to make sure that no one and nothing that you can't recognize personally gets into Copper House. Rr'garn went off in search of a killer, one he expects to get past whatever you put up to keep the thing out. He had the image of a rrôn in his mind, but just one, and one with some sort of special skills."

"They're dark gods," Seolar said quietly. "They all have special skills."

Lauren said, "The Sentinels talk about old gods. You talk about dark gods. Is there any difference?"

Seolar glanced at Molly—just a little twitch of the eyes left, then right and away from her—and he pressed his lips together and nodded. "There's a difference. Let me make sure that the guards are on high alert and all the gates are up and barred, and then I'll tell you the story of the Wreck of Heaven."

He left.

Lauren and Molly looked at each other. "The Wreck of Heaven?" Lauren asked.

Molly shrugged. "I haven't heard this one, either."

Lauren said, "It'll wait until he gets back, then. In the meantime, how are you? Really?"

"Mostly, I'm okay," Molly said. She played with the folds

of her full silk skirt and stared down at the floor. When she looked up at Lauren, she said, "I'm scared, though. I'm scared of this thing we're supposed to do, and the responsibility we have; I'm scared of what happens if we don't try it. I'm afraid of those bastards up there. I'm afraid of making some mistake that destroys home. Earth. I guess for me this is home now, but you know what I mean."

"I know what you mean."

"And I feel . . . wobbly inside." Molly tilted her head and frowned at Lauren. "That doesn't sound right. I feel like something is missing. I'm here, and as far as I can tell, I remember everything that I ever remembered before, but— you know that spot in your eyes where if you hold up a pencil and look at a fixed point and move the pencil around, the tip of it will disappear?"

Lauren nodded. She'd done that little experiment; probably every kid who ever sat through biology had.

"I feel like I have a blind spot like that somewhere inside of me, only I haven't got the pencil to the place yet where it disappears so that I can tell where it is. There's a hole in me somewhere, Lauren, and I can't find it, and I don't know that I can trust myself until I do."

Lauren sighed and hugged her again. "I'm so sorry. Molly, I'm glad you're alive. But I feel so awful that you died."

Molly laughed. "No shit. I'm not crazy about that myself. It doesn't seem to have done me too much damage, but . . . I'd rather not do it again."

"What I can't figure out is how you came back. If you could, why couldn't Brian?"

"Brian was your husband?"

"Yeah."

Molly nodded. "Probably because he wasn't wearing this necklace when he died." She put a hand on the gorgeous, sleek gold chain that she wore. "The Vodi necklace. My predecessors wore it, and every time they got killed, and apparently each of them got killed a lot, the necklace brought them back."

"Until it didn't," Lauren noted.

Molly raised her eyebrows in a silent question.

"None of them is here now," Lauren noted. "So at some point, it looks like the magic wears off or . . . ?"

"No. Each of them eventually got tired of all the pain and dying and just quit. Took the necklace off, put it down where someone who knew what it was would find it, then walked away and died for good. If you aren't wearing the necklace when you die, it can't bring you back because it doesn't know you're gone."

Lauren thought about that—about getting tired of being immortal and about choosing to die. She thought she could understand. She considered the necklace that Molly wore, and thought about Brian, and about monstrous hunters outside Copper House that were, at that moment, trying to find a way to kill her. She thought about Jake, asleep on the soft, plush chair, and how trusting and vulnerable he was, and about how he had no one in the world but her that he could truly count on.

And she considered again the magic that she could do, and the limits placed on it by an uncaring universe.

I need Brian, she thought. I need him here with me; he'd know how to fight those monsters outside. He'd be able to figure out Mom and Dad's notes and put them in some sort of order and tell me exactly what Molly and I are supposed to do. He'd be able to protect Jake far better than I can.

But Brian had no magic necklace. And Brian was gone.

"Where did you go?" Molly asked, and Lauren, startled, came out of her fugue.

"Hell," she said. "I was considering the benefits of running away."

Molly laughed a little. "You scared, too?"

"For Jake more than for me, but yes. I'm petrified."

"But we have to do this, don't we?" Molly asked.

"We could walk away," Lauren said. "But when Earth died, I don't know that we could live with ourselves, knowing that we could have saved it."

Molly looked like someone had punched her. Pain flashed across her face, and her eyes grew bright with unshed tears, and she swallowed hard. "I passed on a chance to save someone once. I thought I'd do it later—and I couldn't. I missed the window. And now I'll carry that stranger on my back as long as I have breath and memory." She shook her head. "Never again. We take the chance we're offered, right?"

Lauren looked at Jake. "Yeah. Yeah—we take our chances, and we do what we can." She held out her hand, and Molly took it, and smiling strangely at each other, they shook.

"We're committed now," Molly said. "We have to save the world."

"It's worse than that," Lauren said. "We have to save all of them."

Copper House

Molly heard Seolar coming back well before he arrived. She kept noticing little changes in herself—acuity of hearing, sight, and smell that caught her off guard, the ability to read the thoughts and intentions of the monsters outside Copper House—and those changes frightened her. Had she been the same as before, she could have pretended that nothing had happened. She couldn't pretend anything of the sort, though. Nor could she get past the question that all those little changes begged: What had changed inside of her that she couldn't see?

Seolar looked tense when he came in. He didn't offer any explanations, and Molly didn't ask for any. Lauren was less polite. "What's wrong?"

Seolar gave her a little bow and said, "Staffing difficulties. The situation within Copper House was uncharacteristically disorganized; I have Birra, my second, looking into it."

Molly sensed evasion in that explanation, and one look at her sister told her that Lauren did, too. But Seolar forestalled any more questions by saying, "I told you I'd tell you about the rrôn and the Wreck of Heaven." He pointed to the chairs and both Lauren and Molly sat. Seolar took a seat across from them and angled his chair so that he could watch both the windows and the door. "This is myth, you understand— one of the stories of the old gods and the dark gods that the veyâr claim came from old gods passing through. It may be. It also may be nonsense, and I have no way of telling how much truth is in it, if any."

He sighed and looked out the window. "Some truth, I think." He gave Molly a little smile, and she smiled back. "At the beginning, in the youth of our worldchain, all the worlds lived and none traveled between them—and because the people of each world stayed where they belonged, there were no gods; but magic flowed freely, available to anyone who chose to use it. So goes the story." Seolar shrugged. "And this was Heaven—when everything was right, and such evils as existed were little things that confined them- selves to each individual world. Then a gate opened and swallowed the one who would become the first of the old gods and carried him to the world below, where this first old god discovered that he had more power than he could imag- ine. And the power sang to his heart and mind, and bent his soul into an ugly shape, and he chose to create more gates. Through those gates he brought a few of his friends, and gave them a world that they could exploit, and native people who could be made to bow down and serve."

"Nice," Lauren said. "So the first gateweavers were ass- holes."

Seolar's eyebrows went up, and Molly grinned and pro- vided the translation. "Evil bad people."

Seolar said, "But the . . . asshole . . . it is the ah . . . this is rather indelicate . . ."

"Yes," Molly said, cutting him off. "That's it. Calling peo- ple assholes is a . . . mmmm . . . suggestion that they have many of the same characteristics."

Seolar considered this thoughtfully for a moment. Then

he smiled. "Oh. How appropriate. What a clever use of the word to imply meaning without long description." He looked at Lauren with admiration in his face and said, "That's most excellent."

"It's hardly original," Lauren said, blushing. To Molly she added, "Tell me I didn't just invent profanity on Oria."

"A modern-day Prometheus—that's you," Molly told her sister.

"F—." Lauren stopped herself. "No. I've done enough damage for one day."

Seolar frowned. "I thought that use of the word most clever of you."

"Maybe," Lauren said, "but if I ever make it into the history books, I don't want it to be for introducing cussing to the veyâr. So what happened with the first of the old gods?"

"They told their friends about the vast magics available through the gates, and those who could brought their friends, and those friends brought friends, until old gods overran the first world they found, depleted its magic, and caused problems in their own world from the effects of using magic for evil purposes in the world below. Their world suffered. So more people left it, moving downworld, and then downworld again. And at some point, these relatively soft and unsuspecting old gods came into contact with the rrôn."

Seolar whispered the word, and Molly saw him glance out into the darkness beyond. She could have told him that the rrôn still circled out there, but she didn't. She doubted that he would want to know how closely they watched the place, or that they fantasized the destruction of everyone within its walls as they flew, or how much they resented the copper that shielded Copper House's inhabitants from their magic.

He shook his head and continued. "The rrôn learned quickly. Before long, they understood the gates in a way that no one before them had. They understood going upworld against the natural tide, they understood the uses of magic, and they understood how magic flows between the worlds. And they discovered that worlds could feed them more magic if the rrôn killed those worlds. They brought others into their scheme over time—some of the most hellish of the old gods, like the keth and the shuminn, joined with them. They began intentionally pulling magic from the worlds they went to, feeding off of them, so the story goes, and draining them until they died. And when a world died, the magic from killing it made them stronger, so they could kill the next one faster."

Lauren and Molly looked at each other. Molly nodded—this was something Lauren's parents had imprinted in her brain. Some of the old gods killed worlds intentionally.

"That is the tale of the Wreck of Heaven," Seolar said. "That none of the old gods should travel the worldchain, but that some of the old gods feed upon the death of worlds; these are the dark gods, and they are merciless and relentless and evil beyond all comprehension. Without them, the story-tellers say that no worlds would die."

He stood. "It may be true. It may not. But whether the rrôn and the other dark gods drink the lives of worlds to feed their own immortality, or whether they are evil simply for the pleasure of being evil, or whether some other hunger drives them, they will stand between the two of you and what you hope to do. They are—and can be nothing but—your enemies. They are the enemies of all existence." He turned to Molly and said, "It has grown late. I'll have the servants bring a meal, and then they can show your sister to her suite. I think, considering our circumstances, that we would be best served not to have entertainment tonight."

"Oh, definitely not for me," Lauren said. "I'll need to get some rest. I'm exhausted."

Seolar bowed. "And tomorrow, the two of you can . . . begin your work, if you are both ready."

Cat Creek

Pete leaned against the bedroom doors in Lauren's house, studying the pattern of the mess. She had packed quickly, rummaging through the toy box for toys for Jake, and through her closet for something kept on the top shelf with the shoe boxes. The picture of the Sainted Dead Husband was gone from her nightstand. But her car was hidden in the back of the old workshop, tucked away under a tarp, and the ex-in-laws were still out in California and appalled by the very idea of having anything to do with their hick ex-daughter-in-law or her kid. Boy, he had *really* hated those people.

And both Lauren's clothes and Jake's were virtually undisturbed.

She'd gone voluntarily, and he was pretty sure she and Jake had gone alone. But not to Charlotte. He figured she'd slipped through to Oria during the Sentinels' shift change.

Which meant she'd lied to him. Nice to know she wasn't very good at it. A man didn't want to plan a future around a *good* liar.

So. Something had come up, and he figured since it wasn't something that she'd told the Sentinels, it had to be related to the secret plans she and her sister had shared.

Technically he was supposed to throw in his lot with the Sentinels, be one of the guys, be trustworthy. Lauren and Molly had had something going, though—and if it came right down to it, Pete would put his money on Lauren to be on the side of the angels over any position the Sentinels might take.

He looked at the clock. It was *way* too late to call Eric with anything purporting to be casual information. Pete would just talk to him at the station come morning. Show Eric the note, say he'd checked out Lauren's story and the in-laws were major assholes, say he'd be staying at the house to keep an eye on things for her until she got back. And then slide right on into the gossip of the day, which looked to be how Mayhem had hit on one of the two new girls, Darlene, and gotten a face full of Pepsi for it.

Pete nodded, liking the plan.

He went down to Lauren's living room and kicked off his

shoes, and sacked out on the couch. He saw a bit of difference between eating the stuff in Lauren's fridge and sleeping in her bed. He wasn't going to do the latter until he was invited. And she was there to share it.

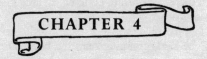

CHAPTER 4

Copper House

CLACK-CLACK.
  "Foom!"
  Clack-skitter-clack-thump.
  "Sssssssmeeeeeeeee . . . POW!"
  Lauren opened one eye. Strange bedroom. Light a bit too peach-colored. Jake sitting on the floor in the next room, with Bearish on one side of him and Mr. Puddleduck on the other, crashing cars into each other.

  She got a lot more awake very fast. Jesus—she didn't think Jake could open doors in this place on his own. They used latches that took a bit of coordination, and all the doors weighed a ton. But she figured she'd make damned sure he couldn't open the doors again before she dared let herself sleep so soundly. In this huge old place, and with strangers and danger all around, she didn't dare take chances.

  She sat up and stretched, and he turned to her, smiling.

  "Hey, monkey-boy," she said.

  "Hey, Mama. Bearish crashded his car."

  "He did, huh? He needs to be more careful."

  "Yes," Jake agreed. "He got hurted. He gots a bump on his head."

  "I'm sorry. Shall I kiss it and make it better?"

  He nodded and carried Bearish to her, and she asked, "Where does he hurt?" She'd learned to ask—medicinal kisses applied to the wrong spot always drew an indignant, "NO! Not there!" from Jake.

"Right there," Jake said, pointing. Lauren kissed the back of the bear's head.

"Did that fix it?"

"Yes," he said, climbing onto the bed with her. "Thank you."

He sat beside her, a hand on her knee. He looked worried. "What's wrong, puppy?"

Jake thought for a moment, finding the words. "I dreamded about Daddy."

Oh, no. Lauren scooped him into her arms and cuddled him. "What did you dream?"

"Cars crashded on Daddy."

That wasn't something she had ever told him. It had to be coming from the memories Jake had gotten from Brian when Brian saved Jake's life by giving him a part of Brian's soul. Brian's gift had kept Jake alive as he and Molly moved between the worlds. And it had changed Jake in a number of little ways. He knew more words, spoke more clearly, used phrases his father had used . . . and apparently remembered things that had happened to Brian. "Yes. A bus crashed on Daddy, actually."

"Could you kiss Daddy and make him all better?"

Lauren hugged Jake tight. "Oh, sweetheart. I wish I could have. More than you will ever know. But Daddy was hurt too badly for kisses. Nothing could make him better."

"Oh." Jake laid his head against her. "He was a good daddy."

She felt tears fill her eyes, and she blinked them back. "The best," she said, her voice suddenly hoarse. She swallowed hard.

"Bring him back," Jake said.

Lauren closed her eyes. "Don't think I haven't thought about it." She kissed Jake's forehead and ruffled his hair. "But I can't," she said. "He's gone someplace where I *can't* bring him back. He's . . . far away. He's gone."

"I want to bring him back."

She hugged him tighter. "Me too, kiddo. Me too."

Copper House

Molly woke with the weight of the rrôn in her head, and spent the first bit of her morning with Seolar avoiding mentioning their presence, either outside the window or in her thoughts. When Seo went to take care of his business for the day, however, Molly decided that before she made any plans with Lauren, she was going to find out why she could hear the rrôn.

Copper House had an excellent library. She couldn't read a word in it, because she couldn't read any of the hundreds of Orian languages yet—when she heard any Orian speak, her brain and some low-level magic translated what was said into English. The translations, however, did not extend to deciphering text.

So she found Birra guarding the door. "Come with me," she said. "We have work to do."

Birra smiled at her. "You look magnificent today, Vodi. I am so very, very glad you . . . found your way home."

"Me, too—and that's a very polite way to put it." She swept down the hallway toward the library, Birra at her side.

"So what sort of work are we doing?" Birra asked.

"We're researching the rrôn. And past Vodian." Molly, in her time in Oria, had discovered that telling saved a lot of time—that when she politely asked, people who had been trained to serve, as Birra had, became confused and couldn't figure out what she expected of them, and didn't know how to react. She was not comfortable in a command position—she'd been enlisted, not an officer, in the Air Force—but she'd seen command done long enough that she thought she was doing a pretty good job of faking it.

"Vodi?" Birra sounded distressed.

Molly didn't slow at all. "Yes, Birra?"

Between them hung a pause that grew, and grew, and with

every step they took down the hall that pause became more uncomfortable. From the corner of her eye, Molly could see Birra's mouth opening and closing as if he were a fish tossed on the bank. He looked both appalled and fearful, and in her time knowing Birra, she had never seen him look either way before.

"Spit it out, Birra," Molly said.

His head swiveled and he stared at her. "I have nothing in my mouth, Vodi."

Molly sighed. Colloquialisms almost always died badly when undergoing translation, yet she could not give them up. She said, "Tell me what it is that you want to say that you don't think I'll want to hear."

"Oh." The pause again, but this time at the point where it got really uncomfortable, Birra sighed and said, "There are so many other things you could do with your day, Vodi. Your sister and her son are here, and certainly you wish to plan with the Hunter . . ."

Molly raised a hand. "Whoa. In the time I've known you, Birra, you've taken the trouble to be honest with me. You aren't being honest now. You're hiding something. What?"

Birra didn't look at her. They arrived at the library doors, and in a stiff, formal voice he said, "I only believe, Vodi, that you will not bring yourself any joy pursuing information on the rrôn, or on previous Vodian. I would dissuade you only because I do not wish to see you unhappy."

"The pursuit of information is only rarely done in pursuit of happiness," Molly said. "You'll give me the information I need, won't you?"

"Yes."

"Fine. Please find me any information we have about the rrôn. Where they came from, what they believe, where they've been, what they've done—anything. I'll also need biographies of previous Vodian, and especially any records of Vodian contacts with the rrôn."

"Especially that?"

Molly nodded. "Especially that. I have something funny

going on in my head, Birra, and I want to know what it is
and how to stop it."

"Very well. Which books should we go through first?"

Molly considered. "All the newest information."

"How new is new?"

"Anything written within the last year."

Birra shook his head.

"Last ten years?"

Birra shook his head again.

"Jesus. Last fifty?"

"We might have something in the last fifty years, but I
wouldn't depend on its reliability."

Molly glanced at him sidelong to see if he was pulling her
leg, but he looked dead serious. "Okay. Do you know specif-
ically of any references to contact between Vodian and rrôn,
at any time in your history?"

"No."

"No. Of course not. Then how about helping me just find
everything you have on the rrôn. And all the Vodian biographies—and anything else on my predecessors."

Birra consulted a file, and took a log that lay atop the file,
and logged in the titles and reference numbers of the books
he needed. Molly, looking over his shoulder, could recognize the difference between the numbers and the letters of
the local writing system, but that was it. She needed to learn
how to read. The fact that she couldn't frustrated her endlessly. She followed Birra through the rows, up and down the
stairs to other levels, and finally helped him carry the two
stacks of books and manuscripts he'd managed to locate.

They hauled everything down to a long table in front of
the fireplace, and Molly took a chair. She indicated that
Birra should take one beside her, and said, "Now, tell me
what we have here."

"This first manuscript is *Imallin Merional's Conversations with the Dark Gods*, written probably five hundred
years ago. I cannot swear that it will have a great deal about
the rrôn, but it may, and will certainly be worth perusing.

Merional has maintained his reputation for clear writing and honesty through the ages."

Molly nodded. "That sounds promising. What else?"

"*Those Whose Names Are Unspoken.* To the best of my knowledge, this is a compilation of knowledge about the rrôn and the keth, gathered by veyâr only a hundred years or so ago. As recent information, it hasn't yet had the chance to prove its lasting value, but you might find some worth in it, if you're willing to accept possible errors."

A hundred years old, and in Birra's eyes it was recent information. Molly sighed. The veyâr were not people who would have much interest in the constantly shifting, ever-updated news-driven world Molly came from. They preferred their information well aged—preferably with a bit of moss on it. She suspected that preferring old information and suspecting new information let them maintain the twin illusions that everything stayed pretty much the same, and that the world was a comprehensible place.

She, however, would have loved a hot-off-the-press, possibly controversial, untested, untried report from a team of anthropologists, biologists, and social scientists who had been dissecting the rrôn and their society for the past five or ten years and who had gathered all the latest dirt into one thick, boring, multisyllabic assessment that would, somewhere in the heart of it, tell her why she could hear the bastards thinking, why she felt a secret, unspeakable, uncanny urge to go running out into the open spaces to scream, "Hey, I'm one of you guys," at them . . . and what the hell she was supposed to do about it.

Birra listed the other books and manuscripts for her—*Life of the Vodi Elspeth*, *Life of the Vodi Melantha*, *Life of the Vodi Aki*, *Life of the Vodi Kelda*. *Travels of the Veyâr from the Lost Homeland*. *The Recounting of Imallin Galorayne*. A couple of untitled journals.

It looked like it was going to be a long day, but Molly was fine with that. She said, "All right. Let's start with *Merional's Dark Gods*. Conversations at least sound promising."

She settled back in her chair, and found Birra looking at her, confused.

"What's wrong?"

"I don't understand, Vodi. I found you the books. What do you want me to do with them?"

"Read them to me."

For just an instant, the confusion held its ground. Then the tiniest look of relief appeared in Birra's eyes, and he said, "You want me to read them to you?"

"I can't read—at least, not these. I read in my own language just fine."

"But when you look at these books I got for you, you do not see words? You cannot understand them . . . at all?"

"Not so much as a word," Molly said. "That's something I'm going to have to remedy, but for now, I need a reader. And that reader is going to be you . . . because I know I can trust you to be honest with me. Right?"

"Of course, Vodi," Birra said. But the tiny edge of relief didn't go away.

She wondered what was in the books that he didn't want her to find out. Whatever it was, she was certain that she hadn't managed to convince him to give her the truth. He still seemed to her just the smallest bit satisfied with the situation, as if he had things under control. As long as she couldn't do her own reading, he was right.

She would just have to hope that he wouldn't be able to figure out which information she most needed and would let something slip.

Birra skimmed pages, offering the titles of each, and Molly said, "Pass . . . pass . . . pass . . ." until he got to, "My Discussion with Baanraak," and Molly recognized the name. Baanraak was the killer the rrôn leader had gone off to find.

"Read that one," she said.

Birra frowned and sighed, but he began to read.

In the forests far from the village, Baanraak the rrôn agreed to meet with me, with an exchange of fine

yellow gold for his time and the guarantee of my
safety; we met as we'd set out to do, and I gave him
the first half of the gold to prove my intent, and he did
not immediately devour me, and so proved his.

Like many of the dark gods I have so far met, he is
in the flesh amiable enough, and tells a good tale. He
recounted to me some of his exploits in worlds above
this one, and though I do not credit them fully, still he
told them with enthusiasm and an eye for detail that
made them fascinating to me. He agrees with others of
the dark gods that there are no other men like us in the
worldchain, that we are the only veyâr—and that is a
thought I cannot countenance. Surely the gods, seeing
that they had done a thing right once, would do it in
the same manner each time.

Molly giggled in spite of herself at that.

Birra glanced up at her. "You do not agree that the gods
made the veyâr well?"

"Wasn't what I was thinking at all. The writer simply
sounds like a lot of humans I know, who either think that the
only living, thinking beings in the universe can be human
and that they exist nowhere but on Earth, or that life exists
elsewhere, but it has to all be human."

Birra said, "Have you no other people in your world, as
we have the Tradona people or the goroths or two handfuls
of others?"

"We don't have any," Molly said. "We might have at one
time, but no more."

"Then what about the old gods? Surely your people cannot see the old gods and think themselves sole owners of the
universe."

"The old gods have gotten thin on Earth," Molly said.
"They've either moved on or are in hiding."

Birra frowned. "I wish I knew how you had managed that.
This would be a better place without them."

Molly gave him a sad little smile and said, "I think it's because our world is getting ready to die. Most of the old gods are moving on because they don't want to get trapped there when it happens."

"Ah." Birra shook his head. "Never mind, then. Perhaps we can find a way to tolerate them." He started reading again.

> *Baanraak seemed more honest than most of the dark gods who spoke to me. He does not claim any pain or grief over the harm he does, nor does he say he regrets the path he chose long before I or any of mine were born. He says that dying—*

Birra flipped the page and started reading again.

> *This Baanraak claims to have no great love for his own people, the rrôn, but by his word, if I am to believe it, the rrôn have ever been solitary creatures.*

"Wait a minute," Molly said. "You were reading something on the other page about Baanraak dying."

"Not at all," Birra said. "He started into a long and gruesome description of killing the veyâr, which I found offensive. I did not wish to read any more of it."

Molly stared at Birra. He was lying to her. Just flat-out lying. And whatever he'd skipped over was in some way related to her—or at least, to things that Birra didn't want her to know. Since Birra did nothing on his own, she had to assume that the actual restrictions came from Seolar.

But why?

She wouldn't find out from Birra, that was certain. She might be able to get information from Seolar, but she couldn't even count on that. What she could count on was that she needed to make sure these books Birra had dug out for her didn't conveniently disappear as soon as she left them. If these books and manuscripts held information Seolar was determined not to let her have, she would be willing to bet they would vanish before she could come back to them the next day.

She manufactured a yawn and said, "Birra, let's leave all of this for later, shall we? I'm being a poor hostess to Lauren and her son, and she and I do have things much more important to discuss than any old trips through ancient history."

She stood, and the air of sheer relief that poured off of Birra would have been funny had it not so clearly demonstrated his reluctance to be where he was, doing what he was doing.

He rose, too, and smiled at her. "Of course, Vodi. We can certainly do this another time, when you have nothing more important."

"Right." Molly picked up one of the stacks of books and manuscripts and said, "Get those others, will you. We'll carry these to my suite. Seolar can read from them for me this evening, or perhaps another time."

Birra nodded and picked up the books. "Of course."

They carried the two big stacks to the huge suite Molly shared with Seolar, but she had no more intention of leaving the books there than she had of leaving them in the library. She said, "Birra, I'm going to change into other clothes. While I do, would you please go to get Lauren for me. She and I must talk."

"Of course, Vodi. Shall I take her by the long route so that you have enough time to change?"

Molly smiled at him. "If you would, give her the complete tour of Copper House on her way here. I could use a bath, too. Something about that library has made me feel all dusty and grimy." She held up her hands, which actually did have a bit of book dust on them, and managed to look like she thought this was something awful.

"She will be here sometime later; I will make sure she sees all the best parts of Copper House."

"Thank you," Molly said. "You've been a wonderful help to me."

When Birra left, she wrapped the books into a couple of her traveling cloaks, bound them with leather belts, and called two of Seolar's guards to deliver the packages to Lauren's room, and told them if Lauren wasn't there to just to put them on her bed.

With that finished, she bathed and changed into comfortable day wear.

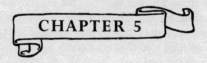

CHAPTER 5

Copper House

L AUREN, WITH JAKE clutching her hand, gave Birra a
hard look. "How much farther *is* it to her room?"

"Just down this corridor."

"This corridor looks suspiciously like the one that con-
nects to the one on which our suite is located."

"It is," Birra said, and gave her a smile that she guessed
was supposed to be ingratiating.

Lauren bit the inside of her cheek to keep from saying
what she was thinking and took a deep breath.

"You did not enjoy seeing Copper House?" Birra asked.
He seemed genuinely surprised.

"It's lovely. But I thought my sister wanted to talk with
me—and she and I have a great deal of business to discuss.
I'm afraid that house tours rank very low on my list of prior-
ities right now."

"She had to change and bathe, but did not want you to
have to sit in your room unattended while she did that; for
that reason she asked me to entertain you with a tour of Copper House."

"It was lovely," Lauren said, wondering as she did what
sort of frivolous creature her half sister might be if her prior-
ities lay with changing her clothes when the two of them
needed to discuss the monsters outside the house and the
fate of the world.

Birra showed her into Molly's room, and before she even

said hello to Lauren, Molly said, "Birra—I have an immense favor to ask of you; I hate to trouble you with it, but I'm afraid it's terribly important. I need a list of all the peoples of Oria, with physical descriptions and what we might know of their philosophies and religions and beliefs, and a list of all the known old gods and dark gods, along with whatever we might know of them. I was thinking in the bath, and this is information both Lauren and I will need as soon as you can get it."

Lauren glanced sideways at Birra, and saw his face fall. "More research, Vodi?"

"I'm afraid so. But this is—essential. We cannot do what we have to do without it."

Birra straightened a little then. "I'll gather some scholars. We'll have it for you within the week."

"Actually," Molly said, "I'll need it today. In as much detail as can be offered."

Lauren heard Birra mutter something that sounded suspiciously like, "Oh, balls!" under his breath. "You shall have it today," he said, and turned without noticing the salutes of the room guards.

"In," Molly said when he was out of earshot. Her entire demeanor had changed.

"What's going on? That errand you just sent him on sounded completely bogus."

"It was," Molly said. "As was me having him drag you all around this damned pile. I had to get some books into your room without his knowing about them, and I had to finagle one of the room guards into getting some alternate books to stash in here. I have a problem."

"I was sort of guessing that," Lauren said. She put Jake in a chair, gave him Mr. Puddleduck and two of the Crashable Cars, and said, "Play for a few minutes."

"Can you play with me?"

"Soon," Lauren said. She kissed the top of his head and said, "For now, you and Mr. Puddleduck can have fun driving the cars, okay?"

Jake nodded. Since deciding that Mr. Puddleduck was also Robin to his Batman, Jake could play for a very long time with his stuffed animal without getting bored. He got down on the floor with the cars and the duck and started driving, carrying on a conversation with his duck at the same time and answering in his duck voice.

Molly stood watching him for a moment, eyes wide. "That's . . . wow. That's really strange."

"Sometimes he'll have two or three invisible friends over, too. He does all the voices, sometimes with accents. Taking him to see the Harry Potter movie might have been the worst mistake I ever made—watching it, he figured out that not everyone talks the same way."

"Eeee." Molly grimaced. "I'll bet that can drive you nuts."

"It does." Lauren looked down at her son, who was now crashing cars into each other with an intensity that made her wish she'd thought to bring other toys for him, while he and the duck said things like, "Oh, that's not good," and "I'll bet that hurt."

Lauren watched him, trying not to think about the revelations of that morning, and stuck her hands in her blue jeans pockets. She felt badly underdressed next to Molly in her complicated-looking silk-and-velvet thing. "What's the problem you wanted to talk to me about?"

"They're hiding something important from me," Molly said.

"Who?"

"Seolar. Birra. All of the veyâr."

Lauren said, "Any idea what? Or why?"

"It's something that relates to the rrôn. And to Vodian in general, and I suspect me in particular. And maybe to the weird . . . connection . . . that I feel to these rrôn out there."

"Being able to hear what some of them think?"

"Yes. I tried this morning to find out more about it, but I had to have Birra read the books to me because I can't read any of the Orian languages—and he skipped parts. And I think he might have changed parts. As soon as I realized he was doing that, I had him help me carry the books in here. So Seolar could read them to me later, I said, but I want you to figure out how I can get the truth out of them."

"Make yourself a reader," Lauren said.

Molly frowned at her. "You didn't have to think about that for long. What do you mean? Change myself into someone who can read?"

"I mean go someplace where you can do magic without all the copper getting in the way, and create some sort of magnifying glass or page cover or something that, when you put it on the page of a book written in any language you don't know, translates the thing to comprehensible English."

"Do you think that would work?"

"Sure. I don't get the chance to do much with magic, but I've done things as complicated as that. If you're careful, you should be able to make something with a really low energy drain—and because it'll be you making it, the thing won't have any magical rebound." Lauren frowned. "That's *such* a good idea, in fact, that while you're at it, you can make me one, too. I have the feeling that being able to read anything wherever we'll have to go would be awfully useful."

Molly was frowning. Obviously she still hadn't reached any real accommodation with the fact that she could do magic other than healing, or that her focused intent could create just about anything she could clearly envision. "Just . . . make it. How?"

Lauren said, "Is there any place inside Copper House where you can do magic, but where you're still protected from, say, rrôn attacks?"

Molly nodded.

"Fine. Take me there and I'll show you what I mean."

Molly glanced at Jake, being a very good boy, and having a great deal of fun playing with his cars on the complicated tile patterns on the floor of Molly's suite's sitting room.

"We'll take him," Lauren said. "He'll be fine."

"Let's go."

Out the door, Molly told the two guards, "Come with us, please. We need to go to the Healing Chambers."

The guards nodded and flanked Lauren, Jake, and Molly. As they came even with an intersection, one of the two guards nodded at others who stood in the hallway, and these stepped quickly forward, taking up the point. Lauren heard footsteps behind her, and glanced back. Two other guards now brought up the rear. They'd done it very smoothly, with no fuss—but she realized how tight Seolar had made security. At most of the hallway intersections, she passed more guards. She smiled to them, they nodded to her. But their attention was on the hall traffic, on people moving.

Lauren realized that they were not running into anyone—not servants, not guests—and until she saw guards far down one long hall moving people out of the hallway, she thought perhaps Seolar had sent almost everyone away the night before. Instead, she realized, the guards were moving people out of her and Molly's way so that no one could come close to them. She couldn't fault Seolar's determination to keep her and Molly safe. She didn't regret inconveniencing anyone, either; those monsters were still circling in the air over Copper House, and Lauren felt her gut flip every time she thought of them.

They reached a pair of elaborately arched, copper-banded doors, and the guards moved ahead, opened them, and then fanned out into the huge hallway beyond.

"Wow," Lauren said, looking in. A magnificent throne stood at the near end, elevated on a dais. The other end terminated in two huge doors, now barred from the inside, that also bore copper banding.

"Do you have any way to shield us from their view?" Molly asked suddenly. Neither of them had yet stepped into the great hall.

"I think so. I know how to create a shield, anyway. I can't guarantee that it will work on anything as old or powerful as they are, but we can give it a try."

"Be ready to run for the doors, then," Molly said. "Because if they do know we're there, they're likely to go straight through the roof to get us. The only copper in there is for show—on the doors at either end. The center is clear so that I can heal the people who come asking for my help."

Lauren nodded. She focused her will and summoned energy from the rich field that permeated this part of Oria, and in her mind created a powerful sphere around her and Molly—something that no rrôn could see through, something that would not even alert the rrôn to its presence. The shield wouldn't actually exist until Lauren, Jake, and Molly moved out from under the copper—but the need for it wouldn't exist until then, either. As long as she held the thing in her mind, Lauren felt certain it would be there when she needed it.

For her own reassurance, however, she visualized it glowing with a pale blue light. It should shimmer into existence and fold itself around them the instant they were out of range of the copper, and thus in danger.

"I'm ready," she said after a minute. "Stay close."

She picked up Jake and stepped across the threshold, and Molly stayed right with her. About eight steps into the room, a tiny glowing blue circle appeared at around knee height and right in front of them. With the next step, it had turned into a glowing blue contact lens about four feet tall. One more step and it was half a ball, with about a third of it disappearing under their feet, a full curve over their heads. In two more steps, they stood inside a big, glowing blue bubble.

"That's really neat," Molly said. She reached out to touch it, but it bulged away from her hand. "Oh. Cool. So we can't accidentally step outside of it."

"Right. It will cover you, me, and Jake, either together or separately, as long as we're in here. The rrôn won't be able to hear us or feel us."

Molly stepped away from Lauren. To Lauren, what happened with the shield looked like those high-school biology slides she'd seen of cells dividing. It worked perfectly.

Another guard came into the room, and Lauren noted him only because, unlike the other guards, he came toward them instead of taking a place on the periphery. Probably just as well to have one close, she thought.

"All you have to do now," she told Molly, "is focus on a device that's thin and flexible, lightweight and transparent, and about the size of an average book page. Imagine laying it across the page, and having the words beneath transform themselves into English—"

Molly had an expression of horror on her face. "Run," she said.

Lauren grabbed Jake, but didn't have time to run. The guard—the one who'd been walking toward them, suddenly charged her, sword in hand. She shoved Jake away from her and saw the guards converging. She turned, summoning magic to hold back the guard, and felt the sword burn into her flesh—more pressure than pain, which shocked her— and she cast the spell that turned her attacker into a smoking cinder that crumbled into dust.

The sword went into her belly. She could feel the point of the blade protruding from her back. She stared at it stupidly, realizing that she couldn't feel her legs, and she heard Jake's piercing scream and the shouts of the veyâr guard, and the sounds of running feet, and then the pressure became a pain that ripped her open and turned the world red and black. She fell, and all she could think of as she fell was Jake—who was going to keep Jake safe?

Darkness.

Darkness and voices, and horrible pain.

Above Copper House

Trrtrag swore. The agent was dead—and not just dead, but dust, with nothing recoverable. Trrtrag *thought* he could tell

Rr'garn, that pompous bastard, that one of the two problems was gone. But so long as he did not know for certain, he dared say nothing.

Trrtrag wondered if he dared activate another of Rr'garn's sleepers, so soon after the annihilation of the last one. Perhaps he could just tell Rr'garn when he returned that the attempt had been made and the agent lost, and let Rr'garn send Baanraak in to see how everything had turned out—assuming, of course, that Baanraak hadn't made everyone's lives easier by just eating Rr'garn.

Trrtrag almost hoped that was the case. Then he came to his senses—he'd rather deal with a hundred Rr'garns than one Baanraak.

Copper House

And then light.

Lauren opened her eyes, and saw Seolar standing over her, and Birra, and Molly, and found Jake clinging to her like he'd been glued there, his eyes wide with terror. He said, "Mama?"

She sat up. She felt okay. They weren't in the great hall—instead, everyone gathered around her in a tiny room heavy with copper ornamentation. She no longer wore her jeans and sweatshirt; instead, she had on a pair of silk-lined wool pants and a silk shirt of creamy texture and elegant cut. She wiggled her feet. They worked. "It's okay, Jake," she said, and wrapped her arms tight around him and kissed him; he cuddled against her and the grip of his arms around her waist tightened. "What the hell happened?"

"Traitor, we have to guess," Molly said. Lauren noticed that Molly wore a long dagger on her hip—something Lauren had never seen her do before. "You didn't exactly leave anything for them to question."

"I'm sorry," Lauren said. "But *what happened*?"

"The sword did a lot of damage. I had to do a quick spell

just to protect you from blood loss while we moved you out of there and into a secret and very well protected copper-free chamber Seolar has deep in the heart of the house."

"It's been here since the times of previous Vodian," Seolar said. "I simply knew of its existence."

"We got you down there, I did a complete healing, and the guards moved you in here to recuperate."

"You're going to be fine," Seolar said. "And after what you did to your attacker, the rest of them will think twice before they come after the two of you again."

"No they won't," Lauren said softly. "They won't hesitate for an instant. They'll just keep coming and coming until they kill us." She ran her fingers through Jake's silky hair and felt the dampness on his cheeks. He'd been crying. He'd seen what had happened to her. He knew. This ordeal was going to destroy him.

Seolar pointed to a belt and a plain dagger in an unornamented sheath that hung on a hook on the wall, well out of Jake's reach. "I brought that for you. It's a fine weapon. When you're up and about, wear it at all times. We will do everything we can to keep you safe—but if you are in any part of the house warded by copper, you will need a final resort—a way to protect yourself if we have . . . fallen."

Lauren looked to Molly and saw the bleakness in her eyes.

"I'll wear it," she said.

Jake touched her face and said, "You wented with Daddy. But you comed back."

She looked up at the faces staring down at her, and asked, "Is that true? Did I die?"

"Almost," Molly said. "Almost, but we got you back fast." Molly winced. "I didn't realize how much Jake saw. Or how much he . . . understood."

"He doesn't miss much," Lauren said. She lay back and pulled Jake close. How was she going to do what she had to do? How could she chance leaving him alone in the world? And what options did she have?

Cat Creek

"I hear you got lucky last night," Eric said as Pete walked in the door at the station. He gave Pete a sad smile.

Pete stopped in his tracks. "You heard *what*?"

Eric frowned. "That you got lucky. That after you and I finished dinner, you went over to Lauren's house and that your car was still there this morning. And when I called over to your place this morning, you didn't answer—which led me to believe what I'd heard."

"I *hate* small towns," Pete muttered.

Eric spread his arms, shrugged, and smiled.

Pete handed him the note Lauren had left. "I'm watching her house for her for a few days," he said. "Her car isn't in the carport. Hasn't *been* in the carport. But the damned neighbors *would* assume the worst."

Eric was staring at the note like someone had just dropped a water moccasin in his lap and the snake was eyeing his crotch. "Mayhem saw your car. Was on the way home from tomcatting around in the wee smalls and thought it was funny enough to wake me up for."

"Mayhem's an asshole."

"No argument there." Eric stood up. "She *left*? She just got up and left, and told us to take it to Vass if we need a gateweaver? Sweet jumping Jesus."

"I suppose she figured things had calmed down a bit. She doesn't sound like she took off for fun."

Eric studied him with steady eyes gone cold. "And do I care about that? Not two weeks ago this world was yea far from ending"—he held up thumb and forefinger, so close Pete barely saw light between them—"and this week she takes a vacation and doesn't even leave an emergency number. What if the Vass Sentinels *need* their gateweaver and we have an emergency? We show a massive increase in gate activity areawide over the last three days. It feels like old god movement. I have June Bug doing a pattern-and-time grid, and while I have to admit that this might be something benign, it doesn't seem likely."

Pete sighed.

"All our gates are in good shape right now, but if we get something moving through that crashes them again, we're going to be sitting here with our thumbs up our asses if we don't have a gateweaver to get us back into it again. What the hell was she thinking?"

"I don't know. I'll tell her you're pissed off if she calls, if you want me to."

"Do better than that. Tell her to get her ass back here. Fast. Before we find ourselves sitting helpless in the middle of a shitstorm."

"I can try to find her if you'd like."

Eric hooked his thumbs into his pockets and glowered at nothing.

"Or not."

Eric blew out a breath in a remarkably horselike start. "You fishing for a trip up to Charlotte?"

Pete laughed. "Yep." Then he shrugged. "I figure I'm the most expendable person we have."

"Bullshit. Calm under fire is never expendable. But you do have some experience finding people who don't want to be found, don't you?"

"Some."

Eric thought about it for a moment. Then he said, "People need their families, and as much as Lauren doesn't sound like she gives a good goddamn for her in-laws, I imagine Jake needs to get to know the only relatives he has. So . . . find her. Make sure you have a way to get in touch with her. But we won't let her know you were looking for her unless we run into trouble. Sound all right to you?"

"I can do that," Pete said, and gave Eric an agreeable smile.

So. He'd go to Charlotte, take care of his own business, which had been on hold during the Sentinels' fight with their traitors and the Carolina flu. And then he'd see what he could do to find Lauren, while keeping whatever she was really up to off the record.

He had to wonder what she *was* up to.

Copper House

Molly diverted her contingent of guards on the way to the evening meal, taking them to the dining hall by way of Seolar's copper-free safe room; she had them wait only long enough for her to fashion two magical readers. She couldn't be certain they would work the way she hoped because she hadn't had time to make a side trip to the library, and had been under observation by her dressers in her room. She'd check the books she'd hidden in Lauren's room later, though, and if the reader didn't work, she would drag the guards down to the cellar behind her while she had another go at getting the magic right.

But she liked the way her little readers looked. She had done them as sheets of what felt like plastic. Each sheet could be folded into quarters to fit into a pocket, then unfolded. She'd thrown in a bit of magic that made the fold lines disappear. They certainly looked like an elegant solution; she just hoped they worked.

She wasn't even late getting to the dining hall. Lauren and Jake sat on one side of the table, and Seolar took the head. Molly saw her place at the foot. In between sat a cluster of five goroths. Lauren and Jake were engaged in conversation with them and didn't see Molly arrive until the goroths stood on their chairs and bowed to her.

Ugly creatures, all of them. Enormous ears and wrinkled blue-green skin and enormous yellow eyes and that ubiquitous stripe of hair that ran from low, beetle-browed forehead over bald, lumpy skull and down the middle of the spine. Molly gave each of them a polite bow and took her place at the table.

As the servants began bringing out dishes, she got caught up on what the goroths wanted.

"As we were telling the Hunter," one of them said, "our Embar got murdered over that which has started—or if not, then over that which led up to what we're in now—and we think we have a place and a part in this. A place and a part, and our chance to fight. Everyone knows the goroths hold claim to a place of honor in the beginning of this—our Embar was the right hand of the Heroes."

"The Heroes?" Molly asked Lauren.

"Her sainted parents," the best-dressed of the goroths said, "and yours. Them who saw what needed to be done and died to get it done. We'll do our part."

"Doggies," Jake said, pointing at them and smiling just a little.

"You remember Embar?" Lauren asked him, and forced a smile that feigned enthusiasm, but not well. Molly studied her sister. Physically Lauren was fine—Molly knew that. But she had a wounded, haunted look in her eyes that echoed the way Molly felt.

"Doggie," Jake said.

"He liked Embar," Lauren explained to the goroths.

"We are honored, Hunter," they said in a gaggle.

They really wore very fine clothes, Molly thought. Beautifully woven and embroidered linen shirts with full, blousing sleeves, fine leather breeches, overstitched and decorated cobbled shoes. If they hadn't been such hideous little things, the clothes would even have been magnificent. On them, however . . . she shook her head. Grotesque little people—she couldn't quite take them seriously.

"How could you help?" Seolar asked as servants placed covered silver platters in front of everyone. "I'm grateful to you for making the journey, and I understand your desire to help, but what could you do that my guards could not?"

The leader of the goroths said, "The Heroes didn't ask that of Embar." He pointed at Lauren. "*She* didn't ask it of Embar. They knew that the goroths are honest, determined, unshakable, and brave. They knew that when others ran, a goroth would stand."

"But standing and getting killed isn't of much use, either to us or to you," Seolar pointed out. "And you're neither big enough nor strong enough to fight."

One of the smaller goroths said, "You know history, great Imallin. For all we are small and weak, goroths have ever stood to fight against the dark gods. We stand here now and offer ourselves again."

Seolar took a bite, chewed it thoughtfully, took a sip of his drink, then leaned back in his chair. "I thank you—formally—as has every Imallin before me. Your offer of sacrifice and service is honorable, and appreciated. But it is unnecessary, and I would be remiss in putting into danger those who are so likely to die wasted."

"You say no," the head of the goroths said. He turned to his quartet of comrades and said, "He says no."

"We knew it." The smallest one hung his head. He looked crushed.

"You can work with me," Lauren said.

Molly cringed and glanced at Seolar, who looked decidedly unhappy.

"Lauren . . ." she said, but Lauren looked her in the eyes and arched an eyebrow in direct challenge.

"Embar was my friend," she said. "He was my friend when I was a little kid like Jake, and he was my friend when I found my way back to who I was. He died helping me. I can never make that up to him, any more than I can make up the fact that I would never have met you or discovered what I was supposed to be doing with my life if he hadn't helped me. They want to help. And if Seolar won't have them, I will."

"It is not the nature of the veyâr to risk the lives of the lesser races," Seolar said stiffly.

Lauren turned to him, and her voice dropped to a growl. "You and your people are on the edge of becoming extinct, if I remember correctly. You're just managing to hang on to a few little corners of what used to be your world. Maybe you ought to start accepting help when it's offered." She rose, clearly angry, and picked up Jake. "I'll take the rest of my meal in my suite," she told one of the servants, who bowed, nodded, and gave Seolar a frantic, panicked look behind Lauren's back.

All five goroths rose, dropped to the floor from their chairs with little thuds, and said, "We accompany you, Mistress Hunter."

"Call me Lauren," she said. "And he's Jake." She turned back to the servant. "Bring the rest of their food, too."

And then she, the guards who were assigned to keep her safe, and the goroths were all gone, and Molly and Seolar were left facing each other from opposite ends of the long table.

"They're worthless." Seolar was looking out the door after the retreating guests and Lauren. "They're stupid and weak and cowardly. If one of them helped her once, it was only because he got something out of the deal for himself; and if he died, it was because he found himself in the wrong place at the wrong time, and not from any bent toward heroism on his part." Seolar turned back to face Molly, and she was startled by the expression of disgust on his face. "They eat food and use up firewood and arable land and other resources and they give back nothing. They breed and spread disease."

Molly said, "But they came here offering to help."

"Don't have anything to do with them, love. You'll bring shame to yourself; your sister is going to be marked by her association with such creatures. Not even old gods can be immune to the taint of those nasty subcreatures."

Molly ate quietly and watched Seolar. She'd never in the time that she'd known him seen this facet of his personality, this prejudice. She wondered if all the veyâr shared it, or if this was something that belonged to him alone—and why his distaste for the goroths was so vehement and seemingly irrational.

They seemed harmless. In fact, in a funny way, they sort of reminded her of the veyâr. Veyâr hit by the ugly stick, but veyâr nonetheless—the odd skin coloring, the large, gem-like, solid-colored eyes, the angles of bone and shapes of hands and fingers and ears and faces. If everything about them was an exaggeration, it had nonetheless come from the same template.

Reminded her a bit of wolves and Chihuahuas—the one magnificent, the other something that ought to be stepped on at one's earliest convenience—but both sprang from the same lines.

She decided, however, not to offer this observation to Seolar. He was in a foul mood—something she had never seen before—and some stroke of common sense suggested to her that he would not welcome any comments in favor of goroths.

She ate, and watched him. "Birra and I went to the library today," she said.

He shook off the look of irritation on his face and smiled. "Really? I'd be happy if you could find something to entertain you in your rest."

"I didn't have him looking for entertainment," she said. "I was hoping to find out something about the previous Vodian, and about the rrôn. I wanted to see what the others like me had to go through."

"And you looked for the rrôn because . . . ?"

"They're hunting me," she said, withholding the true cause of her interest. "I figure I need to know my enemy."

Seolar shoved his plate away from him, even though he'd eaten less than half of what had been served. "Really," he said. "I would think you knew as much as you needed to in realizing that they were trying to kill you. And in being able to hear their thoughts."

Molly said, "Could the other Vodian hear the thoughts of the rrôn? Maybe of the other dark gods? Old gods? If they could, why? If they couldn't, then why can I?" She rested her elbows on the table and said, "I'm not the same as I was, Seo. I feel . . . little blank spots in me. I can't think of a better way to describe it, but I have to understand it. I have to know who I am; I have to know what I have become." She looked down at her tall, slender body, at her inhumanly long-fingered hands, and spread her arms wide. "I'm not the person I was. Not by a long shot. So who the hell am I?"

He looked a little pale as he asked her, "So what did you discover?"

"Not a damned thing. Birra helped me find books, but he doesn't enjoy reading them. And I can't. I thought perhaps you could read them to me tonight."

She watched his face and found on it the same relief, the same intent to deceive, that she'd seen with Birra. "Of course," he said. "I'm afraid the books are likely to be dull reading, but we'll go through as much as you'd like. Anything I can do to help you understand the . . . rrôn . . . and your role as a Vodi." His smile got a bit broader, and he pulled his plate back in front of himself and dug in.

Molly studied him with interest. She wasn't dependent on him to read to her, but she was going to be very interested to see what he was willing to let her know as opposed to what she could find out on her own. And a dark little thrill started in her—a curiosity about how bound he was to his determination to lie, mixed with a feral hunger unlike anything she'd ever experienced before.

Watching Seolar, she had a premonition that the evening was going to be interesting for both of them.

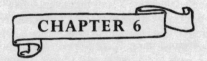

CHAPTER 6

Copper House

L AUREN AND JAKE WATCHED, amazed, as the goroths
swarmed through the suite.

"Wall passageway here," one shouted.

"She'll know about that," another one said.

"Did you know about that?" the best-dressed of the
goroths asked.

"No."

"Peephole here."

"Decent hiding space between the walls back here—be
sure to check it every time we come in."

Lauren held Jake closer and asked the one goroth who
wasn't zipping around like a caffeinated hummingbird,
"What are they doing?"

"Checking your rooms for weaknesses and escape routes.
You haven't already done this?"

"Well—I looked over the rooms," Lauren said. "But I
didn't find anything out of the ordinary about them."

The other goroths were coming back to their starting
point now. "All done," one said. "Nothing else."

The leader said, "That will be enough, then. Be inconspicuous."

Lauren had seen a fair amount of magic by this time. The
thing that unnerved her was knowing the goroths weren't using any magic. While she was watching them, they found
spots around the room and faded out of sight into them, un-

til after just a moment only she and Jake and the leader appeared to be left.

"Hiding," Jake said. "Can I find the doggies?"

"Not right now, monkey-boy," Lauren said. She dropped to a crouch so that she and the leader were nearly eye to eye, and asked, "Why did they do that?"

"Mistress Hunter, we are not strong, and we are not fast, and we are not great warriors. But we are good at hiding, and listening, and making sure that nothing sneaks by us without our noticing it. We will make sure that within your rooms, nothing comes or goes without your knowledge. We will keep you and your little one safe to the best of our ability." He bowed to her—a deep bow, full of flourishes and passion—and said, "We ask only to serve against the great evil that would destroy us and everything we hold dear. You have allowed us to serve you, when in serving you we serve the greater cause; and you have given the goroths a place of honor among all the peoples. By your grace, we can erase the shame of being goroth. We are grateful; we will serve you in life and in death."

Lauren reached out a hand to the goroth. "Embar was my friend," she said. "I don't expect you to be servants, or invisible bodyguards, or whatever you seem to think you have to do. You can just be my friends." She shook her head. "I failed Embar. I didn't manage to protect him from some very bad men, and he died as a result." She gave the little goroth a crooked smile. "I don't want you to follow in his footsteps. If I'm lucky, you and the other fellows will still be around to keep Jake company when he's my age."

Tears slipped down the goroth's wrinkled cheeks, and he whispered, "You honor us. Ah, Hunter, what an honor you do us. To be offered the friendship of one of the old gods . . ."

Lauren heard snuffles from four hiding places. She wanted to tell them it was no big deal, but who was she to say that? She'd seen the way Seolar treated them. To them, being anyone's friend might be a very big deal indeed, and belittling that made no sense. Instead, she decided that she might as well be gracious.

"Thank you for your help," she told him. "And your friendship. If you told me your name . . . ?"

"Rue," he whispered.

"Rue," she said. She gave his hand a squeeze, and rose. "I'll need to be introduced to the other four, too."

"Play with the doggie now?" Jake asked.

"For a little while," Lauren agreed. She had things to think about. And while she thought and planned, Jake would have fun playing with the goroths. She sighed.

"Attend," Rue said, "by Her order." Lauren could hear the capitalization of "Her."

Scurrying feet, and four goroths stood before her. They were fast, no matter their protests to the contrary. They lined up—a chorus line of wrinkled gnomes in great clothes.

"This is Herot, the birdcatcher." The leanest goroth bowed. "And Wyngi, the boatmaster." A goroth with ratty blue hair braided down to the floor bowed. "Next, Tarth, the tracker." The tallest goroth—maybe two inches taller than Jake—and to Lauren's mind, the ugliest, bowed deeply. "And finally, the daughter of Creeg, the seer." The shortest and least wrinkled of the goroths bowed until its head touched the floor.

"What's your name?" Lauren asked the last goroth.

"This one has not earned a name yet, and must prove itself before becoming one of the People. It has been given the greatest honor of the nameless in being permitted to serve the Hunter, and will comport itself with honor." The nameless goroth bowed again, head thumping on the floor.

Jake wriggled, and Lauren put him on the floor facing the goroths. He grinned. He'd been through so much; that he could bounce back said a lot for what he was made of.

"Yes, Doggie," he said, grabbing the daughter of Creeg. "You play with me."

"This one has been given the name of Doggie," whispered the daughter of Creeg the seer. Tears started to run down her cheeks. "This one has been given a name by one of the old gods."

The other goroths gathered around her, hugging her. Lauren cringed inwardly, but considered that there didn't seem to be any dogs on Oria, so maybe Doggie was better than nothing.

She watched Jake show the smallest of the goroths his cars. She saw the others scurry to their hiding places and vanish from sight. She watched Rue, the voice of her new allies, take up a place by the inside of the door, settling in on the floor with his knees drawn to his chest. She felt a little safer, surprisingly. She found comfort in the goroths—and if Seolar and the other veyâr didn't like them, she didn't intend to let it bother her. They were like a little bit of home, and after the attack, and with her fear still fresh, she found anything homelike comforting.

Copper House

The feral urge became a darkness that ran through Molly like black fire. In her mind, the weight of the rrôn overhead. In her belly, a hunger for something to fill the void that formed echoes inside of her. Molly closed her eyes against an unexpected wash of despair, and when she opened them, Seolar had left his seat at the other end of the table to kneel beside her.

"What's wrong?"

Molly looked at him, and the darkness became a dangerous growl at the back of her throat.

Seolar laid a hand on her shoulder, and the warmth of his flesh on hers triggered animal lust, the starved madness of a creature lost in rut, and she leaned close to him, rested her lips against his neck, and bit him hard enough that she heard him gasp.

"I want you," she said, her voice low enough that only he could hear her. "Now. Here." She had not yet had him—their separation by her death, her confusion on her return had stood in the way. Of the promise their love held, of the passion that moved between them when they looked at each other, when they touched, when they kissed.

They had never been lovers. But hunger and darkness drove her, and he stood like a beacon of light before her, and in that moment, she would not be denied.

"Guards, out," he said. "Lock the doors; let no one pass." He sounded like he was speaking around a throat coated in sand.

Molly gave the guards only enough time to clear the room, and then she stood, pulling him up, and lifted up on her toes to bite the back edge of his ear, to lick the soft skin with quick, hard dartings of her tongue.

He pulled away from her, his eyes uncertain. "What are you doing?"

"Don't fear the reaper," she whispered, and undid the laces of her bodice and pulled her underblouse down so that the silk draped beneath her bared breasts.

He breathed faster, staring at her. "Why?" he said.

"Because there is no tomorrow, and now feels hollow, and empty, and I want to fill the emptiness. With you." She loosened the ties on the outer skirt and held the waistband up only long enough to reach underneath and untie the underskirts. She let the many layers of silk slide to the floor in a whisper, and stepped over them.

"Fill me," she said.

He moved to kiss her, but she pulled back, and with a hard yank slid his breeches over his hips. "Bite me." She leaned in and tilted her head to swing her hair out of the way to expose her neck.

She felt his teeth nip at her skin as she gripped his buttocks and pulled him against her. She dug her fingers into his skin and growled, "Harder."

He bit hard and she groaned; the pain drove against the darkness, against the hollowness. Alive, the lost voices sang in her head. Alive.

She shoved him back—hard—and he fell against the table. She stepped against him, and full of a strength she hadn't known she possessed, she caught his weight on her hips and thighs and shoved upward, her legs between his, to throw him onto the table.

Dishes and platters skittered and one crashed to the floor. Seo fell backward and caught himself with his elbows. Molly climbed onto the table after him, poised herself over him, and stopped. She shoved his tunic up over his head and caught his wrists in the linen tangle. Then, slowly, she leaned over him until her nipples brushed his chest.

"I own you," she murmured.

"Yes," he said.

"You want me."

"Yes." His voice hoarse.

Banish the ghosts, she thought, and rose up, and slowly, slowly, impaled herself on him.

"Yes," he whispered.

She rode him, her thighs tightening and relaxing as she fought for silence in her head, as she scrambled for a place away from the whispers of the rrôn, from the grasping of the dead and her own self-doubts and nightmares. She drove herself and drove him, harder and faster, and finally he twisted his hands and wrists free from the bondage of the tangled shirt, and clutched her hips and took her over. With a powerful thrust of his hips and legs he flipped them so that she lay on the bottom, and he caught her ankles in his hands and pulled them up to either side of his neck.

"Nothing will haunt you but me," he said, leaning into her, pressing her thighs to her belly. "No ghosts, no demons, no regrets." He crashed into her, roared over her like a rising tide against a rocky shore, and she lifted up to catch him better and cried out as the exquisite drowning took her over and washed her away.

"Not yet," Seo said, and stilled himself inside her. When she calmed a bit, he ran his hands over her, stroking her gently. As she arched her back to press herself tighter against his hands, he smiled a little and slid his palms over her breasts, circling her nipples with his thumbs until she tingled and ached.

She gasped, and slid her legs down and locked them around his back and tried to force him all the way into her, but he just laughed, grabbed her hips, broke her hold on him, and turned her over. Now he pulled her up against him, and thrust, and she cried out.

In the back of her mind, the voices—whispering. *Today, now—but nevermore.*

The rrôn, the ghosts, her dread—none banished, all waiting. She threw herself into physical exertion, into roughness and mindless animal urge, and fought back the voices and the fear.

They dug and clawed and tumbled, rough strife and passion that raced the sun and burned like the end of the world. They rode wave after wave, thrashed and drowned and surfaced again, bit and rolled and drove harder, faster, wilder, until at last the riptide tore them from the sea and threw them far up the shore. She screamed his name, he cried out in wordless release. She shuddered and trembled, inside and out, her legs too weak to hold her up, her body so sensitive to his touch that with each slightest movement he took her over the edge again. Inside her, nothing. No voices. No pain. Only the rush of the tide of her blood in her ears, the pounding of her wild heart.

In slow motion, they dropped forward, she flat against the table, he on her and in her. Both of them spent. Sated.

After a moment he rolled off of her and cupped his hand on the back of her head. They lay like that for a while, then he said, "Love?"

"Yes?"

"This was not the way I'd planned it."

"I didn't want soft music and candlelight. I didn't want long dance and slow consummation." She stared at nothing, her voice echoing in her ears. "I wanted you now."

"This wasn't about me," he said, and she could not argue with that, and so said nothing.

After a long silence, he said, "You can't hide from the things that frighten you. And you can't bury them away and pretend they aren't there."

"No," she said. "I know. They're still there."

"You have to face them. But you don't have to face them alone. I'll be with you, no matter what you fear. I love you, Molly."

Molly rolled over and looked in his eyes, and reached out with a finger to trace the line of his cheekbone and the lines of tattoos telling his life on his face. "I love you," she whispered.

"I know." His smile was tentative. "And that—that wasn't us." He stroked her. "That was your shadow, and perhaps mine. But shadows pass."

Only when darkness devours them, she thought, but she didn't say that. Instead, Molly said, "I hope so." The hollow ache lay beneath the placid surface of her thoughts, waiting to bubble up again. She could feel it, just as she could feel the pressure of the silenced voices. They were not gone. They only waited.

She wondered how she could banish them—what magical spell would set her free?

She kissed him lightly, then rose and pulled her clothes on. "I'm going to visit Lauren for a while," she said. "I don't want to leave you, but Lauren and I never did get to discuss everything we needed to. The—the attack got in the way of everything we needed to do." She had her back turned toward him while she said it, because she didn't want him to see the evasion in her eyes.

She wasn't going to Lauren's suite to talk to Lauren. With luck, Lauren would be tired and ready for bed, and Molly would be able to sit down without interruption with the books she'd hidden in Lauren's room—Molly would see what she could make of them. Sometime in the next few days, Molly thought she might take them in to see what Seolar pointed out and what he avoided, just to get a better idea of where she should be reading. But she didn't really want to know that he would lie to her. She thought perhaps she would keep the books to herself and tell him she'd decided not to do any more research.

Which meant she'd be lying to him. The way she was lying to him right now—lies of omission, not of commission. But still lies. Still betrayals.

Dressed, she leaned against the tall back of a heavy chair while he pulled on his clothes. He was beautiful. Not human—but then, neither was she, at least not fully. He had an inhuman grace, a sinuous strength that caught her breath and made her heart leap, and had since the first time she saw him.

They were meant to be together. Fated to share their lives—they meshed perfectly; and now more than ever she could feel what she had in him, and she could appreciate its perfection. But she felt like she held a goblet of sugar-glass in her hand and watched the storm clouds building overhead. None of this felt like it would last, like it could last.

Sometime in the 1600s, Andrew Marvell wrote a poem titled "To His Coy Mistress," a poem that Molly had memorized long ago for a class, and that had never left her since. The final words of that poem crept through her thoughts:

> *Now therefore, while the youthful hue*
> *Sits on thy skin like morning dew,*
> *And while thy willing soul transpires*
> *At every pore with instant fires,*
> *Now let us sport us while we may,*
> *And now, like amorous birds of prey,*
> *Rather at once our time devour*
> *Than languish in his slow-chapt power.*
> *Let us roll all our strength and all*
> *Our sweetness up into one ball,*
> *And tear our pleasures with rough strife*
> *Thorough the iron gates of life:*
> *Thus, though we cannot make our sun*
> *Stand still, yet we will make him run.*

Seolar smiled at her and as he did she could feel him slid-ing away from her, not just for the moment but forever. She remembered looking at him and seeing the future. But that had been before she died, before everything changed. It was so stupid—she knew she would live forever, or at least for as long as she wore the necklace. She could be killed, but she couldn't be kept dead; she ought to feel like she had an eter-nity before her. She ought to look at Seo and see them old together, and happy, with this present horror conquered and the world safe and whole.

But she felt as fragile, as fleeting as Andrew Marvell's coy mistress, already long past dust. She felt like she was al-ready gone, and everything around her was just images re-ceding outside the window of a fast-moving train. A train she could not stop, and could not escape.

She took a deep breath. Tears lay too close to the surface, and she would not let herself cry. She had no reason to cry.

When he finished dressing, she asked him, "What will they think? The guards, the servants?"

"They'll think I'm lucky," Seo said with a wry smile. "And they won't even dare to think *that* too loudly. Being the Imallin is no small advantage."

"Kiss me," she whispered.

He did. It was a soft, gentle, loving kiss, and she fell into it as if it were the last kiss she would ever have. She couldn't get off that train, not even when he held her in his arms.

"I should go," she told him. "Before it gets to be too late and I interrupt her sleep."

"I'll walk you to her quarters," he said, and held up a hand when she started to protest that it wasn't necessary. "I'll not trust you to anyone but myself. Not after today. I know all of my men. You don't. Had I been with you today, the traitor couldn't have gotten close to Lauren. I won't let such a mon-ster harm you."

"I simply didn't want to be a bother."

He slid an arm around her waist. "Impossible. I've waited my whole life for you. You're a gift."

They walked out the doors of the great hall, past guards who stared straight ahead with expressionless faces, as if they knew of nothing unusual passing, as if they were on some regular duty. Molly had to fight to hide a sudden smile, had to fight off the abrupt urge to giggle. She would bet that if she snickered, one of them would, too, and that the laugh would spread until she left the whole bunch of them gripping their aching sides, teary-eyed and gasping for breath.

But she bit the inside of her lip and held it in. And the brief blissful silliness passed.

Copper House

Jake curled up in the center of the bed, sound asleep. Lauren had discovered a marvelous silver tea-maker and the matches to light the little built-in heater—the contraption didn't look like a samovar, but she guessed that it functioned the same way. And with her hot cup of tea and a big box of cookies she discovered in the pantry, she'd just settled into the rocking chair to drink and snack when Rue let her know that Molly and Seolar were headed for the suite.

She had time to put tea and cookies on a table and throw a robe over the soft white cotton pajamas she'd found in the wardrobe before they arrived.

She greeted them at the door.

"You knew we were coming," Molly asked.

Lauren didn't want to set Seolar off again, so she said, "Yes," and let it go at that.

"I thought we could do the talking we missed earlier today," Molly said.

Lauren didn't feel even a little bit like discussing her parents' plan or her duties to the worlds just yet. But she was a guest, and could not very well send Molly on her way. She told both of them, "Come in."

Seolar said, "I cannot, though I thank you for the invitation. Even a small Imal like mine requires constant attention, and I'm afraid the events today kept me from many of my obligations." He bowed, gave Molly a tiny, secretive smile that Lauren found fascinating, and headed down the hall, followed by only a few of the guards who had followed him up. The rest arrayed themselves up and down the hall, mixing with the guards who were responsible for Lauren, until it looked like Foreign Legion dress-up night.

Molly came just a step in, then leaned against the doorframe until Seolar was out of sight.

"I want to read those books," she said. She pulled two small, folded squares of what looked to Lauren like laminating plastic from deep pockets inside her silk skirt, and said, "Here. You wanted one of these."

Lauren held the thing in one hand and stared at it. "This is the . . . reader?"

"I hope so," Molly said. "I didn't have a lot of time to concentrate on making it—I did it on the way to dinner. Want to help me test?"

"Of course." Lauren led the way to the bed; she'd hidden the books underneath it. She pulled them out and spread them on the floor, and picked one that had an attractive red moiré silk cover embroidered with pretty patterns. Lauren unfolded the reader, and whistled softly as the fold lines vanished and it became a perfectly smooth rectangle about nine inches wide by twelve inches high. "Oh, this is neat work, Molly," she said, admiring the perfect seamlessness. She folded the reader, and it creased along invisible lines, as smoothly as if it had hinges—then unfolded flawlessly again.

"If it works, *then* I'll get excited," Molly muttered. "I haven't had either the time or the inclination to experiment with anything but healing, so this may be a complete fiasco."

Lauren, standing, looked through the unfolded plastic at the cover of the book she'd chosen. It remained unchanged. "If it doesn't work, we'll go to that safe room tomorrow and try again."

Molly had dragged her huge choice of book over to the sitting room's overstuffed sofa, lit a lamp, and settled in with the book open on her lap. She put the reader down on a page, waited a moment, and looked up at Lauren and grinned.

> "... and then they rode northward from the Battle of Badwater Sea—the heroes, the gallant veyâr— away from the war and the dead, both buried and burned, and toward the city of hope, Naarth, and the river rich with fish and the fields yielding to the plow and heavy with grasses for the beasts ..."

Molly said, "Naarth is south of here, in the Imal of Dalieam. An ambassador from there is in permanent residence here; it's one of the last of the veyâr strongholds, and they trade a lot of their river and plains goods for Ballaharan forest goods." Molly closed the book and placed the reader on the cover. *"Travels of the Veyâr from the Lost Homeland.* I should have checked the cover first, but I didn't realize the decorations were actually words. I thought they were just patterned embroidery. At least I know the reader works." She reached down and hid the book under the couch and went to get another one. "What do you have?"

Lauren sat in her rocking chair with the book in her lap, closed, and laid the reader on the cover. Until the reader actually touched the cover, nothing happened, but the instant it did, the bright embroidered silk patterns resolved themselves into words. *"Life of the Vodi Elspeth,"* she said.

"There are supposed to be some good ones in the pile," Molly said, heading over to the books spread across the floor. "I'm interested in the biographies, but only after I've had a chance to read the things that I think will really be useful." She knelt and put her reader on one of the covers. "Back of the book, I guess," she said, and flipped it over. "No. This one doesn't have a title. I suppose that makes it one of the diaries or journals." She tried another book. *"The Recounting of Imallin Galorayne.* I have no idea why this one was supposed to be useful, and it's pretty thick. Later, maybe." She picked up a thin volume covered in purple silk heavily embroidered with pretty flowers. "I'm betting diary," Molly said, and checked the cover. "I'll be damned. This is *Those Whose Names Are Unspoken*. I really want to read this one, but not now. I'm looking for a big, thick one. I wish I'd been paying more attention to what the cover looked like . . . Oh. Here it is. *Imallin Merional's Conversations with the Dark Gods*."

"Sounds cheerful," Lauren said. "Light, happy reading for the dead hours of the night."

Molly laughed just a little and looked away. "Should be loads of fun, I think." She shrugged, and watching her, Lauren got the feeling that Molly was hiding something. Maybe something big.

Lauren put down *Life of the Vodi Elspeth* and got the one with the interesting title—*Those Whose Names Are Unspoken*.

She started at the beginning, which was a list of those the author considered dark gods. Most of the rrôn, many of the keth, some of the anguawyr, all surviving triiga . . . the list went on for two pages, but nowhere did it just flatly list a species or race and say, "Here. These are dark gods." It always offered some qualifier. Was that, Lauren wondered, some form of veyâr political correctness, where they could not permit themselves to say, "Here. These are all bad people, from bad cultures on an evil world"? Or did their careful qualifiers map out the borders of some unsuspected reality?

But maybe it wasn't all that unsuspected. In the human Christian mythos, God and all the angels started out good, but Lucifer fell and took a good chunk of Heaven with him. The Greek gods had good guys and bad guys. So did the Indian gods, and the Norse gods—look at Loki. Clever, a prankster . . . but if you were going to point your finger at someone who was leaning to the wrong side of the fence, Loki would be your guy.

Was that the only difference between old gods, who got a lot of admiration, and dark gods, whose names literally were not spoken?

Lauren kept reading. She'd planned to sleep—to get past the day's horrors by embracing a few hours of unconsciousness, but she suspected she would just worry in bed, and maybe letting her mind play with something else for a while would let it relax.

"This is kind of interesting," she said after a while. "I haven't gotten anything specific about this, but every time it offers a little biography about a specific dark god, it mentions ways that particular god has already been killed. So nobody is claiming immortality for these guys."

Molly looked up from her reading, an odd expression on her face. "Give me an example."

Lauren nodded. "Here's one for one of the rrôn." From the little hidey-holes around the room, she heard breath being sucked in—the goroth evidently didn't care to hear the word "rrôn" spoken aloud.

Lauren grinned a little at Molly, who frowned at the source of the little noises. Lauren mouthed the word *goroths*, and after she'd done it twice, a look of comprehension crossed Molly's face, and she returned the grin.

Lauren started reading out loud:

> *Baanraak, when he rose to power as master of the rrôn, set out to destroy the veyâr, who would not tithe the dark rrôn or sacrifice to them. He came in a storm that he had summoned and with it destroyed the village of Tiethe Hamar, and slaughtered as many in it as he could hunt down. But the veyâr Nidral, son of Atharene, attacked him as Baanraak devoured women and children that he found hiding in one of the last of the standing houses of the village, and Nidral attacked Baanraak with a silver knife blessed by the old gods, and the knife's name was Thice. And Nidral drove the*

knife into Baanraak's throat, driving it into his blood-
channel, and when the blood gouted out and covered
Nidral, Baanraak died, and did not return to hunt the
veyâr for ten years and a day. And when he returned,
he sought out Nidral first, and devoured the champion,
for Baanraak's memory was long and his hunger for
vengeance burned ceaselessly.

Throughout that whole reading, the muffled yips and gasps of the goroths created a steady undercurrent of noise, so that Lauren began to feel that she was reading the passage over the noise of a popcorn popper in another room. She didn't say anything to the goroths, but their reactions every single time she said either *Baanraak* or rrôn got on her nerves and stayed there.

Molly's reaction, however, wasn't the unemotional interest Lauren had expected. When she looked up from reading, she saw that Molly had gone pale.

"What's wrong?"

"Baanraak," Molly said. "That's the name of the hired killer that the rrôn Rr'garn went off to find. The one he wanted to bring in to kill us."

An ice-cold worm of dread crawled into Lauren's gut and knotted everything it touched. She looked at her sister and said, "You don't suppose it's the same one?"

"It probably is," Molly said. "I don't want to be an alarmist, but the thoughts I managed to gather from Rr'garn suggested that this Baanraak was once leader of them all."

The goroth Rue popped out of whatever hiding place he'd chosen for himself and said, "Please, oh, please, Hunter . . . Vodi. Do not speak of them. You say their names and evil things will happen—you must not speak of the dark gods, not by what they are nor by who they are. They are wicked, and have paid the winds to carry every mention of them to their ears, and they seek out those who summon them."

Lauren felt bad for the little creature. He looked like he was about to have a coronary—he was grayer than Molly, and sweat beaded on his skin and runneled into all his wrinkles; he breathed like he'd just run ten miles at top speed, and his previously yellow eyes had taken on an alarming orange hue.

Lauren said, "I'm sorry, Rue. We don't mean to upset you—but if we're going to defeat our enemies, we first have to know who they are, and how they operate, and what their weaknesses are. We can't allow superstition to scare us away." She smiled at him and said, "But we're in Copper House. This is a good place; you don't have to worry for us, or for yourselves. If the rrôn had been able to get in here, they would have already done so. The fact is, they've done nothing but circle. They can't reach us here. Don't worry."

But Molly was watching the goroth, her head cocked to one side, an intent look on her face. "You know them? You've met them?"

"Oh, no!" Rue said, horrified by the very suggestion. "They ignore my kind as often as not, and if they do notice us, it's only to eat us. They have no regard for . . . for thinkers and minds. Anything that moves is food, they think. They are wicked. Wicked—and if you talk of them, they will hear you."

Lauren wanted to thump Rue, but he had sworn himself to her service. Compared to Embar, he seemed flighty and silly and excitable, but she supposed she couldn't expect every goroth to be like Embar. That would be like expecting every human to be like Brian. It just didn't work that way.

When Lauren looked back to Molly, Molly was sitting there with her eyes closed, and from the expression on her face Lauren could only guess that she had a migraine coming on.

"Molly, you okay?" she asked, but Molly held up a hand to silence her. Lauren sat watching her, puzzling at Molly's pallor, the way her brows knit into a frown, and the way her spine straightened and seemed to go stiff. Lauren closed the book on her lap with the reader in place like a bookmark and lowered it silently to the floor beside the rocker. She leaned forward, ready to get up to offer her sister comfort or help. But the instant she started to get up, Molly's eyes flew open, her head snapped around to face the copper grille of the east window of the suite, and she shrieked.

Lauren looked where Molly was looking, and saw—and felt—a monster hovering outside her window, one hellish yellow eye the size of a basketball staring in at her. And at the same moment, she felt the presence of something behind her, and turned, and saw another equally huge eye, at the north window glowing like a ruby cat's eye in headlights.

"They're here!" Molly shrieked, and leapt to her feet. "We have to get out of here."

Lauren ran into the bedroom and grabbed Jake, and heard the ponderous flapping of the monsters' wings outside the windows, and the horrible scratching of claws on glass.

And then a crash, and a piercing scream.

She tucked her groggy son under her arm like a football and ran like hell.

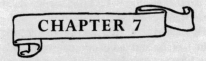

CHAPTER 7

Copper House

MOLLY HELPED LAUREN and the goroths and the guards move Jake, the books, and Lauren's few belongings into safe—if windowless—quarters in the core of Copper House. The guards took up their positions outside the room. The goroths went through the inside of the smaller suite with paranoid efficiency, located what they determined were its weaknesses—a secret servants' door into the sitting room and a narrow blind passage between the dressing room and the bedchamber—and set themselves to guard them.

Seolar arrived, sent guards against the too-close rrôn, and then made sure Molly was safe. He left when she told him she needed to stay with her sister and her sister's son for a while—at least until they could calm down.

So finally the sisters were as alone as they were going to get.

"What the hell are we going to do?" Lauren asked. She rocked Jake in her arms and stared woefully at the bed as if it might turn into something terrible that could devour her.

"About the . . . about *them*?" Suddenly Molly felt a bit more respectful of the superstitions regarding the mention of the dark gods.

"Yes." With a sigh, Lauren tucked Jake into the bed. Oblivious as only a child could be, he blinked a couple of times, smiled sleepily, and curled into a ball. Within seconds he was asleep as if nothing had happened.

Molly said, "The veyâr are taking care of them for now. They can shoot them from concealment and at least get them to back off. Long-term . . . ? Long-term, you and I are going to have to find a solution."

Lauren looked sick. "We caused that, Molly. We brought them down on us and put everyone in danger."

Molly bit her bottom lip and fidgeted with the ties of her bodice. "I know. We have to know the rules, Lauren. We have to know what we can do and what we can't. We have to understand who we are, and to do that, we're—or at least *I'm*—going to have to do some reading."

"I don't know that this is going to work," Lauren said. She sat on the edge of the bed. Molly saw her glance at her son. "Putting Jake into danger is driving me crazy. I can't think, I can't focus. I should be reading Mom and Dad's notebook, but all I can think about is that if I get killed, he has no one."

Lauren hid her face in her hands. Molly heard her muffled voice saying, "This morning he told me he wanted his daddy back, and just a little later he almost lost me, too."

Molly said, "We'll be more careful."

"Careful isn't going to matter. You and I are targets for something big and terrifying and evil. My kid is caught in the middle. And I don't . . . I don't even know who to see to hand in my resignation. This isn't duty, Molly. This is *captivity*, and it stinks. What were our parents thinking?"

"They thought they were doing the right thing," Molly said. "And it isn't like they weren't taking some risks."

"They could have risked me." Lauren rose and walked over to look at her sleeping son. "But they had no right to risk him." She looked over at Molly. "Maybe we could find a way to get him a necklace like yours. Something that will keep him safe and whole. I know we have things we have to do, but if Jake isn't safe, I don't think I'll be of use to anyone."

"A necklace to keep him safe and whole, like me," Molly echoed. She didn't feel whole. She couldn't tell Lauren about the empty place inside of herself. She couldn't tell Lauren that since she'd returned from death, she no longer needed to sleep—that at that moment she had been awake for several days, and not once in that time had she felt the faintest impulse to lie down and rest. She spent time in bed with Seolar—but once he was asleep, she got up and stared out into the darkness.

Darkness spoke her name now, in a way it never had before.

"So—you don't have anything to say about the idea? You think I'm crazy, or that the whole thing sounds stupid, or . . . anything?"

Molly shrugged. "We'll go down to the safe room tomorrow, and see what we can do. I don't know that it's a good idea. It might even be a really bad idea. But he's your kid, and you have every right to do what you can to protect him. If I were you, I think I'd be doing the same thing." She patted the corner of the bed.

"Thanks, Molly. I appreciate it."

Molly thought for a long moment. Finally she said, "Why don't you get some sleep, then? I'll stay here and read and keep watch—I don't really want to go to sleep, and I don't really want to be away from you right now. Sleep on the problem, try to figure out a solution, and I'll see if I can get some research done on *our* problem. We have a lot of work to do—but you're right. Until you can concentrate, we aren't going to be able to do it."

Lauren gave her a wan smile.

"And be a little happier," Molly said, forcing cheer. "If you're successful, Jake will be safe."

Lauren stood, smiled a little, and came over to hug her. "I wish we'd been kids together. You're exactly the sister I would have chosen, even if you are too pretty and you have huge alien eyes."

Molly laughed—a genuine laugh. "I know exactly what you mean. You would have been the perfect older sister to have around when I was little." She grinned. "Anyway, get some sleep, cuddle your little guy. I'm going out to the sitting room to read for a while."

"If you get tired . . ."

Molly waved her off. "If I get tired I'll sack out on the couch. I know how to do that, and this dress is a lot more comfortable than it looks."

As Lauren got into bed, Molly headed out to the sitting room and the long couch. "Leave the door open a crack, would you?" Lauren called after her.

This time Molly went straight to *Those Whose Names Are Unspoken*. Lauren had left her reader in the page from which she'd been reading, and Molly wanted to know more about the rrôn, and the dark gods, and what made a dark god.

She read more about Baanraak, who had died a dozen times but who always came back, and about the hated keth god Aril, for whom the veyâr had only been able to count five deaths and returns at the time of the writing, and finally about a god named Cisgig, whom the veyâr destroyed—to all appearances—permanently.

It was while reading about Cisgig's final destruction that her heart began to pound and a creeping sense of horror overran her.

> Then the champion Val Vâryn brought the body of dead Cisgig to the pyre and before he was burned, stripped off all his gold. And the goldsmith said, "Give the gold to me, for we will not succumb to greed and harbor our enemies in our belly as our slaughtered brethren did." And he prised the stones from necklace and armbands and earcuffs, and ground them to dust, and when he'd finished that, grated the gold into a fine powder and mixed it with quicksilver and took it to the river and poured it in a drop at a time. And the dust from the gemstones he scattered to the four winds, and when he was done, they lit the pyre beneath Cisgig's corpse, and burned him until even his bones were ash, and scattered them to the wind as well. The soulless monster rose no more, nor will he ever.

Molly ran her fingers over the sleek gold chain that she wore and touched the heavy gold pendant, and ran her index finger slowly over the sapphires around the edge of the medallion. The necklace hummed and purred beneath her fingertips, a thing alive. It was the reason she had come back; she knew it. It told her things sometimes—not in words but in pictures in the back of her mind, or when her eyes were closed. Through it, she had known of both Rr'garn and Baanraak; through it, she could feel the rrôn circling high above Copper House, once again out of the reach of the guard and its silver-tipped crossbow points.

Soulless, the book had called Cisgig—and as she thought about it, every other dark god. She flipped to the back of the book, hoping to find an index in which she could look up "soul," but it had none. However, she had better luck in the front, where the writer or writers offered a wordy table of contents without any page numbers.

Toward the front of the book was a section called, "The marks of the dark gods, and their curses and characteristics, as well as their powers."

She moved slowly from page to page, using the reader to identify the first few words in every paragraph—for besides not having page numbers, the book didn't have anything she could recognize as chapter headers. No changes in the handwriting, no special indentation, no little pictures or lines. Nothing.

But she found it soon enough, and started to read.

> *Though most of the dark gods, like the old gods, can change their forms to resemble the veyâr or natural creatures of the world, they carry with them always an aura of menace that they cannot dispel. They are creatures dead and risen, who with their first deaths lose their souls and never after regain them. They are the lost, dispossessed of the afterlife that would have been theirs, and though in their first reincarnations they of-*

ten hold much of the memory of who they were, with
each death more of what was living about them
washes away, and more of what is dead remains. They
become evil, but immortal evil, passed from rebirth to
dark rebirth by the god-tainted gold that remembers
and re-forms them.

Molly closed the book and closed her eyes. This was the truth Birra and Seolar had hoped to keep from her; that she was a *thing*, a construct, a soulless monster that would live forever, but would shed more and more of herself as time went on. She felt the rrôn outside Copper House because she was kin to them; she was the same thing that they were, only younger. Fresher.

Soulless, dead, with the magic of a gold necklace to reanimate the corpse and make it think that it was a real person, and let it have hopes and dreams and aspirations, but let it have them in vain.

Her soul had abandoned her—gone wherever souls go, to do whatever souls did. And she remained behind, a child abandoned by its parent in a hellish bus station filled with devouring monsters and sadistic men and left to fend for itself. And she could never follow. She was cast off.

How could Seolar love her? He knew what she was. Did he pretend love just because his people needed her help? If she were a cynic, that would be the easiest explanation. But she was not a cynic—at least not yet. She thought she could read his touch, his voice, his care and compassion well enough to tell that she was not being deceived.

So she believed he loved her. But how could he?

And how could she live with herself? She'd wanted to live with him, grow old with him, and in the end die with him. But that wasn't the way it would work. Sadly she closed her eyes and pictured him, filled with her love for him and her anguish at the future she saw spreading out before her. She would live now until she chose to die—until she found the courage and the strength to remove the necklace and walk away from it for good. In the meantime, she would watch Seolar grow old and die while time left her untouched—and after him, she would, perhaps, find some other beautiful young man, and perhaps after him another. The echoes of the lost Vodian, whispering to her in the silent room, mourned not their own lost youth, for they had never lost it, but the lives of every creature they had ever dared to care about.

She could go through their biographies to find out the details of their lives, but she now knew the key piece to the puzzle, and knowing it, she could see already the most important fact in each of their lives. Each of them had held in her hand the chance to be immortal, and had eventually chosen—*chosen*—oblivion. That truth terrified Molly. For her there would be nothing after death. She was real; she felt, she yearned, she hoped, she loved—but her soul was gone, and when she died she would simply blink out like a snuffed candle. And all around her would go on to the afterlife. To infinity, to wherever souls went, to do whatever they did.

Molly had never felt so alone or so adrift.

Or so angry—at Seolar for hiding the truth from her; at herself for being stupid and not getting Jake to safety in time; at Lauren for having put her into a position where she had to make two decisions she didn't want to make—first, to leave Oria when she wanted to stay, and second, to save Jake when she knew she would die if she did. She was angry at the world and her life and the soul that she no longer had and the dark gods who hung in the air above, waiting for something . . . something . . . that would permit them to destroy her—and at the knowledge she was more like them than either the sister or the man she loved.

She put her hand on the necklace. She could save herself a lot of time, a lot of pain and heartache. She could take the necklace off, walk out onto the balcony, and call the rrôn down to her. They would end it quickly—she'd suffer one more death, probably faster than the last one, and no new awakening. If her life was a nightmare waiting to get worse, then death would be freedom, wouldn't it? Or at least surcease from horror.

Pity she sat in a room with no windows, no balconies, no outside access. She could have been outside and the deed done before anyone could stop her—before she had a chance for second thoughts.

But.

The easy path was almost always the wrong one. Lauren needed her. So did the veyâr.

Molly had not chosen the duties placed on her shoulders, but if she did not carry the burden, no one else would. No one else *could*. Without her, her world would likely end quickly and horribly.

She pulled her knees up to her chest and wrapped her arms around her legs. With her chin on her knees, she began rocking back and forth. Live and suffer and fight, or die forever?

Back and forth. Back and forth. She was a coward. She could see what was coming, and she didn't want it. She wanted quick and clean and done once. She wanted life and love and Seolar. She wanted to fight beside her sister. She wanted to run away. She wanted everything—and nothing. Finally, she wanted a solution, an escape, a happy ending, and that was the only thing she knew she could never have.

Molly closed her eyes tightly, and rocked and wept, and waited for morning.

Cat Creek

Pete got himself out of bed well before dawn, and was just driving into Charlotte as the sun rose behind him. No problem in looking eager to Eric—that could only work in his favor. And getting into the city early allowed Pete to figure out how he was going to set up a meeting—something that was going to be damned difficult to do.

He couldn't use the usual protocols—scrambled lines, secure phones, code phrases. He was breaking new ground this time, and he had to admit it had him scared shitless.

Copper House

Molly still occupied the couch in the sitting room when Lauren and Jake, trailing goroths, headed out of their bedroom in search of breakfast. And Molly looked like refried hell.

"Molly, what's the matter?"

"I found out how this all works." Molly sniffled and wiped at her face as if just at that instant realizing it was streaked with tears. "I came back, but my soul went on without me. I'm—I'm a dark god. Kept in check by the necklace I wear, apparently—there was a great deal of information in several of the Vodi biographies on how the necklace helps me hang on to my memories and personality, and keeps me from going dark too soon. But I am a soulless immortal, and I'll keep coming back less and less me, and more and more . . . nothing. More and more an empty shell. Only nature abhors a vacuum, and the rrôn are like me. They're *things*—soulless, immortal monsters. That's why I can hear them, Lauren. That's why something in them calls to me. It's because we're the same, or we will be if I'm around long enough."

Lauren started to protest that this wasn't true, but Molly hadn't finished speaking yet.

"They all killed themselves, Lauren. All the Vodian before me—they all eventually took off the necklace and walked out into the midst of whoever was hunting them at the time, and got themselves ripped to pieces. That was better than living as what they had become. And . . . that's what I am."

Lauren looked at her, wordless, and pulled her into a hug. "You have people who love you," Lauren said after a while. She patted Molly on the back and rocked her back and forth a little, the way she would comfort Jake. "Seolar, me . . . all the veyâr . . ."

"I have you now," Molly said. She pulled away and looked at her sister. "But you're getting older every day. I'm not. I'll look like this when you're ninety—I'll look like this when you've been dead a hundred years, and a thousand. I am going to watch everything I love die—all the people, maybe all the worlds." She whispered, "One night of knowing the truth, and already I understand a little why the rrôn are the way they are, and the keth, and the rest of the old gods who somehow ended up dark gods. They have become their universe—everything is temporary but them. They have forever—but they don't have Heaven. No karma, Lauren. No repercussions for evil; no rewards for good. And no way of stopping time for anyone whom they discover they care about. I can't make you live forever. Or Jake. Or Seolar. You're going to be gone someday soon, and I'm going to be here, and I'll be hollower than I was before."

She turned her face away from Lauren and said, "I'm not sure that I'm going to go through with any of the plan, Lauren. I'm not sure that I can live this way."

Lauren didn't know what to say. She couldn't imagine how she would feel if she found herself in Molly's place. She couldn't imagine what she would do. She just stood there, feeling lost, unable to come up with a single thing that might be comforting to Molly and still be true.

Jake had been watching Molly, frowning. When she fell silent, he took Bearish over to her and said, "Superman will save you. He saves mamas and daddies. He will give you a kiss and make it better."

He pressed Bearish's nose to Molly's cheek and made a kissing noise.

Lauren watched Molly's face crumple; she watched the tears start afresh. "And I will never have my own child," Molly sobbed. "Not ever." She scooped Jake into her lap, and Jake looked uncertainly at his mother. Then, without prompting, he wrapped his arms around Molly's neck and patted her gently. "It's okay," he murmured. "It's okay."

In Jake at that moment, Lauren saw a bit of herself and a bit of the man Jake would one day be—if she could keep him safe long enough to get him to adulthood.

She wouldn't be keeping him safe by giving him a necklace like Molly's.

She had no idea how she would protect him. But after she fed him breakfast, she figured she would go down to the safe room—either with Molly or without her, depending on how Molly was doing—and see what bright magical ideas she could come up with.

Once she had Jake protected, she could think about other things. Molly's nightmare discovery. The tasks their parents had left for the two of them. The problem of the rrôn, and other old gods, too. And not incidentally, the fate of countless worlds, no matter how grandiose that sounded to her when she thought it.

But Jake came first.

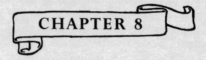

CHAPTER 8

Charlotte, North Carolina

PETE SAT on the green park bench, feeding a pair of fat mallards and trying to appear inconspicuous. He had a good day for sitting—a bright, breezy North Carolina spring morning, with pink dogwoods and daffodils and forsythia and azaleas ringing the lake and lining the paths, and the skyline of Charlotte rising over the top edge of the dogwoods like some Chamber of Commerce guy's postcard wet dream.

Pete kept expecting the brief, awful explosion of a bullet tearing into the back of his head, though, and that spoiled his enjoyment of the weather, the view, or the fact that he was away from the confines of Cat Creek for the day.

He pulled bread out of the paper bag he carried and tossed crumbs to the ducks. On the bench beside him lay a small, square hand mirror. He ignored the mirror.

A man in a gray suit sat down beside him, opened a bagged breakfast from Hardee's, and began to eat a ham biscuit. "This is a real pain in the ass, you know."

Pete did not look over. Fred had been both a good friend and Pete's secret boss for the last three years. Pete said, "I'm sorry about that. Can't be helped. Take the mirror."

Fred picked up the mirror without question. "All right. So what's the emergency?"

"I've made contact."

A short, pregnant pause. "Damn. That's not an emergency, Pete. That's success."

"It's an emergency. You know how we thought we were pretty close to understanding the technology? How we thought we were maybe five years from having things back under control again, whether they decided to make contact with us or not?"

Fred didn't say anything. They both knew it was a rhetorical question.

"Hold the mirror in the palm of your hand," Pete said. He got a mirror out of his own pocket, took a folded piece of paper from the same pocket, then rested his fingertips just above the surface of the mirror. It began to glow with a soft green light, as did the companion mirror in Fred's hand. Fred swore softly. Pete shook his head. "*That's* not the problem. Wait for it."

He shoved the paper into the surface of the mirror, which shimmered and distorted like smooth water disturbed by a pebble. The paper disappeared. An instant later, the glowing surface of the mirror in Fred's hand began to ripple, and the paper popped out onto the surface of the glass. The green glow in both mirrors died away almost instantly.

"Sweet Jesus H," Fred muttered. "What the hell . . . ?"

Pete put his own mirror back in his pocket and began tossing crumbs to the ducks again. "You know the old saying about any sufficiently advanced technology being indistinguishable from magic?"

Fred, staring at the mirror in his hand, nodded.

"Welcome to the brave new world."

Fred sat there for a moment, staring at the mirror lying in his trembling hand. "The mirror isn't everything, is it?"

"Secure lines are a problem, too. Basically . . . well, basically, secure lines don't exist anymore. These guys can send things through mirrors, and they can look into mirrors and see what anyone, anywhere, is doing at any time."

Fred's skin turned the color of week-old fireplace ashes. "Our ETs did this?"

Pete considered telling the truth, then shrugged. "I don't know who developed it. I know the ETs have it."

"What else is there? How bad does this get? Jesus Christ, this was a national security nightmare before. Now . . . how the hell do we secure a facility against this sort of technology?"

"Maybe we hire some of them to work for us. If they built it, they have to have ways to block it."

Fred turned the mirror over in his hand and studied the back. "How did you get this?"

"I've had a breakthrough. I'm in contact with some of the ETs. My lead in England paid off, in spite of how long it took."

Fred looked directly at Pete for the first time since he sat down. "You're in *contact*? With a *live one*? And this is the first you've mentioned it?"

"Not one. Several. And they're watching me. For all I know, they're watching me now—but I don't think so. I got one of them to ask me to come to Charlotte on a few errands; they don't have any reason to think that I wanted to be here."

"All right." Fred put the mirror in his pocket, and said, "I'll have some of our guys analyze this."

"Don't," Pete said. "It's just a mirror. There's nothing to analyze. All the . . . technology, I guess . . . that makes it work is . . ." He rubbed his temples, feeling a headache coming on. "It's somewhere else. I don't even know how to begin explaining that. I gave you the mirror because I can't call you, and I don't know when I'll be able to get back to Charlotte without raising anyone's curiosity. This way, at least I can send you reports regularly."

"How do *I* operate it?"

"You don't. It's one-way." That was another lie, but Pete wasn't about to get into gates and showing Fred how to open one. Lauren had spent hours showing him, and he was still inept with anything bigger than a pocket mirror. Besides, the second he showed Fred that humans could make the thing work all on their own, he opened himself up to a whole range of questions he wasn't sure he wanted to answer yet. If ever. Right now, he and Fred were talking about extraterrestrial invaders who'd first shown up on the FBI's radar in Roswell back in 1947. If he introduced upworlds and downworlds and frontworlds and backworlds and sideworlds, he'd find himself with no control over the way the Bureau handled the situation next. As long as Fred was relatively comfortable with what he thought was going on, Pete could buy himself the time that he needed to figure out what was really going on, and what, if anything, he needed to do about it.

Pete threw the last of his crumbs to the ducks at his feet, sighed, and rose. "I'll be in touch when I find out anything new."

Behind him, Fred crumpled up his paper bag and tossed it into the trash can beside the bench. "As fast as you can, if you don't mind. You've done a nice job of scaring the shit out of me today."

"We'll get a handle on it," Pete said.

"I hope so. I've never particularly wanted to see one of those little gray bastards as president of the United States. Or emperor of the planet."

Pete didn't look back.

Copper House

Guards led them—Lauren, Jake, Molly, and all the goroths—through the secret passage in Lauren's suite down into the bowels of the house. Lauren wanted the protection to be overkill; she wanted to think that she and Jake and Molly would be fine if they walked through the house alone. But they wouldn't—or if they were, it would be out of sheer dumb luck. She didn't know how she could adjust her thinking to accept the fact that she and her child were prey. The dagger at her hip seemed as heavy as a ball and chain, and she kept catching her arm on it as she walked. She had to adjust, though. She had to realize that she and hers now lived in a state of constant war—and she had to make that realization second nature. Then she had to find a way to make both Jake and herself damned unattractive targets.

The route down to the safe room seemed simple enough: straight through the passageway to the first flight of stairs, down those stairs, then left along the damp, cold stone foundation to a big door of iron and dark, ancient wood. It struck Lauren as grim—the approach of prisoners to a dungeon.

"The upper floors of this place are great," she told Molly. "But, God, do they need an interior decorator down here."

Molly laughed—the laughter a little strained. "Maybe we could get Martha Stewart in to redo the place. Or Christopher Lowell."

Lauren grinned at her. "Or both of them. I always thought they'd loathe each other. We could sell tickets to the catfights."

Inside, the safe room felt no more welcoming than it had appeared from the outside. Stone walls all around, stone floor, stone columns, a vaulted stone ceiling. The place felt cold and damp, and Lauren's first thought was that Jake would get sick if they stayed long in this place.

Going through the door, Molly posed like a real estate agent showing a property and said, "And this room is straight out of *Home and Dungeon.* Note the careful use of rocks in the floors, walls, and ceilings, and the way the stones let in the dark. And . . . and . . ." She stopped. "Help me out here. I'm not sure Martha and Christopher together could save this room."

Lauren laughed. "It really is awful. I mean, it's ugly, but it's also just miserable. We can't work in it this way. The damp and the cold aren't good for anyone, but especially not for little guys."

Molly nodded. "You can change things."

Lauren thought for a moment, then did a tiny, careful spell to warm the air, and another to brighten the place, and a third to put carpet on the floor. With each change, she kept her focus small and tight—just this place, just this moment. The heat, the light, and even the carpet would go away when she and Molly were finished in the room. In every way, she focused on minimizing damage and rebound—because a tiny heat spell carelessly cast and poorly thought-out could cause a drought back on Earth; a sloppy light spell might rebound to cause headlights in cars in one city to suddenly brighten to the point that they blinded oncoming drivers; and as for carpeting . . . she didn't even want to consider where a disaster with that might lead. The return of Seventies shag? God forbid.

She stopped herself. Her tendency to make jokes about things that unnerved her sometimes could be a good thing, but she didn't want to let herself trivialize magic in the process. A bit of carelessness by three traitor Sentinels had just weeks before resulted in the deaths of millions back on Earth—and from something so small and so stupid . . .

Lauren shook her head. She didn't want to trivialize magic.

"Better," Molly said.

And Jake laughed, looking at the changes. "Down, please," he said.

Lauren put him and the little bag containing Bearish and Mr. Puddleduck and his cars on the floor. "You can play for a while," she told him. "Molly and I are going to do things."

He grinned. "I play with the doggies," he said.

Molly raised an eyebrow. "Doggies?"

Lauren watched her son, looking happier and more confident than he had since the day Molly died, head for the goroths. "Explaining to him that the goroths aren't doggies would be too much trouble, and as far as I can tell, this world doesn't have dogs anyway. So it can't be an insult. Or a compliment, either. For what it's worth, Jake really likes dogs."

Molly said, "He's a beautiful little boy, Lauren."

"Thank you." Lauren thought about what her sister had

given up so that Lauren could still have her beautiful little boy. She turned to Molly. "Thank you for saving him," she said. "That thanks isn't enough—and I don't think that anything I can do for you will ever be enough. But I'll do what I can."

Molly smiled, her eyes sad. "Let's figure out how we're going to keep him safe. If we can do that, then I won't have died for nothing."

"What we need," Lauren said, "is a way to tell immediately what effects our magic is having upstream. Yours is supposed to be completely clean, right? Because you're from both worlds, the magic you do . . . has a damper on it, for lack of a better analogy. Right?"

Molly nodded. "That's the theory."

"But mine isn't. So anything we have to do that might get messy, you'll have to handle. I can take the small stuff and the happy spells—the things that should rebound for good. But even so, we have to be able to check results. If we don't, we could set off a disaster with something that feels like nothing."

Molly settled cross-legged onto the floor and closed her eyes. "Approach this logically. We have to see what's happening on Earth, pretty much simultaneously with putting a spell together."

"That would be the ideal." Lauren settled to the floor beside her. She thought chairs and a table would be nice, but if this took long, they could have the guards bring some in. That was a much easier problem to solve than temperature control in the subbasement of an ancient castle. "To the best of my knowledge—and I confess that my knowledge is severely limited—everyone working with magic works blind. So we're starting from nothing if we're looking at a way to see the effects of what we're doing while we're doing it. How do we do that? What are we looking for?"

"Can you link the spell to some sort of viewer? Sort of . . . tag the spell, I suppose. Like those big radio tags that scientists put on animals so they can see where they go and tell what they're doing without actually having to follow them."

Lauren got thoughtful. From what she had seen, magic worked well with analogy. If you could describe almost any working process, you could use that process to create a functional spell by analogy. If she used the animal-tracking process, visualized each spell as being tagged, then hooked the tag to a mirror . . .

"We could tag the spells and link them to viewing mirrors. They're mirrors that have closed, relatively stable gates attached. We should be able to check our results just by letting the tag dictate the viewing destination, and then scanning the mirrors."

Molly gave her a cockeyed smile. "That might work for *you. I* have no idea how to use a gate, how to look through a mirror—none of that. I have healing down pretty well, and I am getting used to the idea of making and changing things with magic—basic spellcasting. Gates, though, and mirrors—I have no idea what to do with them. If you hadn't had the gate already open when you asked me to take Jake back to Earth, I would not have been able to go through."

Lauren considered that. "If we didn't want to track results, we could just have you do all the spells."

"We could. Is there ever a time when rebound is desirable?"

"Well—yes. You heal someone here, and a handful of people back home have spontaneous remissions from cancer. You build something good here, and construction can jump in a town that needs the economic boost. Or you could be responsible for yet another strip mall in the middle of an overcrowded, overbuilt city, I guess. Anything that is good for one person is likely to be bad for someone else." Lauren pulled her knees up to her chest, wrapped her arms around her legs, and rested chin on knees. "There aren't easy answers to any of this—everything has a price, and our big job is to be sure that whatever we do for Jake doesn't create consequences we can't live with."

"Are we sure my magic has no rebound?" Molly asked.

"*I'm* not sure about anything," Lauren told her. "The theory is that your magic has no rebound. The Sentinels seemed fairly sure that was the case. Mom and Dad's notes suggest that this is an important part of your power. And when June Bug Tate was trying to figure out where you were and what you were doing, she had a hell of a time even pinpointing you to an area. And she has a whole lot of years of tracking experience."

Molly frowned. "That seems all wrong, though. If good magic benefits people upstream, why the hell am I the healer? That seems—wasteful. If you have to have a job done, and one person can do it and create a by-product that will benefit uncounted people, and a second one can do the work but you get no by-product—who are you going to put in charge of that job?"

"You want a corporation answer for that, an Air Force answer, or the logical answer?"

Molly snorted. "I forgot the Air Force had its hooks in you, too."

"Sometimes for the good. Anyway—there has to have been a reason why our parents set it up that way. Even good rebound could be destabilizing, or maybe it has something to do with negative effects of positive magic. I don't know. We'll figure it out as we go."

Molly frowned. "As far as my magic—and rebound—the books I read last night were all written by long-dead veyâr, none of whom had clue one about how magic actually works. So their biographies of the previous Vodian, while interesting, are pretty useless for me. I needed to know how the previous Vodian used magic, and what they used it for, and what I've been getting is a list of their interventions and dealings with the old gods, and not much mention of magic at all. I could use the dead voices as a resource, I suppose— but I don't want to go there more than I absolutely have to. The dead Vodian are dangerous in ways I can't quite put my finger on yet."

Lauren got to the other end of Molly's commentary with no more idea of what Molly was driving at than she'd had at the beginning. "And your point in all of that?"

"I don't think we're safe to assume that my magic has no rebound. It might just rebound to a different degree, or in a different direction."

"Which means . . . ?"

"That we need to watch the results of any spell I cast as closely as we watch any spell you cast. I thought it might work to have me cast the spells, but I don't think we can take that for granted."

Lauren nodded. "That does make sense." She glanced over at Jake, who was commanding his army of goroths. "I'm Superman," he said. "I am a superhero."

He was fine. He'd need lunch in a while, but he was close, she could see that he was safe, they had guards at the doors and here in this one room, and if necessary she could use magic against anything that challenged the guards. She could breathe a little easier, could afford to take a bit of time. Not a lot—at some point, once she had an idea of how she and Molly would carry out their parents' plan, which was still pretty nebulous in her mind—she would have to get in touch with the Sentinels, at least long enough to tell them she wasn't coming back. If she wasn't, of course.

But she and Molly could take a day to go over mirrors, figure out a way of tracking rebound, and then get into protection spells. She and Jake could easily spend a night sleeping in this room, if it came to that—she felt safe here. Maybe they could just turn this room into their apartment, and work from here. It was big enough that it could be turned into a nice little apartment for the duration of her time in Oria, and if she and Jake stayed here, Lauren thought she might be able to sleep a little better. She returned her attention to Molly. "Let's get you comfortable with gates, then, and viewing. I can show you what you need to know, then you can practice."

"What will we need?"

"Just mirrors. We should have some large ones and some small ones. You should be able to open and close an existing gate, too—that's just a safety precaution. I guess we should have some objects that could be shoved through the gates—once you open one, you *must* use it, because it won't close until you do, or until something else does."

Molly looked a little green. "Something else?"

Lauren nodded vigorously. "Assume the worst, then multiply by ten. Maybe a bird would fly through and close the thing for you. But maybe not. And there are some awful potentials in the 'nots.' "

"What sort of objects should we send through, then?"

Lauren considered. "Boiled stones would be ideal. No sense taking a chance on introducing bacteria or viruses or . . . God only knows. And stones are inert, and one looks pretty much like another to anyone who isn't a geologist."

Molly rose, a graceful movement that went from cross-legged sitting to ankle-crossed standing in a single thrust. Lauren, older and feeling it, thought, I remember being able to do that. Will I ever again?

"We're going to need some mirrors in here," Molly told the guard in charge. "Have an assortment brought in—standing mirrors and hand mirrors." She turned to Lauren. "Does the quality of the mirror matter?"

"It's easier to work through a good surface than one that's scratched or dull."

"Good mirrors," Molly amended. "And boiled rocks. Any size preference?" she asked Lauren over her shoulder.

Lauren mimed something roughly the size of a softball. "And some lunch," Lauren added.

Molly laughed. "You're hungry already?"

"I think so. No time sense in here—we don't have a window, and my stomach is growling. I didn't eat much breakfast, though."

"Chairs and a table," Molly told the guard. "Might be a good idea just to tell Seo what we need and let him arrange to have the house staff bring it."

The guard nodded, bowed deeply, and took off.

Lauren turned to watch her son commanding the goroths, perfectly content in the role of spoiled child god. "I'm going to go keep Jake company until our stuff gets here," she told Molly. "And I'm going to have a talk with the goroths. Jake is enough of a handful already without discovering that when he tells some people to jump, they obey. Megalomania is not something I want to encourage in him."

Molly watched him for a moment, and winced. He was demanding that the goroths jump up and down. "I think that might be a good idea."

Lauren pulled Jake away from his activities, sat on the floor with him on her lap, and told the goroths, "You don't have to do what he tells you. He's supposed to do what you tell him."

"But he's an old god," Rue said, speaking for the rest of the goroths, who all nodded agreement.

"No," Lauren said firmly. "In fact, he is a little boy. That's all. You don't let your own children tell you what to do, do you?"

"No, Hunter. We do not."

"Right. Because if you let them tell you what to do, they'd become unbearable to live with, right?"

"Yes."

"Same principle, then. He's only three. He can't do anything more than any of your littlest children can do. When he grows up—well, that'll be different, but between now and then, we will all teach him how to treat people, how to be responsible, how to think about others and not just himself. So that when he does have the powers of an old god, he doesn't think that he has the right to use them however he wants."

The goroths nodded. Rue said, "Very wise, Hunter. We will, then, treat him as we would treat one of our own. With kindness, but with firmness as well."

"Thank you."

Doggie said, "When *will* he develop the powers of an old god?"

Lauren shrugged. "I really don't know. Years from now, I hope."

The goroths nodded again, looking oddly relieved.

Lauren considered that, from their perspective, being in charge of a very busy small boy who they thought might strike them with lightning at any moment must have been uncomfortable. When he told them to jump, no wonder they jumped.

"You can't tell the . . . doggies . . . what to do," she told Jake. "You are a little boy."

"I'm Superman," he said, studying her with that look that said he was testing her to see how she reacted to defiance.

"You're Jake. You can pretend to be Superman later, but right now I am talking to Jake." She displayed no weakness in either her voice or her expression, and he looked down after a moment and nestled his head against her chest. "Okay, Mama."

She stroked his hair and cuddled him tight, rocking back and forth. "I love you," she said.

"I love you, too." He smiled up at her, and kissed her cheek. She kissed the top of his head. "I want my Superman cape."

Lauren sighed. "I should have packed that. I'm sorry. I'll get it for you as soon as I can."

He looked at her. "I *want* my Superman cape."

"I understand that." She pointed to the bag. "I brought Bearish. I brought Mr. Puddleduck. And I brought the cars. But I forgot the cape."

Jake said, "We are the Justice Leak."

The Justice League was a superhero cartoon that Jake loved beyond reason. He adored superheroes—any superheroes. He was perfectly willing to be a Powerpuff Girl, or Captain Underpants, or Batman. He didn't discriminate—as long as they were clearly the good guys, they were all right with him. If he was Superman, then Bearish could be the Green Lantern, and Mr. Puddleduck could be Batman. He'd decided some time back that she was Wonder Woman. Of course, he liked his superheroes best if they wore capes. So when she had noticed this budding passion, she made him a Superman cape by tying together the sleeves of a short red satin bathrobe she hadn't worn in years. It made a surprisingly convincing cape. On Jake, it was floor-length, and the material draped beautifully.

He loved that cape. Prior to the disaster, she'd had to watch him every minute to make sure he didn't try to fly off the top stairs while wearing it, of course, but she'd also had the fun of watching him stand in front of the mirror, in Superman Underoos and the cape, with his hands on his hips and a stern expression on his face, repeating, "I am Superman. *I* am *Superman*." But this was the first time since that day that he'd really expressed interest in being Superman.

She smiled and hugged him tight. Maybe he would make it all the way back to being himself again. She wanted desperately to believe that.

"I'll get it for you today, all right? And you can carry it around in the bag with the rest of the Justice Leak—er, League."

"Yes. That will be a good thing."

Seolar arrived then, with the first of the household staff, and the room filled up with mirrors and chairs and a table and food, and then with cots for Lauren and Molly and Jake, and nesting blankets for the goroths, and then Lauren and Molly fell into work, and magic, and didn't resurface for hours.

By the time Molly could open and close a gate and was starting to get the hang of distance-viewing through a mirror, Lauren looked up from working to discover Jake already asleep.

She looked at him, curled alone on the cot, his blanket already kicked off. Curled on the floor all around him in little piles lay goroths on balled-up blankets. At the sole door that entered the safe room, guards—alert and armed. Doggie stood watch behind them.

"Like living in a fort within a fort," Molly said, watching the direction of Lauren's gaze.

Lauren nodded. "I wish it seemed like overkill."

"I know what you mean." Molly shrugged. "But at least nothing is getting in here tonight."

Lauren, lying with her own cot shoved against Jake's, realized as she was drifting off to sleep that he was wearing a red cape. She wondered which of the goroths had managed to understand what Jake wanted well enough to find the cloth and fashion a cape.

Sweet of them, she thought. And drifted down to darkness.

Copper House

"Hunter? Hunter? He's . . . gone."

Lauren woke, to find the goroths up and milling, the guards standing around staring with panic in their eyes.

And she saw Jake's cot empty, and looked for him, and did not see him.

She was on her feet, caught in a fine rage and a coarse and terrible dread. "Where is he?" she asked to anyone and everyone. "What happened?"

"He kissed you," Doggie said, wringing her knobby hands. "He said, 'Everything will be okay, Mommy. Superman will go get Daddy.' And I thought he was playing, for he spoke much of this Superman yesterday after he pulled the red cloak out of the bag you brought him—though when he asked me to get the cloak from the bag, I could not find it there—and then he said to me that *he* was Superman." The hands wrung faster, "And you said he did not have the god powers, so I thought he could not do any harm to himself playing with the mirrors."

Lauren's skin suddenly wore a sheen of cold sweat. "The mirrors," she whispered. She'd gone through gates as a small child. Had brought playmates into her room from Oria, too, by opening gates. But Jake had never opened a gate. Had never done magic.

But he watched. He had traveled the path between the worlds.

He knew the feel of gates opening, the feel of the power that opened them.

"But when he put his hand on the mirror and the green fire

opened before him, I was not fast enough. Had I been, I would have pulled him back—or barring that, I would have gone with him. But the passage closed behind him, and I could do nothing but wake you."

Lauren felt light-headed. Sick. Her mind whirled, confused, like an animal caught in a trap trying to find a way out. Trying to roll back time just a few precious minutes.

"Which one?" Lauren asked, and suddenly Molly was at her side.

"What happened? What are you going to do? I just woke up and all I caught is that Jake is gone."

"He opened a gate and went through it. He's gone to get his father."

Molly looked bewildered. "But his father is dead."

Lauren asked Doggie, "Which mirror?"

Doggie showed her, and Lauren knelt before it, her fingers pressed lightly to the glass, feeling the echoes of the last passage.

"Lauren," Molly said, her voice a background noise in Lauren's mind, "Brian is dead. Where could Jake possibly think he might find him?"

Lauren felt the first echoes of Jake's passage, and shivered, wanting to pull away. Coldness, darkness, a slow and terrifying vibration that had nothing to do with worlds and life, and everything to do with eternity and death—it seeped into her fingertips and ran through her bloodstream, freezing her from the heart out. Her child was in there. Jake. Jake, who thought he was Superman.

"Where did he go?" Molly asked again.

"Heaven," Lauren said, her voice dull. "Or Hell. Or maybe just nonexistence. I can't tell."

Molly put a hand on Lauren's shoulder. "How could Jake know where to go?"

"Brian gave Jake part of himself—part of his soul, his essence—to keep Jake alive when you carried him from Oria back to Earth after the accident. Jake can feel his father as clearly as I can feel Jake. Maybe even clearer."

Lauren stared into the mirror, into the reflection of her eyes, and there looked within for the fire—comforting green fire, the embrace of the energies of the universe. She splayed her fingers against the glass, summoning the gatefires, and the storm that rode with them. But the familiar energies did not come. No green light glimmered far away. The fire that came for her, the fire that had swallowed Jake and that would take her, too, seeped toward her, gray and cold and terrifying, and tears filled her eyes as she thought of her little boy calling that—calling it so that he could go get his Daddy—and then bravely stepping in when the darkness came. That cold, that gray, that hell, was nothing short of Death, and the river through which Death flowed opened a pinpoint tributary that ran from the end of everything straight to Lauren, and she had to fight down fear so awful it made her want to pull back and hide.

"Don't go," Molly said, and the fear in her voice cut through the haze of terror that clouded Lauren's mind. "We'll find a way to bring Jake back. With magic. With something. Don't go. If you go and don't come back, worlds will die."

The passageway spiraled bigger—a thumbprint, a peach, a cantaloupe. She kept calling it, and suddenly beneath her fingertips she felt the dead flowing past. A broad, deep, powerful river of souls, cold and angry and terrifying, confused and grieving and lost, relieved and sad, mourning and merely numb, pouring steadily in one direction. The direction in which she could feel Jake, still moving away from her. Lauren locked her knees and clenched her teeth and stood fast, though her heart felt like it might explode and she stank of her own fear-sweat. "Death has been stingy about giving me back the people I care about. I'm going to *make* him give me back my child."

Behind her, Lauren heard Seolar, feet pounding on the stones, running like hell—and others running with him. He was shouting, "Keep her here. Do whatever you must, but keep her here."

"Anyone and everyone who tries to stop me from going after Jake is going to die," Lauren said. "Right now."

Behind her, Molly whispered. "I've got your back." And then, to those who came pouring into the safe room, Molly shouted, "Don't touch her, don't anybody move." And then, in a voice that broke Lauren's heart, Molly added, just to her, "Be safe. And if you see the real me . . . bring me back."

"I love you, Molly," Lauren said. And stepped into darkness.

CHAPTER 9

Copper House

MOLLY WATCHED LAUREN walk into the dark, cold fire of the gate. She stood for a long, quiet moment, lost between hope and despair; and then she thought of Seolar, who had known the truth and kept it from her, and anger filled her and washed everything else away.

She turned and waited, while Seolar waded through his men to stand in front of her, and on his face she read echoes of her own fury.

She glared at her reflection in Lauren's gate-mirror, angled behind Seolar—her green eyes gleamed. She gave no impression of softness, nor yielding. No shadow of the woman who had sought passion and wild sex from her lover the night before remained.

"I would speak with you," she said, only barely containing the fury in her voice.

Seolar's eyes narrowed. He turned to his men, the goroths, and to a thin, short veyâr dressed in tan and dun.

The guest held up one hand to forestall Seolar, and said, "Matters between you and the Vodi take precedence over anything I might have to say. We'll wait outside." He led the rest out the door, and within a moment Molly and Seolar had the room to themselves.

With the click of the door behind her, Molly tore into Seo. "Not only didn't you tell me, but you actively hid the truth of what I am from me. When we were at Graywinds, I told you not to confuse adversaries with enemies. I may not want the same things you want, we may have different means to an end, but I am *not* your enemy. Unless you lie to me."

She shook her head, clenched her fists. "You could have saved me time and confusion; you could have just laid out the facts in front of me and trusted me to deal with them. Instead, you decided to jolly me along as if I were some fragile, brainless little twit, and to hide things from me. *And* you *lied* to me—and lies of omission are just as heinous as lies of commission. You would have let me go on thinking nothing had changed, you bastard. Why? Afraid that if I knew the truth, I might be a little less willing to leap in and risk my life to save the worldchain? Afraid I might go over to the dark side right away, join forces with others of my kind? Afraid I might just say 'To hell with all of it,' and go off someplace else in the universe to sulk or work on my fucking tan or something? Is that what you thought? You shit! You asshole! You creep! Wouldn't even let me know that I'm a monster, that you can't abide the sight of me, that I'm just some soulless *thing* that is going to become more and more evil, more and more lost, and less and less me." During the tirade she kept walking toward him, a half step at a time, until she was inches from him, her face tipped up as close as she could get while she shouted. She realized suddenly that she *was* shouting; that was more loss of control than she wanted to display. So she dropped her voice to a soft growl and continued. "Just keep me confused and bury me in bullshit and let me keep healing the sick and let me and my sister put everything on the line to reverse the dying of the worldchain and pretend that you give a shit about me just to keep me happy and quiet, and never mind that as long as I'm here and fulfilling my parents' plan for my life, monsters are just going to keep dropping out of the sky and cropping up from the ground to kill me. *And* some of them are going to get through, and I'm going to die, and every time I die I'm going to lose a few more little pieces of me, and all the while I could be downworld about ten or fifteen worlds in some nice undeveloped corner of some planet, doing nothing but working on my tan and no one would ever come after me to try to kill me." She gasped for breath and glared into his eyes. "I could live something that resembled a normal life, you shitweasel, if I wasn't here busting my ass trying to keep our part of the universe from going tits up."

Seolar hadn't said a word or made a sound during that whole tirade; Molly didn't think he'd even blinked. Now, though, when she'd temporarily run out of steam and breath, his anger faded from his face and he put a hand on her wrist. "I'm sorry. I wanted to protect you from the truth because it is so sad, and because I love you. I did not mean to hurt you." He looked brokenhearted.

"You did."

"I can see that. But, my love, causing you pain is not and will never be my intent."

"You can't possibly love me," Molly said. "I'm a . . . thing."

Seolar shook his head, reached out and touched her hair. "You're you. Right now, at this moment, you are still you. My sadness comes from knowing that you will gradually slip away. Perhaps we can keep you safe and you will be you for as long as I live—and if that sounds selfish, it is. I know that you will outlive me, and I don't mind that—but I don't want to outlive the part of you that is truly you." He brushed his fingertips against her cheek, and for just a moment looked away.

"That's easy to say—"

He pressed one finger to her lips. "It is *not* easy to say. It is very hard—to admit that there could come a time when I will look at you, and you will look just as you do at this moment, but that whatever is inside of you will have no memory of your love for me, no thought of me, no compassion toward me. I love you—I love you with everything that is in me. In you I found the partner and the lover I waited my entire life to discover. And no more do I find you than you start to slip away from me, and if I can protect you well enough I may be able to keep you as you are—but I am just a man and your enemies are gods."

He pulled her into his arms and stroked her hair. "Would that I were a god. Would that I could be everything you need me to be, as you are everything I need you to be."

Inside her, the anger melted. "You're everything I want you to be. I found love with you, and I never had that before. I just thought . . . I thought that you couldn't love me anymore."

"I will always love you." He leaned back so that he could look into her eyes. "I wish I could say the same for you." He smiled when he said it, but the sadness in his eyes grew vast as an ocean.

She looked at him and memorized his face and the moment and how love filled her—and knew as she did it that it was futile. The realization was a knife in her heart. "*I* will always love you—for however much that's worth, and for however long I'm me."

He pulled her in close and squeezed her. Then he sighed and pulled away, and his mood shifted.

"Someone came here to meet you. He's here to help—he felt your sister arrive, and noticed the . . . ah, *them* gathering overhead, and he said he's been waiting a long time for Lauren and you to get here. Your, ah . . . . temper . . . chased him from the room before he had a chance to introduce himself."

"That bland little veyâr?"

"That is the form he takes here. He's one of the old gods. One of the Tergathi. His name is Qawar and he is almost as ancient as the . . . rrôn . . . and powerful. And absolutely on your side—if not on ours."

"He doesn't like the veyâr?"

"We don't matter to him. He's concerned about Oria, though, and Earth, and all the worlds above and below it."

Molly said, "Then he can't be happy Lauren left."

A trace of Seolar's previous anger chased across his face.

"He was furious. But no matter. What's done can be un-done." Seo opened the door and asked the old god to enter.

On closer examination, Molly decided Qawar didn't look quite like a veyâr. Apart from his short stature, his eyes—black as Seolar's—seemed a bit small and not luminous enough. His cheekbones and nose jutted at wrong angles—if he'd been a sculpture, he would have been a second-rate one. And unlike the veyâr, he had all the presence of lumpy mashed potatoes. He'd pass the first glance, she thought, but not a close inspection.

"Dearest Vodi," he said, and bowed. At odds with his appearance, his voice held the echoes of a Stradivarius played by a genius. Nothing timid or bland about it. "You are a grace note to the universe."

She returned his bow and said, "Qawar, I apologize for my display of temper."

"No apology necessary. Little swan, you hold a weight on your shoulders great men could not hope to bear, and I would not chastise you for at times resenting your burden." He bowed again. "I have come to help you."

"How?" she asked.

That toothy smile again. "Perhaps you could recall the Hunter from wherever she has gone, that I might offer my services just once?" It was not a question, though—simply an order couched in politeness.

Molly had taken a lot of orders in the Air Force. Here, though, she held the higher rank. She could feel it in her gut, and in the fact that he had come to her. "I'm afraid that isn't going to be possible."

Both Seolar and the old god gave her wary looks.

"Why wouldn't it be possible?" Seolar asked. "You worked all day yesterday on gates and viewing. Surely you can just find her and tell her to come home."

"She isn't anywhere that we might be able to reach her."

"Find a way," Qawar said. "Her arrival finally triggered conditions which I have been watching for on a dozen worlds and for, ahhh, ten thousand years at least."

"She's gone where we can't follow," Molly said. "With luck, she'll make it back."

"Where is she?" Seolar asked. "We need her."

Molly said, "From where I was standing, it felt like she walked into the River of Death . . . and is on her way to the afterlife."

Two adult males could not truly create pandemonium—that would take a full mob or one child. But Seolar and Qawar gave it their best shot. Molly crossed her arms over her chest and listened to them shouting—at her, at each other, at thin air. She got the gist of what they both seemed to agree on, which was that she had been irresponsible in not stopping Lauren, and that those who crossed the abyss never returned, and that now the plan that would have saved the worldchain was wrecked, and whole worlds and peoples would continue to die horribly. And it would all be Molly's fault.

"She's going after her son," Molly said as soon as she found a patch of quiet in between their shouts.

If they had been angry before, now they were simply flummoxed.

"Going after Jake?" Seolar asked. "He . . . died?"

"No. Jake walked into the River of Death to go find his father. He wanted to bring his daddy home."

Qawar asked, "How old is this son of hers? How powerful? If he could bring the flow of the river of souls to him—"

"He's only three," Molly said. "He's just a very little boy who loves his daddy and wants to have him back."

Qawar looked sick. "And the Hunter chased after this three-year-old boy into Death?"

"She's doing what she needs to do. When she's done it, she'll find a way back."

"No she won't," the old god said. "She's lost forever. I might as well go back whence I came."

Molly said, "She figured out how to get there. My money is on her to figure out how to get back."

The River of Death, and Beyond

Lauren had found Hell—but she seemed to be the only one who noticed. The dead surrounded her, so thick she couldn't turn, couldn't move, almost couldn't breathe. She hung there, drowning in the dead, and though she could see them and feel them pressed against her, each soul seemed totally self-absorbed, oblivious to place and time and movement. They raced through darkness en masse, carrying Lauren along in their current, with the tunnel of dark fire that Lauren had summoned to enter the throng long gone. The darkness was not absolute, though; she could see the souls around her in the shifting grayness that streaked past at nightmare speed.

Her child, somewhere up ahead, traveled in the same mass of crowding spirits. He would be so scared. He would hate being crowded; he would be frightened by the screaming and the weeping and the manic antics of some of the dead. And he was so little, surely they must be pressing in on him even tighter than they were on her.

Jake would not understand this place. These people. Some of them wept. Some laughed. Some seemed terrified. Some stared backward, reaching and clawing toward whatever it was they had been ripped away from. But all of them save her traveled oblivious to the rest.

"You're dead!" she screamed at one shrieking woman who seemed to be trapped perpetually in the last instant of some horrible accident. "It's over! Nothing can hurt you!" But the screaming went on, and on, and on.

She tried to shove the man who laughed. She wanted to hurt him. But her hands went through him, and he didn't so much as twitch when she tried to make him stop. He had an evil laugh. He'd done something bad—something terrible—and he seemed to think he'd gotten away with it.

The worst was the young mother who kept sobbing, "My baby, my baby, my baby. Where is my baby?"

Yes. And where is mine?

Lauren's eyes filled with tears that she couldn't blink away. Gone, she thought. They're gone to someplace where we aren't. We can't find them, we can't help them, we can't get back to them. And I can't even put my arm around you and cry with you.

Hell. There was a Hell and she was in it. And so—somewhere—was Jake.

The spirits weren't all human—but her mind said, *These are people like me.* And they were going someplace, and when they reached their destination, surely someone would set things right. Would punish the man with the evil laugh, would comfort the mother whose baby was missing, and soothe the woman who had died so badly. Would point Lauren toward Jake, then toward Brian and Molly.

There had to be people in charge to set things right, didn't there?

The hellride stretched interminably, to the point where Lauren would have clawed her way free of the mob to find another way to get to Jake. But this hell had no footholds, no handholds, no ceilings or floors—just the dead packed like sardines on top of her, to either side, in back and in front of her, beneath her feet. An ever-shifting, writhing, inescapable cacophony that had neither beginning nor end—and the thought entered her mind and then would not leave; what if this was it? What if this was the afterlife, and there were no people who set things right? What if the afterlife was this river, and when Brian moved beyond the place between the worlds, this was where he came? How could Jake ever find him . . . here?

How could she ever find Jake?

Panic rose from her gut, set her heart racing, clawed at the back of her throat until she wanted only to scream, and to keep screaming until someone saw that she did not belong with the dead and plucked her free of them.

Then the sounds of screaming, sobbing, laughing, madness began to die away; one by one the faces around her calmed, and one by one each soul turned to face forward and looked upward. And looks of recognition crossed their faces, and little by little peace descended.

The darkness faded a little, into a more uniform gray, and Lauren had a feeling that she was near to arriving. But she could see nothing. She had no clue what the dead around her saw, no idea why they found peace, or if not peace, at least stillness.

Some of the pressure let off—space appeared between her and her fellow travelers. She could move her arms, turn and look around. All she could see were more of the dead, and they still paid no attention to her, though now almost all of them wore beatific expressions. Then one beside her blinked out of existence. And then another. Suddenly all of them were vanishing, popping away with soft little flares of light.

And still Lauren moved forward, at least in what felt like a forward direction, but the herd of dead around her thinned at an alarming rate, so that she could see bits and pieces of the place where she moved. And it made no sense.

Forward—relentlessly so, with fewer and fewer of the dead around her and the universe turned a flat, lifeless gray. This was the Afterlife? No clouds, no pearly gates, no sense of place. When she tried very hard, she could make out the lines where a sort of floor raced past beneath her feet, but with nothing to give it scale, she couldn't begin to guess whether she floated inches above it, or miles.

She watched the dead all around her growing brighter, then blinking out. And then she discovered that she was alone, and still racing . . . somewhere. With a thought, she turned to look behind her. In the distance she could see the souls pouring into this place, growing brighter, blinking out. But finally she traveled so far that she could no longer see them.

And still she could find no detail to give the place either meaning or shape. Nothing but the gray floor lay beneath her, nothing but the gray sky arced above her, and still nothing to relieve the monotony. She tried to turn around to go back the way she'd come, but though she could turn without difficulty, she discovered that without any sort of visual reference she had no idea which way was back. She also discovered that she'd stopped moving—or at least that if she was still moving, she could no longer tell.

She hung in the middle of the void, all alone, and could not think of a single thing to do. Had Jake come this far? Had he found some way to Brian? Or was he, too, lost on this endless plain? She had to find him. She had no idea where to start.

In the moments between when she'd first discovered that Jake had taken off to rescue his daddy from death and the moment when she stepped into Death's river and discovered it to be nothing that would yield to her, Lauren had entertained a brief, shining hope—that she would burst into Heaven, rescue her child, then play Orpheus to Brian's Eurydice—that she would melt the hearts of any who stood between her and Brian with the story of their love and loss, and that she would win over whoever was in charge into letting her steal him away from Death. That her eloquence and her passion would win back Molly's soul as well. That this nightmare would have not just a happy ending, but a magnificent one.

That she would end up lost and alone in a place that was the most literal "middle of nowhere" that she'd ever seen had not even crossed her mind.

"JAKE!" she screamed at the top of her lungs. The sound muffled to nothing, as if she'd shouted through a mouth stuffed with feathers. Shouting wouldn't work.

Would she just hang there forever? She wouldn't accept that. Jake needed her. They were in the afterlife, but they weren't dead—so obviously whatever system existed had not been set up to accommodate the living. The souls of the dead had all gone places—things had started making sense to them, and they had found some sort of peace, and when they reached what looked to her like acceptance, they had vanished. She did not believe they ceased to exist. That would render everything that had happened meaningless. They were souls; souls were energy; energy did not cease to exist. That violated everything Lauren knew about physics—though what she knew wasn't a lot.

So, the souls had gone where they belonged. And because she and Jake did not belong anywhere in this place, they had ended up at the end of the . . . what? The sorting line?

She needed to have her feet on the ground, she thought. She needed to feel something solid underneath her, to get some sense of reality in the midst of this horror. And thinking that, she realized that she was floating downward—and as soon as she realized that, her feet settled gently on solid ground.

She took a deep breath, feeling a little better. Just knowing that she wasn't going to float forever in nothingness helped. What she really needed, though, was some direction. Some sort of signpost that could tell her which way was forward, which back, and which direction would take her to Jake.

She turned—slowly—looking for anything she could use as a reference point. A spot on the horizon, a signpost, a tree . . .

A tree would be great, she thought. Something to offer a bit of beauty in this dismal horror of a place. A big, strong, live oak, its gnarled, twisting branches spreading out a hundred feet in every direction, its leaves dark green and glossy, its massive shape a half sphere flattened at the top. Crowning a grassy knoll, adorned with a tire swing that would be a magnet for a scared little boy, with sunlight sparkling off the leaves, it would . . .

It did. Off in the distance, as far away as she'd imagined it, sat the very live oak she'd been spinning in her mind, and though she could not see any sun, sunlight nonetheless shimmered off the leaves. Beautiful—and the little patch of grass beneath and around it, and the tire swing hanging still and ready—all of it, beautiful.

Go to the tree, Jake. Wherever you are, go to the tree.

Lauren started to walk toward it, but stopped. Maybe Jake was too far away to see it. Or maybe the tree existed only for her imagination. She wanted to cry—she wanted to roll up in a ball and scream at the universe. But that wouldn't help Jake. She had to stay strong. She had to keep moving. She had no guarantee that Jake could find the tree, or that he would go to it even if he could see it. But if she could make a tree, she could make something considerably more useful.

Roads, she thought. With signs.

And she decided that the signs would be useful signs. TO JAKE →. TO BRIAN →. TO MOLLY. → HOME → .

She closed her eyes, visualized the signs, and made them as real in her mind as she could. JAKE—white letters on a green background, arrow pointing in the appropriate direction, a smooth black tarmac path leading across all this featureless grayness to the place where she needed to be. Another just like it that would take her to Brian and Molly. And then a sign pointing to the direction where she and Jake and Brian and Molly could all go home.

Lauren opened her eyes and was heartened to see the tarmac sprawling out in front of her, a fine, thin, arrow-straight ribbon running to her right. One road, a single direction, and she was at its very beginning. And directly in front of her, a sign. And the sign had its little arrow, and was green and white. But it did not say JAKE. Or BRIAN. Or MOLLY. Or even HOME. It said, ADMINISTRATION.

"Shit," Lauren whispered.

The road seemed infinite, with not a curve or bend in sight. In fact, it vanished to a point at a distance so far away that she could only guess at horizon and sky.

The road led past the tree.

She walked to the tree, and there she found another sign, planted in the grass. The sign said, "PLEASE DON'T RE-ARRANGE THE TERRAIN."

Lauren frowned. *Administration* did not like the tree. *Administration* did not want her leaving signposts for her little boy—and didn't seem to care if she found him. Well, *fuck* Administration.

But as she watched, the tree slipped into the ground, turning gray and blobby before it did. And then it was gone. The grass vanished. The sign vanished. Lauren glared at the ground, at the grayness, and turned to look behind her, to see what had become of the green sign with the arrow.

The road ended right at her heels.

"Oh, Jake . . . this isn't good," she whispered.

The road still stretched ahead of her, though, pointing toward dread eternity, bisecting all infinity into two equally dreadful halves. She was not going to walk that whole distance. She closed her eyes and re-created her little yellow CRX in her mind, and willed it to appear in front of her. She opened her eyes. Another sign. WALKING WON'T KILL YOU. AND YOU MIGHT LEARN SOMETHING.

Lauren screamed, "I want my kid back, you monster!"

And the gray nothing swallowed her scream the way it had swallowed the tree. She got no response. With tears leaking from her eyes and her throat aching and clogged, she started walking.

After a while, she decided that the nothing was changing at an insufficiently fast rate, and she started to run. The horizon remained the same, the ribbon of road the same, the gray ground and gray sky remained the same.

I could keep doing this forever and never get anywhere, she thought.

She stopped, panicked and desperate and out of ideas about what to do next. She sat down on the road, pressed her face into her knees, and just sat there for a moment. She was challenging Heaven, and she knew that—but all she wanted was her people back, and it seemed to her that if she'd found her way here, she had earned the right to claim them and go home. And yet it seemed that . . . that *Administration*, to use the bureaucratic name the bastard had chosen for himself, didn't think she had earned anything.

"You're brave," a voice said in her ear. "But you *haven't* earned anything."

She jumped, and looked around. Nothing. The voice had been kind enough. Not mocking. Certainly understanding, compassionate. But it was not a voice with good news.

She had not come all this way for bad news. She was going to find Jake—and then Brian, because Jake had risked his own life to get his daddy back, and they *both* loved Brian and needed him. And then Molly. She got up and started walking again.

"I'm not going to let you tell me I can't have them!" she screamed. She clenched her fists, glowered at the vast nothingness before her, and roared, "I WILL GET MY SON BACK! I WILL GET THEM ALL BACK!"

She started to run, this time determined that she would not stop until she reached Jake; that her Brian would be coming home with her, that Molly would be going back to Oria, that these tragedies would end and be undone. She didn't care if that wasn't the way things usually worked. She didn't care if people didn't get their loved ones back from death. She didn't care if "that is not the way we do things here." Bureaucracy would not stop her, little green signs that said, "ADMINISTRATION" or "Don't step on the grass," or "STAY ON THE WALKWAY" would not stop her, and if she had to reshape this place and upset everything and wage war on the gatekeeper who stood between her and those she loved and needed, then by God she would.

She ran—faster and faster, harder, and her muscles bunched and released, and her heart pounded in her chest, and she felt herself become a creature with wings, unstoppable, a warrior, a hero. While she ran, she did not doubt that she could take on anything.

"I'm coming after you!" she screamed. "I'm coming, and you do not want to be the one standing between me and Jake when I get there. I'm going to tear you people apart, I am going to turn this place into a crater, I am going to tip heaven upside down and shake it until you all fall out and drop into nothing unless you produce my child for me NOW!"

Suddenly the scene shifted. The world cracked open and darkness spilled out, and out of the darkness stepped a figure in black, robes swirling around him and occluding his face.

"And you would take on heaven and hell and everything between to get your son back—and as an incidental—your husband's and your sister's souls as well. Is that right? You would do anything?"

"I *will* do anything," Lauren said, and suddenly she was standing with a bazooka on her shoulder aimed right at the black-robed bastard, and she didn't doubt that she could turn him into ash with it.

Cat Creek

Pete shut down the scene he'd been viewing in the hand mirror and broke his connection with Lauren. No matter how long he watched what was going on, it wasn't going to make sense.

He rested his head on Lauren's kitchen table. He hadn't been able to find her at all. And then all of a sudden she had erupted into view in the mirror, but for the life of him, Pete couldn't figure out what he was seeing—or, for that matter, what he was feeling.

From the second Lauren first appeared in his view, the echoes of something terrifying had reverberated beneath his fingertips, just on the other side of the glass. He stared through the window at Lauren—the single dark spot in a river of light that creeped him out. The pulse of that river felt like every crime scene he'd ever passed and every funeral home he'd ever entered; it scraped along his nerves with the same night fears that had shaken Pete when his father died in the hospital, holding his hand, gasping for one more breath, and when Pete's dog had died, hit by a car, and when, his first year in the FBI, Pete's partner January Ellison took a bullet from a drug lord's sniper—a bullet that had been meant for him.

Pete didn't know where Lauren was, but he knew damned well she didn't belong there. Then the river thinned out to nothing, and she hung in emptiness.

He got dreamscape images of a tree. A road. A strangely out-of-place sign—all of them hanging with Lauren in the middle of what was clearly nothing. And suddenly an enormous black-robed, faceless horror that rose up out of the depths of Hell and was going to be a feature attraction in Pete's nightmares for the rest of forever.

Then Lauren was holding a bazooka that appeared from nowhere, just like the nightmare she faced. Pete couldn't get to her. He couldn't help her. He couldn't even let anyone else know where she was—that would betray any trust she'd placed in him.

She seemed to be holding her own. Or at least not giving up. But he couldn't stand to watch anymore. He felt helpless, and he felt stupid for not understanding where she was or what she was doing. He didn't know if he would be able to re-create the link between the two of them once he let her go. But he couldn't stand watching helplessly while feelings like swamp-bottom death and just-past murder crawled out of the mirror through his fingertips and went straight into his brain.

He considering going to Oria, but *clearly* she wasn't in Oria. He could do magic in Oria, but if he tried following her to save her—assuming that she even needed saving, which was no sure thing—he would probably do more harm than good. He wished he could show the shit he'd just seen to Fred, but Fred still lived firmly within his "aliens-on-Earth" worldview, and Pete wasn't ready yet to bring him up to speed. But Fred had a really nice religious upbringing that had introduced him to many strange, mystical concepts, and Pete almost thought that Fred—seeing Lauren in the lighted river, or Lauren facing off with a bazooka against a Thing in Black—could have made some sense of things that left Pete flummoxed. Pete had been raised Default Christian—which meant that his parents had taken him in to have his head sprinkled in some old-fashioned church not long after he was born, and that he hadn't been inside a church since, except for weddings and funerals.

Yet what he'd seen in the mirror had more than a whiff of the Mother Church, and suddenly he regretted his lack of interest in things religious. He wondered if maybe he hadn't missed something important. He didn't have time for a Sunday school crash course at this late date.

He was, he thought, stuck with helping from where he was and with what he knew.

And what he knew—at least what he knew that might be useful to Lauren—was misdirection and deception.

"You use what you have, I guess," he said.

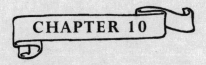

CHAPTER 10

The Wilds of Southern Oria

BAANRAAK, resting comfortably outside the entrance to his cave, enjoying the sun on his hide and the redness that seeped through his closed eyelids, chose not to stir himself to wakefulness at the approach of Rr'garn. He had felt the younger rrôn coming long before he flew into visual range. Rr'garn had neither subtlety nor grace; he rode the world as if he owned it, but more than that, he rode it as if he wanted it to know he owned it.

Baanraak, who had learned the survival value of a low profile early in his career as Master of the Night Watch, and who was the only master so far to step down successfully rather than being removed from office by the extreme measure of eternal annihilation, thought Rr'garn had little chance even to *become* Master of the Night Watch—a position he loudly coveted—before his subordinates wearied of him and destroyed him.

Such loud and chaotic thoughts—perhaps, Baanraak thought, I ought to save the Night Watch the trouble and do the job for them.

Baanraak opened his eyes at the thunderous wingbeats over his head; another foolish affectation. *He* could land without disturbing the leaves or the grass, or even the dust if he was careful. He didn't disturb the mind with his thoughts, he didn't disturb the world with his presence. Mostly anymore, of course, he basked—he had grown weary of the game long before.

And now this twit wanted to drag him back into it.

Baanraak finally lifted his head from its comfortable resting place on his rump as Rr'garn landed and studied the visitor with distaste. Rr'garn had dropped to the ground at an appropriately respectful distance, but then, he wanted something. Baanraak could sift no actual respect from the noisy contents of Rr'garn's mind.

"I'm not interested," Baanraak said. "So you've wasted the trip."

Rr'garn said, "But you haven't even heard me out yet."

"I heard you out long before you got here. You want me to eliminate a Vodi for you, and perhaps her Hunter, though if I can get the Vodi and the Hunter is not convenient, you'll consider the former sufficient to fulfill the contract. You offer me a fine grand mass of purest gold, unspelled and ready for my working, and an equally fine measure of silver—and there is no deceit in this offer; you have both the gold and the silver, and intend to part with it if I succeed. Which is why you're alive and not lying there in the grass with your throat torn out."

Rr'garn pulled in his rilles and cowered like a chastised hatchling, and all the membranes slid over his eyes for just an instant before he got control of himself and shook everything back out to adult display posture.

"Who brought this news to you before I did?"

"Your noisy thoughts, boy. Just as now you think you ought to kill the traitor who came to me before you and soured me on your mission."

Rr'garn managed to keep his rilles out this time, but the membranes over his eyes flashed quick betrayal even before he could sort his thoughts. "What manner of magic is this, Baanraak, that you can pull my thoughts from my mind?"

"No magic. Simple control, Rr'garn. You never bothered to find your own silence, choosing instead to keep your thoughts secret by hiding yourself in with a pack of others like you, none of whom has ever quieted for a minute. When you grow very still, and slow your own thoughts until they creep at the pace of a worm burrowing through earth, or even slower, to the pace of the growth of a tree, then the thoughts of others who are neither so still or so slow become bright, shiny baubles that you can pick out of the air at will."

"I have too much to think about to turn myself into a worm or a tree, Baanraak. I'm still active in the world."

Baanraak blinked slowly and smiled a sleepy smile at him. "And yet, while you cross-quartered my domain looking for me, I learned everything you currently know and worry about. Shall I list the enemies who seek to prevent your rise to Master? Shall I list your treacheries against the keth? Shall I tell you the name of the mate you aim to steal from one who considers you an ally, or the means by which you intend to do it? While you shouted your secrets down to me, I lay in plain sight and watched you flounder." Baanraak's smile broadened. "And yet you are too busy for silence or stillness."

To this, Rr'garn had no reply.

Baanraak said, "Now you hate me and wish me destroyed—and still, your fear keeps you here. And how very strange. You think this is not a Vodi, but *the* Vodi." He stretched his wings and uncurled and stood. He was bigger than Rr'garn, and next to his own opalescent black Rr'garn's pale gray and yellow scales looked sickly. "*The* Vodi? Really? Why would you think that? She's like all the others."

"Not quite." Rr'garn spoke, though he seemed tentative. As well he might be—Baanraak could read most of his thoughts clearly enough. The little coward had managed to keep the cause of the fear that had his mind spinning tucked deep enough inside that Baanraak had to confess surprise. *The* Vodi. He'd thought that little myth had died during his tenure as Master. Rr'garn continued, "She's strong. She was strong before she passed into the dark—and she carries a brand on her that none of the others has."

"A brand?" Baanraak found himself interested in spite of himself.

"She was a deatheater in her home world. But more than that, she was a warrior. She didn't come here as a tender child, and she near killed a handful of her abductors while they were getting her here from there. She carries herself as a warrior now."

While Baanraak thought, the very tip of his tail began to twitch. That had always been the myth—that someday, a Vodi would appear who sought not peace but war, who would not give quarter, but who would take her war to the dark gods and would eventually defeat them and unspin the darkness they had built. The tale was that she would walk the length of the worldchain, and where her feet touched life would spring forth. Life from death—for she was, at heart, as much of a soulless dead thing as any of the dark gods she set her spear against.

That had been the myth, and in Baanraak's day they had scoffed, because the Vodi of that time had been a fragile little buttercup, as had the ones who preceded her. She'd negotiated, she'd appeased, she'd surrendered a bit here and a tatter there and a piece elsewhere until her veyâr sat on a few shreds of ground that had, at the time the first Vodi arrived, been a healthy and promising young civilization.

"A warrior," he said. "Fancy that." Then he shook his head and laughed. "But you would think anyone a warrior who did not shriek at the sight of you."

"Not so. My spy told me tales. He would not approach her; he lived in fear that she might notice him because he said she had hawk eyes and she made no noise when she moved."

Baanraak did not want to let this ambitious stripling know he was intrigued. So he yawned elaborately and settled back to the ground. "And yet, a messenger came chasing after you to tell you that your spy got up his courage after all, and went after the Vodi and her Hunter. And now he's dust." Baanraak chuckled. "You need a better spy. Or at least one that isn't quite so dead."

"He got me what I needed to know, and his reputation was

impeccable. The veyâr trusted and liked him. If he was not brave, well, what of that? I needed his eyes and his ears and his discretion, not his sword. Bravery is overrated in spies. And in his case, it was wasteful."

"Tell yourself that." Baanraak chuckled. "And so, with your slaughtered spy and your noisy mind, you come to me to ask me to destroy a Vodi for you."

"Yes."

"You don't think killing her a few times will be enough to frighten her into oblivion on her own, eh?" He closed his eyes, though he watched Rr'garn closely with his mind and his other senses. He knew he gave the perfect impression of an old rrôn bored and stupefied by the warmth of the sun and the sweet breezes in his nostrils, but he could not have been more tightly coiled or more ready to spring.

Rr'garn was watching him, turmoiled mind churning its flotsam and detritus. So loud and so frightened. Baanraak waited. Rr'garn waited, too—and a surprisingly long time. This pleased Baanraak for some reason he couldn't quite put a claw on.

At last Rr'garn said, "You do still partake of the feasting at the fall of a world, do you not? You have not set aside the drinking of death?"

Baanraak smiled on the inside. "I still feast."

"This one could end the feasts, and in so doing end us."

"The Night Watch has the warriors of the upworlds at its disposal—the best and strongest and cleverest of the Night Watch, immortals all."

"And yet not one of them is you," Rr'garn said. "We do not want an adventure out of this, Baanraak. We simply want efficiency and success. You aren't known for a trail of drama—only for getting things done promptly and well."

Baanraak gave up the pretense of sleep. He raised his head, shook out the rilles around his face to full display, and grinned. "That's not a reputation I mind leaving at all."

"Will you do it? The rewards for success will be rich indeed."

Baanraak cocked his head and considered. "I think I will do it. However, it won't be for the gold or the silver."

Rr'garn's eyerilles stood out straight as cat whiskers—an overt display of shock. Baanraak thought that in a game of bluffs, he'd have the poor, clumsy fool twelve times out of twelve, even if he couldn't read Rr'garn's thoughts.

"Don't mistake my meaning. I may decide to accept the payment. But I'm not doing it for the payment. I want a look at this Vodi who is so different. If she is—if she truly could be *the* Vodi, I'll dispose of her for you. If she's not, I'll go my way, leaving her for your people to dispose of as you will—and I'll eat the next one of you who interrupts my napping."

Rr'garn nodded, not saying a word.

"You have her under surveillance now?"

"Oh, yes." Rr'garn looked quite proud of himself. "I have a detail circling Copper House at all times. She's in there; she's had no opportunity to leave."

Baanraak would have rolled his eyes, but unlike Rr'garn, he knew how to control his reactions. "Circling—as in flying circles above Copper House."

"Yes. Out of range of their best weapons, too. We haven't had anyone take so much as a scratch."

"How many?"

"How—oh. Rotating shifts of a dozen at a time. A combination of watch and threat, really."

"Clever," Baanraak said, though it was anything but. "Won't work with my plans, however. I'll go in and find a convenient watchpost out of sight and range of the veyâr. Once I'm settled in, you'll give the signal and all of your people will fly away."

"And then you'll slip in and destroy her."

"And then I'll probably wait a bit to get a feel for things. You seem dreadfully impatient."

"We have a handful of deals going on Earth that could finish it for us in as little as a month. I want her gone before we trigger the last war."

This took Baanraak completely by surprise. "The *last war*? Earth hasn't even reached maximum population density yet. It's not slated to ripen fully for another ten years."

"Many of us are hungry."

"We used to wait a thousand years between worlds," Baanraak said. "Now it's not even fifty?"

"This world is ripening slowly." Rr'garn gave a disgusted look at the budding forests all around the rocky outcrop that marked Baanraak's lair. "It should have huge factories, powerful war engines, mass transport at least in the budding stages. Instead, it's stalled at wind and water, with no sign of moving forward. We may be a thousand years before we can harvest Oria. And we can thank the veyâr and their backward-looking ways for that."

They could thank mismanagement for that, Baanraak thought, but he didn't say it. Why make waves about something unimportant? He suddenly had an interesting task before him, and he could not recall the last time anything had caught his interest.

So he shrugged, and said, "Well, if Earth is about to go, I wouldn't be averse to a snack. But I'm not going to rush the job with this Vodi. If you want me to do it, I do it my way."

"Do you suppose you could be quick about it?"

"I'll do the job right. If right is quick, it'll be quick. But if haste is your first priority, then I suggest you take the work to someone in a hurry."

Rr'garn sighed bitterly and said, "I didn't come all this way to decide that someone else would be sufficient. I want you, because you're the best there is."

"Then you'll meet my terms?"

"Of course. We get out of the way, you decide whether she is or is not *the* Vodi. If she is, you dispose of her and we pay you."

"I dispose of her *in the manner of my choosing*."

"Have your fun," Rr'garn said, and in his mind Baanraak watched mild curiosity about which method of annihilation Baanraak would choose—but this the lesser rrôn quickly squelched.

"On your way then. I've a few things to take care of here, and when I've finished them, I'll be along." He smiled a little at the obvious impatience Rr'garn fought to hide. "Go. I want to check something in an old manuscript—it may be relevant. It will take as long as it takes . . . and so will I."

Rr'garn nodded. "I'll be watching for you."

Baanraak said, "Don't waste the effort. You wouldn't see me. I'll find you."

Rr'garn was insulted, bunched annoyance when he launched his lean body into the sky and cupped the air in his wings.

On second thought, Baanraak decided, the petulant ninny would be lucky to survive the year.

Copper House

In a dark green room, away from the ears of any who might be listening, the old god, Qawar, paced. "Your sister has abandoned this worldchain of the universe for a worthless, futile venture. She has abandoned life for death as surely as if she'd stood before us and killed herself. This is, in fact, what she *has* done, and you knew what she was going to do and *let* her go, even threatening those who would have stopped her. And do you think we'll be able to find a replacement for her? Truly, how many gateweavers do you think exist that could create a gate to Death?" Qawar's steps rang unpleasantly on the stone floor.

Molly had taken enough blame and listened to as much of his tirade as she cared to. "Amazing how I'm not an ornament to the universe anymore. You want to do this?" she asked. "Here—you take this damn Vodi necklace, and become a target for every evil thing that moves and breathes, and give up your soul and then go out there and save the world." She reached for the back of the necklace as if to take it off; she didn't intend to, but she hoped to make a point.

She didn't expect the reaction she got. "No!" Seolar shouted at the same time that the old god lunged for her, surprisingly fast, and grabbed her wrists. Qawar's hands, small and delicate though they were, clamped around the wrist bones and squeezed with surprising strength, and he stared into her eyes.

"You will not take that necklace off," the old god said. He was hurting her.

She leaned her face in close to his and said, "Screw you. You want me to call the rrôn down on your ass, you just keep it up. Otherwise, get your mitts off of me." She rammed a knee up into his midsection, hard, as emphasis, and got a satisfying "oomph" from him.

Qawar let go, and Molly rubbed her wrists.

The old god said, "I ... apologize. I feared that you would ... ah, damage yourself by removing the necklace, and I did not want that."

"How thoughtful of you." Molly realized she would have bruises around both wrists if she didn't heal them. She decided if she did bruise, she would leave the marks. Let the bastard see what he'd done, and let everyone else see it, too. "I'm so glad you're concerned for me, since I can't do anything to help you and your cause anymore."

"You can't do enough," the old god said. "But you can do more than nothing—as long as you're the Vodi. As long as you're alive, and on our side."

"Let's be honest with each other, shall we? You aren't here out of concern for me. You want something, and I have to guess that I'm the only person in the world, or maybe in the universe, who can give you what you want. So. What can I do for you, Qawar?" Molly asked, her voice cold. "And what can you do for me?"

"Honesty . . ." The old god tipped his head and studied her through narrowed eyes. "Yes. All right. Let us be honest with each other, however unpleasant that may be. What do you know of the dark gods?" Qawar asked.

"That they are soulless, like me. That they keep coming back when we kill them . . . like me. That most of who they once were has been washed away by repeated dying, until they are empty. As I will someday be. That they are evil. And will I someday be evil, too, Qawar? Is that part of the truth?"

"I hope not." The old god said, "You are not like them, and you don't have to be like them. None of your predecessors succumbed to the evils embraced by the dark gods. They are not evil just because they have no souls. They're evil because they have embraced death and destruction, and between mere soullessness and the active pursuit of evil lies a vast and deep abyss. You are who you choose to be. The dark gods are who they choose to be. You and they do not have to make the same choices."

"No. And yet, though this will no doubt frighten you, I can understand the choices they made. To hang on in the face of everything, to choose themselves and their own survival at any cost . . ."

The old god glanced at Seolar. "Perhaps you should leave for a few moments. What I have to say to the Vodi is not truly for the ears of a mortal—"

"He stays," Molly said. "I have no wish to endure your company—or your bullying—without a witness." She looked at Seolar, and gave him a little smile. "And he is my love, and my friend."

The old god snorted, a disgusted sound. "Mortals and immortals don't mix well. The possibility for a happy ending simply doesn't exist."

"Thanks for pointing that out," Molly said, glaring at him. "I'm sure I hadn't even considered how this would all end."

Qawar evidently was able to catch sarcasm in others. He gave Molly an even, unblinking stare and said, "Your choice. But this is nothing to laugh at."

Molly crossed her arms over her chest. She disliked Qawar more every second. But she said, "I'll listen. Tell me what you know that's so much more earth-shattering than that the rrôn are evil."

Qawar said, "Worlds do not fall by the actions or inactions of those who live on them, or through the use of magic or the presence or absence of old gods working good magic. No natural process has left the chain of worlds above us a series of charred embers, each haunted by the ghosts of its inhabitants. Worlds die because the dark gods kill them. They feed their target worlds with information that will permit these worlds to aid in their own self-destruction; they infiltrate governments; they whisper in all the right ears; they foment dissent and work against negotiation and accommodation. Your world, for example, would be unlikely to annihilate everything with its nuclear weapons. Worlds are vast, with natural resources for recovery. If ecologies could not rebound, no world would survive cometary bombardment, or even large volcanic eruptions. And the people most likely to use nuclear weapons have few of them, and those relatively small. I'm less sure about the Terminator Seed technology."

Molly stopped him. "The *what*?"

"Terminator Seed technology. A serious case of greed before common sense. Your country's USDA and a corporation called Monsanto, with secret funding from the Night Watch, created a way of genetically preventing crops from reseeding—that is, creating viable seeds that could be replanted the next year. On the surface, it was to prevent farmers from storing copyrighted plant seeds and growing crops from them the next year. But the Night Watch had its own reasons for funding the research. At barest minimum, they can increase starvation and poverty in third world countries by preventing farmers from storing seeds for future crops."

"That's terrible."

"It gets worse. There's a chance that the altered Terminator gene will find its way into the general plant population, and if it does, that it will wipe out crops and maybe whole species of plants. From the point of view of anyone hoping to encourage mass starvation and the desertification of a planet, Terminator Seed technology is wonderful stuff. And your country's government approved the technology, quietly, several years after halting research because of protests. No doubt the Night Watch will be bringing it downworld with them when Earth is a cinder. However, to wipe all life—and all chance of the recurrence of life—from an entire planet of rich, fertile, diverse ecosystems takes focused effort, and hundreds of years of planning and preparation."

"What sort of preparation?" Molly asked.

"Along with all their subversive activities, the dark gods engage in the actual practice of death magic, encouraging wars and using the deaths from both sides to cast spells that feed the hostility, demand more death, more technology, and more insanity. Every time war goes on beyond reason, you'll find the Night Watch feeding on it and fueling it. They aim for massive casualties and slow, burning hatred. And because they feed existing tendencies, amplifying what already exists, they have always won. When they finally cast their best and biggest spells, the end comes quickly. And nothing all those pathetic little groups fighting against it do can hold off the end when that time finally arrives."

"Pathetic . . . you mean like Lauren's Sentinels?"

"Like them. They aren't the only ones—not on your world, not on this, or the worlds below this one."

Molly walked over to the fireplace at one end of the room and stared into the flames. "So the Sentinels fight for nothing?"

"No. They just fight too small, and with the wrong tools. They don't take their fight to the dark gods—they try to maintain the status quo. But in any game where one side is aiming for a win while the other side is playing for a draw, the side with the big goals will take the day. And the Night Watch already has entropy on its side."

"So the dark gods work to destroy worlds one at a time. But it just doesn't make sense. Why? Why destroy worlds? That seems . . . ridiculous. Ludicrous overblown mustache-twisting evil for the sake of evil."

"You mean what do the dark gods get out of destroying worlds?"

"Yes."

"They get immortality. Immortality of the flesh, but immortality nonetheless—and not the sort of guilt-ridden hollowness that already plagues you and will eventually devour you. I don't know any of the dark gods who suffer any grief for the worlds they've crushed and the lives they've snuffed out. They get power—mind-bending power. And they get . . . at least from what the one who tried to recruit me told me . . . an impossible-to-replicate euphoria from drinking the deaths of worlds and lives, a buzz that lasts for hundreds of years. It's the reason they work so hard to raise populations on their target worlds before they actually close the shields. Ripe worlds are heavily overpopulated."

Molly's head was starting to hurt. "They . . . drink the deaths of worlds and lives?" She turned away from the comforting flicker of the flames and frowned. "I don't understand."

"They kill each world in turn quickly—and as the world and the people on it die in the conflagration, they siphon off as much of the magic spawned by the world's death throes as they can consume. And for a hundred years afterward—or a few hundred years, depending on how powerful they already were and how much of the dark magic they managed to consume—they have unimaginable powers." Qawar said, "They get greedy, though. Your world ripened a bit too soon, but rather than let it wait until they need the energy, they'll push it to destruction now. Their people are in place, their final plans are almost completed, and when Earth goes they'll feed well." He sighed. "By taking your world now, though, they'll only increase their need for the next one. The more power they absorb, the more they need in order to maintain the new levels they achieve. They've already started encouraging technology and population increases here, and they have members of the Night Watch working throughout this world, preparing for its eventual destruction. I've seen them do this before, many times. They're almost ready. Unless I miss my guess, they'll destroy Earth before this year is over."

Molly closed her eyes and rubbed her temples. She felt sick, and a bit lost. She said, "I'm curious about something. Old gods like you—you could do something against the dark gods, couldn't you?"

Qawar held up a hand as if fending off the question. "We have learned to keep out of sight. We have some of the same abilities as the dark gods, though in lesser degree. We have access to the powers of life, as the dark gods have access to the powers of death. But we die and they don't—and they have boosted their powers until they're stronger than we are."

"The answer, then, is 'yes.' You *could* do something."

Qawar spread his hands wide, and said, "There are no billions of us. The surviving people of our worlds number in the hundreds. Hundreds. We're all that remain of entire worlds, and we . . . are . . . mortal. Unlike the dark gods, we won't come back if we die, and those madmen would be more than happy to kill us. We have the option of moving on, most of us, so after a few hundred years or a thousand years on a world, we head downworld before things go bad." He studied her levelly. "You're glaring at me, but you aren't in my position. In *our* position. I still have a soul. I have a real life. I have something to lose in this—far more than you, Vodi. You're what's left after the important part of you moved on."

Molly stare at him in disbelief. "You say that and think I'll help you?"

"You want me to coddle you and lie to you? You just told

me you wanted the truth. So which is it? I won't tell you what you want to hear, though there are plenty who will. You aren't what the dark gods are, and you don't have to be. You aren't alone, either. And you have nothing real to lose."

Molly looked at Seolar, and then back at the old god. "Wait a minute. I have everything to lose. I stand to lose who I am—everything I love, everything that matters to me, every shred of passion in me. And at the point where I can't take it anymore and take off the necklace and let myself die for good, I'll just turn to dust. Nothing of who I am will go on. So no—of the two of us, I have more to lose."

"You would say that. But"—Qawar settled himself against the wall with an air of absolute certainty—"the part of you that was really you is long gone. This physical construct"—he waved a hand at her casually— "is a vital tool, but not a real person. Between the spelled necklace—which was created with the most powerful of chaos magics—and the tough, low-fuel-consumption body, it is an excellent tool. But it isn't a *you*. It's an it. I refer to you as *you*, but surely you can understand the difference. You were made to do a job."

"I feel real to me," Molly said. "My life, such as it is, matters to me."

"That's an unfortunate part of the Vodi spell that no one has ever been able to address. Through far too many incarnations, too much of the original personality hangs on."

"The hell with you," Molly said, unable to stand any more. "You don't value my life. But I do. So the hell with you, you hear me?" She turned to Seolar. "I want out of here. I don't ever want to see this thing again."

Seolar winced, and Molly realized she'd put him in a position to run interference between her and an old god. Not good. She added, "I'm leaving. Please come with me—we have to talk."

In Seolar's eyes, relief. In Qawar's eyes, amusement. "He loves you, you think . . . does he really? Think on this; if he truly loved you—*you*—he would never have given you the Vodi necklace, for every woman who wears it is marked by the dark gods as their one true enemy, and each will be a target for the rest of her existence. When he handed you that necklace, he sentenced you to certain death, not just once, but many times over. And he knew it when he did it. Think on that when you think about this pitiful mortal that you claim to love. Think on that, will you? You have those who will stand on your side in the coming battles, and those who believe in you, and you may even have friends. But they aren't necessarily those you think are your friends."

Qawar looked from Molly to Seolar, who stood—stunned—with shock on his face, and Qawar said sadly, "How's that for the truth?"

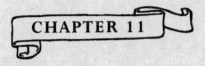

CHAPTER 11

Heaven, or Possibly Hell

LAUREN FACED OFF against the black-robed figure, bazooka on her shoulder, and bared her teeth in a vicious smile. "Produce Jake, or I pull the trigger."

"And *what* do you think will happen then, silly girl? You're the only one here who can die. The rest of us are immortals, without physical form or—"

Lauren tightened her finger on the trigger. "I'm running out of patience."

The bazooka vanished, the black-robed man vanished, and in Lauren's ear, that same voice said, "Well, I'm not."

She stood alone on the plain again, with the road both before her and behind her and everything else without form or feature. Gray. Bleak, barren gray.

Heaven could hold within it no place like this, she decided, so this could not be Heaven. There might be a Heaven, full of angels and harps and hosannas, but this was not it. Lacking any inhabitants, this would not even be a true part of the afterlife, would it?

She turned slowly, fighting through her panicked need to find Jake just to *think*. She could have handled her encounter with the . . . what? . . . the Administrator? . . . better. She shouldn't have acted out of rage, nor responded with force. As she thought back on it, though, she realized she was supposed to have been intimidated. The Administrator was supposed to have been frightening, but bureaucrats had always made her angry, not afraid.

Nevertheless, she'd been . . . Well, face the facts. She'd been wrong. Lauren wasn't good at being wrong; neither was she good at admitting mistakes. Now she faced what could be the biggest mistake she'd ever made.

Temper—she had one. Usually she kept it in check. This was a hell of a time to get trigger-happy.

The road didn't stop at her feet anymore. Now it led both forward and back, with—of course—no sign to tell her which way was which. She had the feeling that if she followed it in either direction, it would lead her on forever. She could not answer her riddle with a road. Nor with her temper and a bazooka—though for the life of her she couldn't recall wanting a bazooka, or thinking of one.

The road was not the answer, but pacing helped her think. So, because she figured neither forward nor back meant anything, she chose a direction at random and started walking.

This quest had seemed possible when she'd been in Copper House in Oria. Make a gate, follow Jake, bring him back with her. Get Brian, get Molly, go home. It wasn't "how things are done"—but it was the way she wanted to do them, and she didn't see any reason why she shouldn't. She hadn't expected Administration.

Perhaps she should have.

The myth of Orpheus and Eurydice echoed in her mind, offering tantalizing hints about how she should have acted. Like Lauren, Orpheus had charged into the afterlife to rescue someone. Granted, he was half a god, and had a magic harp and a voice that could sing birds out of the trees, but he'd still had to go to the afterlife. He'd ended up crossing the River Styx with Charon and presenting himself to Pluto and Proserpine, where he'd pleaded his case in song.

Say Orpheus had actually been a gateweaver. He could have been influenced by the beliefs of his time to see this place as the Greek underworld. If he'd expected to see Charon and the River Styx, Cerberus guarding the gates, and ghosts weeping at his sad song of loss, this place would have accommodated him.

Having now met old gods and having seen magic, and having at least a bit of an inside look at the sources of both, Lauren was inclined to mine for truth anywhere she might find it. Orpheus's journey might fit in with hers more than she had at first imagined. In which case, the Administrator would be Pluto, in a guise designed to make sense to Lauren. He would also be Anubis, and later Osiris, and Zalmoxis, and others that her thin familiarity with comparative religions didn't offer up. One thing she could remember from these was that the gods did not give back the souls they had gathered in lightly, and even when they did agree to let someone go, something always happened to prevent the soul from leaving. Eurydice would have made it, except Orpheus had looked back on her. Proserpine, even though she had been living, had eaten the pomegranate seeds, and so had to spend half her time in the underworld.

God, Jake—don't eat anything while you're here.

Lauren couldn't allow herself to fail. She could not lose her little boy. Jake needed his father and her. And she would do anything to get Brian back. And what about Molly? Molly was going to fight for the salvation and resurrection of a universe; surely she deserved to have a soul while she did so—to be spared the horrors of slowly losing herself.

Lauren had to find the Administrator again. She had to present her case—this time calmly. She had to tell him why she wanted her son back, and why she wanted Brian back. And she had to win back Molly's soul as well; after all, how could Molly be asked to give everything of herself and get nothing in return? What sort of universe, what sort of god or gods could demand that of her?

How, then, did Lauren get the attention of the Administrator again, so that she could win him over to her cause?

He had patience, he had said. And intended that she have patience, too—only she didn't have time for patience. She

didn't have time for anything but to get in, get Jake and
Brian and Molly, and get out.

She had the means to fight for the lives of the people she
loved; she had to take up arms.

If not bazookas.

She stared around her. Nothing different. Until she got to
the Administrator, nothing would be different. So she had to
get to the Administrator. But how?

He spoke directly into her thoughts, but didn't choose to
answer them. He'd responded when she altered the terrain,
but she didn't think that she'd made a friend of him while
changing things around. He had not utterly forsaken her,
though—he'd said that he had patience. Which seemed to
imply that if she could just figure out how to reach him, he
would be willing to work with her.

He wasn't giving her any clues, though. No big neon signs
saying, "GO HERE" or "Step One: Make a tunnel. Step
Two: Pay the guy at the river."

Lauren suspected this place would make more sense to
someone who had expectations about what he would find in
it. She could have used a firmly held belief in an opinionated
religion right about then.

She turned, slowly, squinting against the horrid gray for
some indication that something had changed. Nothing had.
Her feet were on the road she'd made, but the road went
nowhere, and time was passing—might, back home, even be
racing. What if she returned to find that weeks or months
had passed? Or years? What if she got back to find her world
already gone—a blackened cinder?

"What do you want me to do?" she muttered.

"Absolutely nothing," said the voice of the Administrator
in her ear. "You want something from me, not the other way
around."

"I know I want something from you. What do I have to do
to get it?"

"You can't have what you want. You have to change what
you want."

"What do I have to change it to?"

"You have to want to go home."

Lauren looked around her, wishing she could see the Administrator in his damned flapping black robes. She wished she could throttle him.

"I *want* to go home. I want to take Jake and Brian and Molly with me."

"Concentrate on wanting to go home. I might let you do that."

Lauren said, "Let me? I have a son here who doesn't belong here any more than I do. My son's father is here—he was stolen away from us too soon. My sister's soul is here—and she is back on Oria fighting to save worlds, and she needs me. Staying here isn't an option."

"Yes. It is."

Lauren felt the rage flood over her again, but this time she held it close and banked it like embers stored against the need for fire. "You're the Administrator here. You can help me if you want to."

"Your mind perceives me as the Administrator. That's what resonates with you. What I am capable of doing, however, has little in common with your expectations, which are, I assure you, just as hidebound in their own way as those of Orpheus. Yes, he was real. Yes, he came here. No, the story didn't play out quite the way it does in the mythology."

Lauren said, "Could you please come here to talk to me? I'm getting tired of speaking to thin air."

"I don't doubt that you are. Do you intend any more silly stunts?"

"I don't. I didn't intend that one—I can't even imagine how I ended up holding a bazooka."

The Administrator chuckled. "Oh, I gave you that. I wanted to have a little fun."

An instant later, he appeared in front of Lauren, and she could only think it was a good thing she wasn't holding the bazooka. Again he wore flowing black robes, and again they swirled and lifted and whipped, clawed at by a wind that didn't touch Lauren. A deep hood occluded his face, and she realized that with a scythe, he would look like the personification of Death.

"I play him sometimes," the Administrator said. "He's what some people expect to meet somewhere along the way. We aim to be accommodating."

"You haven't been accommodating at all," Lauren protested.

"*You* aren't *dead*," he said.

Lauren clenched her jaw. "Excuse the hell out of me. Neither is my son."

"You aren't supposed to come here if you're not dead. If you had a more amenable belief structure, Cerberus would have met you at the gate with teeth bared, and you would have gotten the idea and gone home. You. Don't. Belong. Here."

"I *know* I don't belong here. I don't want to be here. But I'm not leaving without my son. And Brian is here, and I need him back. And my sister Molly is here, too."

"Sort of an afterthought, is she?"

Lauren flushed. "No. But just before I came here she told me she lost her soul and asked me to bring it back, and I'm having trouble adjusting to the idea."

"Wait. Your sister spoke to you before you came here?"

"Yes."

"Then you don't need her back."

"I need her soul. She doesn't have it anymore."

This seemed to set the Administrator aback.

"Either your sister is alive and has her soul with her, or else she's dead and her soul is here. There are no instances where a person is one place but her soul is someplace else."

"And yet my sister is on Oria, and her soul is here. Imagine that."

The Administrator tipped his head beneath the cowl and Lauren got the feeling that he was staring at her very hard. "You are not the most pleasant person," he said.

"I'm having a bad day."

"Think about your sister Molly for a moment, would you? Picture her in your mind, recall shared moments, things that you have done together."

Lauren really only had one from before Molly's death, so she thought about the final fight between the Sentinels and the traitors, and recalled how Molly had taken Jake and run for the gate. About how she'd failed to get through it fast enough to save both of them. How she'd given up her own life to save his.

"Got her," the Administrator said. "Yes, her soul is here. So the person claiming to be your sister in Oria is not."

Lauren said, "It's a long story. She died saving my son's life—"

"The son who is now here?"

"Yes."

"Ah. So she did. I see from her records that her soul moved forward a great deal that day."

"Let me finish. The necklace she was wearing when she died did some sort of magic that brought her body back. She's alive again, in Oria, and she and I have to stop the destruction of our worldchain. But she's doing so much for our world and all of our upworlds, and she's going to lose more of herself every time she dies. It isn't right that she should do so much and then have nothing in return—and if she has no soul, she'll lose everything. Her memory, her love, her hope, who she is. . . ."

"And you want me to do . . . what?"

"Let me take her soul back to her."

"You want me to let you take a resting soul and send it back to a world to be put into some sort of ragtag, thrown-together-by-amateurs body?"

"Well . . . yes."

"We don't *do* that."

"I didn't think you did on a regular basis. I'm not asking for you to do what you usually do. I'm asking for you to give me my son back, and to make a couple of small exceptions."

"Your son found his way here through the link that he shares with his father. There was some . . . irregularity in his case. They are together, and Brian's spirit is now in one place—if in two bodies. In your case, no such irregularity exists. As far as you need be concerned, your son is dead. You, however, are all in one piece inhabiting a living body, and you can either go home, or you can wait out the rest of your mortal existence right here on the plains. I do not think you would enjoy the latter option."

"I. Want. My. Son."

"I can't give him to you. I can't give any of them to you."

"Who can?"

"You need to talk to them."

Lauren stared at him. "I can do that?"

"No. If they wanted to talk to you, they would already be here."

"I want to go to them."

"All souls are autonomous. You think we run a prison here? As the soul who takes care of difficult situations, however, I can tell you right now that you'll be happier if you don't speak to them, but just turn around and go home. It is within my power to mark a path for you so that you won't get lost."

Controlling the blinding rage that threatened to swallow her, Lauren kept her voice quiet and said, "I want to talk to them"

Sadly, the Administrator nodded. "They always do."

Copper House

"Is it true?" Molly asked.

Seolar didn't bother pretending. "Yes. When I gave you the necklace, I wasn't in love with you. But—yes. I knew what it would do."

"When you fell in love with me, why didn't you take it back?"

He turned away from her.

"You could have, couldn't you? The action wasn't irreversible when we rode on our picnic, when we stayed at Graywinds during the snowstorm, when the traitors brought the Sentinels here, when I went to join my sister. At any time, you could have taken the necklace back."

"I could have," he said, still not facing her. "And had I done that, my people would have died."

"So it was me or them."

"There's more to it than that. I thought I could protect you. I thought I could keep you safe here in Copper House, or protected by guards while you were out. I was certain that for my lifetime, at least, you would be safe—unharmed."

Molly's rage tore far beyond the reach of mere words, but still she kept it in check. "Then the night I came back here and found you dressed in black, the whole of Copper House draped in black, and you so clearly in mourning—you knew I'd be coming back. You weren't mourning the fact that you'd never see me again, but only the fact that the 'real' me was gone."

Now, at last, he turned to face her. "No," he said. "I thought I'd lost you forever. You didn't die here, in this world. You died in your own world, and you were the first Vodi ever to do so. I had every reason to believe that the necklace would not permit you to re-create yourself in your world, and no reason to think that it would let you come back here. When I mourned, I mourned for real."

"But you didn't mourn for Molly. You mourned for the Vodi who would have saved the veyâr from the depredations of the rrôn."

His eyes narrowed and he stiffened. "I mourned for you. For the woman I loved and thought I would have at my side for my whole life. I mourned for you. Yes, I mourned for my people, too. Should I not? I'd spent the whole of my life sending out agents to search for you, praying all the while that we would be able to find the promised Vodi before it was too late. I prayed, I put every resource of Copper House into the search. I made enemies of allies because I would not arm and engage battalions in their defense; anyone I sent to help others I had to take away from my obsessed search for you." He walked across the great room they shared to the bookshelves and ran a finger across the spines. "I'd read all of these. I knew what might happen. I thought I was prepared; I thought I could prevent it from happening, and that only when you died of a natural old age would you return as . . . what you are now."

"A soulless freak. Some magically animated monstrosity. You figured by then you would be old or dead anyway, so what was the harm?"

He turned on her now, and she could see anger in his face. "You were in the military. You understand duty—that sometimes duty comes before life, before love, before personal ambition, before all else. I have a duty to my people, and finding you, and making sure that you received the necklace and took on the mantle of the Vodi was my duty. Had I not done it, I would have betrayed everything I have lived my life for."

"Duty," she spat.

"Duty. You took yours on voluntarily, and left it when you grew weary of it. I was born into mine and will not be free of it until I die. If, knowing what I know now—knowing everything that had happened—I had to make the same choices, I would. Because my people's lives are in my hands, and any love I might feel, and any dreams I might harbor for myself, are and always will be secondary to that."

Molly laughed—a shocked, disbelieving laugh, and said, "I might have left the US Air Force behind, but I, too, was born to a weight of duty, and my life was never my own, either. When I swallowed the deaths of strangers, I didn't do that because it was fun, or because it made me happy. I did it because it was my duty." She glared at him. "But without the Vodi necklace, maybe I could have done what I had to do for your people and your world—and beyond that, for the worldchain—without drawing the attention of every murderous, life-devouring dark god up and down the worlds. Maybe I wouldn't have had to see a child blown to shreds by the fucking rrôn; maybe I wouldn't have had to sacrifice my own life to save his. Maybe you and I would have had some sort of normal life together, instead of spending our time cowering beneath the circling horrors overhead right now. And—yes—they *are* still there."

"I know that," Seolar said. "My guards keep me apprised of their movements."

"I don't need the guards," Molly hissed. "Those bastards are inside my head. And why is that, do you suppose? Because down at the very core of it all, I'm one of them. I'm a dark god, too, a monster, a thing." She turned away from him and dug her fingernails into her palms until they drew blood. Then she stared at her bleeding palms and thought, I'm real. And Shakespeare's Shylock whispered in her head: "If you prick us, do we not bleed? if you tickle us, do we not laugh? If you poison us, do we not die? And if you wrong us, shall we not revenge?"

Poisoned, she would die. She'd just come back again, bringing a bit less of the woman she had once been with her, and a bit more of the monster she would one day be.

Revenge—she could have her revenge so easily it frightened her. She could have her revenge in a hundred ways, and the chain of worlds and everyone in it would pay for the hurt this one man had done her, and for this one bitter betrayal. She could take off the Vodi necklace and walk out of Copper House to embrace the murderous jaws of the rrôn. She could refuse to shoulder her duty. She could go back to Earth and await the end—well, maybe. She actually wasn't sure she could go back to Earth. She was pretty sure she would be able to travel downworld, though, so maybe she could await her end there.

Or she could close Seolar out of her life. He'd earned that—he'd killed her as surely as if he'd thrown the fireball himself. No matter his noble talk of duty, he had betrayed her. He had murdered her. He had taken her soul away from her and consigned her to a slowly worsening hell from which the only exit was not-being.

She bled. She breathed. She yearned and hungered and hoped—and it was all a sham.

She turned away and walked off without another word. She couldn't look at Seolar, and didn't know that she would ever be able to again.

Behind her, Seolar said nothing. Which was right. How could he have anything to say?

Outside the door, Birra and a squad of guards waited.

"I'm going to Lauren's room," she said. "I'm going to wait for her and Jake."

They walked with her—point, flank and rear, watching and wary—and she thought, This is a gift of Seolar, this awful caution, this endless danger. He brought this on all of us when he gave me the necklace, because without it I would have been invisible to the enemy, and none of the awfulness that happened would have happened.

The goroths welcomed her into the room, where they, too, waited.

She went past the goroths and looked around Lauren's bedroom; she saw a thick black ring binder on the nightstand. The books she had swiped from the library, now neatly stacked on a table, could tell her a great deal about the past. But Lauren's binder was an enigma—something potentially interesting, if Lauren had brought it when she had brought so little else.

Molly went over to the bedside, lifted the heavy binder. Behind it she saw the photo of a blue-eyed young man in a flight cap and dress blues seated in front of an American flag. So that was Brian. Molly picked up the photo; Lauren had framed it in simple, old-fashioned sterling silver. In the man's face, Molly could see a great deal of Jake, and a little of what Brian must have been like. He had intelligent eyes, a kind smile, a bit of presence even at what had to have been a trying time—the photo was the one taken during basic training. Molly had had one like it of herself. Brian's was better.

She didn't recognize him. She might have crossed paths with him once or a dozen times, but there were a lot of good-looking young men in the Air Force, and she couldn't have noticed every one.

He'd been between the worlds with her and Jake, though, when Jake was dying. Molly had felt him sacrifice a part of his animating force to keep his son alive. And prior to that, Brian had evaded the consequences of his own death for over a year just to be close—in spirit if not in body—to his wife and son.

And his child had raced into the great unknown to save him, with the woman who loved him in fast pursuit, equally determined to bring him back.

Molly wondered what it would have been like to love someone that much—and to have someone who loved her that much. She'd thought she knew . . . but the truth had no respect for foolish emotion.

Molly put the picture down, and still clutching the notebook, turned away. She could read it out in the sitting room. That would be better, she thought. She found herself uncomfortable in the bedroom, even though Brian had never been in it; it still felt to her like shared space, as if he were there and watching her. As if she were invading Lauren's privacy.

She settled into the rocking chair and started to read.

Journal entries, starting in the 1950s and continuing into the 1970s. Two separate hands, the neater of the two belonging, she realized, to her mother. The other to the man who'd stepped aside so her mother could conceive Molly with a man not of her world, or even of her species.

She couldn't imagine what *that* relationship had been like, either. How did they do that? How did old Walt say to this woman he ostensibly loved, "Go on, Marian—go have a baby with that creature that isn't even human, and we'll figure out a way to raise it as ours." Because that had been their first intention, before things went wrong. She was skimming, finding little notes that she knew related to her because she knew how old she was, knew when she was born, knew the story.

When Marian's writing disappeared for a whole long stretch, replaced by Walt's heavy, dark, angular script, Molly realized that Marian had gone off to someplace in western North Carolina to give birth to her. She read mentions of Lauren, and of problems, and of progress and setbacks on the great plan the two of them had hatched.

"It's not going to end well, folks," she muttered. "It's not going to end well at all, and if you're smart, you'll give up on this idea and do whatever you can to live normal, meaningless lives."

Skimming, skimming—looking for details of their plan and their expectations for their daughters. They were both careful. They hinted, and from their hints Molly could piece together a few details they hadn't included in the memories they'd implanted into her via magic.

They felt she and Lauren could save the worldchain. That the two of them had special sorts of magic that would let them do what no one else had ever been able to do before—stop and maybe reverse the deaths of worlds. But *how* . . .

Molly read the entries and just got more and more confused. Diagrams of thing to make, lists of spells to cast, weird connections to create between worlds—as she read through, she just kept thinking, *Even with a dozen people, this would take years. And we don't have years.*

She closed the notebook, frowning. Why had they made it all so vague, so contradictory from one page to the next, so terribly baffling? It was *so* confusing, it almost seemed intentional.

Something about that seemed right to her. But she had other things to think about, and she brushed the errant thought aside.

Copper House

The goroths held their positions in the room, waiting for their adored Hunter to return. Outside in the hallway, the guards murmured to each other—when Molly concentrated, she could hear that they talked about women and sex and gambling. Everything seemed the same. But something had changed. She put the notebook aside and stood, looking around, trying to get a feel for the direction of the change, and for its importance.

Then she realized what was different. The rrôn who had been circling overhead had flown away. She still carried their darkness inside of her, but their thoughts had dwindled to nothing, and the ominous pressure they'd exerted on her had vanished completely.

CHAPTER 12

Outside Copper House

As BAANRAAK HAD PREDICTED, Rr'garn didn't see him coming, and didn't realize he'd arrived until Baanraak gave a couple of hard wingbeats and took himself up above the level of the trees.

Rr'garn spiraled down to meet him. "You see," he said, looking smug and setting his wings to fly wingtip to wingtip with Baanraak, "I saw you coming."

"Did you?" said Baanraak, who'd been watching the rrôn circling Copper House while the sun moved halfway across the sky. "Well, I must have been mistaken then."

Rr'garn looked like he was ready to agree—but at the last instant he held his tongue. So maybe, Baanraak thought, Rr'garn wouldn't die just today.

"Are you ready to send them off?" he asked, his voice and manner so exactingly polite it was almost an insult.

Rr'garn seemed oblivious. "I'm ready—but are you sure you won't need them as reinforcements?"

"I'm certain. I work alone—always. I find that's the only way I have complete control of the outcome."

"Well, then—I can have them make some sort of commotion while you get into position," Rr'garn offered. "Something that will draw all eyes away from you."

"I'm . . . grateful," Baanraak said, trying not to laugh. The idea of those noisy clods soaring overhead trying to make a scene painted pictures in his mind entirely too funny to bear. "But really, you need do nothing special. Any staged drama will be sure to leave people wondering, and perhaps suspicious. If your lads will just file off in one direction—west, maybe—that should be enough to aid me, without it being too much."

Baanraak didn't care for other rrôn—even those who had not chosen to follow the path of cycling death and immortality annoyed him. He detested the rest of the dark gods. He found Rr'garn execrable. By all rights, he should have still been basking on his rock in the sunshine, listening to the murmuring of water in the nearby brook, and the soft rattle of the wind through bud-heavy trees, and the incessant yammering of the birds building their nests and defending their territories. By all rights he should be nowhere near this place, for he had no interest in helping those who needed his help.

Yet here he was.

He gave Rr'garn a nod as the idiot flew up to tell his cronies and sycophants that it was time to go away.

Why had he come here?

Baanraak had no good explanation; he certainly couldn't be so bored with existence that the arrival of another human/veyâr hybrid wearing spelled gold could elicit genuine interest in him. Could he?

He waited until Rr'garn flew level with the lowest of the circling rrôn. Then, with the patience and care he'd developed with thousands of years of practice, he curved light around himself until he made no more impression on the eye than the ripple of heat rising from sun-baked sand. He stilled his mind, curved his wings in such manner that the air made almost no noise as it rushed over and under them, and, giving loving attention to detail, he soared twice around the walls of the village of Copper House, and twice around Copper House itself. Then he banked off toward the closest edge of the forest and dropped to the ground in a clearing. He settled on the ground, adjusting rocks and branches until he found a comfortable position. He shook his wings out and tucked them into place, and slid his head under one and back to rest on his rump—his favorite pose when he had to stay still for long periods of time.

He rested well away from traffic; yet close to the village wall and Copper House. He could not see anything with his eyes, but he had them closed. He didn't need to see anything with them. Practically invisible, safely away from anyone who might accidentally step on him, he stilled his thoughts until they flowed no faster than sap flows up the ancient hardwoods in the middle of winter. He slowed his heart, his lungs, the blood in his veins. And then he listened.

At first, the sheer chaos of the minds within the village of Copper House made focusing on any one mind impossible. Baanraak, undeterred by impossibility, patiently sifted through minds, blocking them one at a time and shielding his thoughts against further intrusion from the thoughts of each mind that was not the one he wanted. He eliminated males quickly, and nonveyâr, and children. He had to pay more attention to the women, because he did not want to ac- cidentally remove his target from view, which would force him to sift again. He preferred doing something right the first time, so he took time laying his groundwork. He had time. The hurrying, scuttling head of the rrôn branch of the Night Watch and all his many followers had never released the hurry that had characterized their mortal existence. They had never learned to take the long view—but then, Baanraak had already been taking the long view as a mortal. It was as a mortal that he'd mastered stillness. In the uncounted thou- sands of following years in which he enjoyed immortality, he had merely refined his techniques.

One by one he pushed the women of the veyâr away, blocking them off. By the time it got down to a few dozens, he should have found it easy to pick out his target. But he could not. He could not find her among the minds, and he thought perhaps he had missed her. Blanking his own thoughts entirely, he let the thoughts of the strangers run through his mind like water over a streambed, and continued patiently removing them. One, and another, and a third. Curiosity began to tiptoe through his mind, a tiny itch that he dared not scratch. Still. He held to his stillness, and shielded off a dozen more. And then another dozen. He felt nothing but veyâr thoughts, no twinge of the darkness that characterized a once-dead Vodi. The water that ran through his mind babbled. He kept sifting. Kept removing, one by one by one by one. And at last he had removed every single set of thoughts within the village and within the House—and yet he did not wipe away the shields and start again. He knew he had not made a mistake. He knew that he had not let her slip into the common herd. Which meant one of two things. Either she had, in spite of the noisy surveillance of the rrôn, slipped away from the village—or she, too, had mastered stillness. He lay like the dead, no pulse moving in his veins, no air in his lungs, no thud of his heart, or thought in his forebrain.

Patience.

Waiting.

Invisibility.

And more patience.

Then she jumped, and Baanraak felt her irritation; someone had come in and interrupted her, and she proceeded to give the interloper a sharp dressing-down, demanding that if she was still and did not seem to be doing anything that was not an invitation to interrupt her. She had been after something that lay outside Copper House, she said. Something big, something bad.

Forcing stillness in a body that suddenly abhorred it, Baanraak carefully placed a tiny marker in her mind—something that would let him find her again quickly without all the irritating sifting. Then, before he could betray himself, he shielded her from him—and himself from her.

Only when he had done that did he whip his head out from under his wing and leap to his feet and stretch his wings.

By the Egg, she could have had him as easily as he had her! He paced in a circle, so excited he could barely contain his movements to walking—he wanted to bound into the air and pump his wings until he raced the light. He wanted to roar, to shriek, to do loop-the-loops around trees and he wanted to sing. He'd found in this new-hatched Vodi, in this veritable child when measured by geologic scale, a worthy opponent. Someone who could lie quietly and watch and wait and not blink and not breathe and not give herself away. Someone in whom his cautious, patient, surreptitious search had triggered alarms—and Baanraak couldn't think of anyone, ever, who'd caught on to him when he was being careful.

Lovely, he thought. Oh, it was lovely. All of a sudden his existence had flavor again. All of a sudden, he was not alone. He was not the only one in the worldchain who knew how to watch, knew how to wait . . . to hunt. Suddenly, he had a worthy enemy. Rr'garn had been right: She was special. She might or might not be *the* Vodi, the much-mythologized warrior-goddess who would stand against the combined might of the dark gods and shatter their plans and scatter their evils to the four winds and bring life back to the whole worldchain, but by the Egg, by the Infinities, by his own lost and lately lamented soul, she sang in his blood like the fires of a murdered world.

He would hunt her. He would kill her. Or perhaps she would kill him. The idea that she might kill him, as well as the potential that she *could*, thrilled him.

Excitement so consumed him that he did not even bother to calm himself until nearly sunset. He had time. He had eternity. To the empty spaces with Rr'garn and the Night Watch and their premature hunger for Terra and all her lives. Baanraak had something wonderful in front of him, and he intended to savor it—and that meant letting himself feel the thrill that too many soulless years of existence had leached from him.

When the sun dropped below the horizon, however, he began pulling himself back in, leashing emotions long-unused and now running rampant and tying down loose thoughts. He was going into battle, and somewhere within the walls of the village waited a warrior who had felt his silence and had answered it with silence of her own. She suspected his presence. She suspected his interest. He had no idea how he'd tipped his hand, but he had, and the fact that he had not been careless and had not made any mistakes and she knew he was out there anyway electrified him.

He might lose.

Eggs and Bones, he might lose.

He grinned, his hide tingling, and spread his talons. He bowed toward the village, tucking his head between his forelegs and spreading his wings to their full extension, and he saluted the warrior who waited as if they faced each other on the killing field. In thousands of years, he had ever done his prey the honor of salute.

Then he snapped his head up, crouched for launch, and whispered into the wind, "I'm coming."

Baanraak leapt into the air, caught it beneath his wings, and flung himself up into the sky. The crisp night air smelled of damp earth and growing things awaiting the return of the sun. The moon's thin scythe sliced through the purple haze of twilight, near to dropping off the horizon behind the sun. Stars already glared down, casting faint shadows from the clear heavens. He lifted himself above the wall and looked over, into the still-busy village. It had its quiet spots, however, and he found one of them—a square of cleared earth behind the public stables big enough to afford him a comfortable landing space. He circled once to be sure, then dropped to the ground, making no noise and disturbing nothing. Then, for the first time in hundreds of years, he cast the spell that changed his form. He twisted, muscles bunching and condensing and bones melting and sliding, wings absorbing into spine, spine straightening and stiffening. It took a bit of time and the pain forced tears to his eyes and caught in his newly reshaped rib cage so fiercely that he almost couldn't breathe. But when the spell had worked its magic on him, he looked much like a veyâr, the tags of his wings moving behind him disguised as a cloak, and he could walk through the village. When people looked at him, they would believe they knew him.

He knew how he wanted to go after her this first time. He would be delighted with a fast, clean kill; if he got it, he'd feel that he'd earned it. If she proved better than his best, however, he would be prepared for that. He would get her.

Baanraak practiced walking, just to get used to having only two feet to propel himself forward. It had been a while, and he'd forgotten the limitations of a flightless, bipedal existence. He checked his hands, flexing the fingertips to be sure the retractable claws worked. Veyâr didn't have claws, but he'd done away with wings, tail, and teeth, and Baanraak had no intention of leaving himself without his favorite weapon.

When he was sure he had the locomotion issue taken care of, he strolled out to the cobblestone street and looked down its narrow, crooked length toward Copper House. He could see only the upper spires and towers from this vantage point, but he didn't need to see even that. He knew where he was, and he knew where she was. The time had come. He headed for Copper House.

At the gate, he presented himself. The guards looked at him, said, "Good evening, Captain," and stepped aside with a salute to let him pass. He waited while the guard before the inner door opened it for him. Then he walked into Copper House itself, and as he crossed the transom, he felt the weight of the copper cutting through the magical energy of the world-chain. He had no magic to call on anymore. He could not cast fresh spells, he could not fade himself to invisibility, he could not use the arsenal of magical weapons he'd preferred for assassinations for thousands of years. He had his claws, and his mind, and his innate ability to feel the pull of the one creature in all this place that was like himself. He could hear her thoughts, but that was because just before he entered Copper

House he tore down the wall of silence he'd built between them. He moved quickly but casually to one of the side corridors of the vast building, closed his eyes, and listened.

At that moment she was otherwise engaged; she was reading something, and her focus was on the words, and not on him. Then he had not alerted her to his presence this time— at least not yet.

Good.

He set off in her direction, following the faint spoor of her oddly quiet thoughts.

The Gray Plains, and the Afterlife

Lauren faced the Administrator with her heart pounding in her throat. "Let me talk with them."

"You will regret it if I do."

"Regret *how*?" Lauren asked, because the Administrator's voice took on a low, hollow note as he voiced his warning.

"There is no knowing. But when lost loved ones see each other here, there are no happy endings."

"My son is not lost, is not dead. I want him *back*. And I'll take my chances with Molly and Brian."

"Molly first, then—she means less to you and may therefore do you a lesser hurt, and you may yet leave intact."

"You really have no clue, do you? Jake first."

"Molly first, or no one at all."

"Fine, then. Bring her on."

The Administrator said, "When you need me, call. Until then, I have no wish to be present for what is to pass." He vanished in a pale flicker of light.

Lauren stood alone on the plain again. She turned in circles, expecting Molly to appear out of the air as the Administrator had. Instead, however, nothing happened. She waited, watching the road in both directions, afraid to walk or move, afraid that Molly would not be able to find her if she did.

Time passed, and nothing happened. The featureless gray plain remained unmarked except for the road, and on the road nothing moved.

"Hey!" Lauren yelled. "Where is she?"

"You expect her to drop everything and come to you? She will reach you when she reaches you."

Son of a bitch, Lauren thought. "Why don't you let me go to her?"

"You cannot pass through the gates to that which lies beyond. You are alive—there is no place for you among the dead."

"I have a kid waiting for me. My place is with him, no matter where that is."

She waited for the Administrator's voice to remind her that she could leave immediately and save everyone a lot of inconvenience, but he didn't say anything.

"Look," she said, "Orpheus got to go in. According to the myth, he stood in there surrounded by the dead, and in front of Pluto and Proserpine sang about his grief until they let him take Eurydice home."

"And you know how badly that ended."

"He got to go in."

"He charmed the heavens with his singing. Do you sing?"

"Everyone sings," Lauren said darkly. "I can't charm the heavens with mine, but I can sure as hell kill crows. Tell you what. If you let me in, I *won't* sing. You'll be happy, I'll be happy . . ."

Lauren heard the deep, exasperated sigh. "Saying that you have been warned repeatedly, and that I wash my hands of all that befalls you from this point forward, I hereby summon the gate that will take you to your sister Molly, and that will, when you have spoken to her, take you either to Brian and your son, or transport you home. It will also transport you home now should you tell it to." A pause, and then a muttered, "Not that you will."

An arch clicked into existence in front of her. One instant

it wasn't there, the next it was—solid stone, a pale bluish white with gold veining that transmuted the bleak light of the gray realm into something wondrous.

Beyond, Lauren saw a meadow, waist-high in flowers, and sunlight streaming down through white, fluffy clouds. She saw people moving up and down paths, and charming little houses, and the edge of a beautiful lake. Looking through at that scene, she realized in all her time on Earth she had never seen a day as beautiful, colors as bright, or a place as welcoming. A voice whispered in her heart, "This is my true home, to which I have returned."

She stepped through the gate, and looked around for Molly.

A woman older than Molly at her death, though still younger than Lauren, with a pre-Raphaelite tumble of black curls down to her knees, said, "I would have come."

Lauren stared at her. This was not the Molly she had expected, but in the eyes and the voice, something of Molly remained nonetheless. "I know you would have. I'm on the clock. Jake is here. He isn't supposed to be, but the Administrator told me I won't be able to take him home. I have to get him, but I had to talk to you first."

Molly's beatific smile seemed wrong for the situation. "If he's here, he belongs here. Everything is better here, Lauren. You couldn't really hope to take him back to . . . all of that. How grim."

"I'm here. And I certainly don't belong."

A tiny frown knit Molly's brow. "And yet you talked your way in. You must have been persuasive."

"Just very persistent," Lauren said.

Molly looked into the distance and smiled at something Lauren couldn't see. Then she said, "So—you have come such a great way and through such obstacles to get Jake. And yet you're here with me. Why?"

"I want you to come back with me. I need you. Seolar needs you. And . . . Molly needs you."

Molly's smile grew puzzled. "You need me . . . I could see that. We had much we hoped to do. And Seolar—that's sad, but his life is not yet done. He'll join me here soon enough. But . . . *Molly* needs me? I'm *here*, Lauren. There is no Molly McColl in that universe anymore."

Lauren sighed. "It's complicated, but there is. You're—she's—damn. I don't know how much you remember."

"Everything from the moment I took my first breath until the moment I took my last. For that life and a handful of others."

"That helps," Lauren said. She wanted so much to ask questions, but it was not the time. "You recall the Vodi necklace."

"Yes."

"After you died saving Jake's life, some magic in the necklace brought you back, except without your soul. You remember your life, you have the same appearance, the same emotions, the same hopes and goals—but your body is there and your soul is here. I want to put them back together."

Now Molly looked disgusted. "That isn't me, Lauren. That thing might look like me, it might act like me, but it's not me, nor is it any part of me. It's nothing more than echoes I left behind poured into a monstrosity." She looked deep into Lauren's eyes and said, "That use of magic—to create dead things that mimic the form and personality of live people who died—is horrid."

"It wouldn't be horrid if you came back," Lauren said. "Then your soul would be in your body and everything would be all right."

"Climb into a cold, heavy, lightless crypt of flesh to live some uncounted number of years when I have earned my way free of that life? I did what I came to do. I lived that life to learn self-sacrifice, and at the end I did—but now I'm done. I have nothing else I have to do there."

Lauren stared at her. "The plan, Molly. Mom and Dad's . . . and your father's . . . plan. We're going to keep the worldchain from dying. We're going to bring the dead worlds back to life."

Molly was shaking her head. "Mom and our fathers didn't realize that worldchains die sometimes. If that one dies, souls will move on to others."

"I *live* in that one. *Jake* lives in that one. Everyone I know and love lives in that one. I don't *want* it to die."

"Of course you don't—but perhaps that is why you chose that life: to participate in the death of a world. From where I'm standing, I don't know what lessons you set yourself to learn. I only know that I'm not a part of them anymore. I'm done." She sat on the grass and patted a space in the flowers beside her. "Sit. Talk to me. Tell me why you could think that some dead thing was me, or why you would come here to help what you already know is a hideous perversion of the magic of the universe. Surely you must be confused, and I can help you."

Lauren stared at her. This place called to her, and Molly in her beautiful, radiant form seemed both reasonable and right. This was the place they would all eventually end up anyway. Why fight anything? Why struggle? Perhaps her lesson in life was to learn to give in gracefully; perhaps she was supposed to learn that fighting was futile. Jake was already here. Brian, too. She wanted to sit in the flowers. She wanted to talk to Molly. She wanted to listen to the music that floated in the air here, to breathe in the wonderful smells, to let go of the worry and the pain and the strife—because in the end, everyone did. They never finished everything; they simply packed up in midsentence and walked away with everything undone, and yet the world went on.

Or it didn't, and apparently that didn't matter, either.

She and Jake and Brian could stay here. She could miss the pain of living—because unlike the bleak gray plain, this place was a wonder; it was the sort of place where a soul could stretch out and recuperate and never feel a moment's anguish or a moment's worry. It banished sorrow. It soothed away fear.

And then she thought—Yes. And if Jake and I stay, that will be the same as killing him, won't it? And the same as killing myself. I'll be depriving both of us of our lives.

And what of Molly—the Molly back on Oria, willing to fight the fall of a universe even though this wonderful place is denied her? What of Molly, who deserved better than she was getting? No matter what Molly's soul, sitting here in comfort and safety, said, the Molly back on Oria was real. A real person. Worth helping—worth fighting with, worth fighting for.

Lauren didn't sit. The grass, the flowers, radiant Molly, the perfect day—these were not hers. She did not belong here.

It would be here when she got back, she told herself. Exactly the words she told Jake when making him walk away from a favorite toy at bedtime. "It will be there when you get back."

If she didn't go back and fight, though, her world—her home—wouldn't be there for Jake or anyone else.

She drew in a shuddery breath and said, "I think my job is not done yet, Molly. I think I have to go back and fight—I have to do what I can to save the worldchain."

"Without me, you can't," Molly said. "But I'm not going back—it isn't what I'm supposed to do."

"Maybe it's not what *you're* supposed to do," Lauren said. "But the part of you that's still back there—the person who still believes she's you—also believes that she and I are supposed to fight this fight, and she can't do it without me and win any more than I can do it without her."

Molly stared at Lauren, and for the second time a shadow disturbed that perfect countenance and that radiant joy. "If you consort with the walking dead, they will eventually turn on you and destroy you in ways you cannot even begin to imagine. You cannot conceive of the evil of the magic that has to have brought this thing into existence. No good can come of it."

"And yet," Lauren said, "I'm going to see if I can get some good out of it anyway." She took a step back toward the arch she'd stepped through and turned back to Molly.

"Thank you for your time. I wish you were coming with me—but for her sake. Not for yours."

Molly's smile was once again that beatific, saintly smile. "Perhaps in this lifetime of yours, you're destined to make mistakes. I will not fight against your path any longer. I wish you good fortune."

"Yeah. Thanks," Lauren said.

Molly turned and started to walk away. She took normal-looking steps, but every step carried her away so quickly she seemed to be blown in a high wind. Lauren watched her until Molly blinked out behind a small copse; she seemed like a star suddenly hidden behind a cloud.

Lauren turned back to the arch. She dreaded the possibility that Brian might be as unmoved by the pending death of the world as Molly had been. She dreaded imagining that Jake might want to stay in this place instead of coming home with her.

Don't think. Just do, she told herself.

"I want to go to Brian and Jake," she said to the arch.

The Administrator said, "On your head be it."

She stepped through the arch. And Brian stood on the other side, and behind him, a joyous Jake came charging over to her and threw his arms around her legs and shrieked, "Mama!"—and Lauren realized that if she couldn't go back with Jake, she wasn't going back.

She picked Jake up and wrapped her arms around him and buried her face in his hair, for a moment forgetting to breathe.

He tired of her embrace, though, and smiled at her and said, "I want down to play."

And she was left facing Brian. He was a little taller than he had been. A little leaner. The shape of his face had changed in some subtle way that she couldn't quite put her finger on, so that he was handsomer. But his eyes and his smile . . . she had seen them waking and sleeping, both before and after she lost him. And until that moment, she had thought she would never see them again. She would have known him anywhere. He looked at her and smiled, and her eyes filled with tears and she tried to swallow around a throat suddenly constricted.

"Oh, Brian," she whispered.

He pulled her into her arms and kissed her, and her whole body sobbed, "Yes."

Yes. This was Brian—her Brian.

"How did you get to me?" he whispered in her ear. "Lauren, I missed you so much, and for so long. It was hell to be near you and to be unable to touch you." He brushed her hair back with a hand and kissed her again. "How did Jake get here? He wouldn't tell me."

"He figured out how to make a gate when we were in Oria." She frowned. Oria had come after Brian died. "Do you know about Oria here? About the worldchain?"

His head pressed against her cheek, he nodded. "I know. I was with you all the time, Lauren. I was with you in the house and between the worlds. I was with the two of you every minute, up until I went through with Jake when he was dying, and I had to decide—save him, or stay with you." He pulled away from her. "I didn't even have to think about it."

"No," Lauren said. "I would have done the same thing." She touched his face. "God, I love you. I haven't been able to breathe since you died."

He held her tight again. "I know," he said. "I was there. I was supposed to leave, but I didn't. I couldn't. I couldn't leave you alone until I knew you would be all right."

"Sometimes I thought I could feel you with me. It was so hard. Then I found you when I found the gate—you touched me and I felt . . . less alone. And then I lost you again." She ran her fingers through his close-cropped hair and breathed in his smell. He had the same radiance to him that she'd seen in Molly, but he didn't feel as far away from her, or so far above her. He was her Brian, and they were supposed to be together. The universe had been designed that way.

Brian was looking at her steadily. "Once I saved Jake, I

knew that I'd served my purpose—and that, finally, it was time for me to move on."

"It's all right. I can fix it now. I came to take you back with me. Jake . . ." She shook her head, halfway between laughing and crying. She and Brian and Jake were together again, and everything was going to be all right. *Now* she could almost laugh about the nightmare Jake had put her through. Almost. "Jake came to save you. To bring you home. I'm here to take both of you back."

"Lauren . . ."

Lauren shook her head. "Don't say anything. I know you probably finished everything you needed to do there, and your place is here now; I heard all of that from Molly. But Jake needs his daddy back, and I can make it real. We can be us again, Brian."

She felt moisture on her neck, and for an instant wondered if a warm rain was starting. And then she realized Brian was crying.

Her first thought was, There are no tears in heaven. And her second was, No. Don't tell me. I don't want to know.

CHAPTER 13

Copper House

SOMETHING HAD BEEN watching her, but Molly couldn't feel it anymore. When the rrôn outside the window flew away, Molly felt a growing silence in her mind as the little hums of life all around her blanked out. She hadn't even re-alized that she'd been aware of those soft hums, so like breathing, until they started to vanish. First she'd been alarmed, but when she could see people around her moving even as they grew silent in her mind, she got a sudden image of something hunting her.

She left Lauren's suite with its crowd of goroths, got away to a quiet place and dropped into a meditative trance, some-thing she had learned to do in the Air Force. Finding still-ness had helped her survive barracks life—the resonating pain of injuries, the hangovers, and the illnesses suffered by her barracks mates, which she dared not heal but could not ignore.

She waited for a very long time while inside her the pres-sure built and she became certain that if she could just hold out, she would catch his metaphorical blink and be able to tell who and what hunted her.

Only Birra and some of the guards had become concerned at her continued silence and lack of response to their calls. And when they found her—lying so still she seemed to be dead—they had forced themselves into the front of her at-tention. The instant the trance broke, Molly felt her enemy's elation, followed by a total blankness that let her know he had no wish for her to find him or identify him.

She'd gotten something, though. He was rrôn, but he was to the rrôn who had circled above Copper House what a Rolls-Royce Silver Ghost was to a Ford Pinto. He was old beyond imagining, and powerful, and in spite of age and power, or perhaps because of them, he was also cautious.

That she got, and then he shut down what little vision she'd had of him.

Inside the main part of Copper House she couldn't even do enough magic to shield her thoughts from him. She could, however, return to stillness and keep watch. He would be coming for her. He would find a way. And when he entered the grand house, his magic, too, would be stripped away, and he and she would be on more-or-less equal footing. So. How to give herself the advantage?

She considered weapons. Swords, knives, bows and crossbows, guns, rifles, military armament, stuff she might conjure with magic. She had some training in hand-to-hand combat, and wished she'd had more. She wouldn't trust herself with a sword, couldn't count on the distance necessary to use a bow or crossbow effectively, and didn't have standard American weaponry, either civilian or military, nor any means to acquire them in time. Time was the issue. He was going to be on his way.

She did not know how he could come into Copper House—huge nightmare monster that he was. She only knew that he believed he could get to her. If he believed it, he had information she didn't have; his was the most clear, intelligent mind she'd ever brushed up against.

She felt her fear, but remembered Air Force training—that fear was part of the game; that those who learned to work through the fear rather than deny it were the ones who lived, the ones who succeeded. Just for an instant, she did wish she'd been a Marine—they got a lot more practical experience in real warfare. But Molly had the killer instinct, and she wasn't squeamish. She figured she would find a way to

make everything she had count. The thing coming after her
was big and bad, but she intended to win anyway.

She did not want to be anywhere near Seolar. It wasn't
just his betrayal, his placing of duty before her life. It was
also the fact that she was bringing trouble down on the inhabitants of the house, and her best and most honorable
move would be to keep out of the way of everyone she cared
about. She was the only one who would be able to come
back—she didn't want Seolar's blood on her conscience,
even if she couldn't bear the sight of him for putting her into
this position.

If she could get to Lauren's suite, she could pretend to be
studying the notebook. She could leave the guards outside,
run through the back passages down to the safe room, and
make herself something powerful to use against the horror
that stalked her.

In the hall, Birra and guards waited for her. She approached Birra, fighting to appear calm, to look like everything was fine. "I'll be spending the rest of my evening in
Lauren's room, studying her manuscript," she said. "I think I
might be able to find some way to summon her back."

"That is excellent news, Vodi," he said. "However, I believe, that the Imallin is hoping to speak with you."

Molly gave him a level stare and said, "I won't be speaking with Seolar tonight. I may not be speaking with Seolar
for quite some time."

Birra looked shaken; he nodded and said, "As you wish. I
will relay your message to him."

"As soon as you have seen me to Lauren's quarters, if you
please. I don't wish to have any missed communications. In-
form him, also, that he *will not* come to me. I speak as the
Vodi on this issue. I will tolerate no disagreement."

"Yes, Vodi," Birra said.

They hurried through the corridors to Lauren's room. Rue
met her at the door with a nervous, "Has she returned?"

"Not yet," Molly said. She turned to Birra. "Please take
him my message now." Birra nodded, and Molly closed the

door with all the veyâr on the outside of it. She turned her attention to Rue.

"I will be working in here tonight. I must ask that all of you leave—I am going to require the suite entirely to myself."

"We will make no noise," Rue told her.

Molly gave him a hard look. "Your thoughts will."

He said nothing else—simply bowed and gathered up the other goroths. Molly pointed him to the hidden door that led to the servants' passage. "That way, if you please."

Molly waited until all the goroths were gone. Then she headed into the passageway herself. She could see well enough—it had both air and light from grilles in the floor and ceiling and her eyes, no longer human, handled near-darkness better than they would have when she had been just Molly McColl back home. She did not, however, want the rrôn to catch her in these passageways—they were too narrow, too enclosed, with too many blind alleys and cubbyholes, too many doors leading in from too many rooms that she could not watch. She needed to get to the safe room quickly. Once there, she could set up a magical trap that would kill the rrôn as soon as he passed through the doorway. She knew exactly how to do it. She broke into a lope, feeling pressure along her spine and in her gut—an anxiety she could not ignore or allay.

Faster. He was coming. She started running—through the darkness, down the passageway.

Then, without warning, eyes opened inside her mind, eyes that watched her. He was not still now, the hunter, and he had managed to get into Copper House without raising either an alarm or suspicions. Nothing real stood between the two of them, no barrier but space and a bit of time. He was hiding his thoughts, but he could not hide his eyes. *I need a weapon.* But all she had was Seolar's dagger.

She raced down the ramp, feeling the hunter behind her. She tucked up her skirts as she ran, wishing she was wearing shorts and running shoes, not daring to slow down to tighten the stupid slippers that matched her dress more firmly to her feet.

One flew off, and unbalanced, she kicked off the other one. The rough stone floor felt like hell to her bare feet, but her traction improved and she moved faster. She rounded the last corner down the ramp and came out into a wine cellar.

She'd taken a wrong turn.

She had no idea how to get back to where she'd come from, and no chance of fighting off the rrôn without the edge being the only one with access to magic would have given her. Without the safe room . . .

She looked around. Along the back wall, one massive metal-banded wood door that opened inward—it stood ajar. She raced inside, closed the door. Levered a metal bar into the brackets one side at a time, putting all her weight into lifting the thing—she guessed it weighed more than she did. If she hadn't been able to move one end at a time, she would never had managed to block the door.

But she did, finally. Then she stood there, breathing hard, and stared at the dagger. She had to find out where he was, and what he was doing.

She leaned against the nearest wall and slid down into a crouch; in spite of her fear, she stilled her mind to the point of thoughtlessness.

The eyes in her mind grew brighter and clearer, and suddenly she was looking out of them. He was following not her thoughts and not her scent, but a marker he'd placed in her mind the instant she'd betrayed her presence. Looking at herself through his eyes, she could see the marker, and she could see how it was constructed . . . and she could see, as well, how it might be eliminated. Just . . . like . . . so . . .

It blinked out of existence, and the rrôn faltered and stopped.

Molly held still. Her enemy had taken man-form—she didn't know the rrôn could do that, but should have guessed it. She could change her form, as could other upworlders. Magic offered that option. The rrôn gave the initial impression of being a veyâr, but it was not a particularly good impression. He'd used magic to cloud the thoughts of the men at the gates, convincing them that they knew him and had reason to trust him. By that ruse he'd come through the gates.

Inside a vast cage of copper, though, he could not use such tricks. His form would hold, but those who saw him would recognize him for what he was. She got this as a sharp, tiny impression at the back of his mind, a thought he had not bothered to tuck away because he considered it unimportant. He carried no weapons, but he had no doubts that he could destroy anything that crossed his path. And he intended to. When he was done with her, he planned to kill everyone he met on his way out, just because.

Still . . . still. Molly did not let emotion or reaction betray her presence in the monster's mind. When she erased his marker, he'd quieted his thoughts, but he did not have the luxury of sitting still and waiting for her to betray her presence. She had gone to ground; he had to keep on the move to find her.

He admired her. She excited him. He was strangely pleased that she'd found the marker, oddly delighted that she had managed to disappear when he thought he had her. He yearned for challenge, and considered her an equal or a near equal. He despised the rrôn who had circled Copper House.

All of this she gleaned from stray thoughts simply by being still. He started moving again, following the direction he'd been taking when Molly disappeared from his view. It would eventually bring him to Molly, though not at the pace he'd managed previously.

Still Molly waited, heart and blood and thought quieted to nothing. He came for her, he hunted her . . . but why?

She was the Vodi. She was as much an immortal as he. Either of them could be killed, but they would simply return. So what did he want? She waited, silent behind his eyes, cold and patient within his mind.

He was careful; he moved steadily, stopping to sniff the

air, and she realized that he had caught a scent and had determined that it belonged to her. The traces of humanity mixed with veyâr blood, the heat trail she had left as they fled—he had marked these and by process of elimination had come to a clear knowledge of how she smelled. With a scent trail, he began to move faster again. He stopped once, and through his eyes she saw her shoes. He left them. They only confirmed what he already knew.

He would be on her in just minutes. His excitement began to rise, and suddenly, for just an instant, Molly got a clear flash of his intentions. He did not plan on killing her first. He planned on keeping her alive long enough to get the necklace off of her. Then he intended to kill her—in that manner, he would destroy her forever. She would not come back. He and his kind would win, and she and her kind would lose.

Baanraak moved around another corner, and through his eyes Molly could see the floor level out, and before him rows of wine casks, and behind the casks, a door.

Her door.

The Afterlife

With Brian's tears still hot on her neck, Lauren pulled free of his embrace and grabbed his shoulders. "You're coming back home with me, Bri. I've come too far and through too much to accept excuses."

He gave her the saddest smile she had ever seen and pressed a finger to her lips. "I don't belong there anymore, my love. I finished my tasks. And now other doors are opening for you—other steps you need to take along your chosen path. I have no place along that path in this lifetime—not anymore."

Lauren walked over to Jake and picked him up. Jake protested a little, but seemed to sense her mood. He calmed quickly and wrapped his arms around her neck, and said, "See? I'm Superman. I gotted Daddy."

Lauren looked from Jake to Brian and took a deep breath to steady herself. "You will always have a place in our lives," she said.

"Yes. As a memory. Oh, Lauren—there's so much involved in this, but I can't go back with you."

"No," Lauren said. "I can't accept that. He *found* you, Bri. He came through Hell to save you. He needs you, and so do I." She turned away, feeling tears burning their way down the back of her throat. She blinked hard, took a shaky breath, and turned back to him. "You weren't supposed to die in that accident, you weren't supposed to leave me when you did, and you know it. You promised."

He watched her and said nothing.

She stared into his eyes, willing him to say that he would find a way, or make a way, and that he and she would be together again. "Come on, Brian," she whispered. "Let's get the hell out of here."

"I made a deal," he said at last. And then he was quiet.

Lauren didn't want to hear it, but she asked, "What kind of deal?"

"When Jake was dying, I had the chance to keep him alive as he moved between the worlds. But I wasn't supposed to have stayed close to you when I died; I was supposed to come straight here. I didn't, but in order to do what I had to do to save Jake, I had to make peace with this place, because I had to give Jake part of myself—part of my soul. It was no guarantee that he would live once he went through, because if Molly hadn't sacrificed herself for him, I would have lost that piece of myself and he would have died anyway." Brian sighed. "But I did what I had to do, and Molly did what she had to do, and Jake lived."

Lauren nodded.

"But when I gave up a piece of myself to Jake, I showed up on the . . . well, the radar here, for lack of a better word. Because we aren't supposed to do that, either, the difference being that if you hide once you die, no one comes looking for you. If you as an AWOL soul start doing flashy things you weren't supposed to do, suddenly everything here gets a hook in you and starts reeling you in."

"Bastards."

Brian shrugged. "There are reasons. Souls are supposed to recuperate between lives, learn from what they've done, spend time choosing their next challenges or figuring out how they might better approach the challenges they have to reattempt . . ." He gave her that crooked little smile she had always loved. "I was sitting on the side of your bed while you slept, stroking your hair, or going into Jake's room and watching him play when he first woke up. I was hanging out in the kitchen while you made food for you and Jake, wishing you and I could cook dinner together again. I wasn't resting, or recuperating, or getting on with my growth as a soul. I wasn't moving forward. I was . . . stuck."

"And now you don't have to be stuck anymore."

Brian pulled her close and kissed her forehead. "You haven't learned the art of giving up gracefully yet, I see."

"I don't intend to learn that one. Giving up gracefully is just losing when you still might win. I intend to win."

He took her hand in his and pulled her onto a path. He started walking, and she realized they were heading for a lake, away from her stone arch, which was going to take the three of them back to Oria and a life together. "Laurie, listen to me. They had me dead to rights. I'd broken the rules not once but twice. In order for them to let the things I'd done with Jake stand, I had to agree to back out of life for a while. I'm not going to be taking on any new lives for . . . I don't know. A long time. Until I've learned how to let go."

"Neither one of us is good at letting go," she said. "But that's not a bad thing. That's a good thing. We belong together."

"You and Jake belong together." He laughed a little. "You're two of a kind. Me? Well, because of me, you still have Jake, and that was the finest thing I did in that lifetime."

"They're telling me I can't take Jake back, either."

Brian shook his head. "That can't be right. My deal with

them was that Jake got to live his life. They won't cheat." He shook his head. "But you're missing the point, Laurie. I *was* supposed to die when I did. You're supposed to move on."

"Without you? No."

"You have other opportunities now. New directions."

"I don't want other opportunities or new directions," she said. "And neither does Jake. We want you. We love *you*. Enough excuses, enough bureaucracy, enough people telling you what you're supposed to do and what's supposed to be good for you. Come home. I'm taking us."

He put his hand on her shoulder and looked into her eyes, and slowly shook his head. "Put Jake down for a minute. He'll be okay."

Lauren put her son on the grass. Jake sat and looked up at her, suddenly solemn, suddenly patient.

Brian said, "We have this chance to say good-bye, you and I. This one chance, which you fought hard to get. Don't waste it. Kiss me, and tell me that you love me."

Lauren blinked back tears. Shook her head "no."

"Dead is dead, Laurie. My word is my word, too. I love you, and I will love you forever. When you return here—when you really belong here—I'll be here waiting for you. But I am not the last love you will have in this life of yours. Kiss me, and tell me good-bye, and go start living again."

"Oh, Brian, there's no one else like you."

"I hope not." He gave her a little smile, and she saw tears on his cheeks. "I don't want you to find a replacement for me—that would be living in the past. Just look forward. And remember that you're free. Heaven has no place for jealousy—here, all loves have room to flower and grow." He pulled her into his arms and kissed her hard, the way he used to when they were standing in the hangar and he was going TDY and had his bag on his shoulder and she could feel the plane out there, waiting to take him away from her again.

She kissed him back, melting into his arms, wanting so much for this to be the first time, not the last. For this to last forever. But he pulled away, bent over, and picked up Jake.

"I'm glad you came to see me, sport. But you know you don't get to come back here again."

"I know." Jake nodded.

"And you know I'll always be with you inside." He tapped Jake's chest.

"I know."

"Take care of your mommy," Brian said, and wrapped Jake in a tight embrace.

Jake flung his arms around his father's neck and kissed him on the cheek. "I wanted to be Superman," he said. "I wanted to save you."

"You're going to have to be Mommy's little Superman, okay? Be a good boy. I'm proud of you." He put Jake back on the grass. "Go with Mommy now. It's time to go home." Brian's face crumpled, and he had to turn away.

"Not yet," Lauren whispered.

"You have to go," Brian said. "They need you back there." He turned around to look at her again and forced a tiny smile. "I'll be here when you get back."

Lauren finally accepted it. He wasn't coming home. No last-minute reprieve, no miracle, no voice of God above saying, "Go. Go. You fought so hard to be together—you deserve this." Just that gate, waiting. And Jake. And the knowledge that back home, people needed her.

She picked up Jake and swung him onto her hip. "I'll miss you, Bri."

"I'll miss you, too. But it's never as long as it seems. Usually, it isn't even as long as you want. Be happy. That will make me happy."

With Jake in her arms and his legs wrapped around her waist, she put her hand on the gate and said, "I want to go home."

"Good-bye, Daddy," Jake yelled.

And then Lauren stepped through.

Onto a featureless gray plain, with a featureless gray sky, now lacking even a road to bisect it and offer to it some feeling of direction and finity.

"Oh, no," Lauren whispered. "This is not where we wanted to be." She closed her eyes and summoned a road beneath her feet. Then she gave it a sign that said, "Home," and started walking.

"I don't like this place," Jake said.

"You have good instincts, puppy-boy." She tightened her grip on him and walked faster.

"You know why you're here," the Administrator said. He sounded like he was right behind them, though Lauren didn't trust sound in this place. Nevertheless, when Jake gave a little whimper and buried his face against her neck, she did peek over her shoulder.

She wished she hadn't.

The Administrator stood right behind her, clad in his flowing, wind-whipped black, and with him were a hundred black-clad clones, all faceless, hidden beneath their dark cowls, with arms crossed over chests and censure in their stances.

They said nothing. They simply stood.

"I'm not leaving without my son," Lauren said. "Brian made an agreement—he would stay here and learn what he needed to learn—Jake got to live out his life."

"The child *did* live out his life," the Administrator said. "He left it of his own volition. And there are irregularities in his case."

"He's *three*!" Lauren shouted. "You don't *have* volition when you're three."

"Part of him is much older."

"Most of him *isn't*! You don't get to change the deal now!"

"We didn't change the deal. We are merely enforcing its terms."

"He's *ALIVE*!"

"Enough of him belongs here that we are within our rights to claim him and keep him."

"Jake came here because he loves his daddy. He's a little guy, and he wanted to save Brian, and because of that love, you're going to try to steal his life from him—and take my son away from me—on a *technicality*. I thought Heaven was a place of love. A place free from pettiness and bureaucratic bullshit."

"Rules matter. You may think what you like, but the child stays. And if you do not give him to us voluntarily, you will spend the rest of your life on this plain, alone."

"Go to Hell," Lauren said. "You aren't taking my kid."

"Yay, Mama," Jake whispered.

The Administrator began to speak, and with him all the silent ones now spoke in unison.

> *"By the authority vested in us,*
> *by the hand of all that made us,*
> *We who hold the keys to the gate*
> *That stands between life and death,*
> *And afterlife, hereby sentence—"*

But all Lauren heard was the first part—*By the authority vested in us.* "You aren't the ultimate authorities!" she shouted over their chant. "I WANT TO TALK TO THE GUY IN CHARGE!"

That stopped them for a moment. The Administrator did not finish his chant, nor did the massed mob behind him. They all seemed dumbstruck, and for one long, lovely moment they stood silent.

Then the Administrator, sounding peevish, said, "Well, you can't. *I* deal with cases like yours."

Lauren, however, had spent time as a military wife. She knew when to stay within the chain of command. She also knew when to buck the system. She drew in the power of this place, calling to herself the vast potential of the featureless gray plain, the endless gray sky, and the bleak light, and claimed it for her own use. She started to stretch upward, bringing Jake with her. First they towered over the Administrator and his cronies, and then over the line of the road that she'd made, which shrank until it looked like a pencil line, ruler-drawn on gray paper. They grew taller and more vast, hanging on to each other and staring into each other's eyes, until even the pencil line that had been the road disappeared, and the plain again became featureless. Suddenly, however, a voice said, "Do you then intend to fill up eternity?"

The voice was masculine, and friendly, and seemed to come from nowhere and everywhere at the same time.

"Is that what it will take to get Jake and me out of this place and back home where we belong?"

The light all around the two of them became brighter, then impossibly so. It was a beautiful light, warm and loving, and Lauren felt no fear in its presence.

"You are—mother and son—well-matched souls," the voice said. "Your love and courage do you both honor."

"Honor is great," Lauren said. "But what about what that . . . that *administrator* said? About the sentence he passed on both of us?"

"I've rescinded that. The administrator overreached himself. Have some pity for him, though. Souls in the lower realms gravitate toward situations that feel familiar to them. We tend to have problems with a lot of his sort—after death, so many bureaucrats become so wrapped up in their hunger to duplicate the petty power they wielded in life that they cannot release it; they get trapped in the gray places, wielding their power over others even smaller than themselves. Some never do find the joy of freedom—which is power over no one but yourself in a place where everyone else has just as much—and just as little—power. Some of them— perhaps even he—will spend eternity there, unable to break free and move on to better things."

Lauren looked at Jake, hopeful. "Then we get to go home?"

A gentle chuckle. "You both get to go home. Before you leave, a little message for your Molly."

Not *Molly*, Lauren noted, but *your Molly*. She nodded.

"Those born with souls frequently lose them or toss them

away. But such a one as your Molly, born without a soul, does have a chance to grow one."

"Molly could get her soul back?"

"No. Your Molly never had a soul. She was born after the first Molly died, and they are not the same person."

"But she really is a person."

"If she chooses to be." His voice grew soft. "Now, dear children, it's time for you to leave. Take care of each other, find your destinies . . . and don't come back too soon next time."

Another soft chuckle, and he was gone, and the brilliant light was gone, and the gray plain was gone. Lauren and Jake floated in nothingness. Before them, a faint speck of green fire appeared; it expanded rapidly and became a gate. On the other side of it, she could see the chamber in Oria through which she had originally left.

Cast from heaven, she thought. Without Brian or Molly, finishing in exactly the same place they'd started. They had gained nothing, accomplished nothing, won nothing.

Jake cuddled close as the green fire of the gate enveloped them, and Lauren held him tightly.

At least, she thought, they didn't have *less*.

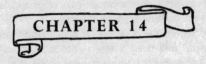

CHAPTER 14

Copper House

BAANRAAK KNEW his little Vodi hid behind the door. He could smell her in there, and hers was the smell of a living thing. But he could not find her thoughts, he could not hear her breathing, he could not sense even her awareness of him. He admired her ability—but she'd committed a few mistakes from which she wouldn't be able to recover. She'd fled rather than fighting; she had prevented others from sacrificing themselves to save her out of some misguided altruism, when numbers of veyâr on the attack might have defeated him, and if they didn't at least might have injured him enough that she could beat him herself. She'd moved away from rather than toward magic, when if she had gotten to magic first she might have turned it against him quickly enough to kill him, or even to destroy him.

Alone, in a contest of strength, she would not defeat him. She could not. He had uncounted thousands of years of experience in fighting, and dying, and living to fight again while avoiding the mistakes he'd made before. She was little more than a child as judged by her own species—by his standards she barely even existed.

He had to restrain a sudden pang of disappointment and the temptation to turn away and give her a second chance to do better. He would not find a worthy opponent. Not now, not ever. He was the only one of his kind, and he might as well go in, pick up his bauble, kill its wearer, and go back to basking in the sun on his rock. He'd been foolish to hope that his existence might once again offer a challenge, something to excite him, someone worthy . . .

She'd barred the door, and it was a heavy one. In this human form, he'd need a few minutes to batter it down. He couldn't change back to his natural shape, which would have let him shove through the thing as if it were made of well-rotted twigs. Damn copper for that; getting through a door was no challenge; it was merely an obstacle, and a poor one at that.

He shifted his mass, which had not changed with his form, and applied a slow, steady pressure to the weakest part of the door, the point on the floor opposite the hinges, where no bracket held anything steady. The door began to bulge inward at that point. He nodded and increased the pressure. Not much longer and he would be able to go home.

Copper House

Molly followed all of his thoughts, his assessment of her situation, his breakdown of where she had gone wrong. She let it flow through her, though she did not at first react to the information. She simply absorbed it and tried to find flaws in his reasoning.

There weren't any. She was alone, trapped, with a weapon she had minimal skill in using, and he was a killer who'd been killing longer than her species had been civilized. She couldn't beat him. She couldn't win.

And then, in one brief flash, she found the single way that she could beat him, and before she could think about it and give herself away, she took it.

Copper House

Baanraak determined that he would be through the door in another moment or two when, without warning, the Vodi's thoughts flared to life for one brief, flaming instant.

Then pain shut him down—pain that drove straight into his brain, so fierce and incomprehensible that he dropped to his hands and knees and puked on the stone and rolled up in a fetal ball, screaming. He pissed himself. His bowels let loose. He writhed and screamed.

It faded, though. Whatever she had done to him faded quickly, and he crawled back to his hands and knees, determined that he was going to hurt her for that. He had no idea how she'd shut him down so completely without using magic, but before that moment, he had experienced such pain and anguish only the few times that he'd been tortured.

Warily, Baanraak got to his feet. His senses were still in disarray, his nose clogged by the reek of his own urine and vomit and shit, his eyes half-blinded by nagging, persistent flashes of light—had he hit his head when he fell?—and his mind was numbed by that initial, terrible blast she'd thrown at him. He shuddered at the thought of pushing on that door again. She'd been remarkably effective in making him think twice about going after her. The question was, could she do whatever she had done again? He knew he'd screamed, and that he'd been loud about it. Soldiers looked for him now in the house, and he suspected that his scream had alerted them. He could find himself neck-deep in armed veyâr in no time, and he would not be able to get his prize.

He couldn't believe it. He'd seen no way out for her, and yet she'd managed to give herself a fighting chance to beat him. Now she was silent in there again—he could find no trace of her mind. She'd submerged herself as deeply as she'd been before.

Emotionless, he thought—or with stunning control—to be able to rise out of the depths of her hiding, shatter him with her single blast, then hide herself away from him again.

He smiled a little. He was still going to win, but by the gods, she was a better enemy than he'd thought.

He applied pressure to the door again, this time bracing himself against the next lightning bolt to his brain—but that second attack didn't come, and as he heard footsteps and shouts heading in his direction from up and in the distance, the door gave way and he burst in, claws flexed.

And then he saw that she had won after all.

She slumped against the wall, face resting against one bent knee, whole body bonelessly relaxed. The fingers of her right hand wrapped loosely around the hilt of a long knife. The blade was ripe with the stink of her blood.

He studied her for one long moment, aware of danger drawing near but feeling that this moment and this enemy required marking in his mind. She did what he had once done in a similar situation—hunted by a wiser and more powerful enemy, he had realized at the last instant that his greatest danger lay not in dying but in living, and he had killed himself quickly. Though he had not been so clever as to share his pain and shock at his own death with his enemy. *That* had been a masterstroke.

She'd gambled, and in her gamble she had won more than she ever would have believed. Baanraak's pursuer, finding in Baanraak not just a worthy enemy but at last a worthy successor, had not destroyed the gold band with which Baanraak had anchored flesh to mind. He had instead taken Baanraak, stripped all vestiges of his mortality from him, and when he was hard as diamond, the old one had trained him. Finally, when Baanraak became the perfect hunter, the perfect warrior, and the perfect killer, the old one had come to him and had found the release from the burden of immortality and the weary pains of existence by the blade of one worthy to give him the final cut.

Baanraak knelt at the Vodi's side and gently lifted her hair away from her neck. He unclasped the necklace she wore; it came away easily now that she was dead, though he would have had a hellish struggle on his hands to get it from her while she lived. He did not wear it in any fashion—the soul-gold of the immortals would destroy anyone who tried to wear an active piece. He simply slipped it into a little bag that he tied to the belt around his waist. He let the bag dangle at his hip, took her blade, and headed for the door. Those coming would think he'd killed her; that didn't matter. The survivors would come after him no matter what he did; let them think what they liked.

He considered going straight back the way he'd come in—his pursuers came that way, and he could have a bit of fun ripping them to pieces with their own weapons, her blade and his claws. But he had in his possession something more valuable to him than any gold bauble to be handed over to those who had hired him, or than any pile of clean gold and silver that might be offered in payment. He held in his bag the mind, the eventual body, and the indomitable will of the one creature he would never have thought to meet at this time and in this place.

He held his heir, and for that reason alone, he would be stealthy and careful, and he would leave by taking the fewest possible chances and exposing himself to the fewest possible risks.

Copper House

Some niggling worry twitched through the quiet places in Seolar's mind, and he rose out of troubled sleep. Molly wasn't with him, but when he considered what she'd found out and the way she'd discovered it, he wouldn't blame her if she never spoke to him again. It wasn't her absence that had awakened him.

What, then? He sat up, listening. He didn't hear the guards outside his door, and he should have. As he focused his concentration, he couldn't hear the guards up and down the hall—and though they were quiet, his acute hearing had always permitted him to pinpoint their presence.

He rose, slipped on shoes and an overrobe, and over that put on sword and buckler. He considered Molly first, of course, but he knew that he had enemies too, from among the veyâr as well as outside.

He opened the door with trepidation; he knew he might find his guards, many of them friends since childhood, dead on the floor, with the enemy waiting without. What he found, though, was an empty hall with no sign of struggle, and nothing to suggest what might have happened. For his men to have left their posts, however, leaving him asleep and unguarded, the situation had to be unthinkably bad.

Birra had told him Molly was going to be in her sister's suite; that Molly had decided she needed to spend time studying. Seolar headed in that direction, listening for anything, but the whole place ached with a silence that defied explanation or comprehension. He tried to imagine any situation in which all of his men would abandon their posts—and the farther he got into the center of the house without passing another soul, the more clear it became that they *had* all abandoned their posts—and he could think of nothing; any danger should have had half of them rallying around Molly and the other half around him.

No blood in the halls, no dropped weapons, no bodies, no smoke, no sound . . .

Coming out the door, he'd walked, but the emptiness weighed on him, and dread consumed him, and soon enough he was running as fast as he could toward Lauren's suite. Once he could be certain Molly had come to no harm, he would figure out what to do next.

No guards barred the path to Molly, though, and the door to Lauren's suite stood open. He wanted to rage, he wanted to vomit, but instead he went into the little group of rooms. No goroths. No Molly. And, aside from the complete absence of everyone, no sign of anything wrong.

Finally, however, he heard something. He headed into the suite's bedroom, and found the hidden door into the servants' passageways ajar. He pulled it open, and heard from far away the sound of men hunting, quietly and with a sense of desperation.

He ran, sword drawn and held ahead of him; he ran toward battle to rescue or avenge the woman he loved, the woman on whose life his people's and his world's survival, depended. He ran, praying that he would be in time to help, that everything might still be all right.

Then the keening started.

He could not think. He could not breathe. He pushed forward and downward, following the screams, moving at a dead run. Down into darkness and quickly into the stink of blood and piss and shit and vomit and death. His men, crowded into narrow stone corridors, most of them searching with hard eyes and weapons at the ready. He pushed through them, toward the keening, into the wine cellar of all places. He noted on entering that something had shattered the door into the wine steward's storage room. That the worst reek of puke and piss and excrement lay outside the door. Inside, fireless torches jammed into torch brackets, casting a few rings of pale, sickly light, and Birra and several others of the inner circles knelt on the stone floor, blocking him from seeing what they'd found, their heads tipped back, eyes closed. Keening.

He did not want to see. He did not want to see. But he had to look.

He moved forward, sword still in hand, heart in his throat. His eye caught on the cascade of copper hair, unbound, on the slump of slender shoulders, on eyes still open that stared forward, unblinking, already developing the dullness of death. On blood still red in places, in others drying to black—so much blood.

"Oh, Molly," he whispered. "I'm sorry. I'm so sorry—I'll make this up to you."

He pushed past his men, touched her cheek, stroked her hair. His fingers slid along the back of her neck to find the clasp of the Vodi necklace, and instead found nothing.

He stared at her body then, and at his men kneeling around her, and he bellowed, "Up. Up and find whoever—

whatever—did this. We have no time to mourn—the killer
has the Vodi necklace."

The keening snapped off into silence, and Birra leapt to
his feet, dragging his sword from its sheath. He looked like
he wanted to run it through himself. "I did not see," he said.
"I thought only of my duties, to mourn her passing—I did
not think to check . . ."

Seolar waved him out the door without a word. For this
failure—for this horrible, total failure, he would have every
right to demand the lives of every man who served him. He
could not speak to these men into whose hands he had en-
trusted everything. *Everything.* He could not find words beyond rage.

He ran out into the passageway; he had no idea what he
hunted, but he tried to think as his enemy must be thinking.
Her killer had stolen something of immeasurable value; he
held the fate of worlds in his hand. He would, Seolar
thought, stay as far from sight as he could, take the safest
passages out no matter how he had come in. Not for now the
question of how he had gotten in—he could have used
magic for that and almost certainly had done so; now only
the question of how he might get back out. On his way out,
he would have no magic in his arsenal.

For all its vastness, Copper House had only four doors
that led beyond the outer grounds: the front gate, the service
gate, the soldiers' gate, and the secret gate.

He grabbed captains and quickly assigned them to each of
the four. The captains stopped their searching of the subterranean passages and fled upward, dragging everyone with
them, heading for the four gates that would offer the bastard
egress.

Seolar stayed behind. He did not want to go back in to see
her body. But her body might be everything the worlds had
left of her; if the killer had wanted her dead not just once but
for all time and if he had succeeded in taking the necklace
off of her before she died, then the veyâr had lost. With no
Lauren and no Molly, they would move quickly to extinction

as the dark gods hunted down the last of them and destroyed them.

The worlds would keep on dying, too, Seolar thought—but the veyâr would not be around long enough to see that.

He took a deep breath, stepped back into the cell, and went to Molly's side. He knelt beside her, scooped her into his arms, and lifted her with some difficulty. Alive she had been light; in death she seemed to be three times her living weight. With tears starting to blur his vision, he positioned her so that her head rolled onto his shoulder. He could not bear to see the horror of the vast, dark gash that ran from one side of her slender neck to the other. With her so arrayed, he started for the ramp that led upward, thinking to put her in the bed they had shared, to rest until the women could clean the body, hide the wound, and prepare her for burial.

Something big and fast moved in the darkness ahead of him, and Seolar caught the blink of pale yellow eyes and a sense of two shapes blurred over each other, as if he could see both a man and something vastly different and far more terrible. He hesitated for just an instant, his arms full of Molly and his sword out of reach, and in that instant the creature—man or beast—bolted up the nearest ramp.

"Oh, gods forgive me," Seolar muttered, letting Molly's body slide to the floor in a heap. He drew his sword and charged up the ramp in pursuit. The creature outran him, though since he grew to manhood Seolar had been able to run down everything but stags in the forest. Yet this thing before him fled so quickly out of his sight that only by concentrating on sound could Seolar track him.

They pounded up the ramps, both of them running at top speed. This intruder didn't falter. He seemed, instead, to know exactly where he wanted to go. Neither of them wasted breath on shouts; Seolar felt certain that the killer would head toward one of the exits that would let him escape Copper House, and any exit was, from Seolar's point of view, as good as the next. He had guards on all of them.

The enemy, however, had other ideas. He kept racing upward along the ramps, and at first Seolar experienced a moment of jubilation. The killer had made a mistake, and Seolar would be able to run him through and get back the necklace as soon as he realized his error and discovered that his only options were to retrace his steps or proceed onto the roof. But even once the killer could surely see that he had passed ground level, he still kept the same pace and the same direction—ever upward. Did he think to lose Seolar in his own house? Did he think that he would be able to find some other path back down? He had the distance on Seolar, and it increased with every step each of them took; Seolar guessed the killer to be nearly a floor ahead of him. They reached the level of the roof, the killer well ahead of Seolar; the killer smashed through the door with a thunderous crash and pounded out onto the narrow walkway that led to the tower parapets. Seolar thought, *He has no other way off the roof,* and gripped his sword tighter as he ran, mentally bracing himself for the fight to come.

Half a floor. One quarter. A few steps and he was out into the darkness that lay beneath the gleaming stars. Before him, he could see the killer, fleeing toward the western parapet; even as Seolar watched something about him changed. His balance seemed to shift forward, with his arms getting longer, his cloak whipping up and back in a manner that made it look somehow more like wings; his neck stretched forward, and a tail erupted from his back with shocking suddenness. Seolar's brain, which had been trying to read him as a man, suddenly made the shift to what it truly saw and recoiled. One of the rrôn crouched on the western parapet, and he looked at Seolar with glowing yellow eyes and grinned with teeth that promised only death. He said, "I win, little man."

Then the killer bunched tight and erupted into the void that lay beneath the tower, wings spread. The monster rose quickly, and though Seolar's men saw him and loosed arrows and crossbow bolts in his direction, he showed no injury from them; he caught the air and flew into the night.

Seolar watched the rrôn fly out of reach. Some of his men would be moving back inside soon, but he saw no point in it. He turned slowly and headed back down the long series of stone ramps to collect Molly's body.

Cat Creek

Pete hated answering the phone when he was in other people's houses, particularly way late at night. There was nothing like having a strange man answering the phone in a house occupied only by a woman and her son for creating potential awkwardness—and picking up the phone at three in the morning . . .

He sighed, and on the fourth ring he picked up. "Deputy Pete Stark."

"Relax." Eric was on the other end. "I'm not some unsuspected relative crawling out of the bushes."

"Good. But since it's 3 A.M. I'm guessing I don't want to hear from you, either."

"Something going on in Oria. Actually here and in Oria. Meet at the Daisies and Dahlias."

Pete hung up the phone, and rubbed his eyes, and swore. Disasters had a way of needing gateweavers sooner rather than later. He didn't have a gateweaver, though he'd lied to Eric when he got back from Charlotte, saying he'd be able to find Lauren if he had to and get her back pretty quickly.

Liars live unhappy lives, he thought. Liars by profession doubly so.

He threw on clothes and got over to the Daisies and Dahlias Florist, now out of business, and hid his car around back with the others. A few new cars in the lot, and a whole lot of others missing—it emphasized the fact that the plague, the betrayals, and the almost-total disaster were all still less than a month old. The earth hadn't even settled over Nancine Tubbs, who'd owned the shop, and her husband Ernest. Or the other dead Sentinels, either.

He went through the screen door quietly and ran up the stairs two at a time. He wasn't last, at least—neither Eric nor one of the new kids, an obnoxious twenty-year-old named Raymond Smetty—had come in yet. Everyone else had gathered around the coffee maker that sat on the filing cabinets on the back wall. No one was in the mirror, which he couldn't remember ever having seen.

June Bug Tate nodded to him. She was chewing on the soggy end of an unlit cigar, an unhappy expression on her face. She kept looking at the dark-haired new girl, Darlene Fullbright, who sat, back ramrod straight, on one of the hard chairs, and who was pointedly looking at everyone and everything *but* June Bug. The smoking issue had evidently raised its head again.

Twice-divorced Terry "Mayhem" Mayhew had the other new girl, a perky, busty little blonde named Betty Kay Nye, backed into a corner, where he was trying out his devastating smile and his insurance-salesman charm on her. Pete couldn't hear either of them, but Betty Kay's cheeks were the color of tomatoes and ripening pretty fast.

Thin, balding George Mercer shoved his glasses up his nose and cleared his throat as Pete headed toward them, and Louisa Tate glanced in Pete's direction. She nodded to him, but whatever she and George had been talking about came to an abrupt end.

"Anyone hear anything about what's going on?" Pete asked.

June Bug nodded. "I'm the one who found the problem."

Pete got that sick feeling in the pit of his gut, remembering that June Bug had mostly found their last problem—and that had been . . . well. He could happily spend the rest of his life far away from any more problems like that. But the sick horror that makes people look toward train wrecks rather than away got him, and he asked, "End of the world?"

June Bug gave her cigar a hard chomp. "Damned if I know. But I'm not going to talk about it until Eric and Raymond get here."

Downstairs, the slam of the screen door, and the sound of

Eric swearing. So Raymond must have been the one who let it fly. Heavy footsteps at good speed—two pairs of them—and Eric blowing through the door with a face like a thunderstorm, and behind him, looking insolent, Raymond Smetty, who had such a big chip on his shoulder Pete expected him to start walking like Marty Feldman in *Young Dr. Frankenstein* at any moment. Raymond had once thought he was going to escape his lineage and his fate as a Sentinel—he'd been a big high-school football player down in Enigma, Georgia, with scouts after him and promises of scholarships to just about any college he might fancy. And then he'd taken a bad hit and turned his right knee into irreparable hamburger, and all the big dreams and big promises just quietly faded away. He was an unhappy transfer, and seemed bent on raining his unhappiness on anyone convenient.

Pete did not feel better knowing the fate of the world might someday rest in the hands of Raymond Smetty.

"Go ahead, June Bug," Eric said, taking a seat. He gave Raymond a hard look.

"We had some old gods in this area," June Bug said. "Three of them, from the looks of things. Today, all three just packed up and left the area. Now, they kept separate households, they didn't have much to do with each other, and they had some real long-term associations in this area. And all three just flat abandoned their homes. A gateweaver came through—one who left old god fingerprints all over his work. He went to each of the three houses, made a gate, and then moved on."

June Bug sighed. "I did some tracking, and then I did some calling around. We aren't the only place to have our old gods pick up and leave. Old god gateweavers seem to be going door-to-door in a number of places."

"Rats," Pete muttered.

Eric looked at him sidelong. "I can think of harsher things to say than that."

"No. I mean—rats swarm off a sinking ship—take their chances with the seas, hope to catch a ride on some of the wreckage. They know."

June-Bug nodded. "The old gods have apparently heard something. This looks like an emergency evacuation to me. Obviously this is not good news."

Obviously not. Pete thought about Lauren, who was out of reach, and about the fact that if she'd been in reach, maybe he could get his parents and his brothers and sisters and their kids and maybe a few good friends down to Oria before everything went "splat"—which was probably against the Sentinel credo, too, but if his choice was between having a live family and upholding the ideals of what was looking more and more like the losing side, he was going to have to vote for family.

"Any idea where the problem originates?" Eric asked.

June Bug said, "I can't find anything. I have looked and looked, and I have talked to trackers all over the country, and not a one of us can find anything that would seem to make people who have been established in this area since . . . well, maybe since colonial times . . . just throw a few things into a bag and run."

"How do you know they've been here that long?" George asked. "Wouldn't we have noticed them?"

"We *didn't*. I suspect we haven't been noticing them for a very long time. One of them was Billy Mabry, out in the old Mabry place. You know how everyone commented how much Billy looked like that picture of his great-great-great-uncle Gideon, taken right before the fight at Monroe's Crossroads? And how those Mabrys managed to hang on to the uniforms and the diaries and the sabers and all? Billy might have *been* Gideon. I didn't know either of the other two personally, but I imagine they know us. I imagine they've had their bit of fun with us in the last century or so." She frowned and put down the unlit cigar.

Pete thought about people who'd lived in the same houses under a variety of names for a century or more, and all just up and moved on the same day, and got the chills.

"But nothing seems to be wrong," he said.

June Bug looked at him and tipped her head to one side

and said, "Darlin', I *know* you read the newspapers, because I have *seen* you do it. You look at the headlines for the last ten years and tell me again that nothing seems to be wrong."

Pete felt the heat of embarrassment creeping up his neck and cheeks. "I meant nothing seems to be more wrong than usual."

"No," June Bug agreed. "It doesn't. But maybe the problem is with the part of the iceberg that we can't see. Maybe our Titanic is about to sink on something that's been building for the last thousand years, and that is below the surface of what we can see."

"You ought to know about the *Titanic*, you old bat," Raymond muttered, so low Pete almost missed it. "I'll bet you were on the last one."

Eric turned to Raymond and whispered, "We're going to have a talk," and June Bug, whose hearing was legendary, said, "I'm afraid the first *Titanic* was a bit before my time. But I don't think I'm going to be lucky enough to miss the second one."

And then Eric and June Bug both turned to Pete, and Eric said, "We need Lauren back here. Today. Right now. I'll cover the calls for you while you drive up to get her. Don't accept any excuses. We're going to need flexible access—to Oria, to who knows where else—while we figure out what's going on and how we can fight it."

"If nothing else," George said, "we need gates that will hold up for heavy traffic. If this is it and we've lost, I want to get my family out of here, and I'm sure the rest of you do, too. I'll stay and fight, but I have to know they're safe."

And Pete swallowed hard and nodded. "I'll do my best."

Oria

Baanraak, gleeful at his success, considered his options as he winged through the night sky over the Mourning Forest. He needed to revive Molly someplace with a lot of raw ma-

terials to contribute to the physical recreation the spell
would require. The place would not require the volume of
resources Fherghass had needed when he decided to create
Baanraak as his successor—the Vodi's slight form was nothing like a rrôn's.

But Baanraak was going to have to kill her and revive her
repeatedly until he managed to eliminate all her mortal patterns and tendencies, and repeated resurrection of even a
low-mass creature demanded resources.

Baanraak considered, too, that he would have to deal with
the rrôn of the Night Watch, who would certainly feel they
had a say in what Baanraak was doing with the Vodi. They
wanted her gone; when they discovered that, far from destroying her, Baanraak planned to temper her the way a
blacksmith tempered a fine blade, they would demand
blood. Hers first, then Baanraak's.

The idea of the Night Watch coming after Baanraak didn't
bother him overmuch, but he did have some timing prefer-
ences—he wanted to be able to train his new colleague and
eventual replacement without disturbance.

He could lie easily enough. He could claim he'd killed her
in Copper House—true, and easily proven—and that he'd
then taken the opportunity to destroy the necklace before she
had the chance to reembody—false, but utterly impossible
to disprove until such time as she reappeared wearing the
necklace.

He *could* lie—but lying was the coward's path. He
wouldn't take it. Instead, he would simply disappear, taking
her with him. Downworld a bit, he thought. Dalchi, four
worlds below Oria, had an excellent supply of flora and
fauna to keep him well supplied, plenty of raw materials and
magical energy to permit repeated resurrections for the Vodi
without straining local resources, and the Night Watch
mostly avoided it because it was, as yet, too deep in the layers of live worlds to get a good feed from the death energy of
the upworlds.

He would, he thought, have as long as he needed there. He

could do the job right, and when he was done, he would have a companion, and a colleague, and an eventual heir. And during the whole process, he would once again have a reason for living.

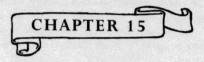
Copper House

LAUREN AND JAKE fell through the mirror into the stone room they had left behind. Lauren got just a peek at the room she'd stepped into; then the green fire of the gate behind her died into complete darkness. For a moment ghost images offered a pretense of light, but when those faded, Lauren realized she could see nothing—and wouldn't be able to. The stone room buried in the depths of Copper House had no windows—and no one had thought to leave a light burning for her.

Jake hugged her neck so tightly she had to fight for air. "Easy, monkey-boy," she said, and conjured a room light. The room lay empty—but it felt more than merely empty. It felt abandoned.

How long had she and Jake been gone? Hours? Days? Years?

Lauren listened, but heard no sound save her breathing and her son's. Her heart began to race—she knew she shouldn't have expected Molly and the goroths to be there waiting for her when she arrived, and she knew arriving into darkness when no one knew when to expect her only made sense. Still, she couldn't quite fight off the feeling of dread that filled her.

"We're going to need a flashlight to get out of here," she told Jake.

She had several under her bed at home. The worldchain did better when magic moved things than when it either created or destroyed them—so she focused on the yellow rubber-coated flashlight with the fresh C cells in it, and pressed her nose against the mirror, staring into and through the glass, until on the other side she saw her bedroom and her bed, and beneath the bed on the left-hand side the flashlight, lying in front of the nightstand and within easy fumbling reach.

Looking at her bedroom and the implied safety that the house represented twisted a knot in her belly. With all her heart and soul, she wanted to take Jake and go back to the old house and find some way to build a normal life for the two of them. She wondered if she would ever get to go home . . . and if she got home, if a normal life would ever be within reach.

She didn't let herself think any more about it. If things worked out, she would be happy then. If they didn't, ruining her life in advance wouldn't help anything. She made a tiny gate, reached through, and grabbed the flashlight, passing on the temptation to get other things or just to sneak herself and Jake across for a moment. If they went home he was not going to want to turn around and come back.

She shifted Jake to her other hip and went through the door, grateful that the last person out had at least thought to leave it unlocked. The maze of corridors beyond it spread out in all directions, eerie and intimidating when viewed with a single weak-beamed flashlight and a three-year-old who didn't like the dark. She stared at the hallway that ran left and right, and at the intersections she could see crossing at right angles. Beyond the range of her flashlight's beam, nothing but darkness in all directions. She leaned against the wall and swore softly and steadily. Obviously going up was the first priority. If she could find a way to change levels, maybe she'd come across a landmark.

Lauren had spent a lot of time in her past being lost. She had a firm rule of thumb for finding her way in situations where she had no idea where she was—go straight until something looks familiar or you run out of road. Then turn right and repeat.

She turned right out the door and went straight. At each intersection she turned off the flashlight, looking for light. Nothing. When she reached the stone foundation wall, she turned right, and started off again. She continued switching off the flashlight at intersections, getting nowhere. The air at one intersection stank with a smell that made her hair stand on end. Something had died down that way—a whole lot of little somethings, or one big one. She hurried past, not wanting to know, and suddenly wishing she had a couple of veyâr with spears guarding her back. She came at last to an arch that led into a tunnel. She considered this for a moment. Under the compass rule, she should continue straight. Using the "anything different is good" rule, however, the arching tunnel that curved away out of sight offered a distinct improvement from wandering around in the maze of the world's biggest basement looking for stairs. She switched the light off one more time and looked down the tunnel. No light from there, either. However, it might be night outside, the tunnel might curve enough to block the passage of light into the depths, or it could end in stairs and a door. Any of these three options offered a distinct improvement. And if she ended up in the wine cellar or a dungeon, she could always turn around and come back.

She took off up the tunnel. She could still hear no sounds but her own and Jake's breathing and the echoes of her footsteps. She tried not to imagine the worst—that she'd stepped back into the copper-free workroom a thousand years later than she'd left—that the world of Oria was only instants from destruction and that Earth had been dead for centuries. . . .

The tunnel curved sharply and started up a gentle rise.

"Yes," she whispered.

From in front of her and behind, soft, drawn-out whispers of "yes."

She jumped and turned, flashing the beam of light in all directions. Nothing followed them.

"Echo," she said in a conversational tone.

"Echo," the corridor said back to her a dozen times, louder, but in what she could identify as her own voice.

"I don't like those voices," Jake said, and the echoes agreed with him. He shrieked. The corridor shrieked back.

"Shh," Lauren said, and the place sounded like a nest of snakes had just woken up.

Jake jammed his hands over his ears and buried his face against her. Lauren wished she could do the same thing with someone bigger and stronger than her.

Nothing like creeping herself out. Bad enough to think she and Jake were the last people on the planet. Worse to think that they were the last people on the planet and *things* were skulking up behind them while they walked on unawares.

Lauren walked a little faster. The incline of the corridor steepened and the curve tightened, and she realized she was heading up a spiral. She tried to imagine its purpose, then realized that wide, sloping corridors would be a lot more practical than stairs for moving crates, boxes, furniture, or anything else large and bulky and awkward. Someone moving supplies could get horses to pull a wagon down this thing, if the horses were well trained and the wagon wasn't too wide.

That raised the possibility that she was in a supply tunnel, and almost immediately after she raised *that* possibility, she reached the end of the corridor—a dead end closed off by a massive copper double door with inside hinges. She grabbed one of the metal handles and pulled.

Someone had locked it. From the outside.

She swore loudly, and all her many echoes down the tunnel behind her added their comments.

"I want out," Jake yelled.

"Me too."

Lauren gave the door a couple of hard pulls, hoping to work the lock loose or maybe put enough pressure on it to break it. Nothing popped free, so she put Jake down and told him "DON'T MOVE," tucked her flashlight into the waistband of her jeans, hung on to the right door handle, and started rocking back and forth. The copper doors began to boom as she fought with them, metal hitting metal as she built up some steam. She was, she thought, making one hell of a racket, but no one seemed to be running to help her.

Then, on one arc, she heard a satisfying crack from the other side, and the door whipped back when she pulled on it with much more force than she expected. "Move," she yelled as she lost her footing and crashed backward. She managed to keep from hitting her head when she fell, but slammed down hard enough that she feared she might have broken her tailbone.

The flashlight flew out of her pocket, and Jake dove for it and snagged it for her. But it didn't matter. Outside the doors, the sun lay on the horizon and pink scored the purple sky like claw marks. Silhouetted against that stunning sky stood half a dozen veyâr, all pointing crossbows at her.

"Aw, shit," she said. "Don't shoot the baby. It's me. Lauren."

She got to her feet slowly, and carefully bent down and picked up Jake. "Really. It's me. Put the bows down and call Molly or Seolar or something, all right?"

They backed slowly away from the door, but not one lowered his crossbow. This scared the shit out of her. One of them with an itchy trigger finger could kill Jake without meaning to. Free of copper, however, she used magic to cast an invisible shield around him; then, with her kidneys itching, she cast one around herself.

The veyâr leader, whom she didn't recognize, said, "Move forward slowly, out into the light. Keep your hands up where we can see them."

Lauren sighed and stepped forward. "My hands are full of little boy. Is that good enough?"

No answer.

"What happened?" she asked.

"To the front," one of them said. "If you move suddenly or do anything we don't like, we'll shoot you."

Again with the threats and the crossbows. She wondered if this was going to be the greeting she got every time she returned to Copper House.

She let them march her to the front gate; she worked out a spell and held it one thought from completion just in case things got ugly, but she wanted to have some answers and she didn't figure she'd be able to get any if she turned these guys into toads—which, considering they were threatening Jake, too, was minor compared to what she really wanted to do.

At the front gate, she got her first break since her return. Birra stood behind one of the two regular guards. He looked about the same—no older, maybe a bit grimmer, but with Birra it was hard to say.

Lauren said, "What's going on, Birra?"

He looked at her for a long moment like he had never seen her before. Then his eyes seemed to focus, and he said, "Oh." And for just an instant, she saw hope in his expression, but it vanished. He said, "Oh," again, and then glared at the veyâr behind Lauren with the crossbows. "She could have turned you into ashes for your impudence," he said. "Perhaps she should have." And to her, "Come with me. Seolar will surely want to see you immediately."

Lauren could tell from Birra's manner that no answers were going to be forthcoming from him. So she simply nodded. They walked in silence all the way to the front gate, then inside.

Finally, Lauren said, "Okay—let me get Molly—I have a message for her. And we can both talk to Seolar together."

She caught Birra's fast, sidelong look at her, then away, and her heart started to pound. She stopped walking.

"We need to see Seolar quickly," Birra told her.

"No. I have to talk to Molly. Everything else can wait."

Birra turned to face her. They stood in the magnificent front hallway, where the copper covered each stone arch in the form of a tree, with uncounted thousands of silver leaves hanging from the branches and tinkling with every slight breeze. In that corridor, with his tattooed cheeks and long, pale blue hair and emerald green eyes, Birra looked like some additional decoration. He stared at her, unblinking, unmoving, his skin waxy and his expression unreadable. He said nothing.

"Tell me what happened, Birra."

"A rrôn got into Copper House." His voice dragged over rocks, fighting to get each next word to come out. "Molly . . . is dead. The Vodi necklace . . . gone."

Lauren felt the room get light and slippery beneath her feet, and she backed against the wall for a moment just to have something to hang on to.

"Oh, God." She looked at Birra, trying to find some hope in what he said. "How did this happen?"

"We don't know. After . . . after the rrôn got away with the necklace, we tried to figure out where we had failed. We searched all of Copper House—we could see where the rrôn had gone through your suite to get to the Vodi, but we do not know how he found her, or how all of us failed to protect her."

Lauren thought about what might have happened had Jake been in that room when the rrôn came through, and fear slammed her in the gut so hard her mouth filled with saliva, and she thought she would puke.

She would have been there, too, of course, but . . .

She closed her eyes and murmured, "Saved by your father again."

"Hunter?" Birra asked. "Are you unwell?"

Lauren waved away his concern. "Molly's dead again, and a rrôn has the necklace. But we still have some options."

"Options?" Birra asked, sounding suddenly the slightest bit hopeful. "We have options?"

"A few. We aren't out of the game yet, not by a long shot."

Birra suddenly seemed to realize that she and Jake were alone. "Did you get any good news from the gods about either Molly's soul or your . . . loved one?"

Lauren didn't look at him. "No." Then she shrugged.

"Well—a little good news for Molly. I hope I get to give it to her."

She turned away from him and blinked back tears. She didn't want him to see her weakness. People whose job it was to fight off the annihilation of planets didn't have the luxury of public tears.

Copper House

Lauren stared at Seolar across a drafting table in his book-cluttered workroom. She held Jake, who had fallen asleep clinging to her and whose breath now blew against the side of her head. At about thirty pounds, he was heavy enough that she noticed his weight—and she had never been more grateful for the twinge between her shoulder blades in her life.

"The gods did not favor your quest?" Seolar asked.

"To put it mildly. The Molly who is there has disavowed any relationship to the one who is still here. But I have news for Molly."

Seolar gave Birra a panicked look, and Birra said, "I told her."

Seolar cleared his throat. "She *isn't* still here."

Lauren looked around the room for a place to sit. She ended up shoving a few books to one end of a bench and settling on the other end. "I know that. I know what happened to her, I know the rrôn has the necklace."

"So it's all over. We have lost. My people are doomed to the depredations of the old gods, your people will see the destruction of their world in their lifetime—"

Lauren closed her eyes. She was too tired for all of this—too tired for the despair of other people, too tired to keep fighting. It would be so easy just to give up and go home, to wait for the end to come. But she had a responsibility to her son to keep going; how she felt meant less than nothing. She held up the hand that wasn't holding Jake. "Whoa. Wait a minute. Don't get carried away; we don't know anything of the sort."

Seolar gave her a look of disbelief. "The necklace is gone. If he took it off her before he killed her, she won't be coming back. If he didn't, then surely he has destroyed the necklace by now."

Lauren said, "You might be right. We might have already lost. But we can't just *assume* we've lost. We have to *know*. I think I ought to do what I can to find her and get her back."

Seolar seemed completely lost in his grief. He just waved a hand as if pushing the suggestion away. Lauren, watching him, thought something about his behavior wasn't right. "Did you have something to do with this?"

He looked up and actually at her for the first time since Birra showed her into the room. "What?"

"Did you have something to do with the fact that the rrôn got in here? That she was killed, that the necklace is gone— is any of this your fault?"

Unblinking eyes stared into Lauren's and a voice like Death on a bad day said, "Of *course* it's my fault. Every bit of it. I brought her here against her will, I gave her the necklace knowing that it would make her a target to the worst dark gods in the worldchain, I lied to her about what the necklace did so that she would wear it, I let her think that I could protect her when I couldn't, I broke her trust . . ." He broke eye contact and turned away, and Lauren heard him say, "I didn't love her enough."

"Do you love her?"

"Yes. Of course I loved her. I loved *her*. Molly. I know I love the woman she was. When I see the . . . woman . . . that came back, I hunger for her, but at the same time, I am . . . I am in some way repelled. She both is and is not the woman I love, and this knowledge is a serpent that devours my heart from the inside, and keeps me awake nights with the sound of its gnawing. I can't look at her the same way. Do I betray the real Molly if I love the creature that is now Vodi? Do I betray a woman who loves me still because she is not the woman she once was?"

He turned to Lauren. "It's all darkness. Everything inside of me is darkness, and I do not think there is a place left where the light can get in. The future is gone, the present is death, the past was all foolish hopefulness without reason for hope."

Lauren stroked the back of Jake's head, and he shifted in his sleep, moving closer to her and draping his arms around her neck. "No," Lauren said. "I don't accept that. And now you're going to quit? Let evil win because you don't have the courage or the will to fight it? Let billions die—my people, and eventually yours? Is that right, Seolar? We've both lost people we love, but you—who have more of the one you love left than I do—are just going to throw up your hands in despair?" She rose, clutching Jake, staggering a bit as she tried to keep her balance. "You don't love her enough, or you love her the wrong way, you're having a bad day and you're all bruised inside, so you abandon your duty? How you *feel* is justification for the death of worlds, is it?"

Lauren headed for the door. "When you start thinking again, come talk to me. People who base world-changing decisions on their feelings instead of their thoughts aren't worthy of the people for whom they make those decisions."

She eased her way through the door and told Birra, "Take me to my room. I'm going to have to sleep before I go after her. I don't know when I last slept, but it was before I left, whenever that was. The floor looks like it's rolling."

"You're going after Molly?"

Lauren looked sidelong at him. "You, too, Birra?"

He didn't answer her for a moment. "Me too, what?"

"You think we should all just roll over and quit?"

He said, "I think we lost. I think it is all over for us—for my people, for your world. But if you think differently, I'll follow you through hell to try to save whatever we can."

Lauren studied him, and finally said, "I've already been through hell once this week. Let's see if we can find a better way to get where we need to go."

In the suite they gave her, with the goroths tucked into corners and hidden from even the sharpest eyes, and with guards outside the door and guards in the secret passageways, Lauren tucked Jake into the bed and climbed in beside him. Exhaustion weighted her eyes to the point that she could keep them open for only a few seconds before they slid shut again. But her mind raced.

She kept losing Brian. She kept having her hopes dashed; he would be waiting for her at the end of her life, but whatever they had in the afterlife would not be what they'd shared as a husband and wife on Earth. She'd wanted *that*, and she couldn't have it. Lying on clean, soft sheets in the darkness with her little son nestled tightly against her, Lauren finally realized that she had to give up the dream of getting Brian back. Every wife who had a husband she loved and lost would do anything to get him back—but there came a time when holding on only hurt, and didn't give anything in return. She'd passed that point.

He's waiting on you, she told herself. He'll be there. In the meantime, keep your eye on what matters. People are counting on you. Your life matters and you're not done here yet. And if you have to do it alone, you still have to do it. You don't have the luxury of quitting, because no one else is coming up behind you. No one has your back.

Even with her eyes closed, the bed still felt like it was spinning. She tried to relax. She tried to let go. But *no one has your back* kept running through her head.

Cat Creek

Pete waved to Eric and drove out of town before the sun even broke the horizon, ostensibly on his way to Charlotte to pick up Lauren. He hadn't given any disclaimers about how he might not be able to find her, he hadn't added anything to his story. For all everyone knew, he knew where she was and she would be back in Cat Creek in about four hours. Maybe five if there was traffic.

He drove through Laurinburg and got on 74, just like he was going to go to Charlotte. Instead, though, he got off again and headed north into the Sandhills from Hamlet. He took dirt roads deep into the rough woods, to a spot that he knew wasn't kept under close watch because it was simply too far out of reach, and the wider a Sentinel worked the circle when he was watching, the more astronomically impossible it became to cover the ground.

Pete didn't take chances, though. He got well off even the dirt road he'd been following, then hid the car. Then he pulled out his gate mirror—which he'd taken off his bathroom door at four in the morning and shoved into his trunk—and carefully laid it across the back seat of the car.

This, he feared, was going to be a real pain in the ass. And if he wasn't careful, he was going to blow his cover all to hell and gone.

He couldn't let himself think about that, though. So he closed his eyes and took a deep breath and told himself that everything would work out. He'd do his thing, and the universe would not stand in his way.

Pete had been to Lauren's family house in Oria. Not under the best of circumstances, granted—he'd been dragging Eric, who was dying at the time, and Pete and Lauren had been pretty sure the world was going to come to an end in a big hurry. Still, the trip had been memorable, and Pete thought he could find the old house again.

He needed to go to that house because Lauren already had a return gate set up there; in the event that he couldn't find Lauren, he would be able to get back home.

Pete crouched over the mirror, rested his fingertips on the glass, and brought his face down close enough that he could see the pupils of his eyes clearly. He stared into them, looking beyond the darkness reflected for the inside of the little house in Oria—the primitive hand-pump kitchen, the fireplace along the kitchen wall, the wood-burning stove, the hand-planed boards. He looked into the blackness in his eyes and remembered the smell of the air in Oria, and the way the forest outside the little house sounded, and the feeling of vast ancient waiting that hung around the trees.

Deep within those two dark points, green fire flashed—a little flicker, the faintest taste of pending success. He teased the fire closer, recalling folded quilts and stacked firewood, cast-iron cookware, hand-braided rugs. In his eyes, he could see the hint of the other world; then the world expanded and his reflection faded away. Beneath his fingertips, the mirror warmed. Pete felt the energy of the place between the worlds thrum and slide beneath his hands, elusive as quicksilver and utterly magical. Green fire flickered from the center of the glass outward, and when it illuminated the whole of the mirror, the sensation of touching something solid disappeared.

Pete took a deep breath and slipped one foot onto what had an instant before been a solid surface, but which was now the open gate. Then he stepped in with the other. With his legs suddenly weightless and hanging in nothingness, he had to use his arms to lower himself into the mirror. He had to pivot sideways to get his shoulders through, and ended up sliding the last of the way onto the path by holding his hands over his head and just dropping. He'd gone into swimming pools the same way, and the process was similar. Beneath both surfaces nothing was the same.

But on the fire-road that led to Oria, contentment, joy, and the touch of eternity poured into him and through him, and for the little time that he moved through the place between the worlds, he became one with the universe.

The experience never failed to move him—and it had changed him. Though he did not look forward to his eventual death, he no longer feared it. He could feel himself as part of eternity, and what claim could death have on that?

Then, of course, he reached the other side of the gate—the mirror in Lauren's family's cottage. And the infinite spit him out into darkness, dust, and the knowledge that he was in a desperate hurry. He needed to get to Copper House, but of course he had no idea how to get there from where he was.

Pete stepped out of the house and closed the door behind him. And all around him spread forest. Forest, capital F, ancient and ponderous and scary as hell—not deer-hunting woods or necking-with-a-girl woods like back on Earth. This was primeval wilderness—Little Red Riding FBI-Agent lost off the path with hungry bears and wolves and dragons all around. Pete's skin crawled. He'd been raised in the country, but he'd *liked* civilization. He'd liked cities and cars and electricity and . . . maps. Trees big around as houses—behemoths whose spreading limbs put to shame *trees* in most of the forests on Earth—spread before him in all directions as far as the eye could see. And spring had leafed out the trees enough that he didn't have any real visibility. Green. And trunks. And not a hell of a lot else.

He swore—softly but with real intensity. Even if he knew which way to go, he needed fast transportation to get him there—and he had nothing. His own two feet.

Well, he might be in the middle of the Brothers' Grimm's worst nightmare, but he had resources. He had magic—and the Sentinels had spent a fair amount of time working with him in the past week or so, just to make sure he didn't do anything unsalvageably stupid with it.

He had to remember three main points.

Control the energy he used.

Borrow rather than create whenever possible.

And do no harm.

He closed his eyes and focused on what he needed—a vehicle that would carry him straight to Copper House at the fastest possible speed, without taking any wrong turns. Something that would be unhindered by the lack of roads. Something he couldn't screw up or wreck, and something that wouldn't draw attention.

He didn't limit the shape or the size of the thing, and intentionally did not visualize a shape for it. He simply willed the right vehicle to appear, ready for his use.

He opened his eyes. Two enormous brown eyes stared into them, down a nose that, from Pete's perspective, looked as long as a railroad car.

The horse snorted, and Pete jumped.

"I *hate* horses," he muttered.

Copper House

Jake woke Lauren by trying to open her eyelids with his fingers. Since he had the three-year-old child's typical dexterity, this worked as effectively as if he had zapped her with a cattle prod.

"Jake!" she yelped, batting at his hands with her eyes tightly closed.

"Tickle me?" he asked.

She rolled over and blew a raspberry on his tummy, then tickled him until he yelled for her to stop. Then she flopped facedown on the bed, hoping he would let her go back to sleep. No such luck.

"I want something to eat," he told her. "Get up."

"Easy for you to say," she muttered. "You slept." She had no idea when she'd dropped off. Her eyelids felt like they were made of sand, though, and while the room had stopped spinning, there seemed to be a gravity anomaly surrounding the bed that made even thinking about standing up impossible. She rolled over and smiled at her son. "I don't suppose you'd consider going back to sleep for a while?"

"I want to get up. We can brush my teeth, and I can have breakfast."

"And I want to sleep."

"You sleepededed already." He'd gotten interested in the past tense recently. He had the concept of tacking the "ed" on the ends of words, but he had decided somehow that three "ed's" were better than one. She tousled his hair and sat up. He was growing up too fast. He used whole sentences, and as long as they were talking about something she knew about, he usually made sense.

"Breakfast," she said, standing up, "is overrated." She stretched, then picked him up and swung him around the room. "Okay. Let's forage."

The suite offered limited resources. They could make a sort of oatmeal concoction with the hot water from the tea set. They could eat bread with peanut butter (the peanut butter—Jif—imported from Earth).

Or they could call a servant to bring something delicious. Lauren had a hard time with the whole servant concept. It grated. But when in Rome . . .

One of the goroths—she wished she could tell just by looking which one—suddenly bolted to the door, jammed his head against it, and after an instant announced, "Master of the House has arrived. He's in the outer room. He brought the old god."

Lauren sighed. So much for seeing if she could talk someone into getting her a big plate of seasonal fruit. "Thank you," she said. "I'll get dressed and go out."

Which meant hiding in the bathroom to change. She had already grown weary of the fishbowl in which she had to live her life when in Oria. "Come on, Jake," she said. "We have to brush teeth and get our clothes on, and then we'll go get something to eat."

By the time the two of them emerged from the bathroom, someone had made the bed, opened the door, and spread a small feast on the table in the outer room.

"Breakfast!" Jake shouted, and grabbed her hand and started dragging her. Not the most dignified way to enter a room in which a prince and a god waited, but if you wanted dignity, she thought, avoiding motherhood would be an essential first step.

"Good morning," she said to Seolar. She studied the stranger, who looked like a veyâr at first glance, but was not. "I'm Lauren," she said. "And you are . . . ?"

"Impressed. I did not expect to get to meet you." He bowed. "My name is Qawar." Seolar sat in the rocking chair. Qawar stood against one wall.

"You were right," Seolar said, skipping any sort of greeting. "We cannot give up. So while you slept I talked with Qawar. He used his magic to divine what happened to Molly. He determined that the rrôn who entered this place was Baanraak—"

"Molly mentioned him," Lauren said.

"He's wicked," Qawar told her. "The worst of the dark gods by far."

"Figures," Lauren muttered.

Seolar said, "Qawar believes he divined the direction that Baanraak took, as well."

"I believe Baanraak dropped downworld, but farther than just one world. I can find a magic trail well enough, but I cannot create the gates to follow it. I do believe he still had the Vodi necklace in his possession when he left, however."

Seolar said, "Tell her what you found."

"He went to great pains to hide whatever he took with him. I could only tell that he had something he did not wish anyone else to know about or trace." Qawar frowned, and finally took a seat on the couch.

Lauren sat opposite him and let Jake get himself a pastry. Everyone else got something to eat, as well.

Qawar continued, "Baanraak had a contract with the Night Watch to kill Molly and turn over the necklace, but he seems to have left without collecting his money for the kill— and the dark gods are unhappy because he did not present them with the Vodi necklace so they could destroy it."

Lauren nodded, trying to put these pieces together. They didn't fit. "Why would he take the necklace and go downworld with it? Is there something he could do with it?"

Qawar shrugged. "She will come back," he said after a moment. He took a bite of the pastry and chewed it thoughtfully. "Perhaps her first death did not satisfy him. Perhaps he wants to kill her a few more times before he finally destroys her for good."

Lauren definitely did not like Qawar.

"But there's no reason why he couldn't have destroyed it here and made the . . . Night Watch? . . . happy with him, if he had been so inclined?"

"That seems the most reasonable course of action," Seolar said.

"If he's doing unreasonable things," she said, "that's not necessarily bad for us. Anything that keeps him from destroying the necklace works in our favor. If nothing else, it buys us time." She closed her eyes. She'd been able to feel Molly's presence when both of them were on the same planet. Even after Molly's death and resurrection, Lauren still felt the connection. Lauren wondered if she opened a series of gates downworld, one world at a time, would she be able to feel Molly's presence on the correct world?

That seemed to her an option worth trying.

After at least a few bites of breakfast. She discovered that she was famished and thirstier than she'd ever been in her life, and she realized abruptly that she hadn't eaten anything since she left for the afterlife.

"How long was I gone?" she asked Seolar suddenly.

"Two full days."

That explained a lot.

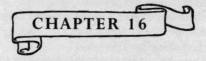

CHAPTER 16

Through Niiadaa to Dalchi

BAANRAAK MADE a neat escape, managing to avoid any confrontation at all with Rr'garn or his cronies. He felt quite pleased with this achievement; the pleasure he got from it, however, struck him as odd. Fherghass had burned emotion out of Baanraak when he began training Baanraak to be his heir. At least that had been the theory—that repeated deaths and resurrections would remove from Baanraak all the taint of his lost soul and his lost life, and make him into the perfect, emotionless hunter, capable of anything.

For centuries on end, that was the way it had worked. Baanraak devoured, hunted, slaughtered without guilt or pain or regret, and became in all ways Fherghass' perfect complement. Fherghass pointed him toward a goal, and Baanraak moved the world to accomplish the goal. Fherghass, on a whim, challenged the Master of the Night Watch, and killed her, and with himself in place as the new god of death, placed Baanraak at his right hand.

When Fherghass eventually grew weary and lost his taste for worlds and death, Baanraak destroyed him, as they had agreed he would if such a thing came to pass, and Baanraak ascended to the throne of the dark gods in Fherghass's place. In due time, Baanraak grew bored with the game. Unlike his predecessor, however, he had not grown bored with existence, so he did what no one had ever done before; he stepped down from the Mastery of the Night Watch, letting his underlings fight it out for the top spot. Then he dropped out of sight. He'd remained a mystery to the Night Watch, but one they respected—or at least feared—right up to the present.

He sighed, thinking his flagrant betrayal had surely ended their willingness to ignore his existence. Ah, well. If they pursued him, he would destroy them. Baanraak spotted a nice natural stone arch in a ravine beneath him and set his wings. He soared over the area, scouting it carefully. No one around—he didn't remember precisely what sort of intelligent life Niiadaa had, but he knew it was quadrupedal and smallish and mammalian—goddamned mammals were everywhere—and nothing of the sort waited below. He dropped to the ground and studied the stone arch. He liked it; worn by water through this barren patch of land where the brush hung on for dear life and even his sensitive nose had a hard time sniffing out a hint of moisture, it wouldn't draw attention to itself. It would absorb the energy traces from the gate he made and clear away most of them within a day or two. Someone of his caliber might be able to find his tracks if they knew where to look, but among the dark gods, none of his caliber existed.

Baanraak smiled a little. This was the last world he had to move out of—he thought that Cadwa, Povreack, and this world would prove to be sufficiently confusing to even the best tracker. And Dalchi was a ripe, lively world, still bubbling with untouched, un-tampered-with, unshielded natural energy. Locating him and anything he did against that sort of background would be next to impossible. He'd have the time he needed to train the Vodi. And to figure out what he wanted after he did so.

He cast the gate, using the arch as its boundaries, and when the green fire gleamed like a vertical sheet of water in front of him, he peered through to the other side. He needed a good, deep cave in a warm, sunny place—not too much

rain, big slabs of flat rock, and all around him, terrain rich
in life, in hot raw meat and good flesh. She would require
the flesh and bone to rebuild not just one but a multitude of
bodies; to feed the Vodi necklace and summon flesh to her
contained will, he was going to have to do a lot of hunting.
Nothing like what Fherghass had needed to do, of course.
But Fherghass had been willing to expend years in reshaping
Baanraak. Baanraak found himself impatient. And he didn't
know why.

Boredom. Impatience. Excitement. Pleasure.

Those should have only been words to him—concepts
that he understood, but not that he experienced. Instead,
those emotions moved through him like dark water through
a swamp, stirring things below the surface where he could
not see, and making subterranean changes in him. He could
not point to the emotions' origins, nor trace their passage,
but he could feel them—and the strange currents they set up
inside of him, as well. He had lived long in the desert of
emotion, and he had appreciated the purity and the austerity
of the place. This verdant swamp of feeling in which he now
soaked seemed a deadly betrayal.

He could not put a talon on the change—either on what it
was or on when it had happened.

He *wanted* things now, though, and he had been free from
want of any sort for time out of mind.

What did he want?

He stared into the green fire and his mind wandered. He
caught visions of his home world—a world long since
burned to cinders with no survivors except those who had
fled—and their descendants. For just a moment he recalled
the warmth of his own sun, and the shape of familiar rocks
beneath his belly as he basked in air that smelled right—and
the air on other worlds never smelled right—and for just a
moment yearning tugged at him.

Silly, really; he hadn't been fresh out of the shell for so
many thousands of years that he had long ago lost count.
He'd lost count of the number of worlds he'd slid down, and

he knew he should feel nothing for those old times. And yet he did, when at one point in his existence, he had been able to watch the destruction of his world and everything in it, and feel nothing but the temporary satiation as he fed off the deaths of innocents.

Strange. Baanraak shook it off and looked over the world on the other side of the gate until he found an ideal site: a fine rock outcropping with a sharp overhang that led into a wide-mouthed cave, and below it, plains dotted by beasts of all sorts and sizes. Good enough. He moved through the gate, hating the energy of the path between the worlds and the way it twanged against his skin. When he was young, before his first death, he had traversed the gates with elation; the green fire sang to him and revived him. Now, made of different stuff and kept breathing by an energy that was the antithesis of the green fire of life, he found each passage an ordeal.

Worth the price, however. He tumbled out the other end, grateful to be at last at his destination. He clambered to the top of the highest slab of rock and sprawled over it, spreading his wings beneath a sun that felt too cold and too distant. He had a bit of time to drowse and recuperate before he started hunting—he could cook the discomfort caused by passage through the green fire out of his system. He could clear any current occupants out of the cave beneath him later—better, he could kill them and throw them into the meat pile that would feed the Vodi.

And the Vodi . . . Baanraak sliced through the cord with which he'd bound the bag containing the Vodi necklace, and loosed it from his gold piercing-ring. He hooked a talon into the bag, pulled the necklace out, and studied it. An old god with both tremendous power and exquisite taste, something of a rarity, had given this particular piece full value, and a bit more. The chain itself was thick and smooth, with each link overlapping the next in such a fashion that the individual links almost disappeared. The result looked like a heavy strand of liquid gold. The medallion, not a feature of much resurrection work, used a ring of faceted sapphires around a central figure in high relief—a winged woman rising from a stormy sea.

He guessed that the piece originated during the Second Dathian School's primacy, which would have put it during his reign as Master of the Night Watch. That was the only school that worked gemstones into resurrection pieces, increasing both their potency and their fragility—an uneven trade-off in Baanraak's mind. It wasn't a Dathian piece, however. Their resurrection work had been characterized by a uniform darkness of mood—and emphasis on symbols of the impermanence of the physical form. They'd run to skulls, vipers, weapons, and dying figures on their medallions. This, with its figure springing unscathed from the heart of turmoil, offered an odd sort of hope.

He felt the hope within it, too. It had all the darkness that any resurrection work had; an inescapable taint of death accrued from creating immortality from the energy of destruction, and this used all the regular magic. But there was more. He held the necklace up to his chin, to the sensing pits there, and closed his eyes.

The hum of the thing ran through his body, and his sensing pits sorted out the various energies and categorized them. The difference lay partly in the sapphires, through which odd contrary energies ran. They gathered light and quickness and fire in them, and held on to passion the way large rocks held heat long after sunset.

If he prised the stones out, he would go far toward removing from the Vodi her yearning for the life she had lost. But in doing so, he could also damage her. He might end up destroying the thing about her that he found most useful.

He laid the necklace on the rock, tucked beneath his long jaw. He lay there with his eyes closed, and after a while he could feel her stirring inside.

Baanraak stilled mind and breath and shielded himself from sight, then he lay there, communing with a mind held in place by gold and gemstones and the magic of chaos. He felt keen intelligence, ferocity, rage, desire, hatred, passion, hope . . . and love. The shape of her mind washed over him, and he wound his way through it, careful in his slow movements not to disturb her thoughts in his passing or alert her to his presence.

She was more *in* the necklace than she had any business being. The resurrection spell brought back as much of what had been as it could salvage, but it wasn't supposed to permit any sort of awareness in the state between death and return. Artists and gods had spent breath and fury in heated arguments over the advantages or horrors of pursuing wakefulness within the gold; in the end, everyone had decided it was impossible to create such a state, and that had been, Baanraak had always believed, the end of the matter. The craftsmen made their things of beauty, the gods imbued them with power, and the necklaces, bands, and rings went out to the deserving, those who had curried favor, those who craved immortality at any price.

Molly, something said inside his head. *I am Molly.*

Baanraak opened one eye. Apparently not everyone had accepted the limitations of the medium. Apparently not everyone had let the matter lie.

He lifted his head from the necklace and tucked his long snout under his wing, to the hidden fold of skin just at the back of one wing where his own resurrection piece burrowed into his flesh. His was a large, heavy ring pierced through his skin, a ring that had been placed and then worked closed so that it no longer had a seam or opening. When last something had managed to kill him, he'd resurrected around the ring already embedded in his flesh.

He laid his chin atop the ring, feeling it through the sensing pits and trying to figure out the differences he felt.

The two summoning spells gave off only slightly different energies. They were, in fact, much more similar than he'd expected them to be. His own ring, he felt sure, had once been completely free of that upbeat taint that marked the Vodi's. Molly's. He would have sworn on it, had he been able to think of anything sufficiently sacred to bind his word.

Yet the taint was there, clear in hers, clouded in his. Unmistakably present, however.

He wondered if he'd been the target of some long-distance spell, some clever joke, some trick. He wondered who might have carried out such a deed, or how they might have accomplished it, since once the dark gods cast their spells, nothing was supposed to be able to alter them in even the slightest degree. The wizards had guaranteed the quality of their products with their lives, and Baanraak had taken those oaths as bond.

Now that all the makers had died, he didn't think he could hope to collect on any oaths. Unfortunately. He wondered what had gone wrong, though.

He untucked head from wing and put his chin back on the Vodi necklace. Then he closed his eyes and tried to savor the warmth of the sun on his skin and the heat of the sun-baked rock beneath his belly. He focused on the soothing smell of the sandstone. He blocked out the Vodi's thoughts—he did not want their disconcerting intrusion creeping into his own. Everything he thought he ought to be able to count on now shifted beneath his wings, as if the terrain of his reality were no more secure than gliding on updrafts on a cloudy day.

Smells—the scent of sandstone; and beneath it grassy plains, the scent of hot flesh and living blood everywhere, rich and delicious; his own scent, which he rarely noticed but did consider mildly earthy and slightly spicy; something not quite right about the scents. His nose over the Vodi necklace—Baanraak had never considered its scent, but now he laid one nostril along it and inhaled slowly and deeply, with his mouth half-open to make sure he caught all the different smells.

Metals gave off little to work with, but his nose could discern by scent the difference in a bit of pumice stone before and after dragging a bit of copper over it. He had a fine instrument and he put it to work. When he had the shape of the scent clearly in his mind, he went through the same procedure with his ring.

And when he had checked that, he tested one of the little

ingots of pure gold he'd brought with him, and then one of the ingots of pure silver.

He stood, swearing, the duplicity of ancient wizards bringing every profanity he recalled from a hundred thousand years to his tongue.

Silver. The gold in the Vodi necklace had been mixed with silver. The gold in his own ring had, as well. Gold drew the energy of chaos and fed on the vibrations of death. Silver drew the energy of order, and gained its power from the vibrations of life. Mixing the two in a piece of resurrection jewelry could only create disaster, as energies and forces battled for control of the mind held within.

Baanraak looked warily at the necklace that lay glittering beneath the cool sun. He could not know that she would respond correctly to his training. He could not even count on his own responses anymore.

Copper House

Lauren had to leave Jake and his toys in the suite with the goroths. She wanted him to be with her, but she didn't dare let him play in the safe room again.

"Look, puppy-boy," she said, "Doggie will bring you downstairs to eat with me, and you'll sleep with me at night. We'll still see each other. Okay?"

Jake didn't understand. He had never been without her. He didn't know she was going to walk out of the room and leave him—and he wasn't *going* to understand, either. Frankly, Lauren wasn't doing too well with the whole idea, either. Jake was everything she had in the world. How could she leave him in this dangerous place, away from her? But how could she take him, knowing that when she slipped into trance, he could be the only one with godlike powers in the room.

He sat on the floor with his cars and said, "Okay, Mama, play with me. You be the truck."

She hugged him. He wouldn't be three forever, and he wouldn't want her to be the truck forever. She felt the impatience of Seolar and the old god, Qawar, but she would not let herself be pushed.

She was going to find Molly; she was going to risk her life to set things right. Everything could go wrong, though, and she would not let the last time she saw her son be the time she told him she didn't have time to play with him.

"I'll be the truck three times," she said. "And then you'll have to play with Doggie. Okay?"

Jake grinned at her. They sat on their knees opposite each other, and for a few minutes they pushed their cars at each other across the floor. Each time they missed, Jake would shout, "Oh. Missed me!" Each time they crashed, he just laughed.

They ran the cars back and forth at each other quite a few more than three times, but when Lauren finally said, "Last time, monkey boy," Jake accepted it. As long as he knew in advance they would have a limit, he was good about it. The last time, Lauren managed a pretty spectacular crash that sent his car flying, and he laughed so hard he shook. She loved to hear him laugh—and since everything had gotten strange in their lives, she rarely did. She kissed him on the forehead and said, "Time to play with Doggie."

Lauren slipped out of the door once Jake and Doggie were involved in their game; trailing Seolar, Birra, Qawar, and a handful of guards in her wake, she headed down to the copper-free safe room. She felt like she was leading a parade, and she had to resist the temptation to turn around and tell the whole lot of them just to go away. The goroths, at least, would be useful. Maybe she could send the rest off for food when she got hungry. She tried not to think about the immensity of the project.

"Why are we doing this?" Qawar asked.

She bit her tongue and refrained from questioning that "we." She said, "*I* am going to open a series gate and start searching downworld for any markers that Molly has passed that way."

"You're going to search a whole planet? Please."

"If Baanraak has gone farther than one world, I'm going to end up searching *several* planets. My sister and I share a connection that should simplify the process, but I don't expect locating it to be quick or easy. I'm going to find her—"

"You're not going to find her," Qawar muttered under his breath. "Not an old god born could do what you hope to do. This is just building hope for nothing."

Lauren pretended she didn't hear that, "—but it's going to take all my concentration to do it, and some fairly heavy-duty magic. I'm not searching one world at a time. As I said, I'm going to open a series gate, and put out feelers for her in a handful of worlds at once. I don't need to know which way she went. I just need to know where she is."

Birra and Seolar exchanged glances, and Seolar asked, "What do you mean by a series gate?"

Lauren thought the phrase itself summed it up pretty well, but she shrugged and said, "I'll open a small gate that runs through about seven or eight worlds at the same time—as many as I can comfortably hold open."

A gasp from Qawar, loud enough that the guards, the Imallin, and Birra all turned to look. "You can do that?"

"Yeah." The question surprised her. She didn't think of old gods as having limits, but they did. Most of them weren't gateweavers, and most of them really had only a vague concept of how the magic they used worked. They were, she thought, a lot like the average computer user back on Earth, who knew how to use a couple of programs but couldn't have created a program from scratch to save his life.

And she was, she thought, a programmer. Top-flight, though still learning new tricks. She was about to try one of them.

She turned her attention to the mirror.

She'd given this a lot of thought—it seemed that the trick in opening gates into a series of downworlds and keeping them open at the same time would be to make each gate small enough that nothing could get through it to close it, but large enough to be usable. She figured all she really needed was a thread into each world, connecting all of them to the mirror, which would serve as a hub. But the time frame she needed might be days, and tending multiple linked gates for days would get wearing. More wearing if she had an audience, but she figured they'd get tired and go away after a while. At least she hoped they would.

Lauren did not expect to be able to feel Molly's presence anywhere immediately. She and her sister had a powerful magical bond that linked them—but Lauren didn't know if that bond existed through the Vodi necklace, or through the body it would regenerate for Molly. If she had to wait for Molly to resurrect, she could be in for a long haul.

She knelt in front of the mirror, closed her eyes, rested her fingertips on the glass, and focused on the worlds suspended beneath Oria in the worldchain. She got through to the first one surprisingly fast—it felt sharp and green and vibrant. She thought about the sad, dark feel Earth had to it, and about the poisonous feel of the upworld Kerras, and she wanted to cry. All of the worlds should feel like the one below. Cadwa, one of the old gods had told her. She opened a pinpoint gate into Cadwa—in theory, a gate so small that events around it wouldn't disturb it, and through that gate she set about creating a seeking spell that would ring within the room if any sign of Molly appeared.

Lauren drew into herself, sliding into a place of utter silence where nothing but the fire of the universes touched her. She put everything she knew of Molly, and every bit of the magical pull that existed between them, into her spell, shaping it in her mind as a ray of light curved to the shape of the world it would circle. She put herself into it—her senses, her emotions, and her urgent need to find her sister quickly, and at last she felt the spell take with a satisfying little buzz. She sent it seeking across the surface of the world, hunting with as much speed and thoroughness as she could manage. It raced away from her like a wild thing, and as soon as it was free, she slid back from her focused concentration and opened her eyes. She was incredibly thirsty; she still had plenty of energy left, but her knees were killing her. Going to have to get a chair before she did the next gate and spell. She decided to take a break for a minute or two, just to send someone after a drink for her and for something comfortable to sit on, and turned her attention back to her audience, only to discover that Qawar and most of the guards were gone.

Seolar sat in a corner, his eyes closed. Birra stood beside him, watchful as ever.

"Birra? What happened?" Lauren asked.

Birra gave her a small smile. "Watching you turned out to be not quite the adventure Qawar was seeking. I believe he gave up after the first hour."

Seolar frowned and studied her thoughtfully. "I had never considered this before, but . . . I don't think he's a very . . . *talented* old god."

Lauren didn't comment on that. She'd reached that conclusion earlier, but it had seemed impolitic to say so. She focused on something else Seolar had said. "Hour?" She was puzzled. "How long was I . . . ?"

"You haven't moved in nearly three hours," Birra said.

She stared at him, unable to comprehend that. "Shit." No wonder her knees hurt.

Seolar asked, "Anything?"

"Not yet. I just finished the first world. I have a long way to go."

He nodded, leaned his head back, and closed his eyes. "Forgive me," he said, "but I have had no sleep, and I fear it is catching up with me."

Lauren said, "Sure. You don't need to stay here, you know. If I find anything, I'll send someone for you immediately. But it could be days."

He closed his eyes for a moment, and sighed. "Yes, of course. I had hoped for some quick news, but there can be nothing quick about this, can there?"

"Not unless I get lucky."

"I fear we have far exceeded our quota of luck."

"Yeah," Lauren said. "You're probably right." She crouched a little and stood again, flexing her knees. "Would you mind sending someone down here with some water for me, some sandwiches, a chair—maybe a cot or something that I can sleep on. And . . ." She realized three hours had worked on her in other ways. ". . . where's the closest bathroom? I'm not going to be able to leave here for quite some time."

"There are no bathrooms on this level," Seolar said. "Nor on the level above this."

Lauren stared at him, then sighed. "You mind if I remodel in here just a bit?"

"What do you mean?"

"Do you mind if I do some magic to make this place livable while I'm stuck here?"

"Well . . . no. Of course not. Do whatever you need to do."

What she needed to do was make a bathroom. Magic flush, she thought, so she wouldn't have to worry about plumbing or water lines. And while she was at it, a nice little kitchenette, and a table where she and Jake could eat meals together, and a refrigerator, and a comfy couch and a double bed because Jake sprawled. Someone that small should not take up so much room when he slept, but Jake did. She could also add a bookshelf and some good books—she anticipated a lot of waiting. Some natural light, though not a window or even a skylight—she didn't want to do something that would breach security. A place for Jake to come and play on warm, soft, well-padded carpet. And something other than damned gray-stone dungeon walls.

She closed her eyes and mentally filled the space with a bright, cheery, open room that existed within the space of the current walls, all one space except for a little bathroom with a toilet, a sink and a shower behind a door in one corner. Magic-powered electric lights; a big square of glass that looked like a picture window inset into the wall behind the futon that would open into a bed, but that showed not what was outside—no doubt dirt and rocks and worms—but what lay outside in the forest beyond the village; a shelf for linens, filled with fluffy towels and flannel sheets in bright colors. A carpeted floor everywhere but in the kitchen and the bathroom, and clean white tile there. An armoire full of blue jeans, sweatshirts, and clean underwear. And as an afterthought, bunklike sleeping spaces for the goroths. No one was going to let Jake sneak to a mirror in the middle of the night again—if he managed to squirm loose from her arm around him, the goroths would be keeping watch.

She willed this into existence, and opened her eyes to bright sunshine pouring into a room with creamy yellow walls and thick carpet. Everyone oohed and ahhed except for Lauren, who only heard the call of the bathroom.

When she came back out, she tried the kitchen tap. Cold, clear water came out. Just to be on the safe side, she added a filter.

She knew she needed to consider the repercussions of doing so much magic . . . but this was, at least, constructive magic. It would have effects back on Earth, but she could hope they would be effects that would do good things for others.

She checked the fridge. Nice and cold, but empty. She considered using magic to fill it, but decided to leave that up to her hosts.

Seolar and Birra were going over the place with interest. "It's very plain," Seolar said at last. "There is no ornamentation anywhere."

"Utilitarian," Birra agreed. "Not ugly, precisely, but . . ." He shrugged.

Lauren said, "I just wanted something comfortable. I'm not all that comfortable with frills. I wanted clothes that felt right, a place where I didn't have to worry about putting my feet up on the furniture, and . . . lots of sunlight."

Seolar said, "You created a forest and sky underground just so you could have light in here?"

Lauren said, "No. I just have the window set to send me images of a place a few miles from here. That way I get my sunlight but we don't have any weak spaces in the walls that the bad guys could use." She tapped the glass. "Behind this, there is nothing but stone and dirt."

She took one of the two padded kitchen chairs and set it in front of the mirror. "I'm going to make the next gate and seeker spell," she said. "I imagine it will take as long as the last one—maybe a little longer." She said, "Would you please make sure the fridge is full of food for me by the time I'm done? And someone to get Jake and the goroths as soon as I finish. I want to be able to spend my free time with him."

Seolar said, "It will be done. But you are truly not going to leave this place until you find her?"

"Or until I'm sure she can't be found."

"I'll make sure you have the best of everything."

A guard appeared in the doorway, looked around with evident surprise, then approached Seolar. The two of them whispered, both of them looked apprehensively at Lauren, and Lauren decided she could wait another minute or two before she got too deeply to work.

Seolar made a hand gesture to the guard, who scurried out of the safe room at high speed. When the guard was gone, Seolar turned back to Lauren.

"You have a visitor," he said.

Copper House

Pete had to admit the crossbows and spears aimed at his back as he and his military escort marched through Copper House sort of ruined his chance to sightsee. And when they left the main hallways and started heading down into the bowels of the place, his skin started to crawl. He wondered if the veyâr intended to murder him and bury him in a sub-basement, then keep Willard the Wonder Horse for themselves. Willard would be worth committing murder for, he supposed. The ride to Copper House had been both incredibly smooth and impossibly fast.

His arrival left more to be desired though. He debated fleeing. Debated fighting. Finally, though, he just marched and hoped to hell they really were taking him to see Lauren, as they said they were.

The little group finally hit literal rock bottom. They marched over stone floors, through stone foundations, with torches lighting the way—then his guards shoved him through a massive door into a room that looked like something off the cover of House Beautiful.

"Pete!" Lauren said, staring at him over the counter of a little kitchenette. Her face lit up.

That hadn't been the reaction he'd expected at all. She seemed to think better of it immediately afterward and started looking all worried and serious. She asked him, "How the hell did you find me? And what are you doing here?" But he held that first delighted smile tight and thought, No take-backs. And no do-overs. That one counted.

"We have a problem," he told her.

"No *shit*," she said.

"No. *We* have a problem. You and me. Old gods are evacuating Earth in droves. Eric wants you back right away—everything could be getting ready to blow up, and the Sentinels are going to need you to help deal with whatever is going wrong. And I covered for you when Eric got suspicious about your absence—told him I'd checked out your story and it was true—so now he thinks I'm in Charlotte bringing you back."

"You . . . lied for me? You knew I'd lied to you?"

He grinned at her. "You're a lousy liar. I knew the second I saw your key ring that something was wrong. But I got your back. I figured if you took off like that to come here, it had to be for a good reason."

She was staring at him—eyes wide and startled, something odd in her expression. She tipped her head to one side and said, "What did you say?"

"I said if you came here, you had a good reason for doing it."

"Before that."

"That I lied for you . . . that you're a terrible liar . . . that I got your back . . ."

Click. Something in her eyes changed, and the weirdest little smile came over her face, and she shook her head. "It's a funny universe," she said. Then, without explaining what the hell that little business had been about, she said, "Can you lie for me a little longer? I know there's a problem, and I'm here working on it. And I'm the only one who can. One of the rrôn killed Molly, and stole the Vodi necklace, and now I'm trying to get her, and it, back. The two of us think we can reverse the problems on Earth."

Pete closed his eyes and pinched the bridge of his nose. Okay. He hadn't even considered the possibility that Lauren had just snapped. She had been under a lot of pressure, but . . . fuck. He got out his cop voice—the reasonable one that worked best on people who were right on the edge and carrying big guns—and said, "Lauren . . . honey . . . Molly has been dead for a while. We all went to her funeral with you. Remember? Why don't you come for a walk with me, and we'll go get Jake, and go home, and we can talk about this. I'm sorry—"

She gave him a cockeyed grin and held up a hand to cut him off. "That's very good. Nice tone, nice delivery. I'm impressed. But I'm not cracking up. The Vodi necklace—that big hunk of gold Molly had around her neck when she died the first time—is a magical artifact. It brings the wearer back from death."

Pete remembered back to the day Eric got shot, and to Lauren's panicked rush to get him out of the hospital and through the gate into Oria before he died. "I thought you said bringing people back from the dead was . . . bad."

"It is. Well, if you or I did it, it would be. The Vodi necklace keeps a lot of who Molly was intact, so that what comes back is mostly her. It isn't perfect. And every time she dies, she loses a little of who she was. But . . . well . . . there may be some good news there, if we can get her back. Maybe. But first we have to get her back."

"So she already . . . came back . . . once. And you saw her."

"Everyone here saw her. She got here the day you were over at the house—the day I left. She was real, she and I have work to do, and we may be able to carry out our parents' plans."

"Only she's dead. Again."

"Yeah. For a while."

"Eeuw. That's . . . eeuw. Has to suck to be her."

Lauren raised an eyebrow. "I'd guess so. Anyway—can you lie for me a little longer?"

"You're working on the problem now? The one that the old gods are leaving Earth to escape?"

"Yes."

"I can lie for you. What should I tell them?"

"Obviously something a lot more convincing than what I told you. I'm *not* a good liar."

Pete considered that for a moment. "Well, I am."

And again she gave him that strange little smile. "Maybe not quite as good as you think. So be careful, okay? If they think they can't trust you, they'll eat you in a New York minute."

"That fast?" Pete sighed. "I guess I'll go, then. See if I can't come up with a convincing lie between now and the time I drive home. When you get back, you have to see me first so we can get our stories straight, though. Deal?"

She laughed a little. "Deal. And I hope . . ." She turned and glanced at the green-glowing mirror in the corner, and shook her head. "Doesn't matter. I hope I make it back to Cat Creek so we get a chance to get our stories straight."

He realized she was in danger, and that the only thing he could do right at that moment was get out of her way. He didn't like that. When he got back to Cat Creek, he would be doing something useful—but not anything that would keep her safe. He found that he very much wanted to keep her safe.

He went over, hugged her, and said, "Take care, okay. And I'll see you when you get home."

She nodded, and gave him a hard squeeze. "Thanks."

The whole long, convoluted trip back to Cat Creek, he found himself somewhere between despair and walking on air.

CHAPTER 17

Copper House

LAUREN, finishing the next gate, discovered that Jake had already arrived and was teaching Doggie to play Superman. Jake, red silk swirling behind him, stomped like he was trying to bring the roof down. Superheroes did not walk lightly. And he put his hands on his hips and glowered. Superheroes never smiled, either.

"Break time," she said. She gathered Jake up and hugged him. Outside her magic window, the sun sparkled through the trees high overhead, and Lauren realized she was ravenous. "Hey, monkey-boy, come help me make lunch."

Jake gave her the Superhero look, and said, "I am Superman."

"That's fine. But Superman can either help make lunch, or he can get his butt kicked by Supermom."

"You will not kick my butt."

Lauren looked at her son sidelong and said, "Say, 'All right, Mama, I'll help you make lunch.' "

He caught the tone of her voice and repeated the sentence word for word. When she turned away, he muttered, "I *am* Superman."

But he behaved himself. The two of them made lunch for themselves and the goroths, and when everyone was done eating, she rested briefly over a cup of hot green tea. She hugged and kissed Jake, turned him over to the goroths, and dropped back into communion with the paths between the worlds, the gates, and magic.

Dalchi

"You're going to like it here. It's a good warm spot, right in the sunlight, and I got you plenty of meat—meat makes it all go faster." Baanraak dug in front of the mouth of the cave he'd chosen—he'd found a soft, humus-rich patch of sweet earth that he could guard easily. Now he flung dirt with his forelegs like a dog digging in a garden, until he had a hole about seven feet deep and about equally wide.

He looked at the Vodi necklace that gleamed in the sun on the little rock to his right. "For the next little while you're going to hate me. But eventually you'll be free of emotion, and hatred will burn away with love—and you'll become so much clearer. And so much more dangerous."

He grabbed a carcass, stripped of its skin and entrails, and dumped it into the hole, then he dropped his forelegs onto the carcass heavily and repeatedly, talons splayed, while the bones crunched and the flesh tore, until the dead thing was little more than a bloody pulp. He scraped a layer of dirt over the carcass, walked around the circle once to study his result, added a bit more dirt, then threw in another skinned carcass and repeated the jumping-up-and-down process. Another layer of dirt, another carcass. And another. And another. Finally, he placed the necklace carefully in the middle of the hole, and covered it with the rest of the dirt, packing it down tightly.

When he was done, he had a mound in front of his cave that he could watch and protect. She'd re-form quickly—he'd softened the meat well, had packed the dirt tightly, and made the cover shallow enough that she'd break the surface when her new body was ripe.

"I'll kill you quickly," Baanraak told the mound of dirt.

"Waking up like that is gruesome—but you have to wake all the way up before killing you again does any good. Otherwise, everything is still there the next time the body forms. I should be able to see your eyes when they open though. One quick swipe when you blink the first time and we won't even have to redig the hole. You'll be able to reuse your own flesh to feed the next bodies, and that will save us time, too." He sighed and settled onto the warm earth and spread his wings to catch the sunlight. "You're small—you should be ready for your first killing in a day, certainly no more than two. This whole thing will go quickly. In thirty or forty days you should be free of every vestige of your life."

He didn't let himself think about the gemstones, about the silver that polluted the gold, about the betrayal of emotion that muddied his *own* thoughts. He'd been alive too long— had taken on some of the oldest habits of the souled. A death would purge the contamination from him. Perhaps once he finished creating Molly, she would do him that favor.

He rested his chin on the hard-packed mound he'd created and said, "It took Fherghass longer to make me, but there was more of me to tear down and rebuild each time."

He closed his eyes and let the sunlight bleed red through his eyelids. Warmth of sun, cool breeze, the rustle of leaves and the sounds of life all around him. He drifted in his thoughts, and remembered waking up packed into the earth—remembered his eyes opening into dirt, and dirt in his mouth and his nose, and the horror he felt as he discovered that his wings wouldn't work, that his legs were encased in what might as well have been stone. He could still feel his fear and his despair as he fought to free himself. Fherghass had been cruel in his method of rebuilding Baanraak; he'd never actually killed him. He had just left Baanraak encased in the ungiving earth until Baanraak died of suffocation, only to be reborn into the same horror.

"You won't suffer much," Baanraak told the mound. "Not like I did. Fherghass said that the way he made me was the best way to purify a dark god, but I found out later it wasn't the way he was made. He had it easy—strapped to a bed in a charnel house, his resurrection ring fed bodies of plague victims as it needed them. He could breath, he could see, he could move a bit, and his purifier killed him as soon as he woke up every time."

Baanraak sighed and settled himself a bit more comfortably on the ground. "Over the years I've come to the conclusion that Fherghass was either lazy or a sadistic bastard, or maybe both." He patted the mound with one taloned foreleg and managed a smile. "But I'm not. I won't let you suffer."

Cat Creek

"She and Jake had already checked out when I got there," Pete said. "I interviewed hotel staff, called around a few places, phoned the airport about plane tickets—things like that. I didn't find anything. So I was hoping she'd be back here."

Eric looked like he might stroke out. "She isn't."

"She's a responsible person. What she's doing matters to her—she's trying to save the world for her little guy as much as for everyone else combined. She isn't going to flake out on you and just disappear."

"I hate to point this out," Eric said, leaning back in his desk chair and closing his eyes, "but she *did* flake out on us and disappear. Otherwise . . ." He tapped a pen on the desk surface. "Otherwise, we would have a gateweaver here right now, when we so desperately need one."

Pete nodded. "She'll get here."

Eric studied him. "You're sure she was in Charlotte?"

Pete raised an eyebrow.

"I'm just checking," Eric said. "It isn't like we haven't had problems lately with Sentinels being places other than where they said they were, doing things other than what they said they were doing. And Lauren's parents were traitors."

"No they weren't."

"Let me rephrase. Her parents were . . . working outside the accepted role for Sentinels. They went rogue." Eric stretched and stood up and walked over to the window that looked out onto Main Street before he said anything else. "When our lives and the lives of everyone else on the planet depend on all of us working together, with one vision and one direction, going rogue is about the same as being a traitor."

The phone rang.

Eric picked it up. After a moment, he said, "Lauren? This is the worst connection I have ever heard. Where the fuck are you? We need you here now." He was quiet for a long moment, then he turned a little pale. "Oh." He stared at the phone, and listened another moment. "Oh. No, I guess you can't. I'll tell you later that taking off without telling anyone was a shitty thing to do. For now, take care of yourself, and good luck. We'll figure out something."

He put the phone back into the cradle, and looked positively sick.

Pete said, "What?"

"That was Lauren."

"I gathered that much."

"Jake's grandparents snatched him. Lauren is in pursuit."

Pete closed his eyes. "Which sort of explains her leaving in such a hurry."

"Yes."

"What the hell happened?"

"She didn't have time to say. Just that she had alerted authorities, that she was on her way to California following the grandparents, and that she would get back here as quickly as she could."

"What about our emergency?"

"People who apparently hate her kidnapped her child. We cannot expect her to drop that to get back here—there are just some things we have to learn to work around."

Pete nodded. "I hadn't actually meant I expected her to come back here with Jake missing. What I meant was, who are we going to get to fill in?"

"I don't know. It isn't like you can just run into Sears and pick up a new gateweaver. We'll start doing extra maintenance checks on all our gates to keep them in good condition. Every six hours, I think. That should keep them healthy enough not to crash. I'll start calling around to other groups—see if anyone can help us out. We'll . . . figure out something."

Pete nodded. "You're a good man, Eric," he said.

Eric raised an eyebrow. "But not a happy one."

Pete thought, You would be so much more unhappy if you knew that wasn't Lauren—that it was a bad connection from an FBI phone circling over Charlotte, with an agent I knew who, if we could get a bad enough connection, sort of sounded like Lauren. He would have to send Fred a thank-you note for putting Mariyne on a plane on such short notice and getting her to lie. Pete patted the mirror in his wallet. Nice device.

Copper House

Every world felt richer than the last. Lauren had Cadwa, Povreack, and Niiadaa gated and linked, and the power that flowed into her and the room from those three gates felt like the air on the first true spring day, turned into a liquid and injected into her veins. She felt like a kid just being in contact with such places, and she wondered how anyone could feel that much life and that much power humming through their veins and along their skin, and then intentionally poison and kill that world.

Hunger and her body's need for sleep drove her to bed at last, but she'd no more than drifted off when one of her alarm chimes rang. She lunged to the mirror, opened the gate just enough to see the spot her search spell had found, and sighed with frustration when she saw what she was looking at—a stone arch that Baanraak had almost certainly used as a gate. It was on the first world, too—Cadwa. So all it really told her was that he and Molly—or the Vodi neck-lace that would resurrect Molly, had passed that way.

She considered shutting down the spell, but left it run-ning. It didn't take that much out of her, and should Baan-raak decide to get clever and double back, she'd have a chance of finding him.

She crawled back into bed and discovered that Jake had taken over the whole sleeping surface while she was gone—he'd spread out like a starfish, facedown, and covered twice as much space as anyone who weighed about thirty pounds should be able to. She sighed, picked him up, and scooted him over. He didn't wake up. Grateful, she crawled back into bed, wrapped an arm around him, and went to sleep. This time she slept until sunlight pouring through her magi-cal window onto the futon woke her.

On her next round, she completed gates and spells for Dalchi, Zodhfr, and Iio, taking small breaks in between each to eat, play with Jake, and stretch. Even sitting in the chair, the work she was doing wore on her. The day was long gone and moonlight backlit the budded-out trees of the forest into lace by the time she finally quit. When she shook herself out of the trance for the final time, she was surprised to find two guards waiting for her.

"Seolar would speak with you, Hunter," one of them said, bowing.

"Fine," Lauren told him. She yawned and stretched. "I'll be happy to speak with him, but he'll have to come here. I don't dare leave the mirror."

"He knows this, Hunter," the other said. "He only wished to be told when you were available to meet with him."

"Tell him to come on. He can have some coffee or some hot chocolate with me."

Both guards turned without another word and loped away. Lauren looked at Jake, curled up in the bed with Doggie be-side him, his arm flung possessively around her as if she were his toy, and Lauren wanted to cry. These were the first times in his life that Jake had ever gone to sleep without her, and she hated it. She hated thinking that she could be replaced, even in such a small way. She hated seeing him grow up so fast, knowing that someday he would grow away from her and become a man with a life and a world of his own. And yet she was so proud of him already. In spite of everything that had happened to him, he still managed to laugh, and to play, and to trust.

By the time Seolar knocked on the door and let himself in, Lauren had two big mugs of steaming hot chocolate waiting.

She smiled at Seolar, handed him a cup of hot chocolate, and pointed to one of the kitchen chairs. "Have a seat."

He took the hot chocolate, sniffed it, and sipped it cautiously. He frowned a little at the taste, and took a bigger one. "This is a liquid form of the brown sweets that Molly loved so much."

"Chocolates?"

"I suppose." He sat on the chair. He looked tired and drained, and his use of the word "loved" dinged on Lauren's ear.

She sat across from him and sipped her own chocolate. "She's not past tense yet, Seo."

He studied her with those weird, huge, all-black eyes, and said, "Even if she isn't, we have other problems, and those problems tie in with this."

Lauren raised an eyebrow and said nothing.

"According to Qawar, who keeps track of such things, the dark gods of the Night Watch are gathering. They can sense your gates, and they know something is afoot. Qawar claims there has never been such a gathering of them in this district. They have come from all over this world, and all over your world, and from downworld as well. He believes that the dark gods have gathered to wage war against you and your sister, and that they will not rest until they have destroyed you both, or until they are destroyed instead. He further believes that the dark gods are not in league with Baanraak—that in some fashion he betrayed them, and that they hope to destroy him, too."

Lauren took a long swallow of her hot chocolate, burning her tongue and the roof of her mouth in the process. It never ended, did it? One solution just bred half a dozen more problems, all of which ended up being worse than the original problem.

Dark gods and war.

She took another sip, and wondered if the old gods that were leaving Earth were really old gods—or if they were dark gods who'd been soaking in all the disharmony.

Who could tell? The Sentinels? She didn't think so.

She bet Molly would have known. But that didn't do Lauren a bit of good.

"The hell with it," she muttered, and took another huge swallow of her drink.

He looked at her over the rim of his mug as he sipped. He put the mug down, and after a moment said, "You are thinking . . . what?"

"I'm thinking this is for the birds."

His forehead furrowed.

She sighed. Metaphor and simile translated poorly sometimes. "I'm thinking I don't want to take my little boy into a war zone, and I'm terrified to leave him behind. I'm thinking maybe I ought to just spend whatever time my world has left with my son, and then either emigrate here or die with everyone else and go on to whatever waits beyond this. I'm thinking that no matter how good I am at magic, I'm not going to be able to stand up to Baanraak *and* an army of dark gods *and* rescue Molly—if I can even find her. I'm going to end up getting killed, and it will all be for nothing."

"When you go to rescue Molly, you won't go alone."

"Your guards are good guys. But they have no magic."

"That's true. Here. But if they go through with you to whichever world Baanraak and Molly are on, they will no longer be just men. They will become old gods, too. And war is a form of magic they know well." Seolar shrugged and took another sip. "Qawar said he would accompany you, as well—though in an advisory capacity. I will go with you. If you lead us, you will lead the best army we can gather."

"And look how well that worked out for Joan of Arc." Lauren looked at her son, now sleeping alone. Doggie had gotten up and crept into her own bunk at some point, and Lauren hadn't even noticed. She looked down and found Rue at her side. "We will go with you if you wish," he said. "All of us. In the next worlds, we will have magic, and we will fight with you—or we will guard the little god with our lives. We are all agreed—nothing will touch him. Stay or go, you have only to tell us."

Lauren smiled just a little. "No cowards in Oria but me, huh?"

Seolar returned her smile. "Oh, no. In all my life I have never been so frightened. But I am more frightened of what might happen if we do not go than of what will happen if we do."

Dalchi

Baanraak watched his mound with interest. The head had formed just at the dirt line sometime ago, a blobby bit of pink soft flesh—and gradually it took on shape and grew hair and developed clear features.

He had never seen the process before; he found it surprisingly repulsive. And yet, now that the girl had almost reformed, she had a beauty that shone clearly even across the barrier of species. She had not taken breath yet, nor opened her eyes, but Baanraak waited, still save for the tip of his tail, which twitched nervously. He wanted to do this right. He'd run over a hundred alternatives since he'd dropped the necklace into the dirt and covered it; a hundred different ways of saying what he needed to say, or of showing what he needed to show—he'd considered, too, the possibility of saying and showing nothing, of just being quick about it. He could not decide which way was best, and he now almost understood Fherghass's decision to just leave him buried until he'd run through all the buried meat and half a hundred lives and deaths. By doing that, Fherghass had spared himself any messy decisions at all. And if it had been a hell for Baanraak, it had been, nonetheless, a hell that ended eventually.

And Baanraak had eventually emerged, ready to be trained into a breathtaking killing machine.

His tail twitched faster. Her skin wore a faint sheen of light in the darkness now, and suddenly she looked every bit the goddess. Soon, he thought. Soon.

The light faded, and as it did, her eyes opened, and he could see the faint movements that suggested she was struggling to free herself. Then she saw him and froze. She looked him up and down, and something in her stilled and he felt her mind touch his. *You*, she said directly into his thoughts.

Me, he agreed.

In the time he thought that single syllable, she'd ripped through his thoughts to discover his plans for her, and had begun to cast a spell against him. He had never seen any response so fast, or so furious.

With a single downward stroke of his forefoot, he smashed in her skull.

"One," he whispered, his tail now still.

He felt less satisfaction in her first death under his tutelage than he had expected.

CHAPTER 18

Copper House

HOT CHOCOLATE FINISHED and conversation basically done, Lauren and Seolar were just rising from the table when the alarm went off again. This time it didn't just ding politely, however. This time it screamed.

Lauren raced for the mirror, her chair clattering to the floor behind her in her haste. She pressed hands to the glass and, already connected by her search spell to the world in which the alarm had gone off, had to do nothing more than widen the gate so she could see what she'd caught.

The alarm fell silent as her fingers touched the glass, and she breathed a sigh of relief. She'd set it to be loud if the spell contacted Molly, rather than traces of Molly's passages; she hadn't realized how loud, though, until it went off.

The image blossomed from a pinpoint in the center of the mirror to a full picture, that would haunt her dreams for the rest of her life. She got a clear side-shot of Molly, buried in a mound of dirt up to her neck, staring at a giant rrôn with an expression on her face of pure rage. In the next instant, the rrôn brought down his massive foreleg and smashed Molly's skull.

Lauren turned away from the scene. She felt light-headed, both hot and cold. She broke out in a sweat. She fought the wave of nausea, but it won; she ran to the bathroom and held on to the cool porcelain of the toilet and threw up. Behind her, she heard Seolar begin a high-pitched keening shriek that made her skin crawl.

Jake started crying. Lauren rinsed out her mouth in the sink and made her way to his side; she felt like she was walking on the deck of a tossing ship. She had never been witness to anything that hit her so hard. She lay on the bed, pulled Jake into her arms, stroked his hair, and cried soundlessly.

Behind her, she could hear Seolar opening the door, shouting into the corridor beyond. The goroths were yelling things, and she thought they might be at her, but she couldn't be sure. Guards ran, and the little room erupted into riot—but it was a riot far away from Lauren, as if she lay at the bottom of the seafloor, listening to unclear, watery voices a long way away. Her world grayed around the edges and narrowed down to her and Jake.

This is the way the world ends, she thought. A blink, a flash, and silence. She was going to go up against not one, but a multitude of those things? She was going to take her child into that danger, or leave him behind so that dark gods could break into this place and find him the way the monster had found Molly?

He's already in danger, something inside her whispered. He's yours—therefore he's a target. For that monster, for the other monsters, for every dark god who sees you as standing between him and the deaths of worlds that feed him.

She stroked the soft hair, the soft cheek. She felt Jake relax and, in spite of the noise in the room, felt him go limp and heavy as he fell back to sleep. He trusted her to make his world safe. She was the only one who could.

She sat up, and her mission had expanded—she could no longer look at working with Molly to bring the upworlds back to life as her destiny. "Hunter" now took on a whole new meaning in her mind, because she needed to destroy the dark gods. In order for Jake to be safe, in order for him ever to know a moment's peace, she was going to have to hunt down the monsters. That wasn't what her parents had planned for her; nowhere in their notes did it say "Kill Night Watch."

Jobs change, she told herself.

And the first job is to get Molly back before that monster kills her again.

She brushed Jake's hair away from his forehead and looked at the guards, the goroths, the old gods, Seolar and Birra, all of whom were looking at her with expressions ranging from horror to grief to dismay.

"We're going after her," Lauren said. "We're going in there fast, we're going to kill him, we're going to get Molly or the Vodi necklace back. It doesn't matter which one, and it doesn't matter whether she's alive or dead when we get there; we're still going to get her back. We know where she is, we know where he is. With luck, we're the only ones who know that, but we have to assume we aren't. We'll have to assume that we're going to war."

She stared at the guards who would be stepping into a situation for the first time in which they would be magic users. She thought about the effects waging war in a downworld would have on the upworlds, and she cringed. "We're going to cause problems here with anything we do there—you have to know that, and we have to be prepared for it. If we go into battle against Baanraak, or against Baanraak and a whole host of dark gods, we're going to spawn civil unrest, wars and possibly even natural disasters all the way up the worldchain. And that means we're likely to go from trouble downworld right into trouble at home. But we can't help that. This evil cannot be permitted to stand."

She crossed her arms over her chest, wishing she wasn't standing there in flannel teddy-bear-print jammies and a terry-cloth bathrobe. She doubted that any military leader exhorting the troops to war had been so dressed. "We have three objectives," she told them. "One—we have to kill Baanraak and whichever dark gods show up on Dalchi. Two—we have to gather up any jewelry worn by our ene-

mies, and we have to destroy that jewelry utterly. And—
three—we have to get either Molly or her Vodi necklace and
we have to bring one or both back here safely."

"Lauren, you cannot go into battle," Seolar said. "You
have to remain safe, because if we save Molly and lose you,
our cause is just as lost as it is if we have lost you but not
her."

Lauren considered this, then nodded agreement. "I'll have
to be there, but perhaps I can coordinate everything from a
position of relative safety." She closed her eyes, thinking. "I
can gate us all through straight into Dalchi, and drop us right
on top of Baanraak. But you veyâr have no experience with
using magic, and we could end up in real trouble if you get
crazy with it."

From behind a mob of veyâr guards, Lauren heard
Qawar's voice. "Especially since the beginning magic user
becomes more powerful as he moves downworld. I hit my
power peak back on Jerr. Everything since then has been
downhill. I become more vulnerable with every new world I
pass. However, the veyâr will have a great deal of power,
four worlds down from their own, and no experience in using
it. The Hunter makes a good point. She and I need to create
safe weapons for them; if possible, we need to give them
kill-proof—"

"No," Lauren said.

All eyes turned to her.

Qawar said, "I was going to recommend kill-proof
weapons, which would minimize the upflow damage—"

"I know what you were going to recommend," Lauren
said. "This is not a situation where we can settle for stunning
Baanraak or the other dark gods. We have to kill them, and
when we're done, we have to destroy them."

Qawar was shaking his head. "You're giving them terrible
advice—you're young. You don't understand. You can't realize that there is no way to rid the worldchain of the dark
gods. We have to work around them. Sometimes we have to

give them a bone, sometimes we have to pretend they aren't there. But to aim to go in and actually destroy them—you'll bring the whole of the worldchain down in rubble if you try such a fool stunt."

"Give them a bone?" Lauren asked. "What sort of bone can you give to creatures who feed on the death of worlds? What? You just let a world fall from time to time to keep them from coming after you?"

"They're immortal," Qawar said. "We aren't."

"We are," Lauren said. "I have proof. I've been to the afterlife, and I guarantee you beyond this death, we go on."

"It's not the same," Qawar said.

"*Nothing* is the same." Lauren studied him, wondering if she would dislike anyone of his species, or if his personality was something completely separate from whatever he was. "Knowing that my world is the next 'bone' you'd be willing to throw to the dark gods to keep them from coming after you, or that the lives of more than six billion people mean nothing to you at least lets me know how useful your advice is going to be."

"That's not how I feel at all. I grieve for the death of each world. But you haven't been dealing with them for ten thousand years. I have."

"Then maybe you've been hiding for so long you've forgotten what really matters. You can't 'throw a bone' to anything that has already sworn it will kill you to have the whole cow. You can't appease anyone whose continued existence calls for your destruction. You might buy yourself some time at the cost of everyone else, but sooner or later the monsters will come for you."

Seolar said, "Qawar has negotiated with the dark gods to protect the veyâr."

"At what cost?" Lauren asked.

"We've had to make concessions," Seolar said, but did not go into detail. "Nevertheless, there have been times when Qawar is all that stood between us and destruction. We had no

Vodi to bargain for us . . . and even the Vodian before Molly gave the dark gods land and privileges in exchange for peace."

"Deals with the devil rarely end well," Lauren said, and left it to Seolar to decide whether she meant the deals with the dark gods or the deals with Qawar. She said, "In any case, we will be making no such deals. Our goal is not just the death, but the utter annihilation, of the dark gods. They are killing our worldchain, and their destruction is our only self-defense. The question now is, are you with me?"

Qawar said, "I think you're making a mistake that will destroy everything you hope to save. But with that said, on your head be it. I'll follow, but I will not lead."

"We're with you," the veyâr guards said. And Birra and Seolar said, "All the veyâr are with you."

The goroths bowed until their heads hit the floor, and said, "You know we are with you, Hunter. To the ends of all the worlds."

Lauren looked at them and smiled, and nodded just a little. "Let's hope we don't get there today."

She pointed to the goroths. "You will be staying here. Your jobs will be to keep Jake safe when I take everyone else through. One of you will have to stay here to shut down the gate if a dark god tries to come through."

She turned to Seolar. "You and your people will have lethal weapons. I can design them so they will only kill dark gods. That way if you shoot through any of your allies you won't kill them."

She turned to Qawar. "No matter what has happened in the past, we have to face the truth about what must happen now. We have to defeat them. We cannot wait for someone bigger than we are or braver than we are or stronger than we are to stand up to them. We cannot hope someone else will save us and end this destruction. The weight of worlds rests in our hands; the lives of those now living and those who wait to be born depend on us. We cannot turn away from this burden, because no one else will pick it up if we let it drop."

Dalchi

Baanraak studied the mound, now all clean dirt again, since he'd buried the little bit of mess. The first purification round had gone well . . . and yet, it hadn't.

He cocked an eye heavenward and stilled his mind. Something had seen him. He'd felt the shock of recognition, he'd felt the surge of a gate opening wide, then snapping down to nothing again, and he'd felt magic. Small, surreptitious—but powerful nonetheless. Whatever had been watching him was either gone or made so small even he could not sense it, but he doubted neither senses nor experience. Both of those had kept his hide intact for longer than he could tell.

He had no doubt, either, that whatever had found him had been looking for him. Now the question was, who lay behind the gate and the spell? Rr'garn and the rrôn branch of the Night Watch? Baanraak doubted they had the subtlety for such a delicate little spell. They were bludgeoners, not surgeons. Some old god suddenly overcome by a rash of foolish courage and derring-do? Not likely—after years of persecuting any who crossed him, Baanraak feared little from any old gods save the few remaining immortals. And even they had not crossed paths with him in ages beyond reckoning.

Someone related to his little Vodi?

If this hidden watcher shared a link with the Vodi, Baanraak might have more of a challenge facing him than he'd expected.

He looked at his mound of dirt and said, "Who do you number among your friends and champions, my Molly? Who would dare me to save you? I think there must be someone . . . and I wonder if I might not gather this hero of yours in and mold him as I'll mold you."

Baanraak had the clean, unspelled gold. He could not claim the artistry of the great resurrection masters of ages past, but he knew the resurrection spells well enough to create something simple and lasting.

Then, in the distance but from another direction, a different gate opened. This one announced itself by a soft, discordant click, followed by a rush of the death-spawned energy that characterized the dark gods. Click followed click followed click.

The incoming dark gods were some way off, but that wouldn't last. They were coming. Heroes and villains, and him with his Vodi in the middle. Interesting times, Baanraak thought.

Copper House

Viewing the terrain surrounding Baanraak's hideaway on Dalchi, Lauren found out that Qawar had been right. An army of dark gods—rrôn and keth and a mix of other creatures from a string of murdered worlds—poured out of conjoined gates, one after another after another.

No chance of getting in, getting Molly, slaughtering Baanraak, and leaving—but then, much as she had hoped, she hadn't thought there would be.

There would be war. Lauren had never been in a war before.

She studied Qawar, who looked hugely unhappy at the idea of being involved with this. She bet he'd be even unhappier at the idea of going first into a fire zone. She didn't blame him, but she also wasn't going to send inexperienced magic users through to stand against God-only-knew what. "You any good at casting tough shields?"

Qawar nodded. "Anything that will keep me alive I've learned to excel at."

"Good," Lauren said. "When we get ready to go through, you'll go first. You can cast and maintain the shields—I'm guessing you aren't much of a fighter."

"I'm more of a flee-er. But I don't need to go through to cast shields. I can shield them as they go through the gates—good, tight individual shields. I'm a master at those. And the shields will just get stronger four worlds down."

"Right."

Lauren turned to Seolar. "You can see the dark gods down there. Anything about the terrain work for you?"

Seolar and Birra studied the view through the gate; then Seolar said, "Can you change the angle a bit?"

"What do you need?"

"A . . . map view. From above."

Lauren complied, and Birra and Seolar studied the ground, then grinned at each other. "They were thinking about defending against this point," Seolar said, pointing to Baanraak's high ground. "If we could approach them from here . . . and here . . ."

"We could catch them between crossfire," Birra said. "They picked their ground with the idea of attack, not defense."

"So you need gates to two points that will open at the same time," Lauren said. "I'm going to need to line the wall with mirrors in here. I'll create enough gates that you'll be able to send through a dozen men in a wave, six at a time to each of your two destination points." That would be tough—holding that many big gates open across that much distance for the amount of time she would need was going to be exhausting. But sending men through one at a time seemed like a bad idea to her.

Seolar said, "If we could bring our people through here, and here—" he indicated ground behind two rises—"we might be able to take them."

"I can do that," Lauren said.

He said, "I have 260 men to send, plus eighteen captains. And Birra. And me."

Lauren looked at the mirror. "So we're outnumbered."

Birra and Seolar studied her, matching expressions of surprise. "I'd estimate we have them to the good by nearly a hundred men—though they may continue to bring people through."

Lauren looked at the future battlefield crowded with immortal evil and wondered at men who could see the monsters, figure an accurate count, and sound even remotely optimistic about the outcome. Of course, with good strategy and better weapons, the veyâr could at least level out the odds a bit.

She told Qawar, "You and I need to make weapons. I want enhanced non-magical weapons to use against Baanraak and other dark gods," she said. "Something they won't be ready for. The dark god I killed died when I used real bullets on him, not magic."

She noticed a funny expression on Qawar's face. "What's wrong?" she asked him.

"You killed a dark god?"

"Yeah. One of the rrôn."

His level stare evaluated her without revealing his thoughts. Finally, Qawar said, "Perhaps you will get us through this after all. I don't know anyone who has killed a dark god in—oh—thousands of years. Except for other dark gods, of course—but we can hardly hope for help from that quarter."

Lauren shrugged. "Pray they suffer a lot of friendly fire. That would help us."

She stared right back at him. "We want something simple. Same concept as the machine gun, the automatic rifle—just aim and pull the trigger. We'll use magic to produce and load ammo so the weapons will never run out, and use magic to augment the aim. Put some sort of 'friendly fire' safety on each weapon so that our guys can't shoot anyone on our side. The only things we're going to kill are dark gods—they emit death-fed magic. You've felt that death-magic. Tune the weapons in on that if you can, to make sure the weapons will only hit them."

Qawar was still staring at her.

"What?"

"You're too good at this."

Lauren still didn't like Qawar. "What do you mean by that?"

He shrugged. "Not once have you said, "Perhaps we can negotiate with them. Why not? Why did you leap straight to planning for war? Why are you not tender and timid and hungry for peace?"

"Women aren't always tender and timid," Lauren said. "Human mothers share characteristics with other mothers. If you threaten our young, we'll rip your goddamned head off. Think *mother bear separated from her young. Mother eagle with an intruder threatening her nest*. Each human being is born fierce, desperate for survival and willing to fight for it. Some of us stay that way."

CHAPTER 19

Copper House to Dalchi

LAUREN HUGGED JAKE CLOSE, then released him and sent him with Doggie.

"Everything's ready," she said to Seolar. She rested fingertips on the mirror she'd chosen as the master and linked it to all the others.

"What if Baanraak is no longer there?" Seolar asked. "What if he's not in that cave?"

"The Vodi necklace is still there," Lauren said. "I can feel it. Do you think he'd go without it?"

"Maybe," Seolar said softly. "We have no idea why he wanted the Vodi necklace in the first place. Perhaps just to bring the old gods and the veyâr together on a battlefield, where we could wipe each other out without requiring any effort on his part."

Lauren nodded. "Maybe. But we still have to go in after it. We can't let him keep it. We can't let him do what he did to her again."

Veyâr captains formed their men into ranks, giving them instructions on where to deploy and what to do when they broke through the gate. Lauren hoped the magic that would move them from one place to the other wouldn't prove too disorienting—she'd experienced it often enough that she should be used to it, but its wonder never seemed to wear off.

The veyâr were queuing up. Lauren personally spun a protective shield around each of the goroths, then around

Jake. She crouched and told Rue, "Make sure Doggie keeps Jake here and keeps him safe. He *has* to stay in this room—if he doesn't, the shield will break and anything could hurt him. But don't let him near the gate. *You* watch what's going on through the gate. I have to leave it open so that we can retreat as soon as we get Molly, but I'm going to make a kill-switch for you. If you see a rrôn, or any of the dark gods coming for it—and you'll be able to see them before they can reach it, I think—hit the kill switch."

Rue looked worried. "The kill switch . . . it will kill you?"

Lauren winced. Metaphor. "No. Kill switch is just a name. The switch will just shut down the gate before anything can get in here. I want to leave it open if I can, because if we have to do a quick retreat, I don't want to have to stop to put a gate together. But I don't want anything awful getting in here again, either."

Rue nodded. "I will . . . hit the kill switch."

Lauren created it as a button on the master gate, high enough up that the long-armed goroth ought to be able to reach it, but Jake wouldn't.

Qawar finished shielding the veyâr in the room. He moved to the doorway and said, "I can't get any more of them until this lot goes through—and we can't send them out in the halls to wait. That will break the shields.

It was time, then. The veyâr started marching through. Lauren hugged Jake again, feeling the tears sliding down her cheeks, unable to stop them, hating the fact that she was leaving him, and that once again leaving him behind was the best of all her bad alternatives. At that moment, she hated her parents for not having been normal people living normal lives.

The veyâr moved through fast—leaping in at a half-run while she used her strength and her focus to keep the gates all open.

Seolar was already coming up on the gate—he would be the last of the veyâr, and then it would be her turn. She swallowed hard, turned away from her beautiful son, and caught up with Seolar as he reached the gate. She could see fighting going on already on the other side. She didn't hesitate, though—because if she did not put her hand on the mirror and push through in that instant, she feared she never would. And she was the one who could sense Molly—the one most likely to find where Baanraak had hidden her. Seolar kept right with her, mirroring her movements. Neither of them said anything.

For one glorious timeless instant, she merged with infinity; she knew her immortality and touched eternity. The universe sang for her as if the whole of it existed for her alone. And then the path between the worlds spat her out onto hard ground, into hot air, beneath a glowing dome of blue light that held back splashes and smears of black fire. She heard screaming, she saw bodies on the ground, some moving, some not. In death, all the dark gods and mortals seemed indistinguishable—lumps of bloody flesh and gleaming bone ends.

She breathed acrid smoke and swore, and tightened the shield around herself so that it cleared the air before she breathed it. She willed her voice loud—loud enough to carry to every veyâr on her side, and said, "If you want the air to be breathable and clean, will it to be so and it will be."

Seolar, standing next to her, said, "I can't see the damned field."

She nodded. "We'll get up above it. First, though, I'd like to figure out where Baanraak is and what he's doing."

"Even on the other side, you said you could feel Molly here. Can you still?"

"Yes," Lauren said. "He hasn't taken her away from this area yet. They're nearby." She closed her eyes and reached for the bond that existed between her and Molly. "She's already a long way back from Baanraak killing her," Lauren told Seolar after a moment. "She isn't breathing, and she isn't aware, but when I focus on her, I can feel—life. I don't know why she's resurrecting so quickly, though—she needed more than mere days the first time."

"I don't know why. All I know is, at least we have not yet lost."

"Not yet," Lauren said. Another moment and she added, "We're meant to think that she and the necklace are still in the mound, though. He's set a trap there—don't let anyone touch the mound." Lauren got images of coldness, of calculating evil that drew pleasure from pain, of deception carefully plotted. She might have been reading all of that from whatever waited in the mound; she might have been getting it from Baanraak himself. She could feel him, even though she could tell he was doing his best to hide his presence.

"Baanraak is down in the caves somewhere—the opening goes way in, and I have the feeling that he has done a bit of work in there to make it meet his needs. He's below us, and below the dark gods coming this way." Lauren shook her head. "He's ready for us. He doesn't know who'll be coming, but he's waiting for whoever does. He figures he'll let his enemies do his work for him—kill each other off, save him the trouble and the risk. And then he'll mop up whoever is left."

"One of him, all of us."

Lauren nodded. "Baanraak has some special talents. He's very good at magic, but it's more than that. I can't quite figure out why he's so confident—he's hard as hell to read." She turned to Seolar, uncertain if she should tell him what else she'd discovered, then decided that at the moment it might help more than hurt, since Seolar knew the myths and history of his world, and Lauren didn't. "He's very possessive of her," she said.

Seolar—who had been nervously watching the splashes of flame and magic that hit their shield, as well as flares of light as the dark gods' bullets struck it—now turned his full attention to Lauren.

"Baanraak . . . the rrôn. He's possessive of . . . *Molly*?"

Lauren nodded. With her eyes closed, she dug beneath Baanraak's shields and into his mind. "He's shielding himself and his thoughts—it's only my connection with Molly that's letting me get through to him, because for some reason he doesn't have her blocked off. He's tuned into her. He . . ." She rubbed her temples and opened her eyes. "He truly believes that if he repeatedly kills her and brings her back, he'll be doing her a favor."

Seolar looked as lost as Lauren felt. "I don't understand. He doesn't want to destroy the Vodi necklace, or Molly?"

Lauren closed her eyes and let herself connect to the tenuous thread that bound her to Molly—and through that link, to connect to Baanraak, as well. Images and feelings flooded through her. A great dark egg; hanging in the sky and then falling like a rock toward some pinpoint moving far below; the sensations of sun on hide, wind racing past; ravenous hunger; the thrill of the clean kill.

Lauren couldn't put the images into any coherent order, any more than she could make sense of a darker thread in the monster's mind. That thread wound its way through entombment, death and death and more death, pain and suffering so intense Lauren could not comprehend anything surviving it and coming out sane on the other side.

Through the predator fantasies and the nightmares, Lauren found images of Molly—and those, too, bewildered her. In his mind, Baanraak equated Molly to a huge black sphere that glowed from within. This visual metaphor meant something to him that was almost holy, but Lauren could not figure out why. And Baanraak saw Molly with wings, dropping from the sky like Death's avenging angel.

"I can't tell what he wants, but though he plans to kill her, he doesn't seem to want to . . . destroy . . . her." Lauren looked at the battlefield all around her. She realized that this was not the real battle. Not for her, anyway. "He's not human—not anything like human. I can get inside his thoughts thanks to Molly and the Vodi necklace, but a lot of things moving around inside his head don't mean anything to me. I'm not a rrôn. He doesn't think the way that I think. You see?"

Seolar nodded. "That you can read his thoughts at all . . ."

Lauren put a finger to Seolar's lips and said, "Don't think it. Don't say it. I'm keeping myself out of his sight, but he'll be able to read you. You run the battle, and think about keeping your people alive—and maybe luring the dark gods to that mound—but only if you are in a position to get everyone out of the way quickly. Don't let your mind wander beyond that. Okay?"

"I can do that," Seolar said, "though I'd prefer to know why."

"If I told you, I'd be telling him. You're shielded, you have one of the gates open to you." Lauren did a careful piece of magic, then said, "The gate will stay with you now. It's anchored to you, which means you have to be the last to leave—but as long as you're here you can get everyone else out."

"We were going to link it to you and keep you safe."

"We were. But if we're going to get Molly back, there's something I am going to have to do. And I'll have to do it alone."

"You can't."

"It's win or lose time, Seo. Either I do this, and we have a chance to win. Or I don't, and every one of your men lying dead on this alien world just died for nothing."

Seolar looked sick, but he nodded. "Go then. Go with the grace of the gods; I'll hold you in my thoughts and prayers."

Lauren shook her head and said, "Thanks. I'll take all the help I can get."

"I can give you some men."

"I know you can. But I couldn't get them past Baanraak— they would only give me away." She took his hand in hers and said, "Good luck, and be well. I hope we both survive to meet again."

He started to protest. Lauren could see the words forming as clearly as she could see the look in his eyes. And then he simply nodded, squeezed her hand, and said, "Good luck."

She needed a good shield before she headed into the cave

after him—but it wasn't going to be the sort of shield that could protect her from attacks or reflect them back on her attackers. Sometimes she saw shields as bright and shiny and reflective, like the clear coat on new cars. But she didn't need that sort of shield now—from inside Baanraak's eyes, she could feel him watching for such things. What she needed now was something that would dull and muffle and hide her presence, blend her into her background, make her quiet and still and unobtrusive. In order for it to do that, she would have to forgo protection. She would be walking naked into the monster's lair, knowing that he'd been creating traps for anyone who dared follow him in.

She needed the magical equivalent of stealth paint— something that absorbed sound and smell and vibration and light and magic and any noise her thoughts might make, something that gave nothing back. She wanted something that made the eyes slide away, convinced they saw nothing.

She could imagine exactly what she needed. She imagined herself covered in it.

"Lauren?" Seolar asked, though she hadn't moved.

"I'm right here," she said.

"Lauren? Where did you go?"

Okay. It did absorb sound. Good. She gave Seolar no explanation; she had no idea how much longer the window of opportunity she had seen might hold.

She slipped through the shield and worked her way up the outcropping to the cave mouth. Keeping well clear of the mound to her left, she crossed the flat, open space. She felt naked. Nothing but the fact that she'd made herself hard to see protected her from the projectiles, both magical and mundane, that flew across the high ground and the plains below. One errant blast of magic would kill her before she had a chance to block it.

By the time she reached the cave mouth, her heart battered inside her chest like it was hoping to get out. She took a moment just to catch her breath and let her eyes adjust to the darkness. The entry posed some problems—fallen rocks

covered the floor so closely that Lauren doubted she would
be able to step between them without disturbing one. Which
might have been the point.

Dalchi

Deep in the darkness, coiled and still, with Molly's regener-
ating body tucked at his side and buried in a pile of stinking
animal carcasses, Baanraak watched the progress of his enemies from behind closed eyes and spun spells into magnificent traps.

The Night Watch had the edge in armaments, but the
veyâr fought from inside some of the best shields Baanraak
had ever seen—and desperation fueled them in their forward
charge. The dark gods, Baanraak decided, lacked both passion and conviction. The veyâr lacked neither.

He smiled. Either could win, and everything for him
would remain the same. He had the Vodi necklace, he had
the lairholder advantage, and he was *him*—which had been
the best advantage of all for longer than anyone could remember.

They might suspect that he hid somewhere in the cave
system, but he lay with body and mind held in perfect, waiting stillness, with himself and the Vodi—Molly—shielded
together out of sight and reach of any searching magic. In
the world above, he could hear the noisy minds and see the
bright jackdaw magic flaring and swirling, endlessly ener-
getic and completely lacking in subtlety, in reserve . . . and
in stealth. He could feel nothing but disdain for those who
had come to hunt him—their very might and fury would be
their downfall.

He delighted in his traps. He'd done excellent work in the
little time he had; they had come with might, but he fought
with gentle, quiet strokes that would draw no attention yet
would take any force offered and turn it against an attacker.
Baanraak had been a Taoist at heart long before humans

found their way down from the trees to give the path of yielding to conquer a name.

. . . Dalchi to . . .

The old gods had not gone to war with the dark gods in time out of mind. The worldchain had forgotten the price paid for wars between gods.

Abruptly, with huge spells of horror and death bursting on the Dalchi fields, rebound magic poured upworld, and . . .

. . . Niiadaa to . . .

. . . on Niiadaa, on a deliciously warm afternoon with the clouds towering like castles above the village of Iri, the earth rumbled without warning and ripped itself apart. Molten rock exploded upward. Fire rained up, spurted, gouted, and the village died in a breath, taking everyone with it. A hill bellied up out of the ground, red fire racing out in all directions, and a mountain shouldered its way onto the hill, shoving rivers of rock and crusts and scabs of lava before it. Poisons poured into the air, and the sky turned black, and still the earth kept shaking. The sun vanished, and the forests and the rivers all around with it—lakes sucked back into the earth as if they had never existed, and death spread out in all directions. Seas rose out of their beds and smashed shorelines, pounding them with forty-foot waves and tossing chunks of lava bigger than houses as if they were toys.

The sun would not shine again on Niiadaa for weeks— and the snow would start falling in mere days . . .

. . . Povreack to . . .

. . . while on Povreack, a hurricane that had been moving
well off the shore of the most populated coastline suddenly
turned inland. It crawled northward, strong and well-defined
and vicious, and laid waste to whole peoples and the better
part of a nation . . .

. . . Cadwa to . . .

. . . clouds. More clouds. The peoples of the drought-
stricken flatlands of Central Hwyr on Cadwa looked up in
startled gratitude. Thunder rumbled, which had not been
heard in those parts in a dozen years, and moist air curled
the dust along the ground and touched cheeks with the gentle promise of rain.

The first drops spattered, big as fists, and people cheered,
and stood with arms outstretched and faces upturned. Then
the skies let loose.

But the ground, too parched to drink the bounty it received, filled fast and flooded fast, and joy turned to horror
as torrents ripped across the plains, taking topsoil and
houses and livestock and people with them . . .

. . . Oria to . . .

. . . across Oria's northern forests, the sound of rattling
wings, individually no louder than the crinkling of a sheet of
paper, grew to a roar as millions of millions of cherik beetles
hatched after a hibernation of twice a hundred years. Starv-
ing, they launched themselves into the sky and swarmed on
everything green and growing. Tender plants, budding out,
were stripped bare in minutes and the clouds of beetles ascended again and moved on.

The plague would last a month, and then the cheriks would dig back into the earth, so deep that men could never find them to destroy them, and lay their eggs, and die.

Behind them, much of the northern world would starve that year . . .

Earth

Across the globe, observatories went crazy as asteroids swarmed out of nowhere, ripping through satellites and exploding secret geosynchronous listening posts and smashing in toward Earth, trailing debris and fire and destruction.

Newscasters rocketed toward their chairs, unmade-up and in shirt-sleeves, cigarettes dangling from their mouths, to shout at the cameras in a thousand languages, "We have just been informed that Earth has moved into an unmarked asteroid belt, and we are being bombarded by meteors. Remain calm . . . most of these will burn up in the atmosphere—"

But many did not. Some of the meteorites hit like exploding bombs, taking skyscrapers and their inhabitants, hitting with freakish perversion on one person standing in line at a bus stop but missing the ones to either side, and slamming into the ground with such force that the earth shook and the people spared a direct hit were shattered by the shock.

Enemies eyed each other suspiciously across borders, suspecting foul play—but not one continent in the world escaped unscathed.

. . . and onward . . .

. . . and the magic moved upworld even farther, through Kerras and Frejandur and even Jerrits—but those worlds lay dead and empty, with no one to notice fresh disasters.

Cat Creek

Pete took a seat next to Mayhem, and watched the other Sentinels finding seats on the wood-slatted folding chairs. The Sentinels, called together in the middle of the crisis, gathered in the upper room of the Daisies and Dahlias, faces grim.

June Bug didn't waste any time on preamble. "I've tracked it through three worlds, but I don't have the strength or the resources to go any farther. This is rebound—no doubting *that*—but we're a long way from getting the worst of it. Our disaster is relatively mild."

"Chicago looks like a war zone," Betty Kay Nye said. Pete glanced over at her, and saw the way her fingers interlaced, the way her knuckles were white, the way her eyes looked panicked. She might be too new, too untried, to be any good for anything. She might, he thought, be as much a disposable castoff as Raymond Smetty, who had not yet managed to get his ass into a seat, or even through the downstairs door.

Pete had the feeling Sentinels from other regions, responding to Cat Creek's cry for help, had answered not by sending their best and brightest, but by sending their biggest headaches.

"What do we do?" Pete asked.

Eric leaned against the wall, shaking his head. "Without a gateweaver, and without a practiced team of responders, we pray. And hope that other groups are more prepared than we are."

"Couldn't we go downworld and do something magical that is both positive and big?" Pete asked.

Everyone turned to look at him, with expressions ranging from annoyance that he'd asked a stupid question to suspicion that he might just *be* stupid. Eric said, "Why don't we try to put out the fire by throwing gasoline on it?"

"I thought perhaps positive and negative magics would balance each other out," Pete said. "That maybe we could lessen the damage."

"Don't think," Louisa Tate said. "You might hurt yourself."

That got a few chuckles, but they were thin and died out quickly.

Pete didn't say anything. He was still the outsider here—even more than the new kids who'd come in over the last week, he would always be *the* outsider, because he hadn't been born into this, and they had. He could never be a real Sentinel in their eyes. Maybe his kids could, if he survived, and had kids, and was willing to let them get involved in this ongoing nightmare.

He was an outsider. But he thought maybe an outsider could see things that the insiders had grown blind to. And he thought of Lauren, the other outsider in spite of the fact that her parents *had* been Sentinels. She was downworld fighting this thing, and he wished he could be with her instead of in Cat Creek sitting on his hands.

He wondered where she was, and what she was doing.

Dalchi

The sounds of battle died away quickly. Tons of stone absorbed them, and no more had she lost the last of the light than Lauren lost sound from the outside world, too. Darkness replaced it. Darkness, and dampness, and the scents of wet dog and ammonia, and occasional faint whiffs of a dank, unpleasantly rotten smell worse than anything else. She could hear water dripping nearby, and a steady trickle of it farther away.

She had no flashlight, and when she discovered that her eyes would not adjust to absolute darkness—that without a source of light of her own, she was blind, she panicked. She dared not use magic to summon light. And even if she were to step outside and create a flashlight or lantern for herself, she would not be able to use it. Baanraak would notice light.

Lauren stood, blind, motionless, focusing on the sounds and scents around her, and she waited. She had no idea how long she stood there, but when finally she closed her eyes to rub her temples with one hand, something interesting happened.

She discovered that with her eyes closed, she could see after a fashion. With her eyes closed and her mind stilled and receptive, she could follow a faint trail of light that led downward—traces of the magic Baanraak had left in his wake. Lauren moved slowly—the faster she tried to progress, the more the light faded, and once disturbed she lost that bit of Baanraak's path forever.

Moving with eyes closed, she could also feel the places where Baanraak had stopped in his downward journey to place surprises for those who dared the cave. These traps scared the shit out of her, but while some were triggered to quick movement and some to magical force or strong magical shields, none seemed to be set to catch someone stealthy.

Lauren opened her eyes from time to time as her nerves got to be too much for her; she couldn't convince the animal hindbrain that she wouldn't fall into a hole walking around with her eyes closed; and every step felt like moving over a cliff anyway. But when she opened her eyes, the darkness got darker. Baanraak's faint trail disappeared, and she lost all sense of where he was, where she was, and where the traps lay.

Lauren hated dark, damp places. She loathed the idea of being underground, which was entirely too close to death for her. She was fine with a roof over her head, but not the remains of a mountain. She shuddered at the idea of cave-dwelling animals brushing against her—she had no idea if this world had bats, or cave snakes, or giant spiders. Anything might live in the darkness, and from time to time she would hear cheeping, or creaking, or soft low moans that convinced her that anything probably did.

She wanted to turn around and get out. But she didn't. She fought down the panic and the disgust and the dread, closed her eyes, and once again found the faint trail of light and stepped where the monster Baanraak had stepped.

A step at a time, moving on nothing but faith and a faint connection through her dead-but-returning sister to the monster she hunted, she crept downward.

Dalchi

Seolar wished fervently that he could rise above the battle to see where his people made progress and where they lost ground. In his mind's eye, he could see the vantage point he wanted; in the air, high enough that he could look over everything before him and behind him, high enough that the rrôn Baanraak's outcropping lay just beneath him, but not so high that he could not make out detail.

With the gate behind him blazing its green fire and the shield Lauren had created for him holding off every attack, he felt safe enough to hold that vantage point—and abruptly the ground fell away beneath him and he found himself and the gate and the bubble of his shield high in the air, rising to the exact point where he thought he might get the best view of the battle.

The aerial view offered more than he'd imagined. He could see the shields that Qawar kept in place over each main group—though he could see no sign of Qawar himself. He saw instantly a place where some of his men were moving into a trap; he called out a warning to them, willing them to hear him, and they managed to get out of trouble before the enemy flanked them and killed them.

He saw a great opportunity to bring two units together at one point where heavy fire already had a cluster of dark gods pinned down, and directed the leaders of those two groups. The pincer was working better than he had hoped— his men gained ground against the dark gods, and might yet win the day.

Then one of the dark gods soared over his head. Seolar

knew he was in a vulnerable position if his enemies could get through the shield; what he didn't know was whether they could get him through the shield.

He didn't need to wonder for long.

The rrôn circling over his head bellowed, and two more monsters materialized from out of the clouds. Seolar wondered what they'd been doing up there; he realized that he didn't know how to fight gods. All three rrôn angled their wings and dropped down at him, striking his shield from underneath with heads or bodies. They began bouncing and tossing him upward, flinging him through the air as if he were a toy. He lost his balance and fell with the first strike, and did not have the chance to regain his feet again.

They were forcing him into the clouds. He wondered why, and realized that he had to do something to keep from finding out. He needed to get back to the rise, close to his men, so he could keep the gate down where he could pull them through it as soon as Lauren appeared. And he needed to do it quickly.

He almost couldn't think. The rrôn had caught him off guard and were keeping him off balance, both literally and figuratively, and he couldn't hang on to any image long enough to will it into reality—and all the while, he bounced toward the clouds, and in particular one twisting black cloud that was beginning to form a funnel at the bottom.

He needed to find a way to anchor himself, he thought as he flopped from his face to his back and from one side of the shield to the other. He barely missed falling into Lauren's gate—and he knew he did not want to do that.

Anchor.

Anchor.

That thought gave him a solid image to hold onto. He imagined his shield tethered to the stone outcropping by an invisible, indestructible rope—tethered so tightly that the rrôn would batter themselves against his shield the next time they hit it and tumble from the sky. He willed rope and mammoth anchor into being, and as quickly as that, he bob-

bled in the air but stopped ascending. One of the rrôn instinctively ducked underneath his shield and tried to hit it
upward—but the invisible rope sliced through his wing right
at the shoulder, and in two pieces, the monster tumbled,
shrieking, to the ground.

Seolar started moving himself down to the ground, holding in his mind's eye an image of a big wooden reel that
turned steadily, filling quickly with the invisible rope. He
got to his feet and looked down, and saw the battlefield moving closer again.

He also saw that the dark gods no longer limited themselves to weapons—they were summoning the forces of nature and destruction as well. And because he made such an
excellent target, they began focusing on him.

Balls of fire erupted from nothingness all around him,
smashing into his shield. Tornadoes dropped from the
clouds overhead and began ripping toward him. Lightning
slammed into the tall rocks of the outcropping just below
him, shattering them and sending stone shards everywhere.
He began to doubt that his shield would hold. He knew he
had to guard the gate—and he feared that he could not attack
anything through the shield without damaging the shield's
integrity. He had to let them shoot at him.

He stared at the mound of earth below him that had held
Molly—and that Lauren said now held something else.
Some sort of trap.

Maybe he didn't have to be helpless. Maybe he could lure
his attackers to their doom. Mother animals pretended to be
wounded in order to lure dangers to their offspring away
from them. He might be able to do the same thing.

He tried to imagine what the shield might look like to his
enemies if it were weakening. He saw it becoming mis-
shapen, the light from it growing patchy and fading alto-
gether in some places. He did not want to weaken the shield
for real, but he thought if he concentrated on it, he might be
able to make it look damaged.

He concentrated on being deceptive—on creating a visual

lie. He wished he'd had a chance to practice with magic, so that he could see what was truly possible with it—but he felt sure that if he could deceive by nonmagical means, he could deceive by magic. Lauren said it was a matter of seeing what he wanted clearly—in precise, exact detail—and then wanting it enough to make it happen.

So he thought about the way wounded animals looked, and the way they acted. The ones trying to draw attention to themselves made noises, and moved erratically, and created a display that drew their enemies away from their nests.

When he could see just what he wanted, he focused his whole will on getting it—and when his shield took its next hit, the bubble of light in which he floated began to weave and rock. The walls wobbled, and the movement threw him from his feet.

He forced the bubble to dive and careen, and threw patterns of shadow across its surface.

Below, across the battlefield, veyâr and dark gods looked up, saw what was happening, and responded. All of them headed for the high ground—the dark gods to destroy the gate and all hope of retreat to safety, the veyâr to save the gate.

Stay back, Seolar thought. He willed his own people to hear him, and was relieved to see some of them falter and slow. But most kept coming.

I'm Seolar, he thought. *Hear me, and stay back. Let the dark gods come—I'm ready for them.* He fought for a clear line from him to them, for the tone of command that would convince his people that the sudden thoughts they heard came from him and not from their own frightened, weary minds.

Most of them continued moving forward, but doing so at a slower pace—they seemed to be pursuing, but he could tell they were only giving the impression of moving in to keep the dark gods from suspecting the trap.

Now the attack focused almost exclusively on him—endless streams of dark energy cast in his direction, fire and pro-

jectiles and torrents of rain and sleet and wind. In his thin
bubble, shielded by something barely visible to his eye, he
prayed to gods he had nearly forgotten—the benevolent, re-
assuring deities of his childhood who had promised rescue
and protection to all who followed them. He prayed that they
might notice him and hold him and the gate he guarded safe
from the onrushing horde; and he prayed that Lauren might
be successful in her mission to rescue Molly—and he prayed
that he and his people would get to go home, safe and soon.
Because now he could feel what Lauren had felt from the
mound in front of the cave mouth. The thing that waited in
there grew and fed—but it fed on the poisoned magic that
poured at Seolar from all sides, and it grew powerful.

Then the first of the enemy reached the ground beneath
him, and Seolar thought that for the rest of his life—however short that might be—he would remember the horror of
what happened next.

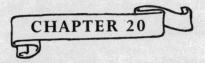

CHAPTER 20

Earth

". . . LATEST REPORTS just coming in on the stunning earthquake centered in south London, which registered 8.4 on the Richter scale . . . photos of the devastation . . ."

". . . tornado clusters throughout the Blue Ridge Mountain area . . ."

". . . They just came out of the clear blue sky—we didn't have no warning or nothing—just all of a sudden there were funnels everywhere, and houses started . . . started blowing apart . . . oh, I'm sorry, I just can't talk about it anymore . . ."

". . . South Florida blanketed under three feet of snow, with more falling . . . Meteorologists are at a loss to explain this devastating freak storm, and while they suggest a possible tie-in to the meteor shower that pounded most of the planet, none has yet suggested what that connection might be . . ."

". . . We have to assume the entire orange crop for the year is lost. Right now we're just doing what we can to save the trees, or we could be looking at completely starting over, with no crop for years . . ."

". . . city of Melbourne was hit by balls of fire that chased each other through the atmosphere before slamming into the tops of skyscrapers. This strange firestorm preceded a hailstorm that left more than a meter of hail on the ground, with drifts as deep as three meters in some places. Damage is estimated in the hundreds of millions of dollars, though fortunately so far estimates of loss of life have been small . . ."

Copper House

Doggie rocked Jake in her arms, but he refused to be comforted. He sobbed, "I WANT MY MAMA!" over and over. He would not sleep. He would not eat. Doggie's heart wept for him.

She pulled him close and whispered in his ear, "Be patient. We will watch the mirror and we will see your mama. But you must be a good boy."

Jake snuffled and wiped his tears on Doggie's outer robe. He looked at her, and said, "Okay. I am a good boy."

Doggie hugged him. "You *are* a good boy. It is hard to have the mama far away. But she is well—I will show you. But you cannot touch the mirror."

She'd kept him all the way away from them—had shoved the bed and his toys and things she'd asked women of the Copper House's veyâr staff to bring for him into the corner away from the mirrors. She'd requested decorative screens, and had erected them around the perimeter of her safe place, and neither she nor Jake had stepped out of it.

But he was terrified—he was a sensitive little boy, and he needed to know his mama was safe. She climbed the couch and stood on the back to look over the screen and said to Rue, "He must see her, just for a moment, just to know that she is well. I will take him over there, we will look at her, then we will come back."

Rue looked at Doggie. "He must not touch the gates."

"Of course not."

They came out from behind the screens, and the first thing Doggie saw was the view through the Hunter's magic window, which was terrifying—before their eyes wind ripped ancient trees into the air and tossed them about as if they were kindling. But sounds of the storm did not penetrate so deep into Copper House, so it seemed just a picture that had nothing to do with them.

But the line of green-glowing mirrors frightened Doggie. Nevertheless, she drew near enough to them that she could look into them. She held Jake's hand and kept him away from the glass, hoping that she would be able to point out his mama to him. But all she could see was war—horrible war, filled with monsters and death—and nowhere did she see the Hunter. What she could see terrified her—the viewpoint tossed and rocked as if she looked through the eyes of someone caught in bad seas. Doggie had been—once—on a ship. She had vowed never to have anything but solid ground under her feet again.

She realized that she was no longer holding his hand, but she could not recall letting go of it. She turned to tell Jake that they would have to wait—that she could not see his mama, that they would go back behind the screens and look again later.

But Jake was gone.

She turned to Rue. "Where is he?"

Rue said, "He was right there." But from where she stood, Doggie could see all of the room but the area behind the screen and the little water closet. And Jake was not in it. She did not move; she sent Tarth the tracker and Wyngi the boatmaster and Herot the so-swift birdcatcher and even Rue— who led them all—racing about the little room to find him while she stood still, listening, thinking. He was not in the room. The goroths looked at each other with shared expressions of horror. He had not gone through the gate—they knew this. But where *had* he gone?

"You stay here in case he comes back," Rue told Doggie. Again he did not chastise her or blame her. In fact, he had not chastised her since she received her name. This revelation surprised her, as did what he said next. "I am at fault—I will take the rest of us, and we will find him."

One of the veyâr stayed with Doggie. The rest went off to search the passages with the goroths.

They would find him, Doggie thought. Surely they would find him. He was just a little boy, and not very fast—he could not have gotten far.

Doggie paced the floor of the safe room, looking from the war on the other side of the gate to the terrifying storm that raged in her own world, and she thought what a terrible time this was to be lost.

Dalchi

The faint trail of light that spun itself out before Lauren's closed eyes grew brighter. And the smell grew worse. As she moved across more or less level ground now, her progress slowed to a crawl. She did not hear breathing; she did not feel any movements of air that betrayed the presence of the monster she sought—but she nonetheless had the eerie sensation that Baanraak waited nearby.

Her knees felt like some jackass practical joker had swapped out the joints and inserted gelatin. She needed to pee. She wanted to run away. She thought of Jake, and wondered if she was going to die in this dark hole in the ground and never see him again. She kept moving forward, because this was what moms did. They fought for their kids, they protected their kids—if they could, they moved the world for their kids. She was just lucky she could.

Lucky. She kept telling herself that. She could do something. She wasn't helpless, passive, just waiting for the world to end and praying that it wouldn't. Active—bad as it was—was better.

Within Baanraak's mind, she caught a stirring of interest—a sudden short, sharp flare of *presence*, as if someone had lit a match, and she stopped. That brief, quick-to-stutter-out flare told her a couple of things. First, she stood almost within touching distance of the monster. Second, though he did not move, though he lay as still as the dead, he watched everything with a hunter's patience and a hunter's intensity.

At first she thought she might have done something to catch his attention. She knew she disturbed the air slightly as she moved forward, and she had crept downward slowly and cautiously as a result, hoping that he might mistake any slight breeze she sent past him as the natural movement of air in the cave. But when he concentrated for just an instant, she thought she had been too bold.

However, something up on the surface had his attention. Lauren caught just the trailing edge of his excitement before he stilled himself, and she eased through the quiet pool of his mind, seeking the reason.

His enemies were heading for the first of his traps, and they had spent a great deal of effort pouring magic into it, which had only served to feed it.

She backed out of his mind and shivered. He'd left a nightmare in wait; she'd sensed it and warned Seolar to keep everyone away from the spot, but she'd had no idea how terrible Baanraak's trap was. She could only hope Seolar had listened to her, and that those getting ready to spring the thing were dark gods.

Of course, whatever it was would still be out there waiting when she had to leave—and her retreat was unlikely to be as stealthy or as careful as her approach had been.

I'm doing this for Jake, she thought. For Jake.

Now that she knew where Baanraak lay, she realized that she could feel a faint warmth and dryness from that direction. Even with her eyes closed, she could not make out the faintest trace of light emanating from him, though she had followed the trail he left without difficulty.

A sudden horrifying thought occurred to her then, and she turned slowly, slowly, and with her eyes closed "looked" back the way she had come.

The bit she could make out before the curve of the tunnel occluded it glowed softly. She had not diverged from Baanraak's path at all, but she could see faint traces of her presence nonetheless. She left a narrower band of barely brighter light wherever she'd moved. In places where she'd stood for a moment, the brightness became noticeable.

But only if one were looking for it in the first place, and knew the trick of closing the eyes and stilling the mind and . . .

Right. He knew how to see her. The only likely reason that he hadn't paid attention to the little trail of presence she'd left behind her was because he assumed that anyone coming down into the tunnel would spring his traps.

She'd bypassed all of them. That, of course, was the easy part of her task. The hard part would be getting Molly and the Vodi necklace away from him. That, she thought, would be very hard indeed.

Lauren had a vague idea of how she might get the necklace away from Baanraak. She thought if she were very careful, she might slip close enough that she could put a hand on Molly. He had her buried within a pile of rotting carcasses, but from what Lauren could tell, these increased the speed with which Molly regenerated. When Baanraak killed Molly by crushing her skull, he hadn't removed the necklace; Lauren had been able to discover that Baanraak wanted Molly to reanimate as quickly as possible so that he could repeatedly kill her. Leaving most of the body intact and attached to the necklace had speeded the regeneration process.

It would be easier to get Molly out if she were alive. Dragging her body would be tough—but for Lauren, that was only the smallest part of the dilemma. The rest of it was how to get Molly away from Baanraak; how to avoid using any magic that would trigger the traps and bring God-only-knew-what screaming down on them, how to get out without triggering the traps, how to avoid whatever was about to happen topside. And once she and Molly got back to the surface, how to avoid the war until they got to the gate.

How to stay alive. That loomed pretty big. How the hell to stay alive.

I'm sorry, Jake, she thought. I'm sorry you have the

wrong mom. You didn't need this—you needed someone who would stay home and make cookies with you and be the horsey and teach you how to read and tell you how great your dad was. I'm sorry you got me. Or chose me. Or however that worked. This can't have been what you planned for.

With her eyes closed, she could pretend that she was Baanraak. If she held herself very quietly in his mind, she could get a feel for the position of his body, the way he lay, the shape of him and the position of Molly and the pile of carcasses beside him. She couldn't get a feel for his position relative to her, though—she needed to move just a few steps while facing in the same direction to see if she could triangulate.

She took one very cautious step—praying that she wouldn't step *on* Baanraak, which would give away the whole game—and then a second.

And then Molly came to life in a roiling fury, still enraged from her previous death, the thought of her magical attack on Baanraak still foremost in her mind. Lauren felt like someone had switched on a field full of klieg lights in her brain. She crouched and something made her think of Seolar's dagger, still strapped to her hip, worn faithfully but not needed since the attack that had nearly killed her, and she grabbed that, and Molly slammed Baanraak with a spell that set him on fire, compressed the air around him with a thunderclap, crushed him and broke his wings, and twisted and mangled him. All up the tunnel to the surface, Lauren heard the traps, set to react to magic in the tunnels, go off; in an instant the roars and grunts of Baanraak's surprises echoed through the caverns and chambers.

Molly rose out of the maggot-covered bone heap, illuminated by the fire that consumed her enemy, and with a scream of pure rage began throwing fireballs at the rrôn. Baanraak turned his long neck to stare at Molly, and Lauren saw her opportunity.

She rushed in and, willing her dagger into a deadly sword, slashed it into the flesh of his neck, powering the downstroke with an image of slicing clean through skin and muscle and bone and seeing his head come clean off. He hadn't guarded against her—hadn't suspected for an instant that Lauren was there. All his attention focused on Molly, and that fact was his death. Seolar's dagger, stretched by Lauren's will and magic to the dimensions of some thunder-thewed hero's bastard sword, severed Baanraak's neck as neatly as if she'd been slicing through pudding. Gouts of hot blood poured over Lauren, and Baanraak's upper body lurched forward and the gruesome, heavy neck and head crashed down on her, pinning her to the floor.

"Molly," she shouted. "We have to hurry. Help me!"

Molly turned, shouted, "Lauren?!" and ran straight for her.

Baanraak's massive body, thrashing in its death spasms, caught Molly, and the splayed, razor talons ripped her into pieces, flinging her head in one direction and body in another. And the gleaming jeweled gold necklace in a third. It happened so fast that at first Lauren couldn't comprehend it. Molly—dead again.

Lauren couldn't think. She fought her way out from under the monster while ponderous footsteps and roars and groans crashed ever nearer. When she finally broke free, she raced to Molly, grabbed head and body and scrambled after the necklace, finally finding it in the pile of carcasses. She dragged everything together, and willed Molly to heal. To live.

But Molly didn't. Head and neck did not rejoin, and the necklace, gleaming in the dying light cast by the guttering fires on Baanraak's body, mocked Lauren. Above, but closer every minute, the horrors cast by Baanraak moved toward her. No sense hiding any longer. No sense trying to be stealthy. All she needed to do now was get out.

But had she won, or had she lost? If the necklace came off of Molly before she was dead, then all of this had been for nothing, because the necklace would not bring her back.

Lauren tried not to see her sister's ravaged body, and tried not to think about the horrors her sister had endured. She created a gate that would carry her to the surface, and prayed that she would be able to get everyone away safely, and prayed, too, that Molly would return.

Using the circumference of the tunnel to cast her gate, she called forth the wall of green fire. She felt the floor of the cave tremble beneath her feet in rhythm to the steps of whatever approached. She could hear it breathing. She could smell it.

Then Lauren heard a banshee wail, a sound so terrible that it ripped the silence of the cave into shreds and forced a horrified cry from her. The surface—she thought. The big trap on the surface had just sprung.

The sheet of green fire formed, and as it did Lauren heard a low, deadly growl, and felt the air move behind her. She jumped into the gate even though it was not completely formed, and for an instant she felt the universe embrace her, and comfort her, and support her.

Then she toppled out the other side.

Copper House

Jake sat in the safe room, tucked into one corner of the couch. He did not want anyone to see him, because when they saw him, they would take him away. In this room, he could make the things he wanted happen. In this room he could feel Mommy, and the next thing he wanted was to be with her. She was on the other side of the mirror, very far away, in a bad place.

But he could not see her. He could not find her if he could not see her. So he watched Doggie walking back and forth in front of him, and he wished that no one could see him so that he could stay close to Mommy. And he waited to see her.

He had his cape. He was Superman. And Daddy told him to take care of Mommy.

Jake was ready.

Dalchi

Seolar, in his bubble, saw the ground rip open like a wound beneath him as the first of the dark gods touched Baanraak's mound. He watched fire blast out and up—not gaseous fire, but fire that spurted and popped and oozed like sludge, like white-hot molten metal poured from a forge. And shoving, squirming, clawing its way out of that blazing hellhole came a light-sucking horror with a ring of eyes that burned white as the fire that gave it birth. It had the look of embodied shadow, of places where living things could not traverse. It held to the merest suggestion of form—Seolar thought he saw arms and legs in multitudes, but he could not look at the horror long enough to be sure. It would have been at home in the worst hell of any world, but from the reactions of the dark gods who saw it shouldering its way up to tower above them, it was no stranger to them.

Big, Seolar thought. Big, oh big, oh gods. Standing on the ground, it would have been able to look into the tower on the fifth floor of Copper House with ease. It hadn't been that big at first. It couldn't have been.

It swallowed the dark god that triggered the trap almost without thinking, then scooped up as many close to it as it could reach and tossed them in its mouth, the way a child would scoop up spilled sweets.

In its birthing, it crushed the opening to the cave, and Seolar cried out for Lauren and Molly, trapped inside—but then green claw-tipped hands dug through from beneath the rubble, and a head poked out, and then a body, and the second monster formed a new opening as it emerged onto the battlefield. Glistening green scales like plate armor, a body heavy and solid as the mountain, teeth jagged as serrated blades. And behind it came another—a thing that skittered out on spider legs, but that made even the most hideous and deadly of spiders seem tender and charming playthings by comparison. And behind that, another horror, in another form.

Seolar, stunned by the spawning of hell before his eyes,

did not realize his danger until the first and worst nightmare turned its face toward him. It opened its mouth and let out a scream that froze his blood in his veins. All he could think was—Away.

The magical tether he'd formed for himself snapped and he soared skyward, out of reach of the monster. Out of reach of all the monsters.

And then he realized that he had the gate. That he was the only retreat for his men, for Lauren, and please, God, for Molly.

The monsters had the dark gods in hand. He needed to clear his people from the battlefield—Lauren would not need an army. All she would need was a way home, and even after his people were safely out of harm's way, Seolar could provide her that.

The horrors had gone back to feeding on the dark gods. And there it was—the friendly fire Lauren had hoped for— one dark god setting his weapons against other dark gods. And Seolar found it much less welcome in reality than he had in his imagination. He noted which of his people were closest to danger. He aimed himself for a clear patch sheltered a bit by trees and rocks and raced the shield and the gate within it down to the ground as fast as he could.

His men saw him coming, and he willed them to hear him. *Retreat*, he told them. *You're done here—now get out.*

His men came at a run, keeping to cover as best they could, but mostly just watching the sky for incoming attacks. When the first reached him, Seolar shoved them through the gate. Each time it flickered a bit, but held. He prayed to gods he no longer believed in that it would hold long enough to get everyone through. He prayed, too, that his men would run faster—Baanraak's monsters, perhaps wearying of a diet of dark gods, were beginning to look his way.

To his left, up toward the rise, he caught a flash of green fire from the corner of his eye. He turned away from his men, who kept moving into the gate as fast as it would take them, and saw Lauren burst out of the wall of light at a dead run. Even from where he stood, he could see the glint of gold in her hand. A hairbreadth behind her, another nightmare made real, maw gaping and claws unsheathed—a horned and hideous four-legged demon-spawn in gleaming red erupted from her gate and charged after her.

Copper House

Jake watched the tall people running into the mirror and then jumping out into the room where they sat. He could see monsters, big scary ones, on the other side of the mirror.

He watched and watched, and suddenly he saw her. He pointed to the mirror and shrieked, "Mama!"

She did not hear him. But Doggie did.

Mama ran toward the mirror, but one of the monsters chased her. She was afraid.

"I'm Superman," he screamed at the monster. "You don't chase my mama!"

He put an arm in front of him and jumped into the air, and flew into the mirror. He would save his mama from the monster.

Copper House to Dalchi

For Doggie, it all happened too fast to stop. The veyâr were retreating, pushing her back against the wall as they leapt, bleeding and battered, into the room, when suddenly over the noise of their arrival she heard Jake's voice in the room, where he could not be.

She looked toward the mirror and briefly saw the Hunter, pursued by something terrible. She heard the little god's voice again, and this time caught a flash of red as he flew over her head into the mirror.

Doggie screamed, launched herself through the veyâr, and

raced for the mirror. She had promised to keep him safe. She promised the Hunter, and now, inarguably, Jake the Hunter's Son was not safe.

Doggie could not get into the gate, because one of the veyâr was coming out—but the instant he was clear, she charged in, begging the Big Fates and the Little Fates that the boy would be safe, and that she would not fail in this, her duty.

She spun through the green fire and for a time lost herself, filled with wonder. She could hear the voices of her ancestors singing, just as the Speakers for the Big Fates said she would when she crossed from death through to life. She could feel her own past, her present, and her future flowing through her, and in them she felt eternity. She would go on—she could feel the truth of that, where before the promises of the Speakers for the Big Fates had seemed like just so many words to her. Peace filled her, and joy. She was safe. She would always be safe.

Doggie had no idea how long she hung suspended in that wonderful place, but she came out the other side changed. And she came out knowing that she could do whatever she had to do to save Jake.

She saw him in the air, rocketing like a tiny shooting star toward his mother and the monster that pursued her, and Doggie had just enough time to register the horror on the faces of the veyâr around her—veyâr who were still plunging headlong toward safety through the gate. Doggie raced out of safety, into the fray.

She bounded through grass up past her eyeballs, and wished with everything in her that she were taller so that she could see over it.

Then, suddenly she was out of the area with the tall grass, although it looked no different. Doggie ran more easily once she could see, but still not fast enough. By all the Fates, if only she could fly . . .

She nearly screamed when one foot, striding forward and

expecting hard ground, failed to find it. The second found only air, too, and for a moment she windmilled ludicrously, fighting for traction that no longer existed. When she realized that she could fly, though, and that she could catch Jake, she tore forward through the air, closing the distance between them.

He reached his mother and the monster before Doggie could get him, though, and screamed at the monster, "GO AWAY, BAD MONSTER!"

The monster turned its attention to Jake, and its jaws gaped in a feral grin. And then it was gone.

No flash of light, no puff of smoke, no sparkles of dust and debris hung in the air. Doggie careened into the ground facefirst, stunned and frightened.

Jake flew into his mother's arms and the Hunter stumbled trying to catch him. She slowed her run, and Doggie said, "More things come behind you, Hunter. Fly to safety." But the Hunter wasn't looking at her. She stared, instead, behind her.

Doggie twisted in the grass. Saw the red monster now attacking the veyâr. The child had moved the horror; he had not destroyed it. And, being just a little child, he had not moved it far enough.

More monsters moved toward them from the high ground, and fireballs and projectiles arced overhead, pounding the shield into which the veyâr fled. Most of them, Doggie saw, had reached safety. A few had not, and those the red monster cut off, chasing them around the shield. The Hunter got one clear shot at the monster as he passed between her and the shield, pointed her finger at him, and snarled, "Die!"

This time the monster burst into flames so hot they were blue, and exploded in a rain of charred flesh and bits of bone. Behind the dead monster, the shield flickered once, and died completely.

"Shit, shit, SHIT!" the Hunter screamed, and pointed at the place where the shield had been. Before she could do whatever she'd intended to do, missiles and fire rained down on the gate, the veyâr moving into it, and the Imallin. The

Imallin and several of the veyâr screamed—bloodcurdling sounds, and the Hunter stopped dead in her tracks, even with monsters of every variety moving toward her, and told Doggie, "Hold Jake. Fast."

Doggie, back on her feet, though skinned and bruised, grabbed Jake, noticing as she did that she was only a handspan shorter than the Hunter now. Strange. She held Jake, who hugged her and stared all around him, no longer the brave little Superman, and the Hunter cast a shield around everyone within range—the veyâr, Doggie and Jake, and herself. She stood with her eyes closed for a moment, and the shield grew so solid that light barely passed through it. "To hell with this," the Hunter said to Doggie, patting her on the shoulder. "Let's go home."

They hurried to the injured veyâr, and Lauren knelt by each one in turn, laying hands on them and removing their injuries. "You can do this, too, Doggie," she said. "Want them to be healthy, and see them healthy. Get them before they die, though."

They worked for a while, and Doggie heard the Hunter reach the Imallin, and heard him croak, "Let me die. Let me go to her."

"Not a chance," the Hunter said. "You have work to do here, pal—as much as either Molly or I do. You'll die when it's your time. But that time isn't today."

Outside, Doggie heard roaring, and saw splashes of light illuminating sections of the Hunter's powerful shield. She shivered; now that she'd reached relative safety, she could feel how close she had come to death. She nuzzled the little boy in her arms, and thought of her family, and her village. She had a name now—a god-given name. From being a girl of no consequence, she had become a woman of repute. She had stature among the goroths. She could take a mate, find safety, live out her life with children and grandchildren of her own, and never look back to this terror of racing between worlds, seeing monsters, flying, fighting gods, doing magic. She could have the life she'd always yearned for.

The Hunter spun a gate out of nothing—a glorious circle of light and harmony and song that stretched a bridge through eternity—and Doggie realized that if she followed the path of her old dreams, she would never walk the fire-road again. She would not commune with old gods, nor would she change the world.

The goroths were not a people given to dreaming vast dreams or seeing themselves in the role of hero. They called themselves a small people, and prided themselves on practicality, reason, and tradition. But inside Doggie, something clicked softly, and she realized that, terror and danger and all, she could not go back to being who she'd been before she came to serve the Hunter. She bore a god-given name. She had flown, she had stretched herself tall, she had seen another world and walked through fire. She could claim the right to dream the dreams of gods.

Copper House

Lauren pushed through the gate last, closing it behind her, and setting the shield to shut down the instant she was gone. No use leaving magic running; she had the feeling they would have hell to pay for this day anyway.

The path between the worlds comforted her, and when she stepped into the crowded room with all the hopeful, waiting people in it and picked up Jake in her arms and held him tight, she felt like she'd come home.

But.

"You still have the necklace?" Seolar asked.

Lauren nodded.

Cheers broke out around the room, so loud that Jake cringed and buried his face against her neck. Lauren held up the hand that wasn't hanging on to Jake and said, "Don't cheer yet."

The silence that followed hurt. Every eye in the room watched her, and all she could hear was breathing—and barely that.

"She came back," Lauren said. "She made it all the way back to being alive again, and she knew where she was, and she acted fast. She's the one who distracted Baanraak—she hit him with a huge magical broadside as soon as her eyes opened. I ran in and killed him before he could do anything to retaliate, but he toppled onto me. Molly ran to help me, and Baanraak, in his death throes, ripped her to pieces, and the necklace came off." Lauren took a deep breath, looked into the eyes of the people whose lives and world depended on what she was about to say, and said, "It may have come off before she was dead."

The silence lengthened, and lengthened. Lauren didn't have anything else to say, so, taking Jake, she pushed her way through the frozen crowd, out into the now-well-lit sub-basement. She followed the line of torches to the nearest stairwell—so much easier to find now than the first time she went hunting for it—and finally slid Jake to the ground and let him walk beside her, holding her hand. She slid a hand into the pocket of her jeans where the Vodi necklace rested, but quickly pulled it out. The necklace had a greasy, unpleasant feel against her skin. It vibrated when she touched it, a vibration that felt almost like a cat's purr—but all resemblance to petting a purring cat ended there. When Lauren touched the Vodi necklace, a dark space opened in her mind and filled her with bleak images that scared her. Places where life wasn't, places of horror and pain and anguish and endless suffering and endless loss. She wondered how Molly ever stood having the thing touch her.

Up one level, and another, and she and Jake came out into one of the beautiful corridors lined with copper arches made to look like trees. This place had such beauty to it, and it might now be doomed.

Home might be weeks or even mere days away from destruction. Everything rested on Molly, and thanks to Lauren's carelessness, Molly might not be coming back.

One of the servants saw her walking with Jake and approached her shyly. "Hunter, you have returned."

Lauren nodded.

"And the others?"

"The survivors are back."

"And the Vodi?"

"I have her necklace," Lauren said. "Don't celebrate yet. We aren't sure how everything is going to go."

The servant looked at her with wide, worried eyes, then bowed deeply and hurried away. Lauren and Jake continued their walk. The corridors lay almost empty. Outside, a storm raged.

Lauren felt the exhaustion go all the way into her bones. She'd failed. She'd failed to get Brian back, she'd failed to get Molly back her soul, and in the end she'd failed to save Molly. She'd fought a good fight, she'd given it everything she had, and she'd failed.

Qawar approached her. "We aren't done yet, you know."

Lauren looked at him sidelong. "You think not?"

"We're getting reports from the downworld, from this world, from Earth. The fallout from our battle with the dark gods has had devastating consequences. In each world up from Dalchi, disasters tear at the fabric of the worlds, and the carnage is horrifying. The effects spread wide and become less intense as you move upworld, but even in your world, the skies are filled with portents and the ground is littered with tragedy." He sighed. "Here . . . well, here things are bad, and downworld they're worse."

Lauren shrugged. "It doesn't make a difference. Don't you realize that? We're done, all right. We lost, and we're done, and everything I ever knew and cared about, except for my son, is going to be gone in just a week or two. I don't get to go home."

"A lot of us don't get to go home," Qawar said.

Lauren turned and stared into his eyes. "If you gave a shit about that, why didn't you do something to fight the dark gods? You have magic. You have a hell of a lot more magic than I do. And you have for . . . how long? How old are you? A couple hundred years? A couple thousand? Didn't you say ten thousand or something like that? You people could have been fighting the dark gods all along, doing something that would limit the damage they're doing, but you didn't want to risk your precious skins, since all you had to do when things got nasty was hop downworld. You and all the rest of the old gods hid until you had people willing to go out and fight in front of you, and even then, you were the only one who showed up—and you held back and let the veyâr take the brunt of the thing. Anyone know how many veyâr died in that fight?"

Qawar shrugged. "They're still counting. Fifty, maybe."

"Fifty. Out of the couple hundred that were all the veyâr could spare. How about old gods? How many old gods died?"

Qawar said nothing.

"C'mon. How many?"

"None, of course."

"I rest my case." Lauren turned and started walking away.

Behind her, Qawar said, "We need your help—"

She felt Jake's hand in hers—small and soft and fragile. The only person in the world who needed her right at that moment was Jake. She turned back to the old god and said, "You need to grow a pair, pal. Handle it. I'm done."

She and Jake got to the suite they shared, and Lauren got the first glimpse of herself in a mirror, and almost choked. Baanraak's blood and Molly's blood coated her from head to foot. Now that she saw herself, she realized that she reeked of blood, that her skin itched and her hair was matted with it. Jake hadn't said anything about it, no one else had made any mention of it—but no one could look at Lauren and think anything but that she'd been in a war.

She shut her door, grabbed soft cotton pajamas for herself and Jake, peeled off her clothes and then his, and said, "Shower time, monkey-boy."

Jake liked showers, though Lauren wondered how she was ever going to get one once he was old enough that she couldn't take him in with her. She tried to imagine trusting

Jake alone in a room by himself for more than a minute and her mind simply balked at the ensuing images of destruction.

She soaped him, then herself; got the flowery shampoo provided for her by the servant, and began trying to get the blood out of her hair. She fought with it for a long time, watching the water curling red around her feet, and watching Jake eyeing the blood warily. Finally, she realized her only hope was to cut most of her hair off and try again. The suite offered a complete supply of bathroom implements, including a gaudy pair of scissors that looked like the handles had been made of gold. The blades weren't terribly sharp, but they'd do.

She pulled Jake out of the shower, wrapped him in a towel, and sat him on the floor beside the sink. "Stay," she said, and he sat there watching her struggling to save as much of her hair as she could.

She cut away great long tangles of it, each a clotted mass, and as she did she cried—she cried for the sister she had watched die, for the world she couldn't save and all the people in it, for the husband she couldn't have back, for the son who would never get to go home.

With every snip of the scissors, her head got lighter, and a little bit of her grief wore away.

When she was done, she'd run out of tears, though her hair was about two inches long all over. Lauren could see that she had no future as a stylist. She looked a lot like her Barbie dolls used to after she got done "fixing" them.

She jumped back in the shower long enough to get the last traces of blood out, then dried off. Jake sat patiently waiting for her—out of character for him. But he'd had a rough day, too.

"You know, kiddo," she said, pulling his jammies on him, "the only thing this place really lacks is a phone to call for room service." She dropped her towel and pulled on jammies of her own. "I could use something yummy right now."

"Yummy?" He looked at her and managed a tired, hopeful little smile.

She picked him up and hugged him. "We'll find something yummy. We both need it. I could eat a moose."

"Why?"

She didn't answer. Jake didn't know a moose from Michelangelo, and wouldn't if she spent half an hour explaining. Instead, she rubbed noses with him and said, "This isn't going to make any sense to you until years from now, provided we live that long, but thank you for saving my ass out there today. My mind just went blank and I panicked. You really were a little Superman, weren't you?"

Now his face lit up. "I was Superman, and I flieded."

"Yeah, you did. And if I thought it would do any good, I'd make you promise that you would never do it again." Jake with magic, and yearning to be a superhero. When she was a little less exhausted, that one was going to give her the heebie-jeebies. The only world where Jake wouldn't have magic was his own . . .

Bad thoughts. She didn't need to go down that particular path anymore in one day.

With him swung onto her hip, she headed into the suite's main room. There she found Seolar and Birra and all of the goroths waiting for her.

"Shit," she said.

"Shit!" Jake echoed, with a bit more emphasis.

Everyone looked at her with expressions she couldn't read at all, until Seolar finally said, politely, "Your hair looks . . . interesting."

"Couldn't get the blood out," she told him shortly, then said, "I want to rest and spend some time with my kid and get something to eat. What do you all want?"

"The necklace," Seolar said. "Where is it?"

Lauren went to her jeans, picked them up and shook them until the Vodi necklace fell out on the bed. She didn't want to touch it. So she backed away, and, palm upward, said, "All yours."

Qawar made a point of not looking at her. Instead, he stared fixedly at Seolar and said, "We need to take it back to

the safe room so that the magic can work and Molly can . . .
return. Slowly, though. Clear everything from the room but
the air itself—the slower she gathers material to rebuild, the
more she will come back like herself."

"I'm guessing being buried in a pile of dead animal carcasses would have been bad, then," Lauren said.

Qawar nodded, though he still wouldn't look at her.
"Baanraak seems to have been trying to strip away everything about her that linked her to life. By repeatedly killing
her and then reviving her very quickly after each death, he
would be able to turn her into something like him in short
order."

Lauren swallowed back the tears that kept trying to form,
and said, "I don't think it's going to be an issue anymore,
boys. Really, I don't."

Seolar said, "We need to be able to hope. At least for a
while. At least until we know one way or the other. We need
to be able to hold on to the possibility that she might come
back. And you have no reason to think that she won't—at
least no more than to think that she will . . ." His voice
trailed off as he saw Lauren shaking her head.

"I wish that were true, Seo. More than you will ever
know. But there's something I didn't tell you before, and
it . . . well." She looked down at her feet. "I tried to save her,
as fast as I could crawl out from under Baanraak's body. I
gathered up the . . . pieces . . ." The tears got the better of
her for a moment, and she closed her eyes and just breathed
until she got herself under control again. "I put the necklace
on her, and I used every bit of magic I could summon to put
everything back together and to bring her back. It didn't
work."

Again she faced terrible silence, and faces lined with pain.
No one said a word. No one suggested that her experience
might not matter. No one had so much as a flicker of hope in
his eyes.

Lauren straightened and nodded a little. "So I don't think
she's coming back this time. But you can sure have the neck-

lace and take it down to the safe room and do whatever you can to give Molly the best chance she has to come back." The tears were working their way to the surface again, and Lauren didn't feel like she could face anyone but Jake. She said, "Please just leave now."

They filed out of the room without protest or comment. Seolar carried the necklace—but not in his hand. He picked it up with a fold of the cloth of his robe, and tucked it into the fancy silk-brocade cummerbund he wore. So he couldn't stand to touch it either.

He left last, and Lauren remembered him lying on the ground begging her to let him die. Lauren understood the way he felt, and now that she stood clear of the madness of the battle and her own fear, she wondered why she hadn't. Because if he died, he would be with Molly again, and she was jealous of that? Because she wanted him to suffer the way she suffered?

She found it easy to think of all sorts of cruel reasons why she hadn't let him go—but his eyes met hers, and they held no accusation.

That, she thought, would probably come later, after the shock wore off and he had a chance to think about everything he'd lost.

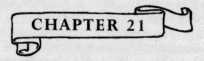

CHAPTER 21

Copper House

THREE DAYS PASSED in silence in Copper House. For three days, Lauren, Birra, Seolar, Qawar and the guards passed each other on the stairs going down to or coming up from the safe room, always checking the other faces as they passed for signs of good news, and always finding nothing.

Lauren considered packing up her few belongings and Jake and returning to Cat Creek. There she could keep Jake from flying around rooms; there she could talk about what had happened to someone (*Pete*, her mind suggested with a vehemence that surprised her), and there she could gather up her few friends and loved ones and gate them out of danger before the world imploded.

She knew she didn't have a lot of time—that the final fall of Earth could begin at any time, and that every day she delayed was another day of deterioration that could trigger the final, unstoppable collapse.

But she couldn't make herself admit Molly wasn't going to make it. She could not claim to harbor any hope, but neither could she take the final public step of saying, "It's over. Time for me to go home and make other arrangements."

By the time three days had passed, though, she had to face facts. Her stupid cry for help had cost the world and nearly everyone in it. She couldn't wait any longer, or she might be late. She and Jake would go back, she would make gates to evacuate any who wanted to leave, and then the two of them would flee to safety.

The radio guy—Art Bell—he could probably get the word out, she thought. Lauren figured he had the only audience anywhere in the world who would both believe what she had to say and be willing to act on it. That might save . . . what . . . a million people? Probably fewer than that, because Art had his share of skeptics in the audience. Five hundred thousand?

Out of six billion.

Shit.

She looked up at the dark sky and thought, This place is never going to feel like home. Then she tucked Jake into bed, curled up next to him, and tried to go to sleep.

Copper House

Seolar sat by the necklace that lay on the marble slab he and his men had carried into the safe room. He could see nothing about it that indicated Molly would ever be coming back. Still, because he had the room to himself except for the necklace, and because he didn't know what else to do, he talked to the metal as if Molly might be in there somewhere; as if she might be able to hear him.

"I have said things to you that I regret, my love. I have thought things about you that I wish I had not thought. I don't know if any part of you is still in there; I don't know if any part of you can still hear me. But I want you to know that I love you. If I cannot be with you in life, I will find my way to your side after death. This separation will not stand."

He rested his head in his hands and sobbed quietly.

Finally he stood. "We deserved better, you and I. We deserved a world where we could love each other without shadows between us. If you come back, the shadows may darken our days, but they will not put out our sun. I swear it. If you will have me, I will love you for as long as I live, and after."

He rose, studied the necklace. It lay there. What else had he expected. If he had hoped for a sign, none came to him.

After a moment of silence, he turned and left. The guards at the door looked at him with hopeful eyes, but he just shook his head.

Copper House

Lying in the dark after Jake went to sleep, Lauren discovered that her mind wouldn't quiet, and that all the calming meditative tricks she knew offered her neither stillness nor peace. She got up, found a lamp, and lit it. Instantly the goroths surrounded her, wanting to know what they could get for her or do for her.

She was going to tell them nothing, but they felt as useless as she did—she might as well make someone feel better. "I could really use a big mug of hot tea, and something good to eat."

Two of them scurried off to find her something.

Lauren paced for a bit, and the remaining goroths finally figured out that all this movement didn't mean she was going anywhere anytime soon, and settled in where they could watch her.

Something worried at the back of Lauren's mind. She paced, trying to knock whatever it was free by dint of constant restless movement. Something about her parents' notebook—a single line written in the margins in an off-colored ink. She'd just glimpsed it and had, for some reason, written it off as her father having a bad day, but now, in the dark of night and with all hope already lost, she couldn't let that line go.

Whose handwriting had it been in? Her father's? Her mother's? Something about that note had been . . . wrong.

She got the notebook out and started going through it, carefully, page by page. Everything was in there. Her father's neat diagrams for spellcasting equipment that she and Molly were supposed to create and power that would

counter the constant downflow of poisoned energy from
Kerras. Ideas for chains of stations connected together
around each living downworld and linked together—years
worth of work for two people, and only Molly could power
the thing, and only Lauren could connect it. It all seemed so
complicated, so fragile, so doomed to failure. Even had
Molly survived, how could they manage the resources, the
time, the effort and coordination for such a massive under-
taking in time to save their dying world?

But the knot in her gut felt hopeful.

So what in hell had dragged her from bed with a sudden
stupid feeling of hope?

Page by page she moved through the old notebook, and
then, on the outer margin of a page in which her father was
complaining bitterly of a failure in one of his experiments,
the line she'd been seeking. "It's all bullshit, except for this."

But the marginal line was in her mother's handwriting.
Her mother, who in Lauren's entire life had never uttered a
word that might even be mistaken for a curse word. Marion
did not even say, "Heck," for heck was simply a substitute
for Hell. She did not say "darn." She did not say "jeez" or
"sheesh." And she most assuredly had never uttered the word
"bullshit" in anyone's hearing except, perhaps, for God.

This had been a woman who didn't *fart*.

It's all bullshit, except for this.

Her mother's handwriting, formed by the Palmer method
and ingrained from years of teaching it to resistant fifth- and
sixth-graders, could in no way be mistaken for her father's
narrow, heavy-fisted scrawl. Lauren could tell whether her
mother or father had written a passage in the dark, just by
running her finger along the back side of the paper. If it felt
like Braille, her father had written it. So the words were her
mother's, and yet they weren't.

They offered a riddle.

It's all bullshit, except for this.

Except for what? Her father's weary ranting about something that had gone wrong? That was the truth?

Lauren looked over the passage, and on it suddenly noted one word in her father's narrative that he hadn't written. One word, in the same color ink as her mother's cryptic note, in her mother's Palmer handwriting. The word was *notebook*.

The middle of the back of Lauren's neck began to itch, and she stared at the diagram at the top of the page, and at the single word down in the right-hand corner, in the middle of a sentence, that fit perfectly with what her father was saying, but that her father had not written.

She turned back to the previous page, and scanned it.

Middle of the page, two words. Ignore the.

A handful of pages before that had been written by her mother, only in different-colored ink—Lauren looked over these carefully, but could find nothing out of place. Prior to these pages, in the older part of the notebook, nothing odd. When she went to the "bullshit" page again and started moving toward the back of the notebook, she found another word. *It's*

With rising excitement, she told Rue, "Bring me paper and something to write with. Quickly. I've just discovered something."

She started at the beginning. Her task took most of the night, but when she finished, she'd uncovered the following message.

Ignore the notebook; it's to draw attention away from you and Molly. The two of you are the secret. You're the answer.

Molly, you must become the Hunter. You alone can hunt down the Night Watch and use the magic that will kill and then undo them without your actions rebounding to our own world. It's a horrible task, but you will have immortality working for you. The veyâr will resist this; they have their own expectations of a Vodi, and you will not be able to live up to them once you change. And you will change. But you must, in order to survive and do what you have to do.

Lauren, you must be the rebuilder. You will have no magic necklace, no protection save that which your sister and those you can trust give you; nothing but your own talent and determination and character to see you through, and those alone will determine whether or not our world lives or dies. You do not get immortality, and if ever it is offered, you must resist. Use your gateweaving to open passages from healthy downworlds back up to Earth—passages that will stay open. Make them as small as you need to keep them stable; hide them well. Each one will be a lifeline to our world. Convince old gods to come into our world and use the fresh magic that these passages will provide to do good. Any positive magic will rebound positively. Good magic echoes good all the way up the worldchain, but as the upworlds die off, the energy that permits magic dies, too, until only drastic measures such as the ones we outline offer any hope of salvation.

Both of you—work from any world that offers you safety. Bring in fresh magic to our world, and to the worlds above. You can open gates to them, even if you can't do much in them yourself. Find the gods who can live in them. Avoid the Night Watch at all costs. Protect each other.

If neither of you was directed to this message by memory, be careful. Some of our imprinting might have gone awry. We didn't have anyone to practice *on—nor much time to get anything right. We're being watched. We love you both, and always will, no matter where you are and where we are when you read this.*

She read through the decoded note three times before it started to sink in.

"Son of a bitch," Lauren said, shaking her head. "You were a couple of sneaky people. Didn't do you a damned bit of good in the end, but you had the moves, anyway."

She considered the information in her hands.

First, the question. Had a memory left for her by her parents triggered her sudden hope and her curiosity about the notation in the margin? Or had she come across that without any help from them? Did she need to be uncertain about everything else she remembered, or thought she did?

Next, the hope. According to the hidden message, Lauren, not Molly, would be the source of the healing energy that would revive Earth and the worlds above it. Molly was supposed to protect her, and was supposed to do away with the Night Watch—but perhaps Lauren could do what she needed to do alone.

Until the Night Watch hunted her and Jake down and killed them both.

She groaned and tucked the paper into the book, and tucked the book back in her bag, and crawled into bed with Jake, who was still asleep. Suddenly she didn't feel like facing the day that already edged in through her east window. She didn't think she would ever be able to close her eyes.

But then somehow she did.

Copper House

In the darkness of the empty room, the Vodi necklace began to glow softly. And the tears shed by the Imallin gleamed briefly, then vanished.

Copper House

Someone pounded on her door. Lauren woke up groggily, remembering vaguely that she'd had a breakthrough, but she was so tired that she couldn't focus on what it was. She sat up, and noticed that Jake wasn't in the bed next to her. That woke her up more sharply than ice water would have. She lunged from the bed to the door, blew past whoever had been standing there, and saw Jake and Doggie sitting cross-legged on the floor, crashing Jake's cars together.

She turned to see whom she'd slammed behind the door.

One of the guards who had been on safe room duty. Lauren didn't know his name, but felt guilty about that; she felt especially guilty since from all appearances she'd given him what was going to be one hell of a shiner.

"The Imallin needs you downstairs," he said. Lauren saw panic in his eyes.

"What's wrong?"

"I don't know. Something. Everyone is in an uproar."

Uproar. Great. Lauren had something that might help—that might offer a ray of hope, if not a solution, and now something else had gone wrong.

She picked up Jake, balanced him on her hip, and said, "Okay—let's go."

The guard took off at a fast pace. Lauren followed, trailing goroths.

When they reached the subbasement and the safe room, however, Lauren found no uproar—only a lot of veyâr standing very still, faces toward the door, making no sound at all.

"You're to go in," the guard said. "The Imallin requested it."

Lauren and Jake went through the door she'd made, into a room that still had the bones of the apartment she'd made for herself. Along the right wall, the live image of the forest outside the village of Copper House remained. Qawar had removed all the carpet and all the furniture, though, as well as the kitchen and bathroom fixtures, and had placed the necklace on a raised black marble slab that seemed stark beneath the bright lights and the white walls.

The necklace still lay there. At first Lauren thought nothing had changed about it. Then she noticed a faint glow. She frowned. "Has it ever glowed before?"

"Not that I know of," Seolar told her.

Lauren said, "Does Qawar know what it's doing?"

"No."

"The glowing isn't part of the spell that activates it?"

"No one knows—but according to Qawar, it doesn't seem likely. The necklace is a dark god magic—under normal circumstances he thinks that it would absorb light rather than emit it when it is . . . ah . . . working."

"Then he thinks that the spell is broken?"

"He doesn't know. From what I could gather, he seems to think that if it were broken, it wouldn't do anything at all."

Lauren stared at him, and then looked at Jake, who was looking from Seolar to the necklace on the slab and back to Seolar, as if he were watching a high-speed tennis match.

"What is it, Jake?"

He pointed with his finger at the space between Seolar and the necklace, with his finger wavering back and forth.

Seolar looked at Jake, looked at the necklace, and turned to Birra. "Bring in Qawar—I want to know what he sees."

Birra came back a moment later with Qawar, who took one look at the necklace and said, "Get the baby out of the room. Quickly."

Lauren ran to the door and called Doggie over. "Take him, wait in the corridor. Jake, stay with Doggie and be a good boy."

"The necklace is drawing energy from life, and the little boy is . . . vulnerable. Birra, bring the veyâr in here. We need as many people in here as will fit."

As more of the veyâr crowded into the room, the nimbus of light around the Vodi necklace grew brighter, until it glowed like a small sun. Then a soft hum filled the room, and ribbons of white light crawled along the walls, ceiling, and floor, like lightning trapped inside the surfaces. Lauren noticed a soft, uneven rumbling like thunder. The only storm, of course, was the one building in the safe room.

Qawar started chasing veyâr from the room. "I was wrong! Out," he shouted. But Seolar commanded Birra to leave, while he stayed. Lauren, scared, stood her ground beside Seolar.

"She's in there," Seolar said. He stared at the necklace, and Lauren could see the tears running down his cheeks. She noticed that the floor around Seolar's feet glowed brighter than the rest of the room, and that every tear that landed on it lit up like a flare before sizzling away to nothing. "She's in there, and she's all alone, and I can't save her."

Lauren reached out and took his hand. "I can feel her presence, Seo. We're both here with her; that's the best we can do."

"Does she know that? Does she know we're here? I don't want her to think we've abandoned her."

"I think she knows." Lauren closed her eyes and tried to reach the place where Molly was. She sought her sister's voice, but all she got was fear.

Instinctively she reached out and touched the necklace, trying to make a connection and to touch and comfort her trapped and dying sister. Lauren wanted to let Molly know that at least the two people who loved her remained with her. But when she made physical connection with the necklace, she got more than that.

She was still holding Seolar's hand. She had only enough time to think, *Maybe this wouldn't have happened if I hadn't been holding his hand,* and certainly not enough time to stop what was happening with the shield she'd prepared. The storm moving through the room erupted inside her and Seolar. The crawling lightning sucked itself out of the walls and floor and ceiling and crackled over the marble slab that held the necklace, pouring from the necklace into Lauren and through Lauren into Seolar, and all in less time than it took to blink.

Fire filled Lauren from the inside out—she couldn't move, she couldn't breathe, she couldn't break her connection with either the necklace or Seolar. Everything went blinding, brilliant white, and she lost her sense of hearing and touch and smell and taste. For a moment she floated in the brilliance, alone and scared—this place bore no resemblance to the comforting green fire of the gates and their passages between worlds, and no resemblance to the realms of the afterlife.

This was hell inside her head, the pain of standing on the surface of the sun with no place to run or hide and no one to save her, with her eyelids seared off so that she couldn't even close her eyes. She stood in hell, and in the middle of it she heard her sister cry out, "Here, I'm here! I'm here!"

Lauren screamed, "MOLLY!" and tried to reach her sister. Lauren felt herself floating, racing toward something, and she thought this place might begin to make sense. Then she fell out of the blinding light, into the safe room, into the blessed coolness and dim light after the magic storm. She grabbed the edge of the marble slab to keep from falling; beside her Seolar, not so fortunately located, collapsed to his knees, sobbing. Lauren stood, shaking and weak, and stared at the place where the necklace had been, to discover it was gone.

What the hell happened, she wondered.

"She's gone," Seolar whispered. "That was it—she is gone and I did not reach her in time, though I tried."

"I'm not gone," Molly's voice said.

Lauren jumped, and still horribly weak from whatever she had just been through, grabbed the marble slab again, then lowered herself to the floor. She could not remember ever feeling so drained in her life.

Seolar looked up and past Lauren's shoulder, and Lauren saw his face change. Joy remade him into a man she had never seen before—joy, and perhaps love.

"Molly," he whispered, and tried to get to his feet. He got

as far as having one foot on the ground, but he sagged back again. "I'm sorry. I don't know what happened to me. But . . . oh, Molly. You're here. You're alive. And you're . . . you!"

Movement beside her, and a naked Molly, still a clear mix of veyâr and human characteristics, dropped to hands and knees between Lauren and Seolar.

The first thing Lauren noticed was that Molly no longer wore the necklace. The second—with a bit of envy—that women in their twenties didn't have any of the sags or stretch marks or lumps that a woman of thirty-five with a pregnancy behind her had. Molly said, "You saved me. Both of you. Thank you—I would not have made it back without you."

"We didn't do anything," Lauren said, and Seolar agreed.

"You did. You loved me. Seolar wept for me, you touched me—and both of you were here when I needed you. The necklace took from you to make me—a lot of energy, and I suspect some matter, but not a lot. You both look thinner to me, but not horribly so."

Thinner? Lauren considered that, and brightened a bit. Thinner would be nice. Maybe the necklace just took fat deposits.

She leaned forward, made a bit awkward by the nakedness, and hugged Molly. "So—you're . . . yourself again? Body, soul, mortality, no necklace?"

Molly looked wistful. "No. I'm . . . I'm the same. I remember seeing the necklace go flying off me when Baanraak's claws got me. I remember that, and then nothing for a while. And then an echo of myself trapped in the necklace with all the echoes of the Vodian who'd died before me. I knew I was trapped—that I was going to be there forever. That I'd failed you, failed the veyâr, failed the plan, failed the worldchain.

"I wasn't going to be able to come back, because the necklace didn't know I'd died. I was in there, but it didn't do me any good. Then . . . magic, of a sort. Seolar told me that he loved me, and he cried—and somehow the necklace absorbed his tears, and somehow his will in contact with the necklace—told it. The spell that powers the necklace understood . . . maybe understood isn't the right word . . . but it reacted to his love for me, and started bringing me back. It had to draw from live sources, though, because you'd removed all dead sources. All the people in the room fed it, but it still needed something more. It got what it was looking for from you and Seo when you touched it. It needed . . . life. A little blood, a little bone, a little flesh. And a lot of energy, and it took them from the two of you."

Lauren said, "Then where is it? If you're still bound to it, why aren't you wearing it?"

"I am. Sort of. I formed around it this time. The clasp was broken, so the spell that powers it got creative—I suspect many of the dark gods are wearing their own resurrection jewelry on the inside by this time." She smiled wanly. "At least from now on I'll have to be all the way dead before anyone can get their hands on it."

Seolar had been fumbling with the complicated knot in the belt to his robe; he finally untied it and slipped off his outer robe, which he handed to Molly. "I love you," he said.

"I love you, too."

"I mean I love *you*. The you that's here right now. I love the you that you were before, too, and I cannot really untangle all of this in my mind, but I know now that having you in my life for the rest of my life is all I want."

Lauren smiled sadly at that, and turned to see tears in Molly's eyes.

"What's the matter?" Lauren asked her.

Molly looked from Seolar to Lauren, and then down. She tied the robe around her waist, but she didn't look back up. She stared at the belt as if it were the gate to the promised land. In a soft voice, she said, "It's all slipping away from me. *I'm* slipping away from me, and I can tell it's happening, and I can't stop it. I'm nothing but memory, and what memory remains is less than it was, and will keep getting less, until the body is here but I'm not. How am I supposed to do this? How am I supposed to keep coming back, and coming back, a little less of me each time, knowing that eventually I'll be all gone?"

Lauren said, "I don't know how you'll do it. But you won't do it alone. You have me. You have Seo. And we love you."

Molly sighed. "And I'll live damn near forever if I choose to, and the two of you . . ." She shook her head. "It doesn't matter right now. It's a worry for another time. Meanwhile, Seo, love, you and I need to spend some time together. I need to get stronger, and so do you, and we might as well do that curled up in bed together talking. Lauren—you and I need to get started. We have so much to do, and I don't know how we can hope to accomplish all the work we need to . . . Why are you shaking your head?"

Lauren gave her a tiny smile. "Mom and Dad left a couple of surprises for us in that notebook. I'll need to show you—but what we have to do isn't as complicated as we thought. Rough . . . but not complicated."

"I'll take good news when I can get it," Molly said softly.

"I'm not sure you got it. When you get the chance to come by our room, do. I'll show you what I found and what we're dealing with." Lauren struggled to her feet, mostly by hanging on to the marble slab. There was no way in hell she was going to be able to make the trip through the subbasements and back upstairs. Good Lord—she'd be lucky not to kill herself getting out the door to the room.

Molly saw that she was having trouble. She stood, helped Seo to his feet, and then slid an arm around Lauren's waist. "We're in this together," she said. "Might as well lean on me. I know there'll come a time when I have to lean on you."

Together the three of them made their way through the door.

Cat Creek

"The FBI will state that they're working on her case, but they won't divulge her location, or give me any details," Eric said.

Pete sat at the desk, looking out onto Main Street. "The worst seems to be over. We made it through this without her. Why are you still pushing to find her?"

"Because June Bug can't track her," Eric said. "Because she can't find any sign of Lauren at all."

Pete shrugged. "Is that so strange? The grandparents were out in California. If Lauren and Jake are out there, in some high-population city like Los Angeles, why would June Bug think she could track her?"

Eric's face revealed weariness and exasperation. "I'm *worried* about her, all right? I'm worried about her and Jake—I want to know they're safe. If she loses Jake, I think it would kill her. Just because there's a logical explanation for this doesn't mean that I have to be happy about it. Or that I have to accept it."

"You still . . . ah . . . have a thing for her, don't you?"

Eric gave him a flat, hard stare. "I won't get in your way, if that's what you're wondering."

"It *wasn't* what I was wondering. I'm sorry."

Eric's mouth twisted into a tight smile that did not reach his eyes. "If the shoe were on the other foot, I wouldn't be."

Copper House

Molly touched things as she walked through the rooms she shared with Seolar. Cool copper; smooth polished stone; rich, dense velvet; wispy silk. She opened the casement windows and let the evening breeze blow past her, and she inhaled the scents of growing things and rich earth, smoke from village cookfires and the animal smells inescapable in a world dependent on animal power. She'd eaten the feast the servants brought her greedily, tasting everything with desperate gratitude. She listened—to sounds of celebration in the village below; to bird and animal and insect noises that sounded similar to those she knew from home, but still different enough that she felt an ache for places she once knew and might never know again; to the sweet strains of a string quartet playing in the anteroom.

She looked at everything, and drank in the world she'd almost lost.

She did not dare think yet about the darkness inside of her. Not yet.

Seolar, a little stronger after having half a day to eat, drink, and recover, closed the door between the bedroom and the sitting room, then came to stand beside her at the window. "You've been quiet, love," he said.

She turned and smiled at him. "I'm appreciating being alive."

Seolar pulled her into his arms and whispered, "Perhaps as much as I'm appreciating having you alive. I did not know how very much I loved you until I realized you were gone, when I discovered I might lose you forever."

She smiled a little, and kissed him. "How do you feel?"

"Better. *Much* better." He took her hand. "Come away from the window, my love. The world will still be there tomorrow, but I want to love you as you deserve to be loved. You and I have waited far too long for tonight."

Molly ran her fingers over his face, then leaned up and kissed him. "We have," she agreed. "And we almost didn't get to have this."

He nodded, and led her to their bed.

They touched, slow and gentle—no desperate coupling this time to bury pain or fear. Seolar led, kissing her, caressing her, holding her as no one ever had. Molly let go of her fears for a while, and let go of her secret, devouring darkness, and held herself in the moment. Her hands slid along his smooth skin, her body rose to his slow penetration. They moved together, bound in a place outside of time, in a world of their own making, where all the magic that existed was the magic they made together.

Molly looked into Seolar's eyes, and saw love, and passion, and—most important to her at that moment—acceptance. She was not and could never be the Molly he had first fallen in love with, but he loved *her*. He loved her enough that he had reached through magic with his touch and his tears to bring her back from oblivion.

He moved her—moved her outside of herself and her fears. When at last they lay together, tangled in the sheets, lost in each other's eyes, she could no longer doubt, and no longer fear. For whatever time she had left, she had found her way home.

Copper House

Lauren and Molly sat in Lauren's suite, and Lauren pulled out the notebook and flipped to the page.

"*It's all bullshit, except for this,*" Molly read out loud. "This? The entries on the page?"

Lauren said, "That's what I thought first. Then I noticed this." She pointed to the odd-colored ink.

"Code. They left us something in code."

"Our parents apparently had a great deal of faith in us," Lauren said. "But it wasn't really a code, so much as it was just . . . a hidden message. I wrote it all out. If you want, you can go through and make sure I got it right." She handed the sheet she'd written to Molly, and watched her sister's face as Molly read it.

Molly frowned. Her lips pursed. She tipped her head to one side. After what had to be a second read-through, she looked up at Lauren and said, "But this is almost the opposite of what we thought we would be doing. I'm the Hunter. You're the healer, after a fashion."

"I know. It makes sense. But it isn't a happy sort of sense, especially for you."

Molly stared at the paper again. "In a strange, uncomfortable way, though, Laurie, it is." Molly folded and unfolded the paper in her hands and stared off into space, looking determined and somehow fierce. "I want to get the bastards who came after me—the Night Watch. Baanraak. *Especially*

Baanraak. I want to take him to pieces and burn the pieces and grind the bones, and when I'm done I want to find his resurrection ring and melt it down into liquid and dump the liquid in the sea." Her voice got softer, but developed a menacing edge. "I spent my life healing, and there is value in healing. But somewhere along the way I discovered that there is value in destruction, too—if what you're destroying is the destroyers. And it isn't like I have a soul that can be tainted by what I am to become."

Lauren took a deep breath. "You could, though."

Molly turned to stare at her. "I could?"

"The . . . God . . . soul of the universe . . . suggested as much. No Vodi has ever regained a soul, but the Supreme Being said it could be done."

"But not if I'm a destroyer."

"He knew what you were, and what you had to do. I think . . . I think above all else, you have to be sure not to become what you destroy."

"I have love," Molly said. "I have people who love me, and I have passion, and I still have a lot of who I once was inside of me. I don't want to become the monster Baanraak would have made of me. I want to be alive, and joyous, and free. And I keep telling myself that the real me already is. That I'm the echo—but that I'm an echo with some bite to it."

Lauren moved around so she could look her sister in the eye. "Molly, listen. You have to find a way not to become the thing you hate. We all experience losses. You'll lose Seolar someday, and you'll lose me, and you may lose you."

"I could take the tried and true Vodi way out," Molly said, giving her sister a wan smile. "We were all in there together, and they were mad as hatters. An eternity trapped inside a bit of jewelry, blind, deaf, and dumb to the outside world, but more than able to hear the voices of your fellow inmates . . . If I could find a way to remove the necklace and live through the procedure, and could then get someone to kill me, what remained of me would be inside the necklace until some kind soul destroyed it." She sighed. "Having seen what walking away from my particular brand of immortality costs, I don't think I'm going to be able to take that route." She shrugged. "Maybe when I'm done, I'll find the courage to destroy the necklace myself."

"Maybe that's what it will take. I don't know. I just know that you have a chance. You have hope."

"That's more than I had." Molly stood up and looked thoughtfully out Lauren's window. The sky above Copper House was clear—cloudless, and free from rrôn spies. "So I'm to be the Destroyer, and your protector." She smiled a little. "And you're to do the magic that makes wonderful things happen back home, and saves the world. I can accept that."

"I'm afraid for you."

"I know, Laurie. I'm afraid for me, too. I'll be walking way on the dark side. And . . . damn . . . Seolar is going to have a fit when he finds out that I'm not going to be the healer of the veyâr and their personal negotiator with the dark gods."

Lauren chuckled just a little. "Well, you will be . . . um . . . *negotiating* with the dark gods. It'll just be in a Clint Eastwood–Chuck Norris–Arnold Schwarzenegger sort of way."

"Make my day," Molly agreed. "So. When do we start?"

Copper House

Lauren and Molly decided to create the first lifeline back to Earth from the safe room in Copper House. Molly didn't feel strong enough to go up against any of the dark gods yet. Lauren wanted at least one chance to figure out what she was supposed to do in a protected and forgiving environment.

Lauren created the gate from Oria through to Earth easily enough, choosing a place on Earth that remained sparsely populated and mostly untouched.

But when it came to actually creating the lifeline that would move life energy upworld through the gate, she stood—lost—for what seemed like forever. What did she do to save them? How did she push life into her dying world?

She rested her free hand on the gate and drew strength from the touch of green fire and the vibrant energy of Dalchi. And suddenly she recalled Brian telling her the whole point of physical life was to learn love. Love. She loved them, the fragile people who lived in her town, her country, her state. She loved their energy and their hope, their striving in the face of huge obstacles and heartbreaking setbacks. She loved their courage, their timidity, and the fact that in terrible times they rose to heroic heights.

She loved them—and love created a river that began pouring into and through the gate.

She loved—and her love proved powerful enough to start feeding her dying home.

She anchored that love to the gate, wrapping it in a spell that would remember this moment and what she had discovered. That magic was real, and the magic that gave life to the universe was love.

Copper House

You'll be thinking about me, a voice whispered inside Molly's head. Baanraak. Not dead, not dissuaded, and already back and aware of her presence, and her location. Molly, ready to leave the safe room behind Lauren, stopped dead. *And I'll be thinking about you, my beloved.*

Molly stepped through the door, into the comfort of copper-shielded security, knowing as she did that safety was an illusion, and that though she had been born to hunt and destroy, she would also be hunted.

Thinking about Baanraak. Yes. She would be doing that.

Copper House

Qawar was waiting in the suite when Lauren returned. "You did it then, didn't you?"

Lauren looked at him. "Did what?"

"Made a siphon. I've been watching you all along, knowing that eventually, if you were the ones I've been hoping for, you would create a siphon. And you did, didn't you? I can't feel it yet, of course. If it's a small one, effects won't start sliding back this way for days. But . . . you have that air about you."

Lauren warily asked him, "Why do you want to know?"

"Because I like Earth. And if you have a siphon situated somewhere on Earth, I could go back and start living my life in the fashion to which I have become accustomed."

Lauren said, "Which would mean . . . hiding in a hole?"

"Absolutely. Well—that and doing magic."

Now Lauren looked interested. "Magic that helped people?"

"I spent a number of years as an itinerant faith healer, back when the Earth still had some magic of its own. I put the good stuff out. I know how it works. And if you'd point me in the direction of your siphon, I'd make sure it started paying you dividends in short order."

"And what about the dark gods? They'll be hunting for anything like that."

Qawar said, "Yes, of course. But I know how to hide. It's the thing I've done best ever since forever. I'm not the bravest person on a planet—but you don't need someone brave. You need someone who can stay hidden and who will use magic to do good things without getting caught. And that's what I can do. It's what I'm best at."

Lauren said, "I wasn't expecting volunteers."

"You won't get many," Qawar said. "Compared to the rest of the old gods, I'm daring. But if you look hard enough and long enough, you'll find more who will be willing to take chances—especially if those chances might open up opportunities to go home."

"How would they do that?" Lauren asked. "The worlds above the Earth are all dead."

"They are now. But if you were to create siphons into those worlds, too, not only would this give old gods like me a chance to revive those worlds, if only a little bit at a time, but it would start feeding something other than death and poison back down the worldchain."

Lauren nodded. It made sense.

"And going home would be their incentive?"

"Wouldn't it be an incentive for you?"

"Yes," Lauren said.

"Point me where you want me to go, then—to where you hid the siphon exit. As long as I get to move upworld once you start putting siphons higher, I'll be happy to work wherever you put me. But, godsall, I miss home."

Lauren said, "I'll make you a gate there whenever you're ready. It's in a deep valley in West Virginia. I spent some time there. Too rough to really develop, and evidently no convenient coal. I figured it would be a good place to spread a little magic."

He nodded. "Send me now. I don't have anyone to whom I have to say my good-byes. You can pass them on for me, if you will, to Seolar. He was a fine host, but at last I've been given the opportunity I have so craved. The chance to undermine the Night Watch's poison in their chosen world. I yearn to see them fail." He grinned a bit, and for the first time Lauren thought he actually looked brave.

Copper House to Cat Creek

Lauren and Jake said their own good-byes the next day. "It's only for a short while," she told Molly. "I have to make sure the house is taken care of, and I need to see that the Sentinels have a backup gateweaver in place. They aren't going to be able to count on me."

"Be careful."

"I will."

Seolar hugged her. "Thank you for helping me get my Molly back."

"Keep her out of trouble," Lauren said with a little smile. "At least until Jake and I get back here."

Jake gave Doggie a hug. He'd cried when discovering he could not take her home with him, but Lauren had promised that they would see her when they returned, and he'd accepted that.

After hugs and good-byes with everyone else, Lauren picked up her bag, pressed her hand to the gate, and cuddled Jake. "Time to go home," she whispered in his ear.

They stepped through without looking back. Oria would be there, making its demands soon enough. But for now . . .

She stepped out into her foyer, and Jake shrieked, "HOUSE!" and got down and started racing through the hall, the living room, back and into the dining room, into the kitchen.

He screamed—a scared scream.

Lauren dropped her bag and raced into the kitchen. And there found Pete, coming in the back door, looking startled.

He saw her and shouted something incoherent, and raced over to her and picked her up and spun her around and yelled, "You're alive. Jesus H. Christ, you're alive! It's been hell around here, and the only time I could get a line on you, things looked . . . bad."

Lauren didn't pull out of his embrace. "Things were bad," she said. "But I got Molly back. We've started putting the plan into action. We won one, and everything might still be all right."

"Only if you turn into a better liar than you've been so far," Pete said. "Because I had to tell a couple of real whoppers to cover for you—and you're going to have to be the one to stick with them. Jesus Christ, you're skinny. And *what* did you *do* to your hair?"

Then, still holding her, he grinned. "But you and the little guy are alive. And it's good to see you."

Lauren smiled at him—and found she wasn't smiling at Pete, the deputy, or Pete, the Sentinel. She was smiling at Pete, the man. "It's good to see you, too," she said softly. "And it's good to be home."